W9-AXE-069

Shadows of Falling Night

S. M. STIRLING

Shadows of Falling Night

A Novel of
THE SHADOWSPAWN

A ROC BOOK

ROC
Published by the Penguin Group
Penguin Group (USA) Inc., 375 Hudson Street,
New York, New York 10014, USA

USA | Canada | UK | Ireland | Australia | New Zealand | India | South Africa | China

Penguin Books Ltd., Registered Offices: 80 Strand, London WC2R 0RL, England
For more information about the Penguin Group visit penguin.com.

First published by Roc, an imprint of New American Library,
a division of Penguin Group (USA) Inc.

First Printing, May 2013
10 9 8 7 6 5 4 3 2 1

ROC REGISTERED TRADEMARK—MARCA REGISTRADA

LIBRARY OF CONGRESS CATALOGING-IN-PUBLICATION DATA

Stirling, S. M.
Shadows of falling night: a novel of the Shadowspawn/S. M. Stirling.
p. cm.
ISBN 978-0-451-46451-4 (hardback)
I. Title.
PS3569.T543S54 2013
813'.54—dc23   2013001052

Set in Adobe Garamond Pro

Printed in the United States of America

ALWAYS LEARNING   PEARSON

Acknowledgments

Thanks to Richard Foss, for help with the fine details of food, wine and restaurants and invaluable hints about Paris and other locations.

To Kier Salmon, for *all sorts* of help throughout construction!

To Marino Panzanelli and Marco Pertoni for help with Italian, and also the other members of the Stirling listserve, including Marcus Baur, my native Viennese guide.

Walter Jon Williams, Vic Milan, John J. Miller, Lauren C. Teffeau, Matt Reiten, Jan Stirling and Ian Tregellis of Critical Mass, for constant help and advice as the book was under construction.

To Jack Williamson, Fred Pohl, Sprague de Camp and other Golden Agers for inspiration; and Roger Zelazny and Fred Saberhagen.

To John Birmingham for advice on speech patterns from Oz.

To Joe's Diner, for putting up with me working in the corner—especially after the accident, when I had to switch to a dictation program.

Shadows of Falling Night

CHAPTER ONE

Paris

"If you're evil and you know it—
Give a shout!

Rape and torture, drink their blood,
Grind their hearts into the mud!

If you're evil and you know it—
Then you really ought to show it!

Shout 'Hurray!'

"This fascination with vampires . . ." the young Frenchman said as she finished the song and collapsed backward onto the sofa.

"Tsk, Henri," Adrienne Brézé said. "Not *vampires*. Vampires are a myth. We Shadowspawn are the *source* of the myth, and of many others."

Henri grinned. "Then my innocent and merely human self has fallen into the hands of beings out of legend, who are inflicting upon me an evening of superb food, drink and intriguingly varied sexual intercourse as a prelude to their more sinister plans?"

"Exactly! We are *loup-garou*, sorcerers, oni, ghūl . . . Nearly all of the wicked ones, in fact. We aren't really supernatural, of course, though we thought so until a few generations ago. In practice that makes little difference."

"Ah, *merci*, Monica," the man went on. "Champagne? Excellent. And is Monica another . . . Shadowspawn, is that the word?"

Monica Darton was wearing a charming smile, a set of faint but fresh red whip-marks on her back and buttocks, and a sheen of sweat from her recent efforts as she handed around the flutes of champagne, a pleasant follow-up to the hot, damp jasmine-scented towels she'd distributed a moment ago. She was still panting a little too. Adrienne took her glass and cast an appreciative glance at the results.

"No, merely my enchantingly flexible minion. Does she not scream and weep and beg in the finest style?"

"Ah, good, I would hate to think ill of her."

Henri stretched. He was a leanly muscular man with short-cropped dark hair and the build of a racing cyclist. That showed to advantage as he leaned back naked in the lounger. It was late, but the lights of Paris were a multicolored splendor beyond the window. The pale white-and-gold glories of the apartment had once been part of a palace, here in the 7th Arrondissement, and you could see the sparkle on the Seine to the north through balcony windows closed against the chill.

And my revered ancestors keep *complaining about how the Eiffel Tower ruined the neighborhood,* Adrienne thought. *There are disadvantages to immortality, at least to immortality for others. Generational rivalries get completely out of hand.*

"This quantum manipulation story is an interesting pseudo-scientific explanation," Henri said. "It would make a good cinema or perhaps a book of the science-fictional kind. Still . . . this obsession you Americans have with the blood-sucking creatures, it is so . . . so *odd.*"

"*American?*" She winced.

"Were you not born in California? So you mentioned. And mostly raised there?"

"Name of a dog, Henri! Jesus Christ was born in a stable, but that doesn't mean he was a horse."

The Frenchman laughed. "Your French is impeccable, better than mine, but you must have learned it from Napoleon the Little," he said. "I've never heard anyone talk as you do outside an old movie. *Or* use those antique and sacerdotal swearwords. No, I lie, my grandmother did once when she dropped her teapot."

Adrienne joined in his chuckle, as if conceding the point; ironic jokes were best when unintentional. She *had* learned the language from people born in the 1870s, the period when the breeding program had re-concentrated the Shadowspawn genes enough for post-corporeal survival. And from their children born in La Belle Époque. Even in their original bodies her breed aged more slowly than humans; she was twice the twenty-something she appeared. That all stretched things out, as if normal humans were unfolding in a time-lapse film.

She shrugged expressively. "It's only to be expected that my language is so . . . pure. I am an old-fashioned girl."

In a way not seen for twenty thousand years or so.

She tried to keep her idioms current, if only because there was something . . . disturbing . . . about the way so many of the post-corporeals were frozen in time. Sometimes what she'd acquired early slipped through anyway; she always used the full ne-pas double-negative unless she thought about it, plus her *r* was less guttural and closer to a trill. And there was a very faint trace of Auvergnat, more a matter of sounds than the actual dialect. Her great-grandparents had spent much of their childhood on the family estates there, in the tail-end of the period when it was normal for aristocratic children to soak up the local patois from servants and nannies and playmates before they learned the French of Paris from tutors and schoolmasters.

She went on: "So please, call me an inhuman monster, a depraved killer . . . but not *une américaine!*"

Monica's smile grew a little sad and wistful as Henri ran a hand over her hip and gave her a slap on the rump. She leaned into the caress for a moment and kissed him on the crown of his head.

"You are as American as Monica here, Adrienne," he went on, sipping his champagne and then stopping and giving the glass a startled glance. "My God, what is this?

"Krug Clos d'Ambonnay," she said. "Nineteen ninety-five."

"I thought only Chinese plutocrats could afford such things these days!"

"That was a superb year, yes. And it is *impossible* to be as American as Monica, unless one is an Indian," Adrienne said, sipping her own flute and savoring layers of taste without the least heaviness to the complexity. "Is that hint of black cherry somehow slightly mineralized? And Monica is as American as . . . as Marilyn Monroe."

"Oh, I *wish* you'd stop saying that," Monica said as she curled up next to her on the sofa. Her French was fluent but heavily accented. "I just absolutely hate it."

"I know you hate it, my sweet," she said.

She took a sliced quail egg with a dollop of Ossetra Reserve caviar off a white tray of nibblements and paused to savor it before she went on.

"I do it to embarrass and humiliate you. I *am* a murderous sadist, after all. What's the point of having you as my lucy if I don't abuse you mentally as well as physically? Here, have one of these."

She popped a second caviar-and-egg concoction into the other woman's mouth, which involved some pleasant finger-nibbling.

"Lucy?" Henri asked, smiling. "A middle name?"

"Ah, an ethnic dialect term, taken in jest from a classic of the Victorian period. It means . . . my bitch, basically," Adrienne replied over her shoulder. "Blood-bitch. Though it's a unisex term. One must not be phobic."

Monica rolled her eyes as she chewed and swallowed. Then she pouted:

"You never brought Monroe up before Ellen started talking about it and how we both looked like the Warhol paintings of her. It makes me feel *ancient*, my *grandfather* used to go to Marilyn Monroe movies. And Warhol was dead before I was *born.* Euuww."

"I didn't realize it until it was pointed out, and Ellen wasn't the first, she just had the artistic references. I seem to collect women of that particular type. Self-knowledge is always valuable."

Monica did resemble the actress, the more so as a minor Wreaking had turned her brown hair pale blond; unlike merely human means it lasted indefinitely, appeared entirely natural and extended even to the finest body-down showing against her tanned skin. She looked rather younger than might have been expected of a thirty-year-old mother of two; her curving figure was full but more toned than had been fashionable two generations ago, the product of dogged Pilates and a genuine passion for tennis and swimming.

"Now for the *relevé*," Adrienne said, showing her teeth.

"The main course? Do I have to watch?" Monica asked unhappily, looking at the young Frenchman. "I'll probably throw up, and you don't like that."

"Not this time," Adrienne said, rubbing her hands together. "It's going to be *loud*, though. Delightfully loud and wet and . . . primal. Earthy, like *la matelote d'anguille à la bourguignonne*."

To the intrigued Henri, as she stood and pulled Monica up by the hand: "I'll be back in a moment. And remember, I'm being far less metaphorical than you think."

He looked between them, puzzled. "What does Monica so strongly not wish to see? She has seemed as charmingly free of inhibitions as you yourself, so far."

"Oh, she is *far* more inhibited," Adrienne said. "Particularly with the messy parts."

"And who is this Ellen?"

"A once and perhaps future victim of mine, currently married to my twin brother Adrian. Who is—but of course!—gorgeous, sexy, intelligent . . . yet distressingly egalitarian."

"Ah, a socialist?" Henri said. "Perhaps you're not so American after all, your family."

"Not exactly a socialist, except that he believes in equal rights for food. Yet I love him dearly, in my fashion. Perhaps that is why my attempts to kill him never quite come off, try though I may. Though one episode of torture and violation was truly delightful . . . and then there are the children . . . ah, the joys of family. I have a complicated culinary life," Adrienne said.

"Culinary or amorous?"

"We're also the source of the succubus and incubus myths, remember. So for me, there is as it were little distinction between"—she dropped into English for a second, for the sake of the alliteration—"feeding and fucking."

"That seems true. When my friends hear that I was seen eating a galette of pigs' feet with a jus de veau and truffles at Dominique Bouchet, in the company of not one but *two* beautiful women in Adeline André exclusives . . . they will conclude that either I have won the lotto or become a gigolo. We've certainly piled one intense pleasure on another this evening!"

"A moment, Henri," Adrienne said, leading Monica away. "And then more intense sensations, I promise you. Ones you've never dreamed of."

The bedroom was a little more modernist than Adrienne really liked, stark and pale except for the 3-D wallscreen, with a faint scent of clean linen and lavender. This apartment was one of those at the service of visiting Brézé scions, and her not-quite-living ancestors *strongly encouraged* them to use what was provided rather than make their own arrangements.

That meant putting up with their habit of simply hiring the most expensive architects and interior decorators around, something they wouldn't dream of doing for the antique splendors of their *own* quarters. Still, you did not ignore polite suggestions from Étienne-Maurice Brézé, Duc de Beauloup and lord of the Council of Shadows. Or from Seraphine, his even more appalling spouse. Not if you wished to avoid the Final Death, and Adrienne was not even post-corporeal yet.

Monica turned down the covers of the great bed and threw herself down on her side, clutching one of the pillows around her head with both arms and radiating an enchanting dread mingled with unwilling fascination. Adrienne lay on the bed as well, carefully putting one of the pillows *under* her head—she found it gave her an annoying stiff neck afterwards if she went into trance lying completely flat. Her arms crossed, each hand resting on a shoulder; the shaman's posture. She closed her eyes and took a deep breath, releasing it slowly, decoupling from the false perception of a world obedient to laws rather than will.

Mhabrogast drifted through her mind, scratching at the brain with dreadful meaning; the *lingua demonica*, the operating code of a universe chaotic at its core, deduced from that raw foam by minds that evolved to manipulate it directly. When her race still believed in legends, they had called it the native tongue of demons, the language spoken in Hell. An adept at her level didn't need to vocalize for the basics:

Amss-aui-ock!

A twisting silvery dart of tingling pain that traced along her whole neural system, and she sat up. Then she stood and swung upright, looking down at her birth-body with happy vanity. Shorter than the human norm, to be sure—all near-purebreds were. Apex predators did tend to be smaller than their main prey species. Slimly taut, subtly curved, the sleeping face regular in a sharp-chinned triangular fashion, skin a smooth light olive and long hair feathery-fine and raven-black . . . Adrienne clenched her fists under her chin for a moment.

"Oooooh, I am *such* a hottie!" she murmured, not for the first time. "My God, I'm turning *me* on."

Then she turned and walked through the interior wall into the apartment's lounge. There was a moment of darkness as the nightwalking pseudo-body slipped through the atomic matrix of plaster and stone.

This was where young Shadowspawn sometimes made amusingly fatal mistakes. If you let yourself get impalpable enough, you fell right through the surface and into the earth and couldn't get out, whereupon your personality matrix disintegrated and the vacant body eventually just . . . stopped. It was a good idea to check for silver threads, too, since those were the commonest defensive measure. Stumbling into them in your aetheric form was the equivalent of running naked and at speed into a mass of razor ribbons.

There *were* silver threads in the *outer* walls and ceiling and floor, installed well over a century ago. Shadowspawn were always the primary cause of death and Final Death for each other, even more so than carelessness about silver or sunlight. That was natural enough for an apex predator, too, but the fact that Shadowspawn existed only in various mixtures with humanity made the problem worse. The conflicting drives didn't produce the most stable of personalities.

Light again, and a pushing effort; her body became fully palpable once more, became something only the Power could tell from the real thing. Henri started violently as she came up behind him and touched his neck, spilling a little of his champagne on his chest. Adrienne grinned. Even in this hominid form her nose was sensitive, and under the sexual musk and the sharp almost citrusy bite of the sparkling wine came the first delicious scent of fear. And the direct sense of it, drifting from the human's mind like the most appetizing of cooking odors. Like meat lightly brushed with garlic-infused olive oil just starting to sizzle . . .

He didn't believe when I told him the truth, but it prepared him for the last, true moment of horror as the lid is yanked out from beneath his feet and the fall into Hell begins. Ooooo, this is going to be fun!

"Holy God, how did you get here?" he asked, craning his head around to look at her. "That is the only door out of the bedroom and I was watching it all the time!"

"I walked through the wall, Henri," she said.

"Your eyes . . ." he whispered.

They were a blank solid yellow now, the color of molten sulphur, the way a Nightwalker's eyes looked unless you made a special effort.

"I really wasn't lying, Henri," she chuckled. "Or making it up. All true, dear little kebab, all true."

Then she snarled, a shrill racking squall, the hunting-call of *Homo nocturnis*. The man started backward and tumbled out of the lounger and fell painfully against the table. He lay on the floor in a tangle, staring as her lips peeled back from white sharp teeth in a way not quite possible for his breed. A hundred thousand years of inherited dread wrenched at Henri Desmarais, a genetic legacy of the first Empire of Shadow, something far older than the age of polished stone.

His first ancestors had painted hints of it on the cave-walls of Chauvet, in those aeons when humans knew why they feared the dark.

"What are you *doing?*" he half-screamed.

"I promised you intense sensations, Henri," she said, stalking smoothly nearer. "First the agonizing violation of your body and mind, then the rending and tearing and feeding. You're going to die now, Henri, in a degradation and agony beyond conception. Now meet your fate."

She reached within, where the coiled helixes of knowledge were stored, the remembrance of blood taken into herself long ago. Pain more exquisite than orgasm seized her for an instant as she changed; sight grew dimmer, but a universe of scents poured into her wet nostrils as her long red tongue hung over the bone-white fangs.

The human squealed in terror as he scrabbled away on his back, not daring to turn away and put the impossible sight behind him. The great black wolf lifted its head and howled a long sobbing note before it sprang.

"Mmmmm," Adrienne sighed happily, as she opened her eyes again and stirred luxuriously against the Egyptian cotton of the sheets.

The renfield cleanup team that came with the apartment would be on its way. Blood was so intoxicating when fresh; you never tired of it, but it went off quickly and then it had a truly vile stink.

And Adrian actually drinks it cold and dead, filched from the Red Cross. Well, at least sweet Ellen has helped him with that perversion. Though drinking happy blood all the time . . . it would be like living on nothing but mango juice and beignets dusted with powdered sugar!

"Is it over?" Monica asked, lifting her tear-streaked face from under the pillow.

Adrienne chucked lazily and touched a finger to the base of the woman's spine, drawing it very lightly upward. "Not for you."

Some time later Monica bent back head and bared her throat, whimpering, then gave a long breathy moan at the sting of the feeding bite at the base of her neck and the sudden flood of ecstasy. It stopped too soon, and she cried an inarticulate protest through the moan.

"Ah, dessert! And now, sleep," Adrienne said lazily, licking the blood off her teeth and lips. "Tomorrow, I will destroy the world. Or make a good start, at least."

Monica sighed. Adrienne went on: "And you can have a Skype call with Josh and Sophia."

"Oh, wonderful!" Monica said. "Mom takes good care of them when I'm traveling, but we miss each other *so* much."

"I visit my children mentally now that they're staying with their father. Skype is an analogue, I suppose."

Adrienne could feel a slight frown in the human's voice as she went on.

"Still, he's . . . well, you and he haven't always gotten along. And Mom . . . she's wonderful, but . . . I think she has problems with my lifestyle choices."

"But *ma chérie*, you *have* no lifestyle choices; you are helpless in my cruel hands, a mere thrall, subject to unspeakable suffering and degradations."

"Well, that's what she has trouble understanding, that I'm okay with that. She's wonderful, but . . . a bit judgmental."

CHAPTER TWO

Paris

Ellen Brézé blocked with a sweeping chop of her forearm as the knife stabbed for her gut. Her own silvered blade cut, but the slight figure opposite her faded back like smoke, like a ghost. Their feet rutched on the ancient concrete of the abandoned warehouse, and her breath sobbed harshly. That bothered her a lot less than it would a year ago; it wasn't just that she was in better shape, but she'd had a lot more experience in prioritizing.

When you were fighting for your life, physical discomfort just had a very low priority.

Another shuffling passage, blades glinting and the *ting* of contact. A twist, and the keen silvered steel scored home . . .

. . . and the other's knife rang on a stone. The clothes collapsed to

13

spill emptiness across what was suddenly the floor of a darkened forest. Cold moonlight shone down through pines tossing in the wind, and somewhere an owl hooted.

Ellen controlled her panic and *pushed* mentally. The Nightwalker could be anywhere, invisible and impalpable to ordinary senses; and she had too few of the *nocturnis* genes to use the Power consciously herself. Her share of that was right in the median range that made nearly all humans *métis* with their ancient predator-overlords. But Wreaking by an adept could put constructs in your mind that resonated to the quantum-foam manipulations. . .

Alarm thrilled along her nerves as she activated the embedded alarm. *Nightwalker.* Not in human form, either. She backed swiftly towards a jag of solid rock—

Paws struck between her shoulder-blades with stunning force; the creature had leapt through the stone impalpably and then rematerialized as it emerged.

She plowed into the roots and leaf-litter. The taste of her own blood filled her mouth, along with the rank dog-scent of the great wolf. She screamed and struck backward, but teeth closed on the wrist until her fingers spasmed open. Fangs ripped at the fabric of her jacket and belt. Weight pinned her down across the tree-trunk beneath her stomach—

"Oh, my," she said, panting and grinning and shivering, staring at the carved plaster of the ceiling until it came into focus. "Now that last bit with the wolf was sort of kinky. Even for me. Even for *you*, lover!"

But absolutely great, if you get off on pain and fear and helplessness. In controlled doses. Which, of course, I do. I think I even appreciate how much self-control it takes for Adrian to keep things . . . playful.

"Not too kinky, I hope?" Adrian said lazily, reclining on one elbow and looking down on her.

"I didn't use the dreaded . . . *earwax!*"

Her husband froze—ostentatiously—at their safe word, until she tickled him in the ribs and they rolled across the bed, mingling his growls and her giggles.

They'd been doing what was officially called soul-carrying among adepts. She'd named it *inside-the-head stuff* to herself. She and Adrian used it a lot for the battle training that had turned her from wimpy Ellen Tarnowski, easily kidnapped art-history graduate working in a gallery on Canyon Road in Santa Fe, into femme-macho Ellen Brézé, Scourge of the Shadowspawn. Or at least Ellen Brézé the *not* entirely helpless victim.

The directed lucid dreaming was indistinguishable from reality while you were under, except that the Shadowspawn who was doing it could always hit the *reset* button. You could learn from mistakes that would be fatal in reality, and great stretches of time could be *experienced* in what was seconds out in the notionally real world. She had *years* of specialized instruction by now, not to mention simple interior tourism.

It could also be a lot of fun, like being able to step right into a full-sensory movie where you could ask the director for anything you wanted. They'd had to ration that part. You could lose yourself; it was as addictive to a human as the ecstasy-like drug in Shadowspawn saliva, and with potentially worse side-effects. Also sex *in there* was like the old joke about Chinese food; wake up and an hour later you were horny again.

"My goodness, Mr. Brézé, what *do* you have in mind?" she purred. *Or less than an hour, sometimes,* she thought. "It wouldn't be holding down your wife and ravishing her mercilessly, would it?"

Of course, a *bad* Shadowspawn, which most of them most emphatically were, could use it to torture you eternally, beyond the death of your physical body. And you couldn't even go insane. Tradition that might or might not actually date back to the Empire of Shadow said that a post-corporeal could survive tens of thousands of years until sheer chance eventually caught up to them.

Adrienne had promised to let Ellen spend lifetimes experiencing her own death . . .

She froze in the happy tumble just before things got really interesting. Adrian's embrace instantly turned from ardent to soothing, holding her until the shivering stopped. Her fingers dug into the hard lean muscle of his shoulders until her nails went white.

"God damn your sister," she whispered. "It's worse because I thought I'd *killed* the bitch."

"She has damned herself more effectively than any deity could do," Adrian said somberly. With a smile: "Therefore out of family feeling, perhaps we should see that she is denied eternal life."

Ellen took a deep breath, controlling the panting. That was not the fun type of fear, no indeed.

"Yah *think*?" she said, forcing herself to relax.

His smile grew white against the tanned olive complexion of his narrow sharp-featured face, a lock of raven hair falling over his forehead, his hand on the curve of her hip.

"And you did make her very, very, very sick for some time. I'm still astonished that she managed to survive a hypo of silver nitrate and radioactives in the foot. We are hard to kill and even harder to bring to the Final Death, but that is a bit much."

"Michiko *cut off* her foot before the full dose got out into her system. I didn't notice that at the time. Of course, I was blowing that particular pop-stand at high speed, riding on a sabertooth tiger doing the full-tilt boogie. You make a *great* tiger, by the way."

"And sabertooths have acute senses but are, to be frank, rather stupid even compared to wolves, so I didn't notice it either. It is a good thing, too, that we were able to . . . deal . . . with Michiko later; she was uncomfortably acute, when she bothered to think. Her luck wasn't as strong as Adrienne's, at least. Or mine."

Luck wasn't just a metaphor, when you dealt with the Power. Ellen bared her teeth, and for an instant looked as predatory as any Shadowspawn. Her blue eyes met Adrian's yellow-flecked brown-black, and she knew he was seeing the scene in her mind—the view through the telescopic sight as the *nocturnis* woman's head shattered, and then the aetheric form sparkling into nothingness. Also that memorable dinner a few months earlier when Michiko had tried to persuade Adrienne that it would be great fun to kill Ellen slowly and have that last mouthful of blood as her heart stopped as dessert.

"Blowing the bitch's head off . . . her aetheric head, granted . . . with a silver-plated .338 Lapua Magnum round was a good start," she said.

Adrian smiled fondly and kissed her on the tip of her small straight nose. "Less dramatic than the fight she and I were having while switching forms—her snow-leopard was very pretty—but extremely effective."

"You distracted her nicely. Let's get cleaned up. And go tell your delightful great-grandparents that Adrienne has been a naughty little girl and is playing with nukes again. I just love visiting them. Not."

"I realize it must be nerve-wracking mingling socially with those who look on you as a canapé."

"It's not just that. They've got a psychic smell like rotting flesh. They think they're alive, but they're not. They're the walking memories of a very bad dream."

"I will not dispute it. But then, I have no family feelings."

"Yeah, you do, lover. Strong family feelings. Even obsessive. They're just all negative."

The apartment on the Île Saint-Louis wasn't big by American standards, but it shone with expert care and smelled slightly of sachets and wax, under the earthier scents of the bedroom; Adrian had lived here while he attended the Sorbonne, and off and on since as the fortunes of clandestine war brought him through Paris. The floors were polished hardwood, with a few Oriental rugs, and the furniture mostly plain in a subtle way that said *expensive and old.* Only the kitchen, electronics and plumbing were thoroughly 21st-century. The bathroom had a tub big enough for two, a smooth shallow curve like an abstract seashell, and a walk-in shower with multiple heads whose walls were glass etched with designs of reeds and bamboo.

The hot water and verbena soap seemed to leach the grue out of her body.

She leaned back against Adrian, and his arms went around her waist.

"I may have to Wreak this evening. With your permission?" he murmured against her ear, then touched his mouth to the damp curve of her throat.

"*Bite* me. But not in the metaphorical sense," she said, with a breathy half-giggle. "And permission? Hell, that's an *order.*"

Dressing took some time; you didn't slop over to the Brézé place in sweats to have hamburgers in the backyard, and her husband was as fastidious as a cat about appropriate appearances anyway. She had expert assistance, at least. Adrian was one of the rare straight men who took a skilled interest in women's clothes and hair for their own sake, rather than just staring at the result like a hungry dog drooling at a pork-chop.

He appreciates, then *drools.*

Ellen did an exaggerated runway-style pirouette before Adrian's knowledgeably critical eye as they left the bedroom.

"You look enchanting in that, my dear," he whispered in her ear. "Though even better in the lingerie."

She was in an ankle-length cap-sleeved lace gown of Valentino red belted with a double string of gold-linked Madras pearls the color of polished steel; there was a modest mandarin collar that was a hint about her carotids being off-limits to those looking for a snack. The collar was covered in a band of the same pearls as the belt, strung asymmetrically on gold chains, and there were two more in her ears.

He poured them both a glass of white wine and handed one to her with what Europeans called a *biscuit roses de Reims,* meaning a crisp pink cookie. Oddly enough they had no word for what Americans called a biscuit. Adrian put his arm around her waist, and they stood for a moment looking out at the 17th-century townhouses and silent streets, and the lights glittering on the Seine.

I really needed this, she thought as she sipped the steely dry Chitry and nibbled, careful not to let any crumbs fall on the gown. *To settle my butterflies.*

He winked at her; there were advantages to being married to a telepath. Even when he wasn't actually reading her mind he was uncannily attuned to her moods. The glimpse of herself reflected in the window looked ready to beard the rulers of the earth in social combat. And it all felt indecently comfortable, for high fashion.

And a little plain indecent. The high-strapped sandals with their coral and tanzanite clasps alone cost more than her coal-miner grandfather had ever made in a month, or two, or four. Or her father before he'd been laid off and descended into alcoholic decay. She turned one ankle to look at them, and the way the natural silk stockings shimmered beneath the lace on her slender sinewy runner's legs.

"Enchanting," he said as he helped her on with the ermine coat.

Then he grinned. At her raised eyebrow he said: "I am old enough to remember fur protests."

"So am I! Well, when I was a teenager."

"As a matter of fact, on the way to the opera at Santa Fe once—years before we met—someone tried to spray-paint the mink of a lady I was accompanying."

"What happened?"

Adrian made a dismissive gesture, smiling as if at a minor joke: "I made his trousers fall around his ankles. I was in evening dress and it would have been difficult to simply hit him without spoiling the occasion."

Ellen laughed, only slightly incredulous. There had been that supremely annoying and inconsiderate street mime here in Paris last year, and a series of unlikely accidents had ended with the seat of his pants catching fire. . .

"Wreaking?"

"Of course. Dousing him in gasoline and using a match would have been excessive, even cruel and irresponsible, and anyway would have drawn attention. So would making the can of paint explode. It wasn't difficult; he had a very badly worn belt. The opera was the revival of *Maometto Secondo*, by Rossini, and very well sung."

Ellen laughed. "I've seen that one. It's got a pants part for the hero, and you keep expecting Anna to do a number warbling: *But Daddy, this Calbo you want me to marry is* toooootally *a* chhhhhiiiick innnn draaaaag!"

He laughed too. "Yes, I had not realized Renaissance Venetians were so enlightened. Perhaps next year, if all goes well—"

"If the world doesn't end in apocalyptic disaster."

"Exactly. If the world does not end in apocalyptic disaster, in '22 we will take a month in Italy, touring the hill towns, and end with the Rossini Festival in Pesaro. The Villa Imperiale there is well worth a visit, too."

"Right, those frescos by del Colle and Genga," she said, feeling a stab of longing for quiet days. "I'd like that, a lot."

And we really could do that, just because we felt like it, if it weren't for the apocalyptic end-of-the-world thing. Now I've really *got a reason to hate the Conspiracy of Evil!*

In some ways the fact that Adrian was quasi-human and drank her blood and could send his consciousness out in animal shapes and twist the fabric of reality with his mind was easier to deal with than being married to someone who was inconceivably, mind-bogglingly, absolutely filthy rich. The rest was true alien weirdness, but she'd always *wanted* wealth, yet found that world as disquieting as it was attractive. Her emotions treated it as real in a more fundamental sense than the Power.

He'd transferred half the capital to her name, too, which was a sum to make Gates choke. Leaving aside the nefarious Shadowspawn plan . . . plans . . . to wreck the world, which would fall like the gentle rain from heaven on rich and poor alike, and the fact that she was madly in love, she could walk tomorrow and be an exceedingly affluent divorcee . . . which was probably the point of what he'd done. It was sort of equivalent to their safe word, letting her exult in the way he pampered her without *really* being like a kept woman.

At least Adrian doesn't think *about money a lot, which merely rich people generally do. Of course, he doesn't have to.*

Since he could have it in any quantity he wished by—literally—

sticking the occasional pin in the financial pages to determine what was going up or down and texting the result to his brokers in Hamburg. That his ancestors had been aristos under the *ancien régime* (and heads of a cult of murderous peasant-sacrificing Satanist black magicians called the Order of the Black Dawn, to boot) was only a slight complication. Her own father had been a degenerate child-abusing shit and her mother a doormat who pretended it wasn't happening. There was no point in disliking people for what their progenitors had done. Because then she'd have to start with herself, and she'd given that up long ago.

The outfit *did* go well with the crown-braided platinum hair, and the light hint of makeup that brought out her turquoise eyes.

And the glyphed silver-edged knife and derringer with silver bullets tucked into the cutest *little purse,* she thought mordantly. *Taking silver to a Shadowspawn party, how vulgar.*

She paused as they went through the living room. One of the paintings on the wall to the left of the fireplace was *The Nut Gatherers* by Bouguereau, a late-19th-century Academic who'd been in and out of fashion and now was very much back in again, driving some of the older and more reactionary critics bananas. It showed two barefoot prepubescent rural girls sitting in a wood. They wore rather plain brown-and-white outfits and looked like French peasant elves, except for an unexpected and rather charming realistic chunky thickness to their ankles and calves. Those were the legs of girls who walked five or six miles a day, usually carrying a wicker basket full of something heavy.

"I wonder who actually posed for this?" Adrian said, stopping beside her. "It is beautiful . . . or at least very pretty . . . but not much like real countrywomen, even that young."

He held his jacket over his shoulder with one finger in the collar; he was wearing a sleek black suit in slightly wrinkled linen, sockless black-on-black worked Louboutin shoes, and a narrow black tie against the white Egyptian cotton shirt.

Despite that and his slightly androgynous handsomeness, he didn't look like a model. There was something too concentrated in his eyes . . . not to mention several fading scars. And the way he moved had a gliding grace that made your spine bristle, even before you felt the shocking strength of his hands.

Ellen grinned. Adrian could be a little intimidating, even when he wasn't trying. Which she very much *liked*, a man without a hint of danger was like boiled potatoes without salt, but it was nice to have something she knew more about than he did. They'd met in Santa Fe, New Mexico, where she'd been working in a gallery, fresh out of NYU, and at first she'd thought he was just an old-money Euro-trash collector, of whom she met legions in the course of her work in that art-crazy resort town. He'd been an unusually sexy one even at first glance, of course.

"No, look closer," she said. "Yeah, they're too clean and they don't have calluses on their feet, but *look*."

She had a degree in Art History from NYU, and these days that included a fair degree of social background.

"They were probably *actual peasants*," she went on. "Back then French peasants were cheap and you could get swarms of 'em. This one was painted near La Rochelle, I think. God, but this man could do skin tones."

"Strikingly clean peasants, with expert hairdressers!"

Her finger traced above the outlines of the girls' legs, caressing the air. "Yes, but see? He didn't show the muscle articulation. That would have violated the canons he worked with, but those aren't dainty little pegs. And look at the sitting girl's arms, the younger one, her forearms here just below the elbow? She *so* whacks wet laundry on rocks for Mom."

Most of the time Bouguereau is as stylized as a Kabuki mask—when he does something mythological the women are always hoofers from the follies or high-priced *demimondaines* or both, with those big butts the Victorians liked that always look like they've been carved out of marsh-mallows—but every now and then something like that breaks through. It's the contrast, you see? They're pretty, idealized village girls. And pretty real ones, both at the same time."

"Hmmm. Looking at art with you is always an education, my darling. Someday we will take a year and tour galleries. Assuming the world does not end."

"All these things we're going to do if the world doesn't end! And sometimes it's better just to appreciate. All those years at NYU mean I can't, usually. I got into it because I just liked it, loved it in fact, but now I start to analyze by sheer reflex."

"You still enjoy," Adrian said with a smile, touching one finger to her cheek for an instant. "And the knowledge . . . enlarges . . . things for me. Harvey's tastes ran to neon paint on black velvet; he is a very competent cook, but otherwise aesthetically . . ."

His face went hard for a moment at the mention of his old mentor's name. The man who'd raised him to think of himself as human was an enemy now. He thought he was about to destroy the Council, and all the while he was Adrienne's catspaw.

Ellen sighed. "I *like* Harvey. In fact . . . you know, of all the Brother-hood people I've met, he's the only one I really *do* like. The rest don't seem like *people* as much, if you know what I mean. Grim and fanatical, or weird, or weirdly grim and fanatical, or just plain scary."

"Scary . . ." Adrian said, and his mouth quirked. "My darling, who is the most dangerous man you know?"

"Ah . . . that would have to be you, honey."

Adrian shook his head. "I am the most *powerful adept* you know, at least of those still in the flesh. Or are likely to meet, apart from my sister; she and I are equals in that respect, I a little stronger, she just a touch more subtle."

He reached out and took a cube of sugar from the tea-set resting on a sideboard, flipped it in the air, and let it fall on his palm. Quietly, without any fuss, the cube crumbled as if it were rock eroding away over eons of time, and the individual grains disintegrated into a powder finer than talc. The powder stirred and rose, twisting into a rising double spiral like a DNA molecule, then puffing away.

"But that is not altogether the same thing as *dangerous*. Harvey is at least as *dangerous* as I; and if I am *as* dangerous, it is because he trained me."

Ellen shivered slightly. You never got used to the Power . . . unless you'd grown up with it, she supposed. She remembered watching Leila, Adrienne's daughter—and Adrian's—cupping her child's hands around a feather, her seven-year-old face intent, the tip of her tongue clenched between her teeth. And the feather beginning to dance.

He sighed. "Something will have to be done about Harvey. Sending Jack Farmer and Anjali after him is a good start; they know his methods well. The problem with that . . ."

"Is?"

"That saying *something must be done* about Harvey neglects the fact that Harvey is very good at *doing something* to others, and not just killing them, either. I would not fully trust even myself, going up against him."

CHAPTER THREE

Eastern Turkey

The truck's suspension was shot. Harvey Ledbetter grunted as he pulled himself out from under the vehicle, slipped his flat LED torch into the back pocket of his trousers and slapped dust off his clothes. A series of freak accidents had cracked the springs on the rear axles, and an undetected lubricant leak had seized a set of bearings in the rear differential until they smoked. Somehow the temperature alarms in the big MAN hybrid's all-glass controls hadn't picked it up. If his thumbs hadn't started prickling the first he'd have noticed might have been flames destroying the shield generator and spilling the weapon within all over the landscape. The possibility made him sweat in retrospect.

It was so *easy* to fry solid-state circuitry with the Power, because screwing with quantum-mechanical fluctuations was what the Power basically did anyway. Which particle tunneled where . . .

He straightened up and stretched until something went *pop* in his back. Above him through the still, thin, dry air the stars were a multi-colored splendor in the night, with a three-quarter moon bright enough to dim them around its silver sheen. He saw just a bit better in light like this than the standard-issue human. His nose was a bit better too; there was a smell of dry powdery soil and hot metal from the wrecked truck, and things vaguely like bruised sagebrush. This upland stretch of mountain and steppe felt older than the Southwestern deserts of his youth, somehow; you could taste the dust of empires and ages and armies.

Anger coursed through him, tasting sour and iron-rich at the back of his throat.

"Yea, though I walk through the Valley of the Shadow of Death, I shall fear no evil, for verily I bear a slab of plutonium nuke-goodness *fuck you!*" he shouted at the darkness.

The Texan was a lean man who liked to think of himself as spending several years being fifty-nine; his sandy-brown hair was only lightly grizzled, but the short beard he'd grown to fit in as he crossed Anatolia was iron-gray-flecked white. He was wearing local clothes, too, of a hick-from-the-sticks variety; a collarless shirt, cloth cap, coarse jacket and rather baggy pants. Despite that, and the fact that he spoke fair Turkish, he didn't expect to pass for a local if someone looked hard unless he was willing to expend precious energy on a Wreaking. It wasn't his blue eyes, or the complexion under his weathered tan, though they were out of the ordinary. Enough Turks were just as Nordic looking, their sainted Kemal for starters, that it didn't attract undue attention, and it was pretty common among Kurds too—this was Kurd country.

The shape of his bones was wrong, though, and his body-language;

he'd never had the time or motivation to acquire a convincing act for hereabouts.

What he usually did with anyone who penetrated his first layer of cover in this part of the world was pass for an American or European intelligence agent pretending to be a Turk—he could do a convincing *mitteleuropan*, and his French and German were fully native-fluent. If they thought you were CIA or DGSE or *Kommando Strategische Aufklärung* it didn't occur to them that you might be a witch-finder, which was how the Brotherhood had started out. Though these days it was more a matter of keeping the witches from finding *you*. It also made it logical that you dealt in large amounts of cash and didn't talk much. He'd even managed to pull that off with the odd *Milli İstihbarat Teşkilatı* type, though the odds of running into the Turkish secret police were remote this far from the borders.

This part of the world swarmed with spooks, metaphorically. He grinned tautly; with the Council of Shadows holding their first full meeting in decades over in Tbilisi, across the border in Georgia, there were going to be plenty of *literal* spooks around in a few months. Until he triggered the twenty-five-kiloton device and blew them—corporeal and post-corporeal alike—into oblivion. The blast would do for the embodied ones, and the radiation would be as deadly as sunlight to the rest.

For a moment sheer aching need clenched his teeth. If he could take out most of the pureblood adepts, the Brotherhood could finally *win* the ancient war. Collateral damage . . . was unfortunate, but whole orders of magnitude less than what the Council of Shadows had planned for humanity in its Trimback options, not to mention the endless torment that would follow when the Empire of Shadow returned full-force. Most of the really bad stuff in the past hundred-odd years had been their work anyway, like the Holocaust and the Great Leap.

Plus he didn't plan to survive the explosion. The Brotherhood could unload all the guilt on him, and then scoop the pieces off the board.

A quick glance either way showed nothing coming or going; there was an abandoned and burned-out light truck with its right wheels in the ditch about half a kilometer away, nothing out of the ordinary; Turkey wasn't a third-world shitheap like say the ruins of Syria, but it wasn't exactly Denmark either, or even Texas. And this was Turkey's equivalent of West Bumfuche, Arkansas, plus it could give lessons in *bleak* to the country south of Lubbock.

The wreck was unexceptional . . . except that it was a fairly *new* four-wheel-drive light truck, the sort you used for adventure tourism. The soot had fooled his eye for a moment. He walked closer, and when he got to within a few yards he could still feel the heat of its burning . . .

He took a stance and closed his eyes, taking one deep breath after another, slower and slower. Let everything go; fear, worry . . . then thought, identity and hope.

"*Tzze-mogh*," he murmured, snarling at the feel of icy knives sliding through his head.

A sense of *wrongness*. Bane, of paths tending black, of complex parts breaking, rupturing, wearing, grinding, on down to the bubbling chaotic foam that underlay everything . . .

Harvey came back to himself with a jerk, panting and sweating and staggering two steps before he went down on one knee, resting his weight on a hand braced against his thigh. He fumbled in a pocket, took out a plastic bottle of a sports-energy drink and gulped it, and waited until the shivering and headache dulled a little. Then he walked over to the abandoned truck and gave it a once-over, careful to avoid touching the still-hot metal. Two fuel lines in the nearly-new engine had come undone, flooding the hot parts with sprays of mixed gasoline and air. The doors were all still shut, and it was unlikely that anyone making a fast exit would have bothered to close them.

Aha, he thought. *The doors jammed at the same time. Secondary effect tacked onto the big one. Charming. Real Council-type curse, high-level adepts working there with rivers of blood to power 'em.*

The front passenger-side window had been broken out; kicked out, probably; it was much harder to jam a boot or bugger up the effect of a straight-up impact. There were tracks on that side of the vehicle. Two people, one much bigger than the other, both wearing hiking boots. That was about as much as he could make out without showing a light. A little way away he found a bootlace, which had apparently split all the way up when someone tried to tighten it. That was even more unlikely than the engine failure, just the sort of combination of immense power and skill with petty vindictiveness you'd expect.

The term of art was *probability cascade,* a directed aetheric structure like an immaterial sensor-effector mechanism; sort of like a Power-driven edition of Murphy's Law dropped on your head, only for real, and something only the most powerful adepts could do on this scale. It worked right down to the zipper jamming on your dick when you went to take a leak afterwards.

There was an interesting pattern to the damage in the rear trunk of the light vehicle, too. The panels were bowed outward in a flower-petal pattern studded with small holes, as if there had been an explosion and high-velocity debris. Contrary to Hollywood, cars very rarely blew even when they burned. That required an extremely precise fuel-air mixture. The fire had probably gone up very fast, with a roar and a flash and the speed of passage driving the flames back towards the windscreen even before it hit the fuel tank, then a rupture and spill and the whole thing burning, but it hadn't gone kaboom.

Now, certain other things *did* react to heat that way . . . he focused for a moment to make sure there weren't any live rounds still waiting to cook off like those last few popcorn kernels, then wrapped a handkerchief around his hand and reached carefully through. Even in the dim light the little brass shape was definitely a round of ammunition that had blown itself into shreds. From the damage to the trunk, someone had had a couple of boxes of mike-nine back there when their transport did its Mr. Crispy and tried to reduce them to long-pig chitterlings.

"Well, sheee-it," he said, and went back to his own vehicle. "Could have been worse. Whoever made it out could have just spontaneously caught on fire themselves."

The metal of his truck felt solid, in a way that went beyond the physical. Adrienne Brézé had made a very bad mistake when she didn't kill a physicist named Peter Boase. She'd been sent to Los Alamos by the Council to end researches which had come uncomfortably close to the truth of *why* the world was sliding down into a pit of seething chaos ruled by hatred and cruelty. On a whim she'd decided to take the young scientist along as a toy and keep him with her other lucies on her Californian estate to destroy at leisure and milk for useful data in the process.

Peter had escaped . . . sorta. He'd certainly beaten the feeding addiction, and the truck contained the first fruits of his investigations at the secret labs of the Brotherhood. Adrienne had probably made a mistake there, however clever it looked in the short run.

And then there's the nuke, Harvey thought.

He'd engineered that himself, diverting a little extra stolen plutonium. The Brotherhood used the stuff in hits, putting chunks in with a dead Shadowspawn master to make sure their final resting place was really restful and completely final. He'd simply liberated a few extra kilos, let some jihadi lunatics think they were buying it from him and then dropped back in later to collect the weapon. When that was over, all was quiet at Casa Jihad until the neighbors noticed a stink really bad even by the standards of a Veracruz slum. The Mexican cops had probably written it off as another of the innumerable gangland killings.

A nuke by itself wasn't very useful; brute-force engineering rarely worked against adepts. The explosion would cut across too many world-lines, rippling back in time through the possible paths to resonate with those who were threatened by it, if they had the Power. Anyone with the right genes blueprinting their neural circuitry would sense it and just avoid the location without thinking about it; those with the training as well would probably be able to make a good guess at what was making their hair crawl. The chance of taking a whole slew of powerful Shadow-spawn adepts by surprise that way were somewhere between zip and nada. That was the drawback of fighting people with turbocharged luck.

What *encased* the bomb was a . . . field . . . that turned aside the Power. That blocked all traces of what it shielded from the whole web of possibilities, regardless of how strong they were. Peter Boase had gotten his start by investigating why silver baffled the Power, but unlike the traditional silver sheathing this didn't shout its presence either. It just . . . wasn't present unless you could eyeball it.

When he tried to focus the Power on the truck himself, it was just *there*, without the fuzz of world-lines everything else had. He couldn't see its past, or its potential futures, or anything that it affected. It was as if around it the world was the deterministic set of blind billiard-balls that Newton had imagined, rather than the will-driven sea of ultimately arbitrary malleability that it really was.

The problem right now was that while a seer couldn't locate the bomb, or even trace it back from the impact it would make on the world, ordinary logic and evidence worked just fine. And while the

Power couldn't *see* the area inside the shield, as far as he knew there was nothing to stop a Wreaking from *affecting* it. Someone was using the shotgun principle, and ready to spend a lot of the Power on it. Luckily it had been a truck-break-down curse, not a nuke-go-off one.

Harvey had just enough of the *nocturnis* genes to Wreak consciously and to give him consistently useful hunches; not nearly enough to night-walk or even feed on blood, which meant that everything came out of his own reserves. That made him a Chihuahua to the wolf of a real high-blood, though a Chihuahua to a mouse against human norms. Smarts and subtlety could substitute for raw power to an extent, though.

"All right," he muttered to himself. "It's a generalized curse. Someone knew, or more likely suspected, I was in X number of square miles, and put a *vehicle-heading-east-go-wrong* Wreaking on the area since they couldn't pick me up specifically. Heap big mojo, probably wrecked dozens of trucks even here in East Bumfuche. And maybe some donkey-powered stuff. Hell, I may have brought the Council and the Brotherhood together on somethin' . . . but they don't *know*, not the specifics, or most of 'em don't, or they'd be doing more. Am I using Adrienne, or she me? We'll see about that at the end of the day. After which the secret part is moot."

He took out his tablet and tapped. It was a special model untraceable even when he hooked into the Web via satellite uplink, and it had GPS and a map of the vicinity. The nearest settlement was only three kilometers northeast, a wide spot in the road just above the farming-village level; the nearest city was a crapsack named Elâzığ whose main claim to fame was cement factories. Luckily it was fifty miles behind him and he hoped he didn't need to go there again.

"My Google-fu is strong, grasshopper," he muttered, and got his backpack out of the truck.

I hate to leave my beloved nuke alone for a moment, but I can't very well stuff it in here.

What looked like company logos on the side of the truck body were actually preactivated Mhabrogast glyphs. Ordinary folk would leave it alone without knowing exactly why.

Twenty-four hours before the internal fuel cell runs out and the nuke is a blazing signpost. Just have to arrange things by then. Christ, I hate doing this alone, too. Nice to have backup . . . Adrian, if I had my druthers. As it is, I suspect someone with an unhealthy interest in me is in that little town up ahead. Let's go and see who it is. Maybe kill 'em, maybe talk, maybe both.

There was a machine-carbine and a couple of clips in the backpack, a compact little H&K G36C, but he didn't think he'd be using it against even a low-level Power user—complex weapons were too easy to fuck with via Wreaking, even for low-levels like him. It was a fallback in case he stumbled across hostile locals, or needed to deal with strictly human renfields and mercenaries working for the Council.

He left it in the pack and took out the coach gun instead; the Brotherhood had a lot of experience dealing with the Power. *That* was a weapon as simple as a firearm could be, a big pistol cut down from a double-barreled twelve-gauge shotgun. The surface was webbed with silver thread and the parts plated with it; the clear spaces in between had pre-activated Mhabrogast glyphs in jet that gave a prickly, itchy feel through your palms, if you could sense the Wreakings. He slipped a dozen shells into the pockets of his coat and tucked the coach gun into a set of Kevlar loops sewn into the inside of his jacket on the left. The stiffening disguised the outline of the weapon a little, and his knife was across the small of his back with the worn dimpled bone hilt slightly down, where he could get his hand up under the tail of his jacket and out again in a single flick.

He set out along the side of the road with a nasty chill wind in his face. Dust smoked off the plowed fields like pale mist, and a little rose even where they were left in the sparse native pasture; wind erosion aided by men and goats had been at work around here for a very long time. There were no trees, and it undoubtedly looked even barer in the daytime. This high up and this late in the season the night was cold enough for his breath to smoke. Snow-capped mountains were a hint of white and purple to the north and east.

The big noisemaker approaching an eastern Anatolian village was the dogs, which were great vicious brutes fully capable of using the average wolf as a chew-toy. They were a threat to any chance traveler on foot, but they could smell the Shadowspawn blood in you and hated it unless they'd been exposed as puppies. Domesticating the dog had been one of the things that triggered the original human revolt against the Empire of Shadow; they could sense disembodied nightwalkers, too, even when they were impalpable and invisible as far as men were concerned. Three of them were circling him while the lights were still a dim glow on the other side of the hill. He stooped, picked up a couple of golf-ball-sized rocks, and sighed as he juggled them and picked targets.

"Thing is, fellers, I *like* dogs. So this hurts me too, but not nearly as much as it's going to hurt y'all."

He wound up and let the first one go just as the beast was slinking in at a sidling trot, massive head low. It hit his nose with a dull *thuwmp* sound, and there was a startled yip before it turned and ran. The other two tried to rush him from behind. He turned and threw the next rock, and the dog went over with a drumlike thump as it plowed into his ribs. The last skidded to a stop, visibly had second thoughts, and backed off growling. Harvey waited until it turned tail, plowed the last rock into its rump to discourage any other reconsiderations, sighed again as it yelped and fled, and walked towards the outline of the stubby minaret that marked the little town's mosque. Everything else important—the gas station, the *meyhane* tavern-cum-hotel, and the stores if any—would be fairly close to it.

Change the mosque to a church, and it could be something in parts of Mexico or even the American Southwest. The village was a straggle of old plastered-stone or mud-brick homes, one-story and flat-roofed, and newer cinder-block structures with tin roofs, with a scattering of tired, scrubby-looking fruit trees, apples and pistachios. He could smell sheep-pens farther out. One fairly largish new building was probably the school. Harvey pulled his cloth cap down over his eyes and sidled towards the meyhane, keeping to the edge of the buildings rather than crossing open spaces. The door slammed out, and he heard a woman's voice raised over a man's strangled cry.

Well, well, he thought. *And they say there's no such thing as coincidence . . . and where the Power's involved, there ain't no such thing. Could that be who I think it is? Sending my ol' buddies after me? Tricky, but tricks can work both ways, Adrian.*

It was definitely the pair from the wrecked vehicle; you were about as likely to see a bullfrog playing a mandolin as a local woman in a village tavern hereabouts.

Three men came though the door; one sagged, and his friends were holding him under the arms as he gasped and whimpered and made cradling motions around his crotch, as if he wanted to rub himself but was afraid to. A moment later he began to puke, at which point his friends cursed and shifted their grip to his back.

Harvey ducked aside and ghosted down a rubbish-strewn alleyway behind the inn that stank of stale urine even in the cold, then eeled through a back door. Down a narrow hallway between walls that had the lumpy smoothness of plastered adobe, past a kitchen where an antique gas range threw heat and the cook's back was to him as he began to pack up for the night. He took out the weapon, waited until there was a metallic clatter and racked the hammers back; there was nothing quite like that little springy *click* to alert the experienced ear.

Then he halted a foot back from a screen of wooden bead strings that gave onto the largish front chamber, the gun held down by his thigh, as inconspicuous as possible with a massive deadly weapon. People saw what they expected, even when you didn't encourage them with the Power.

The air was hazy with harsh tobacco smoke; rural Turkey hadn't caught on to the no-smoking thing yet. There was also the scent of garlic-heavy grilled meat, and the distinctive bitter-spirits and aniseed smell of raki, double-distilled white lightning made from grape pomace or (in a place like this) sugar-beet molasses. Most of the patrons seemed to be gone, though it was early in a winter's evening, the slow season of the farming year. Possibly the village was unusually religious, but he wouldn't bet on it. Those few left were bristly-chinned middle-aged men built like swarthy barrels on legs, and they were clumped at the tables over by the door, trying *not* to look at the pair closer to the back wall here.

Those two weren't making any attempt to blend in, just sitting and radiating pissed-off contempt for their surroundings, along with vibrations of extreme danger. Which was Anjali Guha and Jack Farmer to the life, both among his favorite blunt instruments. They were in denim jeans and laced hiking boots and expensive if slightly battered oiled-cotton jackets, the type with lots of pockets and brass snaps and leather patches on their elbows.

She had an oval face with skin the color of milk chocolate and eyes so black the pupils disappeared in the iris, and was fine-boned without looking the least fragile. Her hair was clubbed at the back of her neck, with a few strands escaping as if she'd done something energetic lately, and it was that raven's-wing black that has bluish highlights. The locals flinched when she looked up from her glass at them.

Her companion had *American*—and specifically *Upper Midwest*—written all over him, blond crew cut, pale-blue eyes, face like a pug-nosed clenched fist and the build of someone who'd be stocky if he hadn't also exercised fanatically. Both of them could have been anywhere between tired mid-twenties and fit early middle age; the man had a frosting of light stubble on his face.

The woman spoke, her voice flavored with the slight mellifluous sing-song of a native Hindi speaker who'd grown up with an old-fashioned dialect of British English as her second language, before spending many years in the United States:

"I am thinking: Why do I spend so much of my life dealing with troglodyte sexist *banchuts* in places like this? Defending them from fates worse than death. Risking my life to do so when I could be in La Jolla throwing treats to the cormorants? It is a wonderment."

"You gave that one a toe-cap vasectomy, so he probably won't be breeding any more of 'em. And hey, usually we're in more civilized parts of the world," the man said. "Don't you love to travel?"

"With *you*?" she asked snidely.

"Hey, I'm not a sexist troglodyte banchut!"

"Not a sexist. Full stop."

Harvey waited until they were both looking at the front door and pulled nothing-here around himself as he sidled in, hooked a chair over with one foot, and sat down at their table. They were both naturally stronger with the Power than he was; that was just a matter of the genes. But his technique was perfect, which also mattered, and the *don't-notice-*

this trick was his best. Good enough that he hadn't died forty-odd years ago, on his first op against a *real* adept. He held the coach gun below the level of the table, tapping the barrels once on the underside for emphasis when he let them see him.

Neither started when they recognized him, or at the equally distinctive sound of the stubby gun knocking on rough wood. Instead their hands moved smoothly towards their own weapons and he sensed preset Wreakings welling up towards the surface of their minds, like smooth fanged shapes rippling the surface of still black water. Harvey showed his teeth.

"Now y'all don't have to get unfriendly, and it would be a pity to go throwing Wreakings around in this fine scenic example of Turkish peasant authenticity because anything they built to replace this shitheap would be even worse," he said. "'sides, I got a barrel for each of you. At this range . . ."

At this range, the sixteen pea-sized silvered shot in the smoothbore weapon would spatter bits of skin, bone, intestines and blood back a dozen paces, and both the Brotherhood operatives had seen more than once how swiftly he could react in a hard place. Plus there was something illogical but primal about having a weapon pointed at your crotch. They froze, and then returned their hands to the table, keeping them carefully in sight. Their eyes rested on his, unwinking as snakes. They were shielded well, but he could feel their taut readiness. And a curious relief, as if they realistically feared deadly violence and welcomed the prospect as well.

Don't you love life in the Brotherhood? he thought whimsically. *Eventually your head becomes a bad neighborhood you don't want to go into by yourself. You need more of the stuff that fucked you up to distract you from how badly you're fucked up.*

The four remaining locals all put away their backgammon games, got up and walked out into the night, talking loudly among themselves about the local football—soccer—team's chances. Possibly they were going to go to the town cop, but Harvey Ledbetter didn't think so, not from his read of their auras. Certainly the man he'd seen being helped out earlier wouldn't be. Pigs would strap on jet-packs before a highland Turk or a Kurd complained to the authorities about getting slammed in the nuts by a female tourist. Bursting back in behind an AK on rock-and-roll was more likely, and still not very high on his list of worries right now.

With his left hand he picked up a glass of a milk-like fluid and sipped. It was raki, which for some reason colored up like that when mixed with chilled water. There were plates of meze on the table: *beyaz peynir* goat cheese, sliced ripe melon, hot pepper paste with walnuts, yoghurt, stuffed bell peppers, and köfte lamb meatballs.

He scooped some up with a piece of the lavash flatbread; using his left hand was mildly impolite hereabouts, but nobody would expect better from a *Frenk*, and he wasn't going to take his right index finger too far from the trigger just yet.

"Anjali," he said, nodding to the woman. She stared back expressionlessly. "Mighty nice meze for a three-hole-privy town like this; I was somewhat peckish. Long time since that kebab stand. I heard you was messed up pretty bad. Didn't expect you back on your feet this quick."

She nodded. "Accelerated healing. Adrian did the Wreakings," she said.

Laying on of hands actually worked reliably with someone at Adrian's level; it was sort of like transferring his own biochemical *luck*. Unfortunately the cost was high.

"Always was a good sort. How's it hanging in Iowa, Jack?"

"I'm from Wisconsin, you dumb Hill Country shitkicker!"

Harvey grinned at the other man's snarl. "Charmin' as ever, Jack. That was your little cross-country number still smoking a bit out there about three klicks back, right? Someone got their blessings an' curses and ever-filled purses crossed, or did they just not give a damn about you being downrange of the muzzle?"

Jack Farmer was favoring his left hand and there was a spot on one cheek that looked a little reddish, which was consistent with putting up the arm to shield his face as he plunged through a growing wall of flames. Both of them smelled a little singed at close range.

"Let me count the *ways* you cowboying away with a fucking *nuke* has nearly gotten us killed—" Farmer started.

Harvey chuckled. "Hell, you two helped me get it. Don't recall you being too behind-hand doing the down-and-dirty boogie when we had that little black flag party in Veracruz with our late buddy Dhul Fiqar. Or thinking it was a bad idea to hit the Council meeting in Tbilisi whether or not we had official permission from the Brotherhood's not-so-omniscient committee of bickering. I can't see you two getting' all weepy about collateral damage the way Adrian would. How'd he talk you around into stopping me?"

"We helped you before we—" Anjali said.

"Before you learned Adrienne was alive and was manipulatin' us all from behind the curtain like the Great and Powerful Oz?" Harvey asked genially. "Great and Powerful Ozzette? Ozma? Whatever."

They both started this time, and looked at each other. He laughed, scooped up a few of the meatballs, and chewed. When he'd swallowed:

"You thought I didn't *know*? Or that I had some sort of Wreaking planted in my brain? Hell, you can tell from this distance *that* ain't so. Check on it, I won't bite. Just be careful 'cause it would be truly tragic if this gun went off."

Harvey drank another swallow of the raki as he felt the featherlight touch of their probes, and exhaled in satisfaction as the warmth hit his belly. They looked at each other.

"He is clean," Anjali said. Then, cautiously: "As far as I can tell."

"Yeah, that's the way I read it too," Jack said after a moment.

Harvey nodded. There was a *click-clack* as he broke the action of the coach gun open, palmed the shells, and set them down neatly on the table. Both the other operatives relaxed infinitesimally.

"Let me tell you two a little about the wheels within the turning wheels," he began.

As he spoke, he wondered what had been going on among the enemy, a category that had ballooned uncomfortably of late. *Something* had happened, or he'd be tooling along towards his target. There had probably been enough wheels within wheels on the other side to make up a fair chronometer.

'cause if you've got two Shadowspawn in a room, you've got a conspiracy and three double-crosses.

CHAPTER FOUR

Paris

"Good of you to see me before the reception at Great-grandfather's tomorrow," Adrienne said. "Just family for this, eh?"

The problem with being a Brézé, she thought, looking at the unreadable face so much like a male version of hers, *is that we all look so alike. Well, of course incest is an ancient family tradition. There was even a eugenic justification until recently; now it's just fun. For some of the participants, at least.*

Her great-grandfather's brother Arnaud Brézé and she were meeting at Carré des Feuillants, a restaurant appropriately enough located in the jewelers' district on the Place Vendôme, since it catered to the appetites of a similar clientele.

She was a little surprised that Arnaud had picked it, because while the exterior was 18th-century—the entire neighborhood had originally been built by Louis XIV as a monument to himself, which gave her some suspicions about his genetics—the inside was a series of smallish pale monochromatic rooms, with Modernist art on the walls. Quite *good* Modernist art, but she'd noted that the really old ones just couldn't grasp modes more than a generation after their transition to post-corporeality—it wasn't simply that they didn't like it: she didn't herself. They had trouble *seeing* it, for good or ill.

It was white noise rather than a disagreeable message. She'd seen theories by the few scholars among her race that the extreme stability of the Old Stone Age—tens of thousands of years without so much as a change in flint-knapping styles—had been due to the unseen dominance of the planet by post-corporeals who lived millennia or tens of millennia themselves.

The two of them had this roomlet to themselves, of course, which made the layout convenient. Even today simply commandeering a large establishment was discouraged by the Council, though the need for secrecy was not what it had once been.

"Not quite what I would've expected of you, Arnaud," she said, waving her hand at the decor.

"One attempts to do something new occasionally," he said. "Otherwise, well, what is the point of simply *continuing* so long?"

He shrugged, and she had to remind her subconscious that he wasn't her brother, especially since he was taking extra care with his human form. They both had the same black yellow-flecked eyes as she, the same build like a compact leopard, and the same raven hair and triangular olive-skinned face.

The auras differed too, of course, though that might not be as obvious to someone not of the family. There was a slight but definite over-tone of rot to Arnaud's, half sensed out of the corner of the eye, and that curious metallic flavor the post-corporeals had. Something somehow *inorganic* to their spirits.

And she couldn't imagine Adrian wearing that *boulevardier* outfit, the latest thing for the man-about-town a hundred and twenty years ago, right down to the white spats and the carnation.

"This building is even older than I," he said. "*My* father massacred the communards not a thousand meters from here and one might have looked from the same windows to enjoy the spectacle, even if the interior was a town house then. So it is no new thing for the blood to flow here, eh?"

Or at least I can't imagine Adrian wearing it except as a joke, she thought. Then, disturbingly: *Perhaps Arnaud is also joking, in his way?*

It was as well to remind yourself occasionally that the post-corporeals hadn't lived . . . well, survived . . . this long by accident.

"Though I had thought we would speak alone," he added, glancing at Monica.

"Oh, I have no secrets from her," Adrienne said. "That fact produces the most charming fits of guilty self-accusation late at night. Though no attempts at suicide for the last few years. Still, the weeping misery has its charm, and then there is the pleading to yield the blood, or suffer well-deserved pain."

Monica smiled and patted her long mane of platinum hair; tonight it was worn *up* and secured by long golden pins headed by carved carne-lian buttons, which complemented the warm russet of her silk sheath dress. Adrienne was in an outfit of boots, glove-tight black leather pants, a long full-sleeved white silk shirt-tunic, and a black embroidered velvet vest.

"Well, Doña, you have to admit I do self-abasement *well*," she said, and took a forkful of her appetizer. "It's my job, after all."

"Granted," Adrienne said. "You have developed a real talent for it."

"You say the *nicest* things sometimes," Monica replied with a sunny smile.

Adrienne ate as well; the dish deserved its title of lobster *with three affectations*, and the sweet meatiness of the Breton crustacean went charmingly with the mushrooms and okra.

"It is sometimes obvious that you both come from California," Arnaud said dryly.

"Name of a dog, that is the second time in two days someone has thrown the purely geographical locus of my birth at me, and I cannot even torture you to death for the discourtesy, the way I did the first."

She looked at Monica. "I am going to punish you for that."

"Goodie!" she said brightly, a flash of fear and longing running through her aura. "The whip?"

"Among other things. One must be flexible. Or at least you must be."

"I'm sure you'll come up with something original, *Doña*. It keeps me on my toes."

"I thought that was the chains and cuffs?"

"Well, metaphorically. More wine, anyone?"

Arnaud had chosen it, a Domaine Dublere Les Preuses 2010, very pale gold now and absolutely at its peak with hints of citrus and mango. Only the very best Chablis benefited from that much aging, or any time in oak. Arnaud seemed to catch the thought, though not through her hard-held shields, and nodded. He held the glass up to view the straw-colored liquid through the candle.

"A few more years and even such a wine as this would decline and eventually become undrinkable. Just so one must maintain *steerage way*

46

down the stream of time. Those who seek to build an enclave in which they may be insulated from it are merely embracing their own Final Death. Building a coffin and getting inside, one might say."

"You are a progressive at heart, uncle," she said. "I am gratified that you rallied to my cause at last. It has been very helpful in securing backing for Trimback Two."

"Perhaps I am more progressive than you," he said with a thin smile. "For what is this scheme of yours, this Trimback Two, but another plan to halt the flow of time?"

"I am not a reactionary!" she said, stung to indignation.

He laughed. "Oh, not in the sense of those fossils who wish to create a world of peasants and oxcarts once again; I experienced the last of that, and the ennui would be paralyzing. They yearn for a past they themselves never experienced. You are more forethoughtful; you seek to hold the wave of change in place *here*, the wave I have seen erode away all I knew . . . and, *ma cherie*, I speak as one who has worn the pith helmet in his time and seen the Hovas fall before the Lebels. You seek to hold this *modern* world in place before it leaves you, too, stranded in time. I grant that you are being . . . preemptive . . . rather than reactionary."

"Well, then."

"But from the viewpoint of that future you would abort before it was born, perhaps the difference between your stasis and that of the ox-cart nostalgics might not be so great. A thousand years from now, you would be playing with the same toys."

The Pyrénées lamb slow-roasted in clay arrived, with its accompanying simple artichokes, vegetables and watercress, its measured tang of garlic blending smoothly with the herb-scented meat. They argued amiably for a moment about the wine and settled on a Chateau Belgrave from early in the century.

"You have some reason," she said. To herself: *Which affects my resentment not at all.*

She continued aloud: "But my motivations are not merely psychological. Or at least not completely so. If the humans continue their project of science much longer, it will be impossible for us to control the world in secret."

He made a graceful gesture of agreement and the waiters cleared the plates. "Ironic, is it not? For it was science that let us reconstitute our race."

That was true enough; their own family had discovered Gregor Mendel's work long before the world in general was conscious of it. The Power was subtle enough to act as a tool of genetic engineering, if you knew where to point it . . . or just knew that you *had* genes.

Then he lit a cigarette. One of the attendants made a horrified sound, and Arnaud gestured again, his eyes going a little blank with concentration for an instant. The man clutched his head and staggered out of the room, weeping softly; there was a soft heavy *thump* from the next room. The faces of the others might have been carved out of seasoned beechwood, save for the sheen of sweat. Adrienne lit a cigarillo of her own, a private blend of Turkish tobacco and Moroccan hashish, a slim brown cylinder in an ivory holder. The smoke was mildly soothing, and complemented the selection of cheeses, coffee and brandy that ended the simple meal.

"One might argue that we have done very badly at directing the world, secretly or otherwise," he said. "I speak purely from our own viewpoint, of course. A wise parasite keeps its host healthy and does not draw attention to itself. And if we had done that, we would not be confronted by these . . . unpalatable and risky choices now. We seek to cure a disease of which we were the agents, or at least responsible for."

"Are we parasite or predator?"

"That depends on one's self-image. My brother identifies with the wolf or tiger."

"Natural enough, surely?"

"Both are endangered species which survive on human sufferance. Mosquitoes, on the other hand . . ."

Adrienne laughed, though the comparison was far too supine for her taste. "And there is no element of resentment towards my great-grandfather your brother there, eh?" she said, giving him a very slight wink. "Since he is the secret ruler of whom you speak."

They shared a laugh. Arnaud contemplated the end of his cigarette: "Though of course your plan to . . . How shall I put this . . . trim the dead wood from our species as well . . . is somewhat drastic. And I *hope* you were not thinking of including me in that category once we are all in Tbilisi."

"Ah," she said noncommittally, hiding her fury behind a slight smile. "No, of course not, my old, that goes without saying. Your assistance aside, you are notably unambitious politically, a rare and precious quality. We are overequipped with would-be leaders and deplorably short of followers, we lords of Shadow."

"Nevertheless, on reflection I heartily approve of the basic idea. Not least because Étienne-Maurice would meet a suitably fiery end in your little scenario of Hell brought to Earth." He chuckled. "My brother takes you a little less seriously than he might, because you are female. An error, and hopefully a *fatal* error."

She laid her own cigarette down, took a sip of her black coffee and another of brandy. There was no point in pretending ignorance. He knew about the bomb. There really wasn't any point in asking him when he'd found out, either; it was enough that he had. Though she certainly intended to find out *how* he'd penetrated that secret.

"Indeed, I think that was why I tried to kill your brother last year, he being so set on preventing your charming little joke."

"You think, rather than know?"

He shrugged expressively. "Often prescience produces no concrete reason for action, especially when other adepts are muddying the waters."

Adrienne nodded. That was true; it was also a splendid excuse for simply acting on a whim, something for which Arnaud was notorious. The way he phrased it implied that he hadn't learned about the bomb until well after that. Which in itself proved nothing, since he might be lying, but might well be indicative. It was as naïve to imagine someone *always* lied as to think they *never* did, one of those facts you had to fight your natural instincts to keep in mind.

"I'm sure your talents will be extremely useful in Tbilisi," Adrienne said graciously.

"Perhaps. Although I have already done most of what I can. Still, let us contemplate a few contingencies."

Outside the restaurant a half hour later Adrienne pushed her hands into the ermine-lined pockets of her Astrakhan wool coat. The Place Vendôme was thronged, the crowds thick beneath the triple lights in their cast-iron stands, around the Austerlitz pillar with its bronze bas-reliefs cast from the metal of captured cannon. It was a close replica of the Column of Trajan in Rome, down to the enemies shown suffering defeat being mostly Germans and other Central Europeans. Unable to improve on his Classical model, Napoleon had simply made his bigger and more expensive and put a statue of himself on the top.

"I think dear Arnaud was right; he has done most of what he can. And, to quote a classic line, he knows too much," she said thoughtfully.

"Whatever you say, *Doña*," Monica said. She smiled as she looked around. "I do love Paris at night. There's always a certain magic in the air, even at this time of year."

"Have you forgotten what I said about punishment?" Adrienne asked archly.

The night air had that particularly Parisian damp winter chill that made you wish for a crackling fire in the hearth and some sort of hot drink involving cocoa and rum. Not to mention . . . She looked around herself. A classically chic woman of indeterminate age was walking a very large poodle whose coat shone like a silvered confection carved from whipped cream, its collar rich turquoise edged with sparkling diamanté. Adrienne stepped over.

"Give me that," she said, and twitched it out of her hand. "I need it for *my* bitch."

The Frenchwoman started to protest, looked into the yellow-flecked black eyes and backed up, her mouth quivering. The dog half snarled and half whined, crouching and urinating on the pavement as Adrienne unbuckled.

"Bend, my Golden Retriever Barbie," she said, and cinched it around Monica's neck.

The blue eyes were wide. "Uh, that's sort of . . . tight," she said hoarsely.

She stumbled on her high-heeled shoes as Adrienne turned and tugged sharply with the lead over her shoulder; the Shadowspawn could feel the flush of humiliation and fear and dreadful excitement.

"Be glad you're not doing this naked," she said sharply.

Then she smiled and turned. "In fact, that's a brilliant idea. Who knows what might happen? To you, that is. To the skin, *chérie*, right now. Just the shoes and the garter-belt."

Heads were turning in their direction, and Adrienne laughed merrily.

CHAPTER FIVE

Paris

Twenty-four hours later, Ellen Brézé whistled softly as Adrian handed her out of the cab in the chill dampness of the Paris night and she looked up at the palace. "Well, that's quite something. Rococo, Louis XV, and well done. Very impressive."

"In more senses than one," Adrian answered grimly. "Particularly if you know the history. The history of my family, near enough."

The great house—or small palace—was shaped like an elongated H in form, the front court enclosed by the outer arms and more courtyards within down the length of it. The frontage was pale stone, three stories high with engaged columns. Light streamed out of the tall windows, but outside, the illumination was from iron crescents of burning wood, shedding highly illegal sparks along with a yellow-red light that flickered across the wet stone. Footmen in eighteenth-century liveries and white powdered wigs were bowing the guests up the sweeping stairs to the gates. They were just as politely attentive to the pair of Siberian tigers padding by as they were to the ones in top-hat and frock coat, or Jazz Age beaded dresses, classical kimonos, Chinese *cheongsan* or Zulu outfits of cow's-tails and leopard skins.

A frieze of running low-relief wolves gamboled above the entrance-way amid lambs and babies.

"That's a joke, right?" Ellen said.

"The center of the ancestral estates was known as Beauloup, from the thirteenth century and possibly earlier," Adrian said. "Domain of the Beautiful Wolf. A very ancient family joke. Individuals strong enough to nightwalk came along every few generations back then. They did not understand genetics, but they did marry their cousins, or worse. And the genes . . . reach back along the lines of descent, from future to past, protecting their own potential existence. They *want* to find each other."

"Jesus, them and the One Ring. Ah, and the little symbol too."

That was a motif set into the wrought iron of the gates, a jagged gilt trident across a broken black circle representing a shattered sun. The sigil of the Order of the Black Dawn, and the Council of Shadows.

"And they say you're stuck with your in-laws. How true," Ellen said, tucking her hand into Adrian's arm as he offered it with a classic crooked elbow.

The Hôtel de Brézé had been built when the French nobility abandoned the more central, medieval Marais district for the Faubourg Saint-Germain, then a greenfield suburb made newly fashionable by Louis XIV. The Revolution had come and gone; young Henri de Beauloup had reopened the townhouse when he emerged from the family's discreet retirement to fight for Napoleon; indeed, that emperor had referred to his exploits in Spain as showing that at least one of his cavalry commanders *knew how to deal with rebels without false sentiment.* Goya himself had painted several of those episodes, then kept the work secret for forty years.

Eventually, a Brézé with the Victorian taste for science and statistics had made the acquaintance of an obscure monk by the name of Gregor Mendel, and suppressed his findings while he applied the cleric's work to a breeding program that had previously relied on mere superstition and on incest practiced mainly for its own sake. Combined with the new science, even his limited command of the Power had produced startling results. His far more adept son Étienne-Maurice Brézé had celebrated his own twenty-first birthday by torturing and butchering his father, in the waning days of the nineteenth century.

Inside the main doors the host was waiting, smiling, chatting with each guest as they entered and handed hats and cloaks to the servants . . . or in a few cases transformed back into human form and accepted robes. One had arrived as a golden eagle, flown into a window, and was now rubbing at his forehead and cursing in some language Ellen didn't even recognize, a brown-skinned man with heavy bold features. Behind him a great silverpoint gorilla knuckled by, deep in soundless conversation with a blade-nosed man in a black burnouse and *gutrah* headdress, who fingered a curved knife thrust through his sash as if that was his hand's natural resting-place.

The Duc de Beauloup had been post-corporeal for over a century. The form he wore was his own, in what his own era considered the prime of life, so that he looked like a slim, swarthy, vital man of around forty. His height was average for the twenty-first century, which made him tall for a Frenchman of the nineteenth. The face was eerily similar to Adrian's, though blunter and somehow a little coarser. His black hair fell down his back nearly to his waist, the top layer gathered in a horse-tail by a jet clasp above the loose torrent below; he wore a full robe of thick black silk that swept the floor, embroidered with black yli-silk thread down the front panel and around the neck and cuffs.

The Shadowspawn's eyes were hot yellow pools, blank glowing fire. An attendant carried a sheathed sword, carefully keeping the hilt within reach, a gray shadow against the gilt and convolutions and worked plaster of the interior.

"Great-grandfather," Adrian said politely, bowing to kiss the extended hand and the golden ring with the Council's sigil.

"We have met twice in a year now, my descendant," the head of the Council said. "There is hope for you yet. And many of your earlier attempts to kill me for the Brotherhood terrorists were truly ingenious, worthy of a Brézé, if a trifle childish and impulsive."

And I thought I *had a dysfunctional family!* ran through Ellen's mind as she sank into a curtsey.

"One attempts to maintain some traditions, sire, even as a rebel," Adrian said coolly. "You have met Ellen."

The molten-sulfur eyes turned on her. For an instant Ellen felt a sensation roughly like the mental equivalent of having your skin plucked off with tweezers. Constructs Adrian had planted within her mind came alert with a clanging of internal barriers, and the Shadowspawn lord smiled.

"And your lovely and now very well-guarded wife," he said. "Enchanted, my dear." To Adrian: "There is even something to be said for it from a eugenic point of view. I have come to think that reconcentrating our heritage beyond a certain point is . . . problematic, is that the word currently used for *possibly unwise*?"

She could tell Adrian was actually interested now. "Why, Sire?" he said.

Étienne-Maurice smiled thinly. "Have you ever tried to compel a cat to obedience by inflicting pain upon it?" he said.

"No, I cannot say that I have," Adrian said carefully.

"An interesting but ultimately futile pursuit, producing only a thoroughly uncooperative cat. The most you can do is drive it away. Whereas with dogs, and of course humans, that approach often works well. I suspect that our remote ancestors were too much like cats for comfort; at least, for the comfort of those who seek to impose discipline and rule upon them."

Adrian nodded. "You were perhaps thinking of me, Sire?"

"And your sister. You are as near pureblood as we have achieved to date. And while your command of the Power is admirable, formidable . . ."

Adrian bowed wordless, polite thanks at the compliment.

". . . post-corporeally the command of the Power increases little by little anyway. I have more raw strength now than you, for example, however much you surpass what I had at your age and in the body. Given that there are certain drawbacks to excessive purity of blood . . . Perhaps it would be better to stop after we achieve consistent survival past the body's death, which would require a much lower score on the Albermann than you have, for example. Between fifty and sixty percent would do."

"Oh, you are always so *serious*, Étienne," a woman's voice said. "Wasting this splendid golden creature on mere breeding when she is obviously meant for pleasure!"

Seraphine Brézé's natural appearance—insofar as the term had any meaning with a post-corporeal—would have been very much like Adrian or his sister. Today she was wearing one of her victims, a petite Asian woman in a tight sheath crimson *áo dài*, slit nearly to the waist at the sides over some sort of hose and jeweled slippers. She had acquired it during the French conquest of Indochina, an after-dinner story of which she was fond. Her piled hair was secured by long golden pins whose ends were wrought into Art Nouveau butterflies by Lalique. She took her spouse's arm and smiled at them:

"Such a fascinating mind . . . it would be a pity not to kill her, a wonderful project spanning years, spanning circle upon descending circle of horror and pain, spiritual and physical torment and degradation complementing each other. Only a great soul is capable of a really satisfying despair, which adds so much to the experience . . ."

"My dear, you paint an enchanting picture, but perhaps another time?"

The doll-like face smiled at Ellen impishly. "They can be such . . . such grim puritans, the men, can they not?"

Ellen contented herself with another curtsey, and they moved ahead to let the next in line follow.

"You know," she said when they were hopefully out of earshot, "this assumption that I'd be a party pooper not to appreciate the grand fun of my own slow-tortured demise gets really old, quickly. She isn't the first Shadowspawn to suggest it, either."

"Even humans are prone to solipsism," Adrian replied. "Imagine being a thing of murderous power and darkness and unfettered will for generation after generation . . ."

"I'd rather not," she said. Then, dropping into English because there were things you just had to say in your native tongue: "I'm not one to insist on vanilla heteronormativity. But why does coming into contact

with this bunch make me feel I should be wearing a whole-body con-
dom?"

"I presume that is a rhetorical question? The answer being *because
they are vile, degenerate and evil?*"

"Yup, pretty much. What next?"

"My great-grandfather will want to torment us by delay, of course,"
Adrian said matter-of-factly. "And indeed with this Council meeting
coming up—the first full gathering in decades—he will be very busy."

"Why Tbilisi, by the way? Why not here in Paris?"

"Two reasons. First, paleontologists working for the Council determined back in the 20s of the last century that the Shadowspawn probably evolved in the Caucasus late during the Riss glacial period, trapped
in a little pocket by the ice. They escaped and overran the planet during
the Riss-Würm Interglacial, when the warmth returned."

"Some *Empire of Shadow*, putting the bite on lice-crawling cavemen
and Neanderthals and those little hobbit thingies out in Indonesia."

Adrian shrugged. "The Order of the Black Dawn were depraved Satanists, but they were also Victorian romantics and loved dramatic gran-
diose titles and dressing up in elaborate costumes, imposing their own
concepts upon the past. They thought of it as the French or British
empires of their time, or those of Rome and Greece they had studied at
school. Only more evil, with Wreaking, prehistoric beasts, better clothes
and run by themselves."

"Great, Sir Walter Scott and *Quo Vadis* with magic powers and all
done to an obbligato composed by demons."

Adrian nodded. "And so the meeting is a return to where we began."

"Oh, sort of a 'roots' thing."

"And . . . would you want this assembly of devils in your backyard any longer than you must, even if you were the arch-devil? In the meantime, we should circulate."

"Mill-and-swill at the serial killer's convention," Ellen said hollowly. "Joy."

He looked around and hissed slightly in anger, drawing a few dark looks or sets of bared teeth. Occasionally his body-language reminded you that he might think of himself as a human being, but his genes were another matter.

"I have never been in a single building with this many adepts present, all tangling the world-lines. It's like being *blind*. I dare not extend my senses! There are reasons Shadowspawn are not gregarious with their own kind."

"Yeah, you sort of cancel each other out."

Inwardly she shivered. In a way—several ways—outright fighting the Shadowspawn would be easier than socializing with them. More terrifying, more dangerous, but less . . .

Gruesome, she decided. *Not least because if you're fighting them, you don't have to acknowledge they rule the planet, and don't run it only because then they'd have to work too hard, reading reports and going to meetings, and they don't do that because they're lazy. The Brotherhood's* la resistance *and not a very strong example of the type, either. Great-granddaddy back there is the Emperor of the World, or near as no matter, as long as he doesn't use the power so much it's obvious. And they're planning to remove* that *limit too.*

The interior of the Hôtel was more or less standard Rococo, if of *high* standards. The gathering was a substantial one. Not only were many adepts here, but some brought their higher renfield aides, or a favored lucy or two, or both—Shadowspawn custom was to have humans about their gatherings, to damp down the primal emotions of their highly territorial breed. She'd heard it compared to control rods in a nuclear reactor. You could usually recognize the lucies by the haunted look in their eyes, and the renfields . . . well, if you knowingly served evil, it left its mark.

Some of both shot her looks that bordered on hatred. *I'm popping their illusions about what they are.*

Many of the Shadowspawn inclined their heads deferentially to Adrian, as to a walking legend. He'd killed more of their kind than any other individual in history, with the possible exception of Harvey Ledbetter, which was something that brought profound respect. Ellen surprised herself by feeling a perverse but warm sense of pride in the accomplishment. It wasn't as if they didn't *deserve* it. Or he had any choice.

No, he did *have a choice. He could have joined his relatives and been a lord in darkness. He chose to fight* for *people instead of preying on them.*

"Ah, my dear boy, you are in Paris once more!" a voice said.

It was apparently a man in his thirties, and to all appearances corporeal—his eyes were a common Shadowspawn color, very dark brown with yellow-amber flecks, like Adrian's. In fact he looked very much like Adrian, except that he was dressed in full Edwardian formal turnout, of a rather foppish nature—black swallow-tail coat, double-breasted white piqué waistcoat, white tie, a double strip of black braid down the outside seam of his trousers, pearl and moonstone links and studs, and white kid gloves. A carnation graced the buttonhole.

"Great-great-uncle Arnaud. Not accompanied by thugs and trying to kill me on this occasion?"

Arnaud made an elegant gesture. "It would have been great fun to do so, and then throw your bride down across your corpse and ravish her in some amusing form and drain her, but it was the mere impulse of a moment. Something . . . told me it would be advisable."

"Ah, well, no hard feelings, then," Adrian said, and even Ellen could barely detect the ironic edge.

"None whatsoever!" Arnaud said cheerfully. "Another time. There are tiresome matters of business my so-arrogant brother has delegated."

"You volunteered? I was under the impression that you had spent an entire century in absolute idleness."

"I volunteered, but under threat of death."

"I am not surprised. Is there *anyone* even in the Council's ranks who does not desire to see you meet the Final Death?"

"Only those who have not met me," the dapper figure said with a charming grin. "But then, that is no particular distinction."

"Farewell, Arnaud. You may not be so lucky if you try to indulge another such *impulse*."

"We shall see."

The name rang a bell as he turned away; that and the style of dress.

"Was he the one who tried to kill Professor Duquesne last year?" she said. "Him and those hired goons."

That had been the first time she'd had someone try to kill her, and had to kill in self-defense. It had been necessary . . . but she would very much have preferred not to lose that particular virginity.

"And to kill us, yes."

"No hard feelings, then, but at the first opportunity . . . let's kill *him*. Nothing fancy, no artistic embellishments, just *dead*."

"I agree."

"He turned into a giant . . . that Madagascar lemur-eating cat thing just before he blew Dodge, the . . ."

"*Fossa*, yes. He spent some time there a century ago, or a little more. In *la legion*, oddly enough."

"What was a brother of the honcho doing as a Foreign Legionnaire back in the *Beau Geste* days?"

"Having fun, mostly. They had to be more . . . cautious, then, here in Europe. That was why Étienne-Maurice and Seraphine went on long holidays to the Congo Free State under Leopold, and to Mexico in the Porfiriato, to Yucatan and the Valle Nacional in Oaxaca. Of course, Diaz and King Leopold were Shadowspawn themselves, albeit not of very pure blood. Leopold *almost* transitioned to post-corporeality, but not quite."

Something else teased at her mind as they strolled through the corridors and chambers. She thought for a moment and snapped her fingers.

An elegant sloe-eyed woman in a late Edwardian hobble skirt outfit that would have wowed them on the *Titanic* raised a lorgnette and stared at her for a moment before turning away to take a champagne flute from a tray. Her companion was a young-looking man in full fig of shaggy brown hair held back by an embroidered headband, long mustaches, tie-died shirt, fringed buckskin vest, bell-bottoms and love beads.

And for some reason it's more disturbing than all that Masterpiece Theatre *and* Downton Abbey *stuff.*

Her own grandfather might have dressed that way, if he'd been a privileged college kid in 1969 rather than a blue-collar draftee humping bad bush in Vietnam. She briefly met eyes as blue as her own before they reverted to slits of hot yellow.

She turned away and cleared her throat as she returned to the thought that had struck her: "Juste Aurèle Meissonier!"

"Who?" Adrian said.

"The designer who did this place. Juste Aurèle Meissonier. He was one of the Rococo greats. He did commissions all the way from Lisbon to St. Petersburg."

"Did I mention that?"

"Nope."

Adrian's brows went up. "Very thorough research. I remember hearing the name as a child, before Harvey . . . removed . . . me from the Brézé family, but offhand I would not know how to find out otherwise. The records all perished long ago in fires or other convenient accidents. Even the municipal maps show no building here, the databases have false images and data."

"Research, hell," Ellen said, glad to distract herself for a moment. "I *thought* I recognized the touch. All that overlapping asymmetric carved plasterwork on the ceiling and the surrounds? And those mirrors with the ormolu frames, and the engraved mahogany legs and intaglio tops on that side-table? Right out of *Livres d'ornements en trente pieces.* He was the Frank Lloyd Wright or Julia Morgan of his day, he designed everything from the building down to the shape of the chamberpots—he'd do your snuffbox, too, and the buckles on your shoes, if you'd let him."

"Isn't she a charming asset, not least culturally?" a warm voice said, a tone like a knife stroked over velvet. "I compliment myself on your taste, and vice versa."

"*Merde alors,*" Adrian said very quietly.

Ellen turned, making herself do it at a natural speed and sternly suppressing mingled impulses to scream and flee and draw her knife and attack. No nausea; she wouldn't permit it. Control the sudden pounding of her heart, and the rush of rage as Adrienne cocked an ear at the sound and sent her an air-kiss and playful-predatory snap of the teeth. The Shadowspawn woman was wearing a gown that was a shimmering black sheath, with her neck and shoulders covered in bands of wrought platinum and a headdress of the same framing her face. Ellen decided that she looked like a very elegant wasp.

For once, truth in advertising.

Then Adrienne smiled at Adrian, a roguish expression, as if inviting him to share a private joke. As they stood within arm's reach of each other, their likeness was shockingly apparent, the way identical twins would look if they came in different genders.

"How are the children?" she asked.

"Well, and well cared for," Adrian said neutrally. "Unfortunately I have not had time for much . . . personal interaction yet. They seem happy, from their auras and behavior."

"I told them that they might be visiting with their father's household and that they should not worry," Adrienne chuckled. "And of course I walk in their dreams."

"You told them?"

"I had a Seeing to that effect."

Adrian's brows rose; that was a term of art for detailed prescient dreams. They showed *a* future, since the course of events was probabilistic, not fixed, but a powerful adept could deduce how likely it was. Often the distinction between a high probability and utterly inexorable fate became very thin. The world had a massive inertia at times.

"I have always been more prone to those," he said clinically; an expert exchanging data with someone in the same field.

Adrienne nodded at her twin. "Yet they come to me occasionally, particularly on personal matters. I understand you have had several dealing with the results of the Trimback One and Two options. Great-*grandpère* takes your Seeings seriously. That has been quite useful to me in discrediting Trimback One."

Adrian's teeth showed. Trimback One was a global blitz on modern technology using electro-magnetic pulse from high-altitude fusion explosions. The more radically reactionary Shadowspawn lords favored it, to destroy the modern world and return the world to preindustrial stasis forever. It would be simple enough to do; all of the governments powerful enough to bother with had long been the Council's puppets. How could you resist ruthless telepaths who could walk through walls in the form of ravening beasts? A few orders to a few generals, and the thing was done.

His Seeings had shown that the *consequences*, from nuclear power plants melting down to firestorms in refinery complexes, were much worse than anyone had thought. Shadowspawn tended to be conservationists, because they all intended to live in the world for a very, very long time. And they dreaded radiation, since the aetheric body was so vulnerable to it.

Adrienne's *Progressive* faction favored Trimback Two, a tailored plague they had used renfield scientists to develop. Dalager's parasmallpox was more contagious than the flu throughout its month-long sub-clinical period, and then swiftly more deadly than Ebola in its final stage. The Council could emerge at just the right point with the vaccine, when everyone was utterly desperate but before things broke down completely, and take over open rule of the world by default. A world with just enough population and industry to furnish the Shadowspawn with luxuries, and a unified planetary government to keep the masses in order and suppress inconvenient research.

Virtually all of the Council's Shadowspawn favored one or the other, reluctant as they usually were to disturb the status quo; that was why a full meeting had been called after decades of squabbling. More and more humans had been stumbling on aspects of the great secret, and none of the clandestine rulers of the world were willing to chance the masses becoming aware of who had been pulling the strings this past century. If all the swarming billions of true humanity turned on the few Shadowspawn and their collaborators at once regardless of casualties . . . the Power was strong and subtle, but more subtle than strong. Brute force could turn the *nocturnis* back into a harried remnant hiding from the witchfinders.

"It was not my intention to aid you," Adrian said crisply. "Both *options* are psychopathic revenge fantasies. The main difference is that Trimback One is a *stupid* revenge fantasy."

"While Two is Brézé, hence brilliant . . . and psychopathic and cruel. And of course it wasn't your intention to help me, beloved brother. That is the delicious aspect, no? Your Seeings are trusted *because* you are known to be sentimental about the apes and favor neither option; yet your Power and skill and purity of blood are incontestable . . . like mine. In the meantime, as far as the children are concerned, perhaps we should launch a custody battle in the California courts?"

She laughed musically. "As opposed to the battle with assault rifles and Wreakings you staged to seize them from my wicked clutches, slaughtering my renfields and mercenaries left and right? Showing *such* noble determination to put the children's moral welfare ahead of the mere bagatelle of risk to their lives."

The woman beside her winced. *Monica*, Ellen thought. *But blond. Even the eyebrows . . . must be a Wreaking . . . oh, icky-poo, it makes her look* even more *like me. Adrienne probably role-plays that she is me . . . oh, très icky-poo.*

The two Shadowspawn had locked eyes, something halfway between wrestling and communication taking place on a level she couldn't follow, with a feeling like trains rushing past in total darkness close enough to feel the hot metal brush you. Adrian made a very small gesture with his left hand, and Ellen fell back six paces; it put her back against a pillar and gave her room to act if it came to a fight. It probably wouldn't . . . that would be a social solecism by Shadowspawn standards . . . but you never knew.

Then the tension broke slightly; Ellen could feel it recede, more conspicuous by its absence.

"Phew! Now *that* was nerve-wracking! It's so good to see you again, Ellen!" Monica said, in her perky SoCal accent with the rising inflection on every sentence. "I'd give you a hug, but—"

She looked down at her dress. It was a sleeveless jade-green silk affair with a plunging décolletage; a wide diamond-encrusted belt cinched in her waist, matching the diamonds edging the asymetrical neckline. "—I'm not really dressed for it! I mean, we're not *that* sort of friends!"

"Yeah, that outfit's *stunning*, really, but it must be held up by a Wreaking," Ellen said, which was true enough.

Monica chuckled. "You should have seen what I was wearing last night for the walk home. It wowed 'em, let me tell you, but there were goose bumps."

"Ummm . . . I see you're blond these days? I'm surprised."

Monica gave a little crow of laughter. "Not as surprised as I was! I staggered into the bathroom that morning, and I was *platinum*. Platinum *everywhere*."

"That must have been . . . alarming."

"It's a good thing my kids were staying with Mom, because I screamed the house down. But it was sort of funny once I calmed down. It usually is after a shrieking fit. You know how the *Doña* is, she loves a joke. The blond stays that way, too, no need for follow-ups and it doesn't even dry the hair or give you split ends. Beats Madame Clairol all to hell!"

Monica beamed at the younger woman, and Ellen responded with a smile of her own, a little unwillingly.

Miss Stockholm Syndrome of Simi Valley, Class of 2012, she thought mordantly. *Which is very true, but not the whole story. Poor Monica!*

"I've missed you. The Tennis Club in Rancho Sangre have all missed you," Monica went on. "*And* Josh and Sophia have missed you."

Those were her children, and charming. Ellen blinked in surprise as she realized she actually *had* missed Monica's kids a bit, when there was time to think. They'd been next-door neighbors for months, after all. Granted they'd been months of sadism and torture and abuse both mental and physical, subtle and overt, seasoned with mind-crushing fear and horror. And that all of it still gave her nightmares and cold sweats. None of it had been Monica's fault, and she'd done everything she could to make Ellen welcome, right down to dropping by the first day with home-made lasagna and brownies.

The Welcome Wagon of Nosferatu Manor, Ellen thought. *I thought she was insane then, and she is. Functional, but insane . . . and there are times when insanity is what keeps you from going crazy, here in the unreal Real World™.*

"Lucy Lane is sort of lonely these days, since Jabar left—"

He'd run away, and been hunted down, by Adrienne and her post-corporeal parents. She didn't want to imagine what they'd done in the course of his polluted death, but couldn't help getting ideas.

"—and with you gone, and Peter, and Cheba, and Jose retired—he's married, did you know? His wife's expecting, she's a really nice girl, Vietnamese parents, they invite me over fairly often. I suppose the *Doña* will bring more people in eventually, when things settle down, but it won't be the same. The good old days, eh? Remember those Saturday potluck barbecues we all used to have, and the afternoon tennis at the club?"

"Ah—" Ellen said. "You know, I really like you, Monica, and you were always good to me. But the Rancho was a nightmare, and did you ever notice that Jose aside people on Lucy Lane mostly just *die* eventually unless they escape? As in, she *kills* them?"

"Well, it's my home, you know, Ellen, and it's really not very cool to be judgmental about other people's relationships . . . oh, let's not quarrel," she said, and cocked an eye at Adrian. "Mmmm, nice. I never saw him in his own human form before. He was in disguise that time he came to the Ranch and took you away. Is that the body, or aetheric?"

"The real him."

"He looks *just* as sexy in person as when the *Doña* puts on his seeming. She's done that with me a couple of times when she was nightwalking in his form, and *my, my, my*, no complaints, floor to ceiling and *lively*. It makes a nice change from, you know. Not that that's not fun too."

Ellen opened her mouth and then closed it. The Shadowspawn could assume the form of anyone or anything when they went Nightwalking, as long as they had a DNA sample to model on; that was one source of the succubus-incubus legends, as well as the myth about vampirism being catching. Adrienne had done that switcheroo into Adrian's form with *her* once. It still wasn't an image she wanted to have in her head, and thinking about Monica in that context . . .

Oh, twice over I do not *want that image in my head.*

"So how is he at the tying up and whipping thing?" Monica said cheerfully; she'd always been a chatterbox with a poor sense of boundaries. "The *Doña* is still using that lovely little nine-tailed silk switch she found in your stuff on me, and those restraints. You really broadened her horizons, you know, made her try more *subtle* methods and I'm having such a good time! Well, I always did, after I, umm, got used to things, but it's even better. Thanks!"

"Ah . . . glad to be of service, Monica." *I think.*

"Well, I'll see you around," she said warmly, as Adrienne turned and sauntered away, raising one hand, snapping her fingers without looking around and crooking a finger. "Duty calls."

Ellen put a hand over her eyes for a second. Adrian touched her gently on one shoulder. "My darling?" he said softly.

"You know, your sister just *loves* to put thumbtacks in people's heads. Not just in person, either."

"We have been married less than a year, yet already our thoughts move in tandem. It would have been even more unpleasant without you. Though the metaphor I used to myself was *fishhooks*."

Ellen thought for a moment, then nodded. "Better choice of words. Fishhooks come with lines attached, so you can pull on them. How is it that she's planning to destroy the world and she still finds time for this?"

"It's all part of her plan. Also . . . I did tell you how she would punish her dolls when we were children?"

Ellen shivered and nodded; she knew *exactly* how the toys would have felt, if they'd been sentient beings.

Being Shadowspawn means you never have to grow up.

She liked children, but children were like housecats, safe to be around because they were small and relatively powerless. Jillyboo the Kitten was lovable and amusing. Jillyboo the five-hundred-pound tiger wasn't. And a tantrum or cruel impulse with the Power behind it . . .

"You know, I don't think Adrienne would make a very good ruler of the world," Ellen said. "Though she'd enjoy the hell out of it. I can see her issuing National Misery Quotient targets at meetings, and starting a Disaster Production Agency."

"My great-grandfather has no intention of retiring from his position as Emperor of the Earth at any time in the next few millennia. He does not approve of . . ."

"Klingon promotion," Ellen said. "At least, not for other people doing it to him."

They looked at each other and smiled grimly. Ellen felt a knot relax slightly in her middle, and she was conscious of her hunger in a way that nerves had suppressed. A servant passed by with a tray of canapés. She reached for one, then had a sudden horrid thought and glanced at Adrian. He shook his head.

"With the al-Lanarkis, you would have to be careful about the kebabs and shwarma. They always thought of themselves as ghūl, ghouls, and their favorite transformation is to cave hyenas."

Ellen shuddered and rolled her eyes. "And cave hyenas, I suppose, are *big*."

"Two hundred and fifty, three hundred pounds. The size of a smallish lion."

"What is it with Shadowspawn and the huge? Freudian, much?"

Adrian smiled at her. "Size is not altogether to be despised. I have transformed into a giraffe on occasion."

"A *giraffe?*" she said, and he nodded solemnly. "What's it like?"

"Peaceful. Extremely peaceful. And the view, my darling, is *superb*. Not just the height, but the two-hundred-and-seventy degree arc of the eyes . . ."

She laughed, relaxed despite herself. He went on:

"And with some of the other families, one must be cautious as well; the von Trupps, for example, who are deeply committed to the *werwolf* legend."

She nodded understanding as he used the Germanic *v* pronunciation. Before the eugenic program of the Victorian period, the part-breed witch-clans had mostly believed the legends that were based on their own remote ancestors. They still formed part of the family traditions.

He went on: "But the Brézés traditionally took only the blood. When they were in human form, at least. *Cooking* humans would be . . . intolerably crude. This is, you understand, an aesthetic and culinary judgment, not a moral one."

The liveried servant had halted with blank-faced politesse, the big wrought-silver tray held at a perfect angle. Ellen wondered how he'd ended up here, if some household renfields hadn't simply kidnapped him because they needed a footman. He was so polished that even thought seemed to glance off—which was probably a survival skill in his position, working for people who might suddenly decide you looked better with your hair on fire or transfer you from the staff to the menu. She took one of the *beignets D'Huitres au vin* and followed it with a concoction of fig jam and foie gras with a very slight touch of cinnamon on a piece of baguette.

Adrian offered her a glass of wine and his arm, and they strolled off down a corridor. He gently steered her from chamber to chamber, which was normally something she didn't like outside the bedroom. After something glimpsed out of the corner of her eye through a set of great doors she was grateful. She wasn't sure what it had been and forced her mind not to speculate.

At least I don't have to sense *what's going on in the private rooms the way he does. Christ, I'm partying in the middle of a mass murder. Getting case-hardened or what?*

"Like Grand Guignol," she murmured. "But for real."

"My darling, who do you think *founded* the Le Théâtre du Grand-Guignol? And formed a good many of the audience? And it *was* real, often enough."

"You're joking, aren't—" She winced at the sadness with which he shook his head. "Oh, *man . . .*"

They gravely examined painting and sculpture, and in a few minutes her interest was genuine. The Hôtel de Brézé wasn't exactly a museum, but it had been in the family's hands a long time, and they collected. In recent generations, by just walking off with anything they fancied, starting with the Louvre, too. The management of the museums and galleries simply substituted fakes.

A servant coughed discreetly, and her heart thudded. The disadvantage of living in a place like this was that things could be very far apart indeed; it took ten minutes to bring them to the library the master had chosen. An odd-looking group—dark men and women wearing striped ponchos and derby-style hats—was leaving as they arrived.

When they entered, the Duc de Beauloup was sitting in a leather chair before a fire, cradling a brandy snifter while Seraphine leaned against the mantel with hers; she was wearing a new form, a slender freckled redhead with great brilliant green eyes, in a 50's-style Chanel classic, the Little Black Dress.

"Peruvians," Étienne-Maurice said, with a weight of disgust, and his wife laughed.

Adrian raised an eyebrow. His great-grandfather went on:

"Your Californian branch of the family is responsible. They brought the message of our discoveries to the Andes for the Council. The Spanish-speakers are well enough, for Spaniards, if a trifle provincial and given to hidalgo airs. But the cult up in the Andes called themselves *lik'ichiri*, fat-stealers, and dealing with them is . . . ah, but enough of that. Even the Power cannot turn a dirty dog of a savage with a bone through his nose and a tom-tom fixation into something worthy of civilized company."

Ellen blinked. *Remember, born in the 1870s,* she told herself. *Hasn't seen sunlight since Hitler was a two-bit agitator in Munich.*

It was surprising how dealing with an inhuman monster became so much more difficult when he also had the all-too-human casual prejudices of someone born shortly after the Franco-Prussian War.

The decor of the library was Victorian rather than Louis XV, dark woods and books and carved oak, globes and mounted maps and a few stuffed animal heads. Which was natural enough, he was old but not Louis XV old like the Hôtel; this study would have been very mildly out of date when he was a young man. There was a faint smell of fine tobacco beneath the leather and old books, and Isfahan rugs that looked as if they were from the same generation as their owner.

She'd gotten used to that scent because Adrian smoked occasionally—a purebred couldn't get cancer. Even with environmental insults like tobacco smoke, that required *bad luck* on the cellular level.

I don't think the Pompidou Center has much future if the Empire of Shadow ever comes back full-bore. I suspect Great-granddaddy there would have everything built after he went post-corporeal torn down.

Adrienne entered a moment later, alone: she wouldn't bring a lucy to a conference. In a way, it was an affirmation of Ellen's status—the Shadowspawn operated in families like the Mafia, only with a bit less old-time sexism since the Power had never been a respecter of gender. In another, it was a one-up for Adrienne, that she dared leave Monica unattended. *She* was probably terrified, and not in a good way . . .

The servant picked up a crystal decanter that gleamed with a silvery sheen like polished hematite, marked with platinum fleur-de-lis designs. He poured three more glasses, offered them about, then retired to the doorway, standing with his hands crossed before him. Ellen suddenly noticed that he had a tiny radio-bud in one ear, nearly hidden by the antique wig. She sat silently, sniffed aromas of vanilla and spiced flowers, then let the Black Pearl run over her tongue like the essence of passion fruit and sandalwood.

"Very nice," she said.

Actually true. I never liked brandy until Adrian introduced me to the real thing. And I have to keep the Demon King there sweet, if we're to have any chance of blocking Adrienne's coup and then springing our own *surprise on her. Which means I have to help save Great-grandpa . . . for now. Politics makes strange . . . oh, God, get that image out of my head!*

"Thank you, sire," she went on.

Étienne-Maurice inclined his head with a gracious-host smile. "Quite good, is it not? A blend of over a thousand eaux-de-vie, I understand, some of them laid down before I was born and none less than forty years old. There *are* things this modern age does better, even if the aesthetics are deplorable. When I still dwelt in the flesh I sampled cognac put in the oak during the reign of the first Napoleon, and it was not quite so fine. Less subtle, though of course my perceptions have improved."

He nodded to Adrienne. "A point you have made to me, *ma fille*. If we deny the humans all their inventions, there is so much less we can take for ourselves. After all, where would we be if my own father had not been scientific and *progressive*, in his way?"

Adrienne made a wordless sound of appreciation as she sipped her own, with her eyes held reverently closed for a moment before she spoke. The Brézés might not be really human, but they were certainly old-style French about some things. Ellen thought her appreciation was genuine, not just flattery:

"I shall add this to my mental cellar, sire, for only in trance will I see its equal, alas. Also, if we returned the world to the Dark Ages I would miss my aircraft. And motorcycles and fashion shows, for that matter. Castles are so drafty and boring! And I prefer my victims to wash and not have skin diseases."

The lord of the Shadowspawn put his snifter down and made a small gesture over it to keep the servant from refilling.

"So, Adrian," he said after a brooding stare over steepled fingers. "You claim that Adrienne is attempting to use a rogue Brotherhood agent to smuggle a nuclear bomb into the Council meeting, despite my embracing her policy preferences? Presumably to wipe us all out and leave her and her faction to inherit the Throne of the World after the humans are put in their place."

Seraphine smiled, covering her lips for a moment with two fingers as if smothering a chuckle. Adrian kept his face expressionless as he nodded.

"In essence, yes, sire."

Adrienne chuckled and shook her head indulgently. "And I am supposed to be concealing a *nuclear weapon* from nearly a thousand powerful adepts . . . in what way or manner, exactly? If I could Wreak on that level, I would be God. Not *a* god, *the* God. Which would be delightful, but which is beyond even my ambitions at present."

Étienne-Maurice raised his glass and tilted it, viewing the low flames through the dark honey-colored liquid. "That is the crux of the matter, is it not? I could not conceal such a weapon, not if I intended to use it so. If you know of such a means, Adrian, will you drop your shields so that I may verify?"

"If Adrienne will do the same," Adrian said.

Something went *clank* in Ellen's head, Wreakings activating to conceal her thoughts, and suddenly all her emotions felt curiously muffled and distant, as if she had just taken a heavy hit of Percocet. It was actually rather welcome in itself, since what she'd been feeling was mostly fear and loathing, but this was the crisis point. If Adrienne was willing to do that, then the Brotherhood's secret would be out. That would be a disaster, and destroy the first real advantage the Brotherhood had ever had in the long war: Adrian had given every oath he could think of to its commanders, and submitted to Wreakings that made it impossible for him to betray it to his kin, despite the fact that it would instantly make his story of the smuggled bomb credible.

Adrienne had ferreted it out, of course. If she agreed to open her mind, the secret would be revealed.

Thankfully, the chances of that are—

"No, of course I will not," Adrienne said cheerfully. "What, and expose my plots?"

Ellen closed her eyes in relief and completed the thought:—*very low.* Then she finished off the brandy to hide the gesture.

"What, you are plotting against me? I am shocked, *chère pucelle,* shocked to the depths of my wicked soul," Étienne-Maurice said.

He and his wife and great-granddaughter all laughed, his deep, Seraphine's silvery, Adrienne's warm and soft. Ellen shivered slightly. Adrian's face showed nothing at all.

I have met a family that's worse than mine was. And the drawback of *being totally—justifiably—paranoid is that it makes you* more *vulnerable to treachery, not less. Because he assumes she's always been plotting against him along with everyone else, the real plot vanishes in the background noise. It's . . . diabolical. It is so fucking Adrienne!*

A touch on her arm told her that Adrian had picked the thought out of her head, though she wouldn't have been surprised if both of them had had it at once anyway.

"And so this accusation . . . one cannot take it seriously," Seraphine said.

Étienne-Maurice cocked an eyebrow. "That does not mean it should not be dealt with at all, or that there is no element of truth involved. I will arrange a ritual this evening . . . there is certainly enough talent available. Eastern Anatolia, you say, Adrian? I never liked the area, though the Armenian business had a certain crude grandeur—that was the al-Lanarkis, of course. Throwing a curse in that general direction will be a . . . pardon the expression . . . good deed."

"Yes, sire," Adrian said, rising and bowing. "I would not presume to advise you on the details of a black curse."

"If I did not know better, I could find an accusation in that!"

Seraphine wiggled her fingers at Adrienne. "Perhaps you would join me instead?" she said. "There is a . . . guest. A very sincere young priest— a rarity in these degenerate times. I have an amusing scenario in mind, involving a form I picked up in the 40s of the last century, a gloriously beautiful youth of fifteen, just barely sufficiently ripe."

"That would be lovely, madame," Adrienne said cheerfully.

In the corridor outside Ellen shivered. "That went better than I thought it might," she said. "Essentially, we won . . . sorta."

"And yet Adrienne is not dissatisfied. That is a bad sign."

"Would she let you know if she *was* doing a slow burn?"

Adrian quirked an eyebrow. "She and I are twins; she could not entirely conceal it. She is planning some devilment, probably by proxy. And we have many vulnerabilities."

CHAPTER SIX

Santa Fe, New Mexico

"Weasel! I'm a weaaaasel!" the boy shouted as he dove over the chamiso bush in an explosion of powdery snow.

"Woof! Woof! I'm a wolfie and I'll *eat you up!*" his sister caroled as she raced after him, eight-year-old arms pumping.

"Come back here, you little *par de esquintles!*" Eusebia Cortines yelled.

Eric Salvador listened and grinned, cradling the shotgun in his arms and keeping his eyes moving over the field of view. You couldn't keep kids in *all* the time, and this pair were more active than most.

He was a stocky, muscular thirty-one years old, and his upper lip was very slightly lighter than the weathered dark-olive of the rest of his face, where a mustache had been until recently. A scar ran down from his cheek to the corner of his mouth, giving it a bit of a quirk. Black hair was cropped close to the sides and top of his head, showing with the hood of his jacket thrown back.

He looked like an ex-Marine NCO from here in northern New Mexico. One who'd pulled a tour in the sandpit, Iraq, and one and a quarter on the rockpile—which was what you called Afghanistan, if you were in the Suck and hence among the connoisseurs of bad neighborhoods. And then spent years being a cop, after he healed up from the IED.

All that was exactly what he was. The *indios* among his ancestors had been around here since the last glacial period; the rest was seventeenth-century Spanish and a little Irish several generations back. He'd started to grow love-handles while he was a homicide roach and especially after the divorce—irregular hours and junk food—but they were gone again now.

Because now I'm a Brotherhood soldier, I suppose, sorta-kinda and without most of the regular training yet. Mierda, back in the Suck only with less air support. Hell, I'm the mouj now, running scared because the other side has all the cool toys. Like, they can make your blood boil . . . literally.

Eusebia—Cheba to her friends—managed to grab Leila and Leon Brézé before they vanished into the darkening juniper and piñon-clad hillside, and escorted them back with a hand under each arm.

"It is late," she said firmly; she believed children should obey adult caretakers promptly, and didn't give a damn who their parents were. "It is nearly time for dinner."

The word *dinner* got the twins' attention; they were both chow-hounds and loved Mexican. Their near-identical triangular faces turned up towards her under mops of raven hair.

"Did *you* cook dinner, Cheba?" the boy asked.

"Yes, I did, *mi rey.*"

"Okay, we're ready!" his sister said.

"Show me your hands, *reynita*. I thought so. Go and wash," she said, giving them a little shove towards the front doors.

Her English was much more fluent now, but still a little slow, and had been developing a tendency to a bookish, Worf-like lack of contractions. Eric gave the surroundings a long last look. The house that Adrian Brézé had built northeast of Santa Fe was long and low, built of fieldstone covered with stucco for the most part. The surroundings turned imperceptibly from a xeroscape garden of native plants into shaggy, rocky hills. The sky was turning dark purple to the east, with the first stars just starting to glitter in the high-desert air. The west was still an implausible striation of clouds turning to cream and hot gold and molten copper, fading to teal green and blue above; the snow on the peaks of the Sangre de Cristo Mountains westward was blush-pink for a moment.

He'd grown up around here, albeit in far more modest circumstances, and he'd never tired of looking at it. Why leave the best part of it all for the tourists? Outsiders thought the paintings of Santa Fe sunsets were garish kitsch; you had to live here a while to realize that no paint palette could rival the real thing, or the clarity of the air. You had to go away and come back to really appreciate it if you'd been born here.

They went through the big copper-plated doors; the copper had silver sheathing within and the walls had silver thread. The central block of the house was open-plan with eighteen-foot ceilings of exposed viga beams; the southeast-facing wall was mostly tall windows, a narrow tile-paved terrace and planters outside it dropping off several thousand feet in a jagged steepness of cliff and arroyo. The view was spectacular, and there was nothing human in it except the lights of a tiny hamlet twinkling in the middle distance and a freight-train drawing away. Off to the left was a large kitchen full of European equipment separated by a stone island from a dining area centered on a massive cast-glass table. It was a big house, not a mansion that couldn't function without a huge staff of servants, though it was also certainly not like anything he'd lived in before.

"*¡Dios! ¡Huele 're sabroso, niña!*" he said, sniffing with appreciation at the cooking odors. "God, that smells good!"

He cleared the chambers of the double-barrel as he sniffed and hung it and the bandolier on a wall rack. It still seemed odd to carry a weapon so primitive, but even the five moving parts in this relic needed to be protected with glyphs if they were to function at all when an adept was around and trying to screw things up. They made his palms buzz a little. He'd always had a nose for danger, which was why he hadn't come back from the rockpile in a plastic bag—it had been close even so.

The Albermann test the Brotherhood used said that he was just barely capable of doing simple Wreaking, though it still seemed a lot like magic to him. The down-side of that capacity was that without training it made you *even more* vulnerable to Shadowspawn thinkery-fuckery than ordinary people. He was absorbing the techniques as fast as he could.

"*¡Inglés!*" Cheba said. "I need the practice. And this country is *freezing*. Freezing, dry, rocky. Why did anyone from Mexico ever come here?"

He carefully didn't say: You're beautiful when you're angry, though it was true. Though you spend a lot of time being angry. Understandable, I suppose.

She was a dime and some younger than him, with more *indio* and less Spanish, plus a dash of African, originally from a little corn-and-beans ejido called Coetzala in the hills of upcountry Veracruz, a place so backward every third inhabitant still spoke Nahuatl. She had a full-lipped heart-shaped face, curly black hair, skin the color of cinnamon and a figure closer to the hourglass type than was common where she came from. She had very little formal education, but he'd come to respect her almost fanatical pursuit of self-improvement and focus on the main chance.

Instead of the compliment that sprang to mind he answered the question:

"Why come here? Chasing rumors of gold. Back then a Spaniard would crawl naked over cactus for that. And later because this was where you sent relatives who embarrassed you, cousin Diego who couldn't keep it in his pants with the alcalde's daughter—"

She gave a snort of laughter as she wielded a spoon in a dish of something bubbling and brown.

"— the backside of nowhere with Apaches behind every rock, knives in their teeth. There was one caravan from Sonora or Chihuahua every year, sometimes every two years. My people here used to hunt buffalo with lances, and trade the hides to the wild Commanche for guns *they* got from the French, that was how poor they were."

He helped her set the table as he spoke. He was pretty sure she thought that was a bit odd; she'd probably have considered him something of a sissy if she hadn't seen him in action when they'd busted her out of *Rancho Sangre* and got Adrian's kids. That was the estate of the California branch of the Brézé family.

There was a lot of hurry-up-and-wait in the Suck, and you could spend only so much time pumping iron. He'd had a fair amount of time to read, and it gave him the vocabulary to describe that little bit of quiet, picturesque isn't-this-pretty New Urbanist hell-on-earth.

First it's like Norman Rockwell. Then you realize it's more like Stephen King.

"Then why did the gringos want this country?"

"Because it was between Texas and California and too big to jump over even with a running start."

She laughed again. He thought she *also* thought it a bit odd he hadn't hit on her to speak of. She'd ended up in Rancho Sangre as part of a job-lot of illegals Adrienne Brézé had bought from a coyote, a people-smuggler, quite literally as snacks for a party. Except that Shadowspawn liked to play with their food. He'd been a cop in the Southwest for years; he knew what was likely to happen to a girl in the pipeline for illegals, and then she'd caught Adrienne's eye as a blood-donor-cum-toy, which was worse because an adept could seriously fuck with your head. Though that was better than what had happened to her companions.

Eric was surprised she was as together as she was, and at how fast she'd bounced back; they made them tough down there.

"And the people are all soft, like *mozitas*," she grumbled as she set out bowls of a rich *menudo*.

"You were a little girl once," he pointed out.

"Not like that."

"Like Peter?" he said.

"No," Cheba said. "He's a man, that one, even if he *looks* like a girl. I got to know him at the hacienda."

Actually Peter Boase wasn't particularly girly-looking, just blond, fine-featured and small; he'd escaped and gone cold turkey from the feeding addiction, all alone in a little rundown motel room in southern Arizona. Cheba had done it with experienced Brotherhood medics to help, and it had still hurt like hell, like coming off mainlining black tar. She gave the tribute grudgingly, though.

"Let's eat, then," he said instead.

Dinner was *menudo* thick with the hominy used south of the border. The tortillas to sop up the rich broth and tripe with chiles and tomatoes were made fresh from the hominy as well. *Café con leche* warmed little bodies that had chilled in the suddenly falling night.

And when I said kids shouldn't have coffee, she just looked at me like I was crazy, told me that La Doña had had no objection and her people always had it before sleeping, for cena, *mostly with sweet breads or cookies.*

The children shoveled it all away with gusto and apparently with four hollow legs between them, though their table manners were excellent and they were slender-fit. Then they settled down to watch the third installment of the *Hobbit* trilogy on a 3-D screen that scrolled down over the big picture window while doing some serious damage to bowls of mint chocolate ice cream from the Aztec Café downtown. Eric pulled two beers out of the refrigerator and started to chuckle.

"What?" Cheba said.

"This," he said, turning it so she could see the label. "It's called Stone Arrogant Bastard Ale."

When she looked puzzled, he translated it:

"*Más o menos, El Cabron más Presumido.*"

He had to hunt for the equivalent of *Bastard* because the dialect of *ladino* Spanish he'd grown up with as his second language had a lot of English loanwords in it including that one as well as being archaic even by Mexican standards.

And bastard is too common a condition south of the border to be an insult the way it is in the North, and arrogant? They're all arrogant under the right circumstances.

"That is . . . what's the English word . . ." Cheba said, flashing a smile. "Like him? The right word, the . . ."

"Appropriate?"

"*Sí*, the a-prro-priate word for the man who owns this house."

"Adrian's not a bad guy."

"He has good manners and he is a man of honor. He has balls, too. He is also, yes, *a stone arrogant bastard.* Like a cat, you know? Or a don in the old days."

"Yeah, but he's *our* stone arrogant bastard. He killed . . . well, he and Ellen killed . . . that Shadowspawn bitch who murdered my partner and his girlfriend. Right over there where the kids are now, after I pumped the whole magazine from a Glock into her and she laughed at me and told me I looked delicious. I owe him."

"Me also too. And I don't like owing things to people. I pay the debt as soon as I can, so I guard his children." She sipped, and looked around. "Good beer. And someday I will have a house like this."

He'd grown up on Bud from cans, and at first this stuff hadn't tasted like *beer* at all. It was caramel and coffee and chocolate and a smooth richness with a kick like a ball-peen hammer upside the head, and he'd come to like it. He'd been a little surprised by *Casa Grande* Adrian Brézé's house and everything in it; it was simpler than he'd expected, certainly a lot plainer than what the bad branch of the Brézés had in that creepy place in California. Then he'd realized it was the simplicity of someone who did exactly what he wanted and didn't give a damn for either expense or what anyone else thought of his choices.

"I could get used to all this," he said. "It's not exactly what I'd have if I could have whatever I wanted, but it's fun. And honest."

"So, your family, what did they do? Mine were *campesinos*, farmers. From always, and then when my father died my mother and I sold baskets to tourists in Tlacotalpan."

He leaned back in the chair and looked out at the moon-washed mountainscape, tilting the beer back again. The conversation required a little backing and filling and dropping in and out of Spanish and English:

"My grandfathers both had little ranchos and a few sheep, sometimes my mother's father worked in the mines and my father's father on the railroads, and they were soldiers in the time of Vietnam. My grandmothers worked in the gardens and around the house, the chickens, that sort of thing."

Cheba nodded; it was all obviously fairly familiar to her, the outline if not the details.

"My father had a garage . . . fixed cars, did fancy work on them sometimes, restored old cars, classics, for rich people. Before then he was in the Suck, the Marine Corps, in the first war in Iraq. He died years ago, cancer, when I was still young."

"You were a soldier too, no? Before you were a policeman?"

"Soldier, hell. Marine! I enlisted out of high school and stayed in until I made sergeant and got a correspondence degree from UNM in Criminal Justice, then came back here. My sister is married to a dentist named Anderson—pretty decent guy but we don't have much in common."

"Because he is a gringo?"

"Nah, because he's a civilian who thinks the world is a nice place; sort of like a big Labrador retriever puppy with glasses, you don't get to think that way if you're in a war. Or working as a cop, sometimes that's harder 'cause you don't expect it to end. But he's good to Alvara and the kids and I get a cut on my dental work. The police work was why Julia . . . my wife . . . took off. Said she couldn't stand being married to my job."

"No children?" she said.

It was a bit of an interrogation, but he found he didn't mind. "Nah, Julia said she wanted to wait."

They sat in silence for a while the movie murmured from the arched entrance to the living room. Both of them watched the cold moonlight move on the slopes. He grinned, then laughed like a coyote, the furry kind.

"What is funny? I would like to hear something funny."

"New Mexico looks a lot like Afghanistan, the parts I was mostly in. Other sections are more like Arizona, but this is a dead ringer for some places along the Paki border. Dry, scrubby, rocky, cold in winter, like you said. Even the houses look a lot alike, at least like the old ones. Even the people, except for the clothes and stuff. More like me than you."

He blinked, blinked again, his hand tightening on the fading coolness of the beer bottle.

Helicopter blades beat through the night in his mind, thupthupthupthup.

Puffs of white dust over the ridge just before the Apaches topped it and banked against the full moon and slid down smooth and hard and low, their black skins tight as sharks with malign intent. Rockets trailing incandescent light and smoke like dirty cotton candy from the pods under their stub wings. Lines of fire snapping down and broken adobe flying back up in black gouts with red blinks in their centers.

Whatever-it-was creeping under his body armor stopped driving him crazy as everything turned to crystal ice and he pushed himself up a little on his elbows. He reached up with one hand and snapped down his PVS-9 and the world went from dark night to pale green overcast day with blooms of light where fire billowed as he snuggled the butt into his shoulder. Noise in the dry rustling corn across the irrigation ditch as the explosions died away, feet pounding the hard clay. Stalks waving like banners despite no wind. Baylor's voice rasping in his earbud from the other wing of the L-shaped ambush, that burring Louisiana coonass accent:

"Top, we got movement on your twelve! *Mouj, mouj!*"

Figures, glowing a little through the cornstalks as the thermal sensors in the goggles caught them against the colder background. Dozens, maybe thirty. Running fast away from the tunnels and spider holes in the village, no idea at all they'd been drone-tracked for days and were being herded into the killing ground, just trying to get out from the lash of the rockets and the chain-guns that swiveled under the gunships' bellies like the stingers of great malignant wasps sparkling the night with muzzle flashes.

"Smoke 'em, bitches!" he snapped through the throat mike.

And brought the M-4 up and brought the laser on target and started to squeeze off crisp three-round bursts, the bullets hitting the baggy tunics, dust flying up as the men danced like jointed puppets on strings and the shattered cornstalks fell on their bodies, *choonk . . . choonk* as one of his squad cut loose with his grenade launcher, the mouj screaming *Allahu Akbar* and spraying the night with AK rounds, or just screaming in fear and pain, everything would be darkness and chaos and strobing lights to them, green tracer going wild far overhead, swap out the magazine . . .

"Eric!"

Cheba was staring at him, concern on her face. He brought his mind and the expression on his face back from a place many years and thousands of miles away.

"Ah, sorry," he said, and went back to the kitchen; he washed out the bottles and set them to drain and got two more before he returned to the darkened table. "Thinking too hard."

"You liked Afghanistan, because it was like your home?"

"No, that made me hate it even more. And now I'm back home, and goddamn if I'm not feeling the same way I did when we were doing night patrol. Except there's beer."

He raised the bottle towards his lips, then set it down on the table, his eyes going wide.

Fuck me, he thought. *It feels exactly like that. Like bugs are crawling over me.*

Leon came through the arched opening from the living room, just after the sound of the screen rolling up.

"A bad man is coming," he said solemnly, eyes a little wide with controlled fright. "Leila says so too."

"*Go!*" Eric shouted at Cheba.

She came out of the chair as if she was on springs, snatched a machete with a silvered blade out of its sheath where it lay on the polished granite countertop between the kitchen and dining room, then dashed through grabbing Leon as she did. Eric passed her as if she were standing still, stopped by running into the wall, whipped the shotgun from the rack, broke it open and jammed in the shells.

"Down, down, *down!*" he shouted as he snapped the action back.

This house was built like a fort, except for the windows over a sheer cliff. There was a lever he could hit to drop grills over the windows, but he couldn't reach it without crossing the room. So—

Something flitted through the night, swelling towards him. Cheba dropped the machete, set her foot on it and went down with the children squealing beneath her. A rock the size of his head slammed into the glass of the great window at interstate speed and shattered it. Eric ducked his head for an instant to shield his eyes.

The forty-pound eagle came through just as fast in the wake of the stone it had released thousands of feet up, talons like four-inch curved daggers outstretched to grab his face and rip it off in passing. The moa-eater, the human-killing *pouakai* of Maori legend.

"Eat this, motherfucker!"

He let go with both barrels. A cloud of silvered double-ought buck exploded at the onrushing bird. It had started to twist violently even before his finger tightened on the trigger—fighting precognition just wasn't *fair*. It slammed into the arch over the dining room entrance, pinwheeled—

—Sparkled—

—and was a naked man, brown and muscular, blood streaming from his face and chest, leaping at him with a snarl—

—And Cheba was between them, shrieking and swinging roundhouse at his throat with the machete—

—and the man went under the swipe of the blade with a smooth duck and hit her backhanded under the ribs with the edge of his palm. In the same instant he shouted something in a language that made the hairs on Eric's forearms crinkle and slammed his other hand forward in a crook-fingered gesture. The shotgun slipped out of Eric's hands and blood burst out of his nose and his eyes were like spikes of dry pain as the amulet around his neck turned hot—

—and Leon and Leila were standing between him and the man. They stood with their arms around each other's shoulders, the other hands pointing at the attacker, their faces stark and huge-eyed.

The man who'd been an eagle seemed to ram into an invisible wall in the air. Cheba came up again, bent over and gasping where she held her left hand to her side, but the blade wavering in her right as she wound up for a cut at the back of his leg. The Shadowspawn turned with another snarl and dove out through the broken window into the night and the long drop to the ground below. A *whump* came from the darkness, as if giant wings had struck the air.

"Go!" Eric wheezed again.

He ignored the shotgun; the action had broken open and the barrels were out of alignment with the breech, some freak crystallization of the metal making it snap. There were plenty of weapons where he was headed, anyway. Cheba hobbled quickly through the door into Adrian Brézé's bedroom. The door of what looked like a big walk-in closet hissed open, sliding sideways to reveal its thickness. They all tumbled in to a small square room that was utterly featureless except for its lining of brown-and-orange cocobolo wood.

"Down!" Eric snarled.

The elevator dropped, fast; it was a special type, one that didn't use cables. He didn't really need to say anything, the Wreakings and control circuits just sensed his intention and identified him as someone on the list of permitted guests, but it helped to focus. Something went *thud* up above, felt through the floor, and Cheba looked up at him from her corner.

"Blocking doors across the shaft," he said. "Glyphs and silver and really thick steel and all that good . . . stuff."

He wiped at the blood on his mouth with the back of his hand, grimacing at the taste. The children were looking at him with sudden interest, then politely glanced away.

God, they can be creepy at times, he thought. *They're not bad kids, but they're odd. Sometimes they're playing like my nieces and nephews, and sometimes they're not fucking human at all.*

The elevator halted and the door slid silently open a thousand feet below the surface. Beyond was a corridor, with white walls that had a layer of Redondo tile along the bottom and above a high groin-arched ceiling carved from the native rock and smoothly plastered. The floor was pale marble, with a strip of sisal carpet down the center dyed in vivid geometric shapes. Indirect LED lighting gave it a pleasant brightness; the arrival of the elevator turned it on the system throughout the underground refuge.

He'd had the tour within; there were bedrooms, kitchens, library, armory and workshops, a video room the size of a small movie theater, data servers, supplies enough to keep you in pickled artichoke hearts and foie gras for years, and an industrial-strength fuel-cell power system fed by a trickle of natural gas from far below. There was even a swimming pool and a gym with sunlamps, everything but a monologuing bad guy with a Nehru jacket and a cat. The place could shelter dozens and survive anything up to and including a low-end apocalypse or a near miss with a fusion bomb. You probably wouldn't even go crazy.

Not at first.

Eric helped Cheba hobble with him to the infirmary. As they treated each other's injuries and he checked that she didn't have a popped rib or internal hemorrhage, she glanced up at him. "They cannot walk through the walls?"

"Nope. Too thick, they'd be like a man swimming underwater for too long. And it's low-grade silver ore all around us."

"*Plata?*" she said, and then bit her lip and gasped as he probed.

Just a bad bruise, he thought with relief. *Must not have had the leverage to hit her really hard. You can lose a kidney from that one if it hits just right. Must hurt like a bitch, though. Still, she didn't lose dinner.*

He went on aloud to distract her as he stripped the plastic off a hypo of local anesthetic.

"*Sí*, that's why Mr. Stone Arrogant Bastard bought this land. It would be like walking through *boiling* water to them. We're safe . . . until we try to get out."

The children ran off; they loved the place, the way they would a tree-house.

"*Should* we try and escape?" she said levelly.

There were also money, clothes, and documents including a wide assortment of passports, and hidden tunnels . . . and contingency plans for this.

"Oh, hell yes. I'm not going to sit tight and wait for them to come to me. Adrian left a couple of alternate ways to get out of here if it got too hot."

You . . . idiot. Adrienne's mental voice was like a lash of chilled steel, even with the low bandwidth imposed by long-distance telepathy. **You . . . moron. Izidingidwane! Baka tare! Èrbǎiwǔ! I . . . am . . . surrounded . . . by . . . morons!**

The exchange became wordless for a moment, like a chorus of shrill hissing snarls, before she changed the thought-stream to words again. Dale Shadowblade could *feel* the background around her, gilt and pale stone and minds like walking razors.

I . . . told . . . you . . . to . . . wait . . . and . . . watch . . . not . . . endanger . . . my . . . children, she thought.

Back . . . off, Dale replied. **I . . . saw/felt/sensed . . . a . . . nexus . . . and . . . went . . . for . . . it . . . to . . . bust . . . them . . . out.**

A mental snarl. **Of . . . course . . . but . . . my . . . children . . . are . . . so . . . high . . . on . . . the . . . Albermann . . . scale . . . even . . . still . . . latent . . . they . . . distort . . . the . . . world . . . lines! There . . . was . . . no . . . way . . . to . . . tell . . . if . . . it . . . was . . . black-path . . . for . . . us . . . or not! Their . . . future . . . a . . . thousand . . . years . . . from . . . now . . . could . . . be . . . bleeding . . . backward . . . to . . . protect . . . itself!**

I'm . . . here . . . you . . . ain't . . . so . . . get . . . off . . . my . . . case . . . bossbitch.

There was a long pause. Then: **Watch . . . and . . . keep . . . me . . . informed . . . we . . . don't . . . need . . . additional . . . random . . . factors . . . before . . . Tbilisi.**

I . . . grovel . . . and . . . obey . . . so . . . fucking . . . much.

He opened his eyes and snarled as the pain hit. Three of the shot had struck despite his dodge, and while the actual damage didn't transfer across when you returned to the body, the hurting sure as shit did. Something deep down *believed* that it was your flesh arm and shoulder and face that had stopped the high-velocity metal—if they were silvered. Going impalpable was an elementary trick, you could just let ordinary lead pass through the aetheric form, but silver plowed right in. Hurt you the way ordinary stuff would your meat-body.

It was one reason silver jewelry was popular around here. They'd known about Big Owl and Rock Monster Eagle and that the skinwalkers were among them back before the white-eyes came with *their* versions. Sometimes he wished the Brézés and the Council hadn't taught his great-grandparents about genes and let their descendants become more than common-or-garden 'áńt'įįzhį, getting by on low-level curses and a little friendly incest and catching the occasional tourist out in the badlands and skinning them alive . . . but it was like anything else, you had to move with the times.

Kai was waiting when he sat upright. He lunged his mouth against her throat and fed, and the pain and weakness receded, beaten back by the wind within. The thin pale-skinned girl with the spiked black hair crawled away to the fire when he finished, whimpering, and brought him a bowl. He squatted by low coals and spooned up the deer-and-corn stew and ate chunks of the frybread while she drank Gatorade. He could do the fancy restaurant thing, but there were times you wanted to eat the way you were raised.

"Good," he said. "Keep your electrolytes up."

She grinned nervously at him as he tossed her the bowl.

"Eat. We'll be moving out unless the Mex decides to hide. And that's not how I read him. The bosslady is sending Dmitri to give me a hand."

He'd picked her up at a music festival years ago, and hadn't killed her because she had enough of the Power to be useful with a little training, but not enough to be a threat even if she weren't his whipped bitch. Hadn't killed her in the flesh; it was somewhere around forty times inside, soul-carrying. He'd also never met anyone who liked dying as much.

"We going somewhere, Dale?"

"Yeah. We're following bossbitch's brats and that roach her brother's got shepherding them."

Kai grimaced. "I don't like her. Why are you looking out for her kids?"

"Nobody likes her except her" Dale grinned; he was feeling better. "But *she* really *loves* her. We need her until Tbilisi goes down and then the plague. Your real beef is that she thinks you're low rent. She wouldn't drink your blood if you were both alone in the middle of the Sahara Desert."

"Yeah, Madame Brézé likes blonds with big ta-tas and elegant Eurotrash guys with monogram cuff links and they all gotta be intellectual giants . . . I mean, she's gonna fuck 'em and bleed 'em and then *do* them and they have to have degrees and talk about art?" Kai grumbled.

"Her lucies thought you should be scraped off a shoe too."

"I wouldn't touch her twat with a Taser. *Or* theirs." Something flickered in her eyes and aura. "Maybe with some pliers, yeah, or a lit cigarette."

Dale laughed and rolled one, lighting it with a twig. Then he closed his eyes for a moment and slipped into a semi-trance, seeing the world without past or present, as a web of potential.

"Yup, I can see what she meant," he said dreamily, coming back to the moment. "Looks like we're going to be traveling if we can't clear this up here soon. There are gaps in the lines, too much Power sloshing around and something . . . something odd and spooky. But I see . . . Europe. It's coming together like rocks rolling downhill."

"Cool!" Kai said. "Like, Paris and shit?"

"Maybe we'll do some Euro-trash dudes and blonds ourselves."

"Damn, sounds like fun. Can I link while you bleed them and feed? Fuck, that's the best. Wish I could do it myself."

"Don't," he said, and took her jaw in his hand. "I'd have killed you by now if you could. And no soul-carrying either, you'd be dangerous inside my head that way."

Then he threw her down on the rocky ground beside the fire, looming over her like Death.

CHAPTER SEVEN

Paris-Mitteleuropa

Arailway attendant in an archaic uniform met them as they stepped from the cab before the main gate of the Gar de l'Est, holding up an umbrella against the light slushy snow.

"Monsieur *et* Madame Brézé? For the Venice-Simplon Orient Express Special to Istanbul? This way, if you please."

Porters in period costume swarmed over their luggage. Ellen turned to him:

"*Don't* tell me it was your great-grandfather who had this restarted," she said. "You said we were taking the train, but I didn't expect *this*."

Adrian looked at her straight-faced, enjoying her surprise. She was very fetching, he thought, in a long-sleeved taupe Celtic knotwork cable twinset with intarsia hints of rose and cream in the fine cashmere, and a

deep box-pleated skirt of fine brown wool. A few snowflakes were melting on the glossy black Astrakan fur of her coat and Cossack-style hat.

"I cannot tell you it was him," he said gravely.

"Aha! I win!"

"Perhaps I should punish you for that."

"Is that a promise, lover?"

"But I will not. Because it was my great-grandmother's idea, not his,"
he said, feeling his spirits lift as he sensed hers. "Indirectly; an ordinary
company acquired and refurbished the original cars of the Orient Express to the level of the 1920s, and runs them as a luxury excursion.
Except when the masters wish to use them, of course."

Then he grinned. "There! True to the letter, false to the spirit, and you
can't complain."

"I can't complain but I *can* kick you," she said, and did—lightly, on
the ankle. Then she did a double take as they walked through the huge
barrel-vaulted concourse and onto the platform beneath the iron and
glass.

"My God," she said. "Is that a *steam engine?*"

It was, a big gleaming-black 2-8-2 French version of the old Pacifics
belching smoke and steam amid a smell of burning coal and hot wetness, and the Parisians and tourists who crowded the Gar de l'Est were
gawking. Discreet security details kept them at a distance. Adrian put
his head to one side and concentrated. A flicker of emotions—wonder,
annoyance, that stolid bureaucratic feeling of doing one's job without
curiosity . . .

"Maybe we should be taking Platform Nine and Three-Quarters,"
she said, shaking her head.

"I think they are indeed claiming it is all a part of a film," Adrian
said.

Ellen shook her head again. "Why on earth would the Council adepts want the trouble of running the world, when they can do *this* sort of thing just on a whim?"

And she is as intelligent as she is ornamental, he thought, happy despite the tension. *Indeed, that she loves me—for what I am—is undeserved good fortune.*

"They might not, if it were not for the increasing risk of the great secret being discovered," he said. "Or the earth being ruined. It took decades of dispute for them to decide and a great deal of pressure from . . ."

A prickle ran through him, and he laid a hand on Ellen's arm: "Do not be startled. *She* is near. The agent of this crisis."

Ellen turned slowly, and inclined her head very slightly. Adrienne was dressed in the height of fashion . . . for nineteen twenty-two, or so; bobbed hair, a cloche hat with a band, and a straight tubular dress under a coat with a spotted ermine collar. One hand held a cigarette in a long ivory holder, wrist bent at an extravagant silent-film-star angle. Monica was beside her, carrying a small overnight suitcase of ostrich leather; she wore a soft sapphire blue wool coat with a collar of golden ocelot fur, and it made her shoulders look exaggeratedly big. Beneath was a jaquard-loomed silk dropwaisted dress, patterned with silver wolves and nymphs on a nile green background.

"*Nothing lacking but another maid with a lapdog,*" he heard Ellen murmur inaudibly.

"'allo, *chérie,*" Adrienne said to her cheerfully. "Just . . ." She indicated the steam train. ". . . going with the ambience. Though that is a very pleasant outfit, I must admit."

"20s suits you," Ellen said coolly, looking down her nose slightly. "If *I* was doing period, I'd have gone Belle Époque, with a Gibson Girl blouse and walking skirt with a nice loose Harris Tweed coat. You'd look mousy in that, of course."

Adrian felt a flash of genuine annoyance from his sister, and smiled slightly. It was an absolutely correct fashion judgment; which was *why* she was annoyed, of course.

"Such charming insolence, sweetie! I would have to spank you soundly for that if you were still in my household," Adrienne said. "As I recall, you enjoyed that quite a bit."

"Yup. But it really requires a man's hands to do a first-class job," Ellen said. "Teeny-tiny little paddle paws always . . . disappoint in the end."

Monica made a strangled, shocked sound. Adrienne's eyes flashed for a second, then she smiled and inclined her head in acknowledgment of a verbal gambit worthy of herself before turning to her brother.

"Adrian, beloved, what a coincidence that you accepted Great-grandfather's invitation as well. But shouldn't you be in character too? If you're going to be out of date, at least be *thoroughly* out of date! Spats, perhaps, a cane and a monocle?"

"You have mistaken me for Great-uncle Arnaud."

"No, you are not insane, tedious or notably treacherous. I have become somewhat . . . annoyed with Arnaud."

"He tried to kill me last year. And Ellen."

"Yet despite that, I find him irritating. He has a talent for annoyance. Even Great-grandfather is becoming short with him. We discussed it, among other things."

"You always were a suck-up," Adrian replied; he kept his tone light, but realized that he really meant it. "And a tale-teller."

That always enraged me, when she blamed me to our parents . . . even though they could read our minds . . .

"But of course!" Adrienne said. "And if our revered ancestors are going to all this trouble, we can at least fit in. Shadowspawn or human, flattery never hurts. As true now as it was in the 80s . . . evidently *your* perpetual decade of choice."

Adrian inclined his head again, hiding a wince; once again his twin had managed to plant a fishhook, if a small one. His slacks, loafers and jacket *did* have a slightly dated flavor, the narrow-lapel, long-jacket style he'd favored as a young man when everyone was finally reacting against the excesses of the 60s and 70s. Adrienne displayed unwonted tact by heading off ahead of them.

Ellen was taking deep slow breaths, and he could feel her calming, directly through her aura and through the strong base-link that joined them. A surge of admiration went through him. They had worked on technique in their time together, but even at the beginning she had been better than any human-norm he'd ever met at simply keeping functioning despite whatever happened inside her head. It had been one of the things that attracted him in the first place, that combination of toughness and vulnerability and intelligence. And it was what had allowed her to survive months under Adrienne's hand without more insanity than a wholly understandable and only mildly obsessive lust for revenge.

"Thoughts?" she said quietly, as she turned and felt his eyes on her. "C'mon, oh telepathic one, play fair."

"Thinking that I am the luckiest man on earth," he said.

She flushed a little. "Damn, and I can feel you actually do feel that way. You know how to pay a girl a compliment."

"And usually it is men who complain that their wives *expect* them to be mind-readers . . ."

Though with most women, being a real mind-reader is less help than one might think.

It took close contact for a while to actually read thoughts, the discursive interior monologue of the mind speaking to itself. Feelings you could grasp immediately.

Usually that simply punctures illusions faster . . . or prevents one from having illusions in the first place. Now with Ellen, however . . . I have never felt so connected to another being.

He gave her his arm. The staff of the Express were lined up beside the train, waiters and cooks in white jackets, stewards in blue with gold-banded kepis and white gloves, the train manager in a suit. As he got closer the scale of the thing was apparent. The train was a third of a mile long and the rolling stock was taller than the modern equivalents, with the *WL* between gold rampant lions that was the blazon of the *Compagnie Internationale des Wagons-Lits (et des Grands Express Européens.)* The staff were more numerous than the passengers, even including the renfield servants.

Most of the employees were feeling suppressed wonder, but no more than normal apprehension. They'd probably been fed a cover story involving a set of impossibly rich eccentrics, with the occasional mental nudge to damp suspicion. The managers had Wreakings clamped into their brains like a web of barbed steel hooks, and he winced slightly and raised his barriers at the feel of minds like raw wounds and a muffled screaming down under the imposed control. Hopefully they'd have their memories excised without too much damage afterwards. His Great-grandmother Seraphine was perfectly capable of petty malice on the order of pulling the legs off one side of an insect to watch it walk in circles, but usually didn't discard useful servants—as opposed to toys— that casually.

Though if they fail, may God have mercy on them . . . and there is no God.

"Was it really like this?" Ellen asked as they climbed aboard into Art

Deco splendors of burnished tropical woods and parquetry and inlay and burnished brass.

"I am older than you, my darling, but not *that* old! When I was at the Sorbonne the primary local sport was rioting, with '68 already a fading nostalgic memory from a previous generation."

Ellen grinned, shaky but recovering her poise. "My fault for dating a boomer."

"Not quite a boomer, though short of Gen X."

"But you're *like* a boomer."

"Ouch. And this train *is* probably fairly close to the original," Adrian said.

He nodded to where a group of servants—high-ranking renfields—was boarding. "Though of course few in that time traveled boxed, as it were."

Her eyes went to the small, heavy containers several of them carried. "That's . . ."

"*Probably* my disreputable ancestors. Sleeping the light away as comatose marmosets."

"Ferrets," Ellen observed clinically. "No way they'd do something without fangs."

"Or ferrets; it is the logical way. Travel is always difficult for postcorporeals, that is why they are such homebodies."

"It would be like . . . traveling through a radioactive wasteland, during the day, wouldn't it?"

"Not quite so bad. Even modest shielding will suffice . . . you see how the windows are tinted . . . but any accident to that shielding, any sabotage, and . . . the Final Death. The instinct is to seek deep shelter during the day, deep and safe and familiar, and to have many bolt-holes. Those boxes are thick alloy like the armor of tanks, and completely sealed. One awakes and walks through the walls. The train will have dozens of them, secreted in places impossible for humans to reach. Even so . . ."

"And they really trust the renfields to guard . . . oh, telepathy, mind control."

"Exactly. Those in renfield families grow with the knowledge that they can conceal nothing and are never safe."

Ellen shivered; he could tell that she was remembering her time at Rancho Sangre. Though she hadn't been in precisely that position, since he'd been able to help her bury secrets via their base-link; still, she'd had to give a *very convincing* imitation of utter helplessness. Wordlessly he touched her shoulder, then occupied himself with directing the porter to stow their baggage. The train was being run in the true lavish old-time style, born of an era when labor was cheap.

Their compartment was a miracle of compact elegance, down to the inlay of peacocks'-tails on the opposite wall. The train lurched as they finished stowing their traveling bags; the rest would be in the baggage car. Adrian had traveled extensively on the Continent by Eurorail pass when he was in his twenties—first as a student, then on Brotherhood business—but he had to admit that this was more picturesque.

"This feels different," Ellen said, putting a hand to the frame of the compartment's window. "Different from a normal train."

"The pistons make the motions less regular than an electric locomotive," Adrian said. "The thrust is less continuous."

The *chuffa-chuffa-chuffa* of the great steam engine sounded through the fabric of the long train. There was no *clickity-clack* as there would have been in the glory days a hundred years ago, and less swaying from side to side; they were running on seamless welded rail on ferroconcrete, not short lengths mounted on wooden ties and secured to each other by bolted fishplates. They sat with their arms around each other and her head resting on his shoulder, watching as the wet gray bulk of Paris slid by outside and night fell on the French countryside beyond.

"You're *thinking* again, Adrian," she said, some time later.

He chuckled. "I was thinking how appetizing you smell," he said. "And how good it is to think that without feeling guilty about it."

"My conscience-ridden one," she said.

"You would not like me if I did not have a conscience," he said soberly.

She chuckled. "I've met you without a conscience. Well, without a conscience, without some other things, and with tits. I didn't like it. Though it was the lack-of-conscience part that was *really* unpleasant."

"Something else smells a bit appetizing. There are no less than three dining cars on this train, and a lounge as well."

"Beats stale Amtrack sandwiches all to hell," she said. "Let's go!"

They walked down the side-corridor. The lounge was exactly that; a Jazz Age nightspot complete with a musician tinkling the ivories in a white tux, while well-dressed men and women drank highballs and elaborate cocktails and chatted and laughed. If you could ignore the hot yellow eyes of more than half, that is. The dining car beyond was an island of light and fine white linen and tableware—not silverware, of course—with Lalique low-relief panels of frosted glass showing dancing bacchanals and bunches of grapes. He winced slightly as they passed a group in kimonos and took a seat at the far end; they'd recognized both of them, and the wave of hatred was almost palpable.

"Who are they?" Ellen asked.

"Those are the Tōkairin family, including the clan-heads from Japan."

"Tōkairin as in Tōkairin Michiko of unfond memory? The guys who thought they were ninja magicians."

"Yes, until the Brézés taught them the truth in a fit of missionary enthusiasm. Michiko's kindred. I hear that they are feeling extremely aggrieved. After all, they lost their California patriarch *and* their most purebred female still in the body, and at our hands. In fact, I was informed at the Hôtel de Brézé that they have kept Michiko's body alive. It is being shipped to Tbilisi, in fact."

Ellen's brows went up as they sat. "I thought the body died if a nightwalker was killed while they were out of it?"

"Eventually. The physical . . . plant, as it were . . . is all there, the autonomic functions continue for a while, but there is no consciousness to use the machinery. While one is nightwalking, there is a link. Quantum entanglement, didn't Peter Boase call it? Destroying the nightwalking body severs that, the trauma of death instantly transmitted and chaoticizing the . . . mmmm . . . software files. The physical form enters a very deep coma. They have kept Michiko's on life-support machinery so that it does not perish of dehydration or lack of nourishment, I am not sure why."

"No way to cure it?"

"Not even the Power can cure death. The essence, the person, is *dead*."

Adrian paused, a thought teasing at him. "I do recall a speculation that it might be possible to . . . transplant . . . a personality, as it were . . . to such an empty shell. By soul-carrying. That's merely theory, though: I do not think it has ever been done, not in the modern era at least. It would account for some of the legends of possession. Or perhaps they will try to breed the unconscious body. That *might* be possible."

"Oh, euwww . . . I seem to say that a lot about Shadowspawn."

Adrian shrugged. "Spawn of darkness, eh?"

"Or maybe they intend to produce the body at the meeting?"

"That could be so. Shadowspawn tend to be short on empathy, but that is a fate that any nightwalker would fear. We should be cautious about the Tōkairin even beyond the usual, if they are that determined to do us harm. Ah, I see we have reached Germany."

Another party was entering the dining room. One was—

Ellen blinked, and Adrian sensed her astonishment at the black and silver, the skull and crossbones insignia and the burnished jackboots.

"Is that—"

"Yes, SS dress uniform. Standartenführer Alberich von Trupp, in the flesh . . . well, not literally in the flesh since 1945. But present anyway."

"The Council was behind *that*?"

"No, just some individuals, thought Alberich was an enthusiast—he was at the Wannsee Conference, behind the scenes."

"Why didn't they win, then?"

"My great-grandfather insisted on an Allied victory. Not for any altruistic reasons, I assure you . . . Shadowspawn are perfectly capable of maintaining the prejudices of their upbringing. Even my great-grandfather considers him a pig of a Boche. The von Trupps still hold a grudge."

"Was Hitler . . ."

"Not enough to nightwalk or feed, but there was a substantial element, yes. Not that he knew it. Most great dictators are at least one-third *Homo nocturnis*. And many saints, too."

"As a reaction against their impulses?"

"Precisely."

He looked at the menu. "Hmmm. *Le filet de boeuf en salaison à l'aneth* . . . fillet pickled in coarse salt, sliced with dill and coriander berries . . . and a bordelaise sauce . . . I would suggest the Château Latour 1998 with this . . ."

Ellen paused in the middle of breaking a roll. He could feel a roil of emotions in her aura; love, and something like . . . exasperation.

"You just told me we were *even more* likely to be horribly killed than we thought, if we don't manage to get ourselves vaporized by that damned nuke, and you're *certain* which Bordeaux we should have?"

The sommelier opened the bottle. Adrian rolled and sniffed the cork, tilted the glass to look at the candle flame through the swirl of dark intense red, sniffed and breathed in a sip. Something like bitter chocolate and graphite . . . just now reaching its peak. Not quite infanticide, but still a bit young, though the grapes had been harvested in the year Ellen was born.

"But of course. One would be mortified to die with the *wrong* wine upon the tongue."

She sighed. "I'm worried about the kids. Do you think Eric can get everyone to Vienna?"

He considered. It *felt* right, but of course . . .

"We must do what we can, and hope for luck. He is a very capable man. Unfortunately . . . now . . . Harvey is too. We are racing against time."

Eastern Turkey

"The first thing we need is a truck," Harvey Ledbetter said.

"How are we going to get one?" Farmer asked.

"Steal it, as usual," Anjali said dryly. "How else?"

"Take a *look* at this place, Guha. Steal an *oxcart*, maybe."

It was a cold bleak dawn, with a sad dry smell and. Harvey absently chewed on some fresh flatbread as they walked back towards the wreck of his vehicle. The nameless village rose as early as any farming settlement, but the locals pointedly ignored them, which was for the best when all was considered. They passed the burned-out van the two Brotherhood operatives had been driving back when they were chasing him, still smelling faintly in the chilly morning.

"That must have been just a bit lively," Harvey said; they'd been trapped inside a suddenly burning car with no obvious way to get out. "Closer to bein' unsalted cracklings than was comfortable, I'd say."

"No fucking shit, if I hadn't felt it coming maybe two, three seconds in advance we'd have been fried," Farmer replied.

Anjali was almost pouting. "*And* we lost our weapons, mostly. And our luggage. I do not like not having a toothbrush or clean underwear in the morning!"

"You could get something local," Harvey said.

Anjali threw her hands up. "Have you seen any woman here over thirteen whose backside is not a bloody yard across? *And* none of it would be *clean*, washed or not."

"Yeah, and if you're going to smell, your own smell's always better." Harvey chuckled.

Anjali shuddered, looking as if she would like to climb out of her skin. She wasn't a high-caste Hindu except in a cultural-descent sense—wasn't teetotal or a vegetarian, for instance—but . . .

You can take the girl out of India, but you can't take all the Brahmin out of the girl, he thought, not for the first time. *Fastidious ain't the word, ditto about feeling unclean even if she doesn't take ritual purity literally. Still, she keeps going even if she grumbles and you can't expect more.*

Nothing was moving east. Harvey wasn't surprised; that curse probably had traffic knotted up back a hundred miles from here, with minds boggling and refusing to accept it even as things broke down, blew up or caught on fire. If you tried to travel in that direction by anything more modern than a donkey, anything that *could* go wrong would, every single microsecond the quantum foam bubbled. Like fate, if Fate was a malicious child grinning and poking you with a stick. So . . .

"Okay, but there's probably going to be something traveling the *other* way. Get us to a seaport, then find us a ship."

"A lot harder to hit a stretch of sea the same way," Farmer agreed. "Those generalized curses tend to bounce and shatter if you try them over open water. You can get a nasty backlash, too."

"A water surface is already chaotic," Anjali said, a little pedantically; she'd always been strong on theory, and had been an instructor down at the new Brotherhood HQ in Ecuador for a while. "That makes it easier to affect in detail but harder to maintain a standing effect."

They passed a herd of sheep with two attendants in coats about as hairy as those of their charges, and more of the big Anatolian sheepdogs. Their masters called them back from a barking, growling frenzy and passed the foreigners with wary nods. The three halted at Harvey's truck.

"Eighteen hours," Harvey said. "I am *not* going to lose this opportunity to hammer the Council's nuts. Probably nothing like it will come along again. Eighteen hours, and this lights up like a Christmas tree."

"Or *Diwali* lights," Anjali said, sounding pleased that he'd used one of her favorite activities as a metaphor. "Hmmm."

She and Farmer knelt. He drew a circle in the dirt and inscribed the glyphs with quick practiced motions of a wooden stylus; they looked vaguely Egyptian, but were much older. A memory of them had lingered when the first Egyptian scribes wrote.

Though they also had a distinct touch of Belle Époque Art Nouveau, legacy of the adepts who had re-created them by fishing with the Power into the depths of time. She began flipping a coin . . . what looked like a coin at first glance . . . into the circle as they both muttered in Mhab-rogast, an antiphonal chorus like rats scratching in the walls of the world. Nobody had ever been able to prove whether the *lingua demonica* was objectively necessary to Wreaking or simply served as a focusing device, but like the glyphs it *worked*.

After a moment, breathing deeply and wiping her face, Anjali went on: "Hard to be absolutely certain indeed, but I'd say the odds are good."

She frowned; they both gulped a sports drink. It didn't really help all that much, but it soothed some of the feelings Wreaking gave you, like sucking on a candy when you were trying to quit smoking.

"The odds of getting a *truck* are good. Better here than anywhere else within reach. But the fall . . . it does not seem very *good* somehow, over-all. There are blackpath hints to the reading."

Harvey nodded. "We're goin' on the next thing to a suicide mission with a *nuke* to blow up a whole *city*," he said. "You expect goodness? As opposed to visions of bane and ruin?"

"A point, indeed, a point."

"No shit, Sherlock," Farmer said, fishing out a pair of Ray-Bans and leaning back against the bulk of Harvey's MAN diesel, moving carefully to avoid jarring the fading post-Wreaking headache.

"Hell, none of us does *good*, much," he said, sounding less angry than usual. "We do what's necessary. Other people get the goodness. We get the satisfaction of knowing we'd feel *even worse* about everything starting with ourselves if we did anything else."

"Seems that way, sometimes," Harvey agreed.

Not long after a trail of dust showed to the east; he squinted into it and the rising sun. It was considerably less fancy than the MAN rig he'd organized back in Austria, but then, this wasn't Austria. Or even Slovenia, or for that matter western Turkey, which had been getting almost offensively modern in recent decades. His practiced eye took it in as a Seddon Atkinson Strato 350 hauling a cargo container; ten axles all up. The make meant it had seen its best days in the 1990s, which come to think of it had been *his* best days too—in your thirties you were past being a dick with legs without being too creaking—but you used what you had on hand.

"Anjali, you flag him down," he said. "Take off your jacket. We'll persuade him of the error of his ways."

"Sexist *banchut*," she grumbled, but complied.

"Me no, the driver of that rig, pretty much guaranteed," Harvey said. "Jack, don't kill him."

The two men crouched behind the cab of the disabled truck; they could both sense the sudden spike of interest in the bored competence of the man's aura. She stood in the road, waving the jacket and looking distressed. The big vehicle slowed, with a hiss and squeal that made Harvey wince a little; someone had been neglecting the brakes. It crept past them, putting them a little behind the cab. The door opened and the driver jumped down, putting on his best would-be dashing grin.

"You need helping?" he said, in thick almost-English.

Which showed an unusual degree of perception—he'd noticed at once that she couldn't possibly be local and hadn't tried Turkish and Kurdish first. The driver was midway between wiry and burly, with a short black beard and bristle-cut hair and dark-olive skin; with the nondescript sweater and pants and battered shoes he could have been from anywhere between Bosnia and Afghanistan, though Harvey would have guessed at Iranian Azerbaijan from the accent and body-language and aura. The two Americans stepped forward without unnecessary haste or words, their movements sliding smoothly between the driver's first sight of them and the possibility of reaction. The younger grabbed the man's left elbow and wrist, twisted and locked and pushed upward.

"*Sadece sakin, arkadaş,*" Harvey said, dropping into Turkish for a moment: "Just keep quiet, friend. No need for anyone to get hurt. Hurt much."

The truck driver gave an incoherent grunt and then froze as Harvey laid the barrels of his coach gun beside the right side of his face. The man's eyes rolled frantically, trying to see them without turning, but Farmer's hold meant that he'd wrench his arm out of the socket if he did anything but stay uncomfortably still. The unmistakable feel of the gun's twin barrels in the skin over his cheekbone encouraged this pragmatic attitude. Still, you could never be completely certain. Men under stress sometimes did astoundingly stupid things, even professionals, and he could feel this amateur's fear and bewilderment.

Fear had its uses, but encouraging rational thought was not one of them. Harvey reached up with his left hand and placed thumb and forefinger on either side of the man's head just above the neck; contact made things much easier for his modest command of the Power.

"No!" he said sharply to Anjali, who was buttoning her coat and also winding up for one of her patented toe-cap ballectomies. "He hasn't done anything but get unlucky and we've got him under control."

The woman scowled and shoved her hands into her pockets instead. Harvey took a deep breath, let it out, and adjusted the auras—there was some scientific term about entangling the functions, but that was what it felt like, as if the edges of their personalities had started vibrating in tune. Then he *pushed* mentally.

"Szzeee. Mogu, ze *ta!*"

Blackness-devouring-thought. Command!

Farmer released his grip and stepped back as the driver went totally rigid for an instant and then as limp as a set of empty clothes. Anjali stepped forward and grabbed a handful of the sweater, setting herself to guide the fall a little. When the trucker was on his back, they could see trickles of blood running out of his nose.

Anjali stared at it fixedly for an instant, then turned away, unconsciously licking her lips and swallowing repeatedly. Then the lips curled back from her teeth.

"Watch it!" Harvey said sharply.

"I am," she muttered. "Just leave me alone for a moment."

The hands in her pockets clenched and her shields went up like ceramic laminate armor on a tank. She was the highest of the three on the Albermann scale, but well short of the ability to feed. Human blood was nothing but dirty salt water as far as her digestive system was concerned. Unfortunately, the *craving* for blood hit at a much lower level; without endless and very careful control, that was what produced a Jeffrey Dahmer or a Blood Countess. Housekeeping in Hell as you tried over and over again to reach an itch you couldn't scratch, tormenting as an insect dancing on your eardrum. He felt only the faintest shadow if it himself, and that was bad enough.

So you gotta make allowances. It's no wonder some people are testy a lot of the time.

"That will hurt more than a kick, yes," she said shortly.

Harvey grunted. He was feeling bad himself; you had to ration Wreaking very carefully indeed when it all came out of you.

"I gave him a dose of short-term amnesia," he said. "Safer than a concussion, though. Rearranging his man-tackle wouldn't have made him forget this."

"A good thump on the head would," Farmer observed. "And it takes less out of you than a Wreaking."

"Tell me," Harvey muttered; he was still feeling logy and aching all over. "That's risky, though. Concussion's no joke."

He looked at the truck. "You're young and full of beans, Jack. Get this thing backed up to mine. The load's on rails and I've got a good set of tools and a winch. We should be able to transfer it and hook up the power leads in a couple hours."

"What about the cargo?" Farmer said.

"It's . . ."

He hopped up into the bed of the truck and used his knife to rip open a few cartons marked as condensed chicken soup in Georgian. That was Georgian as in the Georgia in the Caucasus, an obscure and isolate language with its own script.

". . . yeah, cigarettes and booze, probably dodgy as hell. We'll just dump it out and you can be damned sure it'll all disappear and *I know nothing, Officer, nothing!* Anjali, give me a hand with this osco. We'll leave him in my truck's cab, wrap him up in a foil blanket, there's a couple of spares. He ought to be all right."

It was a little odd taking the trouble, since he was going to blow up an entire city right down to the little girls and their big-eyed kittens. On the other hand, that was *necessary*.

Leaving the driver to die of exposure would just be *convenient*. Keeping the distinction in mind was crucial.

On the mountainside a mile distant, Dmitri Pavlovich Usov watched patiently through the scope of the M82 sniper rifle. It was a .50 weapon, thirty pounds of recoil-operated precision throwing slugs the size of a woman's thumb fast enough to blast through a quarter inch of armor plate, and the maximum range was two thousand meters. More, if you could do a little Wreaking with aimpoints, and there were few adepts better at that than he was. The range was farther than the usual individual hexes could reach, especially if the target was taken by surprise, so it was hard to defend against with the Power.

He imagined the sudden distant explosion of terror as the first round hit; those massive bullets could rip limbs off or kill from shock alone. The instant despair as the others died trying to leap for cover . . . He smiled. He had no intention of killing them, but there was no harm in dreams. He was a happy man, because he often lived his dreams.

Dmitri looked around thirty and was in his forty-eighth year, a sharp-featured blond man with a long lean body covered in ropy muscle, and currently wearing grey-brown hiking clothes and padded jacket. He watched the three Brotherhood agents as they toiled and sweated at their task. Even now, even at this distance the sheer *absence* of the cargo was disturbing. He knew it was there, and he could see it with the eyes of the body, but it simply did not affect the balance of the world as the Power perceived it.

Eerie, he thought. *I do not like it.*

There were practical matters to attend to.

Adrienne . . . Juliyevna . . . he thought.

A sense of awareness, of sharp-edged attention. Damped down behind shields, of course; his emotions were too. You never handed a tool to a potential opponent . . . which everyone was. Your allies most particularly.

Dmitri . . . Pavlovitch . . . came the reply.

Normally Adrienne and her fellow Progressives preferred to just text someone if they wanted to communicate; telepathy took energy and had low bandwidth long-range. It was very difficult to tap, though. They also used an obscure dialect once found only in a few villages in Central

America. One no Shadowspawn had ever known, except for a peculiar renegade in New York most of a century ago, when things were more free-wheeling. The Council clean-up squad had buried his body and that of his seven odd associates under the Empire State Building, and killed off the villagers who'd helped him on general principles. Adrienne had come across the handwritten notes taken in the last raid and dumped in an old warehouse by the Council's mercenaries, liberated them, and had a few of her inner circle learn the language from her. Abstractly he admired her energy, because she had had to do it the slow way from the paper notes and the recordings.

It made a very good code. Shadowspawn could pull a language out of the brain of a speaker, but it was much harder to do to an adept. Impossible, under most circumstances.

The . . . subjects . . . are . . . mobile . . . again . . . I . . . did . . . not . . . need . . . to . . . intervene.

Good . . . do . . . not . . . underestimate . . . them.

He nodded, let *agreement* flow over the link, and waited. Soon enough they would leave. They had little of the Power, but they used what they had well. He would clean up the site—and of course dispose of the truck driver, which would be amusing—and then follow, cautiously. Things were coming together.

Another communication: **the . . . situation . . . in . . . new mexico . . . is . . . confused.**

He acknowledged that without replying; no complex operation came off as planned, even where Dale Shadowblade was involved. Here it was fascinating to watch a major action develop with so *little* of the Power and prescience involved. The Council and its foes had relied on their abilities for a very long time; there was a curious advantage to limiting it to passive deflection.

Though even that took some effort. He licked his lips and snarled lightly. He hoped they hurried; he was growing hungry.

Finish . . . there . . . and . . . join . . . Shadowblade . . . in . . . Santa . . . Fe . . . to . . . exert . . . control . . . act . . . only . . . with . . . a . . . low-risk . . . opportunity.

CHAPTER EIGHT

Santa Fe, New Mexico

The tunnel ran half a mile from the underground . . .

Lair, Eric Salvador thought. *Face it, it's a lair. And we may be walking right towards an ambush . . . with absolutely no way to go* back *if things go wrong.*

It didn't have the spaciousness and smooth interior decor of the rest, though; this was one of the clandestine emergency exits. Cheba could walk upright but he had to stoop a little—it would be just doable for Adrian Brézé, who was a bit of a shrimp. The naked rock was patched here and there with concrete where the tunnelers had run into cracks, sparsely lit by occasional LEDs stapled to the ceiling and smelling of slightly damp stone and the metal of the ventilation ducts. You felt the weight above you here, and he could have sworn he heard it creak in the arch over his head.

Every hundred feet or so was a portcullis of silver-plated steel, cranked up by a simple ratchet mechanism like a car jack, also silver-plated; when they went through, a touch on a toggle and the welded bars crashed home again behind them with a sound like giant teeth. Which left you between two of the things, with no way to raise the one behind you.

Good thing I'm not claustrophobic . . . much, he thought.

"Why no motors?" Cheba asked.

Eric shrugged, looking at the tunnel with tactical eyes and feeding in what he'd learned of the creatures he was fighting against . . . and with. "Don't know for sure. I'd guess motors could be jiggered by their minds, that Wreaking stuff. Electric controls just needs a little nudge but this is straight-up hard work."

"Can't they lift things? By thinking at them? I've seen that."

"Not silver, and these would be too heavy anyway. Notice how the crank handles are all *behind* these gate things? This is a one-way route, for going out not in."

The children were grinning; they'd had a good night's sleep and bowls of Grape-Nuts and cream and orange juice and toast and were raring to go. The tunnel became an instant accessory to an improvised game, and from what he overheard and understood—half the time they were talking French—it was something like *Dungeons and Dragons* with the Hobbit movies they'd been watching thrown in. Cheba was a little subdued, and Eric felt . . .

Okay, truthiness time, I'm getting a rush out of this. Hey, Eric, why did you reenlist twice? Did your brain flip your skull open and run away screaming like a pink blob on legs both times before you put your hand up, or were you addicted? As in, you'd have been in twenty years and made Gunny and been the terror of recruits at Camp Pendleton in your middle age if that IED hadn't given you a lot of time for thought and a rearranged face? At least I don't have that bug-crawling sensation this time. Just normal fear.

Cheba was in expensive stone-washed black jeans, ankle-boots with silver chains and toe-caps—

The better to kick you with, he thought. *Useful masquerading as bling.*

—and a midnight-blue silk turtleneck with more very fine silver thread sewn invisibly into the collar, and a sheepskin jacket; the fashionable backpack had the machete sheath built into it, with the handle looking like an innocuous fixture. She didn't have much formal training, but she had what was much more important, an instant readiness to put everything she had into doing an enemy lethal harm. Most people took a while to learn to throw the switch like that; some just couldn't.

Eric was wearing a suit and overcoat that fitted like nothing he'd ever worn, with a label that said *Cuthbertson and Sheppard, London, England.* It had come with a stiffly worded note saying that going by laser measurements was crude compared to an in-house session and that they resented it despite how much they'd been paid.

Complaining about being given great heaps of cash . . . It was all new but as comfortable as an old work-glove, and had some remarkable storage capacity added for various illegal, immoral and lethal things. It had been included in an assortment of clothes and gear that had simply arrived about a week ago; some of the items were in the luggage they were trundling behind them now.

"Is this how the rich live?" Cheba asked suddenly, touching the coat, as he wound yet another portcullis up. "Everything they want just . . . just coming?"

"How the hell should I know?" he said, grunting as the metal grid locked in the up position.

They walked through; he did a double check to make sure everyone was clear, then tripped the release and it dropped with a huge *clang*. Then he started on the next one and went on:

"The closest I ever got to *rich* before all this was buying a new Nissan Pathfinder one year, and I couldn't really afford that, not and live in Santa Fe on a cop's salary."

Cheba showed an expression that wasn't a smile. "Next to the way I was, that *is* rich."

"Next to Adrian Brézé, it's like being a panhandler living on the streets."

Surprisingly, she chuckled. "*Sí.* I understand that. You climb up the ladder but there's always someone higher, eh? You are always staring up someone's backside."

He snorted. "I think ordinary rich people don't have big honking eagles flying in through their walls and trying to bite chunks out of their ass, either."

"I thought that it tried to rip your face off with its claws. Talons? Whatever the word is."

"*Ass* is a figure of speech there. And they don't have underground fortified bases below the sub-basement or have to do this sort of shit."

The tunnel ended in a square chamber with a metal ladder running up one wall. At the top was a featureless metal rectangle with a set of old-fashioned door-bolts, thick as his wrist, covered in silver and arranged so they ran down at an angle into metal sleeves in the frame. He worked them back with his left hand and held his gun in the right; it was a big-ass pistol cut down from a shotgun, evidently Brotherhood standard and looking like what he imagined stagecoach drivers carried in the old days.

He'd practiced with it—there was a shooting range in the *lair*—and he had to admit that at close range it was a real chain saw. Hard on the wrists and slow to reload, but just the thing for nightwalkers or the Zombie Apocalypse.

There was a *click* that was felt through his palm rather than heard as he put his hand to the trapdoor, some sort of Wreaking booby-trap that had recognized him. Wreakings had this quality of *intention* that put his teeth on edge; it wasn't like dealing with machinery. More like little invisible but vicious trained animals chained to a spot or object.

He pushed. When nothing happened he fought down a stab of fear at the thought of being trapped here, then realized that the trapdoor was just a heavy sucker, even for someone as strong as he was. He strained until it fell backward against some sort of soft buffer that kept the noise down to a muffled *thud.* The space above was dim, with light from narrow dusty windows; it was a closet at the back of a garage with the usual stained concrete floor, and old-fashioned swing-out doors and work tables and racks of tools along one wall.

His eyes flicked around, and the weapon followed. Eric let out a long breath as the *empty* feeling sank in. There was a cool-looking sports car, a big BMW touring motorcycle, a couple of SUVs and—he grinned at the old friend—a military-type hard-top Humvee, different from the ones he'd used only because it was clean and new and had a spiffy paint-job and didn't have a CROWS remote-operated weapon turret on top. He immediately decided he'd take that, just in case things got hairy. A Humvee could pretty well climb walls, and they might have to go off-road.

Though it's still sorta strange thinking of driving through my hometown to the airport as a combat op, he thought. *I'd be even more nervous if I didn't have the kids along. Weird, but near as I can tell, anyone who just blew all our asses to hell with an RPG or a big IED would have Adrienne Brézé torturing them for the next couple thousand years and knows it. And if she couldn't for some reason, the whole of the Brézé family would take after an outsider who did that, ditto. If anyone comes after us they'll do it personal, like the last try, which gives us a chance.*

He grinned at the thought. Werebeasts and spells were all he had to worry about. And those *were* less dangerous than some renfields or mercs with explosives, when you looked at it objectively. At least to someone like him who couldn't hex the other guy's weapons. The Power was scary in a sort of visceral way he couldn't really account for, but less dangerous. Dead was dead, but for some reason Shadowspawn *felt* worse.

"Clear," he said down the hole. Then when all three of them just stared at him: "That means we're okay to go."

Cheba handed up the luggage, then the children, then extended a hand to him. He grasped her wrist and lifted her up until she could swing her feet onto the floor.

"Strong!" she said, looking at him a little oddly and rubbing her wrist.

"Still alive," he replied. "Okay, stay here for a minute."

He checked the ground outside; there were inconspicuous openings that let you see all around, and he took his time scanning the flat, scrubby semi-desert landscape. There were fewer juniper and piñon and chamisos close by than you'd expect, though the clearing was cleverly done to be as inconspicuous as possible. It was early morning, but definitely post-sunrise. That meant no nightwalkers, but a Shadowspawn was bad news even in the flesh; the only good thing was that there just weren't very many of them and they mostly didn't have patience enough for a stakeout.

But they can hire mercs, he thought. *From what I'm told, they fight each other all the time too.*

The building was on a flat stretch below the cliff; he could see a glint off glass at its top, Adrian's sky-aerie. Seeing it from here gave him a bit of a pang. Except for the last bit, it had been a pleasant, restful episode in a life that had gone from routine is-this-all-there-is approaching-midlife bad to really, really nightmare bad over the last year.

"¿*Qué?*" Cheba said, when he laughed softly.

"I was thinking it was restful up there, the last couple of weeks. Then I thought that my definition of *restful* has gotten pretty weird, 'cause it's only a bit spoiled by were-eagles. It's sorta like I've gone back to thinking of a Forward Operating Base as safe and homey 'cause there's nothing worse than an occasional mortar coming over the wire and you've got a nice cargo container to sleep in."

He walked over and pushed the trapdoor with his foot, bracing himself against the wall of closet because the angle was awkward. It dropped home with a *thunk* and *click-chunk* as the retaining springs jarred loose and the bars slid out again, and then it was just a smooth patch of floor.

I'm getting the drift of defenses against the Power, he thought.

Even if you could jigger the lock mechanism, the bolts were simply too big to move with mental effort and there wasn't any machinery to be screwed into releasing them. And even if you could handle the bolts, it would be a stone bitch to get the trapdoor open from this side; you'd need lifting equipment, you'd have to drill and tap so you could sink a big eyebolt in it, and to do that you'd have to tear down the wall of the closet because it was slanted to make it hard. All time-consuming and noisy.

The Power's like a scalpel, he thought. *So silver aside, the best way to fight it is to keep everything simple and big and heavy. Brute-force stuff, don't get subtle. The Power does* subtle *real well. Make it a baseball-bat fight, not a scalpel fight.*

*   *   *

It was the hour before dawn, and surprisingly cold outside—not that Dmitri Usov minded anything this New Mexico place could do, after years in Novorossiysk. The place advertised itself as an *Inn and Spa* and was built in a thick-walled, flat-roofed style around a courtyard now lightly covered in snow; it all reminded him of things he'd seen in the more backward parts of Central Asia, with an interior heavy on thick vividly-striped blankets, exposed pine beams and handsome pottery decorated in zigzag styles. Dale Shadowblade called it the *boutique Injun* style, or *Hokumfakum Tribe* with something of a sneer.

Dinner had been superb, though, with one of the waiters for dessert. Now, though . . .

"Handle your own empties," Dale Shadowblade said. "Look, Russki-boy, this isn't any clan's territory and there aren't any Council clean-up squads to call for. We're operating frontier-style here."

Dmitri snarled back at him, and pointed to Kai. "Have *her* handle it, then!"

He carefully did not add the *chernozhopyi* that came to his mind, except to himself. Someone who'd survived years as a roving executioner of Shadowspawn was not one to be casually called *black-ass*. Better to say nothing while he had to work with the man; there was nothing more futile than threatening a hedgehog with a naked buttock. Some day, of course . . .

"No prob," Kai said helpfully. "He makes a sorta cute corpse, you know? Not much use to a girl, dammit. I think he was getting cold before you guys stopped humping, though."

Dale slapped at his renfield-lucy. She dodged and rolled with the blow and came up grinning; she was wearing a T-shirt and nothing else.

"She works for me," Dale grated at Dmitri.

"Please, may I *borrow* her services to get rid of this fucking corpse? Did I not spare some of the blood?"

Unexpectedly the Apache Shadowspawn grinned. "Okay, since you asked nicely, *ndaa*. He's starting to get a bit high, yeah."

Blood went off so fast . . .

"*Ndaa?*" Dmitri asked.

"That means 'brother.'"

"You lie."

"All the time!"

Kai sighed and rolled her eyes as she zipped herself into her jeans. Then she stripped a blanket from one of the beds—they had taken two bedrooms that shared a common lounge—and rolled the slim body of the waiter onto it with her foot, tucked it around him and then pushed the bundle onto another. There wasn't much blood; Dmitri felt fairly bloated with his share, buzzing with the Power. The somnolent humans throughout the big building were like low-banked fires smoldering in the night, with the occasional brighter fleck from one waking early.

"What's the drill?" Kai said to her Shadowspawn.

"We're not planning on eating here much, so it doesn't matter where we crap," he said.

Dmitri barked a laugh when he translated the unfamiliar idiom. Kai gave a slight grunt as she dragged the wrapped body towards the door; there he could sense her feeble tremor of the Power scanning the hallway before she opened it.

"I'll just stuff him in a broom closet or something," she said. A giggle. "Won't someone be—"

Her eyes went theatrically wide as she bumped the door with her backside and hauled her burden out.

"—surprised as *shit*!"

Dmitri laughed himself; it was a humorous image. The little whore was engaging in her way, and probably useful, which was undoubtedly why she was still alive. Those with a touch of the old blood were the most amusing to hunt, generally speaking. They made challenging game, and had receptive minds.

The inn was within easy walking distance of the town's central square, and they left traveling light; the heavy gear was in Dale's truck in any case. The whole place was very much like a resort town in the Crimea, if you subtracted the ocean—even to the snow-topped blue mountains looming northwards, just now turning pink and crimson with sunrise. Kai brought them warm pastries and quite good coffee from a place called the Plaza Bakery, logically enough, and they sat on a bench in the park. Restaurants and jewelry shops and other expensive stores framed it on three sides, all in the low brown adobe style, with the old Spanish Palace of the Governors to the west—a large single-story structure with a row of log pillars supporting an arcade where Indians were already setting out their wares on blankets.

There was also a monument to what the *yanki* called their Civil War; Dmitri sneered slightly at the fuss over such minor skirmishes. Then something teased at his perceptions. He stretched them while he inhaled the fragrant steam of the coffee, muttering a phrase in Mhabrogast.

Dale looked at him sharply. "What's up?"

"Our esteemed imperial bitch was here . . . and killed."

He frowned, and the heavy high-cheeked brown features grew abstracted for a moment. "Yeah, some homeless dude, she blew a weak spot in his brain. Nice neat job. Not like her to be so kindhearted."

They smiled. Dale went on: "That was when she stole her brother's blonde. The one he got back. Tasty piece, but it'd make you puke the way he moons over her."

Dmitri sucked his teeth thoughtfully. "It would not do to underestimate him," he said. "He has killed so many of us . . . including several of my cousins."

"Tell me. *Or* to underestimate his sister. So should we try for the kids, or not? I really want to get my hands on that Mex who shot silver at me, too. Hands, not to mention teeth and other stuff. I like breaking the brave ones."

"Hmmm. A big payoff if it works, they are a shield to our enemies and Adrienne wants that complicating factor taken off the board, but she will be . . . how do you *yanki* put it . . . peeved, if there is any injury to her children. She made that very clear to me."

Dale was visibly tempted to say: *Do I care?* Or words to that effect, but he did not. It was so transparently untrue; you would have to be insane not to care what Adrienne Brézé thought. Dmitri's respect for him went up a notch when he avoided empty bluster.

"Only if we have a truly obvious and very good chance," he said, and the Shadowblade reluctantly nodded. "From your account of your own attack on Adrian's home, his renfields were much luckier than they should have been—and they have excellent defensive Wreakings, both implanted and their amulets."

Then both their heads came up, turning towards the northeast. "They are moving!" Dmitri said.

"Yeah," Dale breathed, and his voice was somehow chill and hot at the same time. "How would you feel about watching kids for a while, Kai?"

"Watching 'em catch on fire?" she said hopefully. "Drown? Fall off cliffs?"

"No," he said, cuffing her good-naturedly. "Watching 'em really carefully."

"There is something in my baggage that we need," Dmitri said. "Assault with the Power did not work very well for you; and it is daylight now. Perhaps more mundane means . . ."

CHAPTER NINE

Santa Fe and points east

Tooling down I-25 on a bright weekday morning in winter and turning off at Cerillos was a weirdly normal experience, right down to Leon saying are we there yet? And passing the scatter of pseudo-Pueblo-style outlet stores and the Kitty Big House where Julia had stashed her cats when they went on vacations out of town—the interstate skirted the ragged eastern edge of Santa Fe, well away from the glitz and antiquity of the historic district. It still wasn't a big city, but there were men alive who had been born before the first paved roads went in downtown.

He watched every possible ambush point. He also kept carefully under the speed limit and unlike the majority of local drivers—who considered it *giving information to the enemy*—used his turn signal well in advance.

Santa Fe had about sixty thousand people and the city police force was small in proportion, and he'd be bound to be recognized by one of the uniforms if he was pulled over. The official story was that he'd simply vanished with no forwarding address after being put on paid leave when his partner got killed. Or possibly he'd just died. He'd fought the temptation to contact his sister for the same reason—all he could do would be to endanger her. The best possible thing would be for her family to think he *had* died or run off into the wild blue yonder baying at the moon.

The little municipal airport was out at the end of Airport Road, in the part of town where people whose grandfathers had lived in the downtown adobes resided in little *fake* adobes with littered yards, earth-colored stucco over frame and flat roofs that leaked like bastards at the slightest provocation. The surviving real adobes and Territorials had all been thoroughly pimped up for the brie-and-chablis crowd by now.

Eric Salvador grinned at the thought. One of the early American governors of what was then the New Mexico Territory had made a farewell speech that included telling the locals to stop building in adobe or keeping goats because the *gringos* would always look down on anyone who did that sort of low-rent greaser stuff, though he'd been *slightly* more tactful in his choice of words.

How things have changed.

That bunch ate a lot of goat cheese now, too, while the goat-herders' descendants bought Wisconsin Velveeta at Sam's Club.

The airport could take jets; there was a regular shuttle to Denver, Dallas/Ft. Worth and LA, though he'd always flown out of Albuquerque because it cost the earth to start here. Mostly it was private planes, of which Santa Fe had more than its share. And one leased by a certain Adrian Brézé when he needed it, which would be waiting for them, engines hot and pre-cleared to leave fast. He felt a little nervous even so.

"This is Adrian's plane we use?" Cheba asked as they turned into the parking lot.

She seemed a little nervous now too, and he hid a smile as he realized that in her case it was simply that she'd never flown before. He pulled into the parking lot and halted several rows away, just in case . . . he didn't *think* there was an ambush waiting with the body scanner, but you never knew.

He was tempted to just leave the keys in the car, but the thought offended his tidy instincts and police training both. If the Brotherhood didn't send someone, eventually the Humvee would be towed. It wasn't registered to Adrian Brézé, either. He'd found out last year during the investigation into Ellen Tarnowski's disappearance—Ellen Brézé now—that the man just didn't exist as far as the records were concerned. If you were Shadowspawn and wanted to, you could exist in the cracks between the walls of the world, passing like a ghost. So could your retainers.

"No," he said. "It's some sort of rental thing. When we talked it over Adrian said he thought owning a private jet he'd only be using a few times a year was . . . showing off. Peter will be on board—"

Some sort of rent-a-servant was waiting by the entrance for them, with a dolly to take the luggage. Eric swung out and gave the surroundings a cautious scan, while Cheba organized the twins, who were fussing over what toys, books and devices they'd carry with them in their hands and backpacks and what would be put away. They weren't exactly spoiled, but they'd been used to getting their own way a lot.

Eric turned back just as the baggage guy came towards the car, trailing the empty dolly. The man gave a meaningless tip-scenting smile that was almost as tooth-grating as the sort of asskissing from lowlifes you got as a cop, and which was apparently one of the drawbacks of giving off serious-money-and-power vibrations.

Crack.

The man pitched backward spinning, with a one-inch black hole turning red in his chest and a head-sized crater in his back, black and red and pink-white. The impact of the body on the ground was the limp, almost boneless thump of instant death. Behind him on the facade of the terminal a glass window starred and cracked, the bullet scarcely slowed down by its passage through body, ribs and spine.

Christ! .50 cal round, flashed through Eric.

Nothing else did that sort of damage, or tossed bodies around Hollywood style with a single shot.

Ptunk-ptunk-crack!

He was diving for the ground before he recognized the sound: a .50 caliber going by, and *close*, after going through the body of the Humvee, in-and-out somewhere. Ticking and clunking sounds made it obvious that it had gone through the engine compartment, probably hitting something vital in the process.

He hugged the ground and tried to spot the shooter's location while looking under it. That was pretty futile, given the distance a fifty-caliber could cover and the amount of scrubby hillside and small buildings within that distance. There was gear that could pinpoint a sniper with half a second of his first shot, but for starters he didn't have the gear and for seconds if the sniper was an adept he could probably screw with it.

Another heavy *crack*, and this time it took out the left front wheel. He looked back, and Cheba had the kids down the space between the rear seats and the front. She was also covering them with her own body, over their objections and squeals; that was very brave, but also pretty futile. Fifty-caliber hard points would blast right through light armor plate, or a respectable thickness of concrete. Or three bodies in a row.

Four more shots, no more than a second apart and beautifully placed to make sure the Humvee wasn't going anywhere.

Okay, the sniper's trying to immobilize us, not kill anybody. Correction, is being very sure not to kill the kids. He's got a honking great Barrett or something like that, semiauto from the timing, and he's got a good firing position . . . but he waited until we stopped to shoot. Didn't want the Humvee tumbling and burning or moving the wrong part into his sight picture. Definitely not willing to take risks with the kids, which means they're trying to pin us down while they do something else—

When someone tried to immobilize you, the obvious tactic was to refuse to stay still and to do that *right away*, before whatever plan they had in mind could get into action. You didn't let the other guy's plan work if you could avoid it; he didn't know what their plan *was* precisely, but it depended on him hiding behind the Humvee. A perfect solution a couple of seconds too late was worth a hell of a lot less than a passable one done in time. And he had a weird sort of safety factor here, though using it went against all his instincts.

"Cheba, take Leila, follow me, and keep *close!*"

For a wonder she did exactly what he told her without haring off on a tangent or stopping to argue; but then he'd known she had natural combat-nerves, hardly like a civilian at all. They each grabbed a child, hugging them close. She thought they were putting their bodies between the children and the sniper . . . but anyone good enough to shoot that well would know their weapon, which meant that the two were using the children as human shields even if she didn't know it. He snarled as he led the way; it was *not* something he wanted to do, but he'd think about that later.

"Sniper!" he yelled to the TSA guard who'd come to the entrance, and flashed his—very outdated—police ID. "He's using a fifty-cal, something mil-spec. Get some rapid-response out here, call SFPD and the Armory, warn 'em!"

There was only one guard, and this place had minimal checks—this was a *very* minor airport, and mostly for private planes, a one-horse operation. Or more precisely a three-runway one with a single modest single-story building for a terminal. He could see the act being swallowed; terrorists rarely ran in already under fire, protectively clutching children. That was why his gun was firmly *inside* his coat.

There was also a fairly big National Guard HQ only a mile away on I-25, upgraded a few years ago, and they could almost certainly scrape up a reaction team.

"I'm on it, get under cover!" the man said. "Everybody, get *flat*, God damn it to hell!"

He was doing so himself, and holding his piece as if he knew what to do with it. Probably he'd seen action somewhere, there were a fair number of guys their age like that around.

"Fuckin' A!" Eric said, and led his party right through the building and onto the runway. No swinging Jetways from an isolated boarding area here, just tarmac and ramps on wheels.

Everyone else inside the building was running around and some of them were even screaming while they did it, which meant he had a short window of opportunity. If he'd thought the shooter was trying to kill everyone in his party he wouldn't dare head for the aircraft; it was well within range, once it taxied out from behind the terminal building. But as it was, the safest place for them all to be was in the air; if they'd been reluctant to shoot at a moving car with the kids in it, they'd be twice as unwilling to shoot at an aircraft they were aboard.

The jet was a Bombadier 900, a big business model with twin engines at the rear that could be configured for two dozen passengers. A worried-looking female in airline gear—the copilot, apparently—was hesitating at the foot of the ramp, and there didn't look to be anything else even thinking of taking off, even a Cessna.

"Just get us in the air!" Eric said, as he hustled everyone up the ramp.

That was the sweaty bit. Cheba and he were probably safe enough right now with the building blocking things and all . . . but if he was wrong in his snap judgment of where the shooter was, and the bastard had an angle on this spot and felt confident enough to try for a head shot, he was screwed, or probably just dead. He'd seen what those big bullets did to a human body, and not just today.

"We can't just—" the copilot said, following him in.

"Yes, you fucking can," Eric snarled, turning and shoving the door closed and dogging it himself.

For an instant he felt almost limp with relief. Now he was invisible from the outside, and the enemy weren't willing to just shoot up the vehicle he was in. Probably.

"Now just do it!"

Peter Boase was there; Eric handed off Leon and turned to glare at the flier. He was prepared to get things going at gunpoint if he really had to, and trust to Adrian to clear things up later, but that was insanely risky—if they ended up in detention the other side could walk in and get them. The copilot gave him a long look, a short nod and turned back into the cockpit without further encouragement. Eric blew out a long breath and collapsed into one of the recliners, fumbling at the seatbelt.

"I need a drink," he croaked, making his right hand relax and unclench on the butt of the coach gun inside his coat.

There was nothing he could do with that now except commit suicide, which was admittedly starting to have a certain abstract appeal. The engines roared as he strapped himself in, and acceleration pushed him into the softness. The whine rose and then the nose, and then the final bump as they left the tarmac.

"That was like *Call of Duty!*" Leon enthused, bouncing in his seat and calling around Peter's body where the scientist was strapping him in. "Wow! *Magnifique!*"

"Kid, shut up before I shoot you myself," Eric said—but sotto voce.

The white-green-dun-brown expanse of the New Mexican country-side turned beneath them as the aircraft banked, climbing. For a moment he could see the toy-tiny shape of the Humvee, now burning with a flicker of yellow flame and drift of black smoke—evidently the sniper had lost his temper and emptied a magazine into it. Eric felt his stomach muscles unclench as they gained altitude; they were over the height a rifle could reach fairly quickly, even that sort of monster-truck model. He unsnapped and stuck his head into the cockpit.

"Any problems?" he said.

The pilot was in his fifties, with a gray-and-brown buzz cut and faded blue eyes. "Nope," he said. "Tower's chewing my ass for blowing Dodge in the middle of a quote terrorist incident unquote, but I'd already had clearance so it won't amount to much."

"Thanks," Eric said.

The man shrugged. "Just doing my job."

Reaction made his hands shake a little as he turned back into the body of the plane. The interior in this one was pale and mostly open, comfortable in an impersonal way, with six recliner-style seats, a table and chairs, a small kitchen nook and a bathroom with a compact shower. Peter caught his eye and mimed wiping sweat off his brow. Cheba was already busy with something; then she shoved a bottle into his hand and he took a swig of the beer—Stone Arrogant Bastard Ale again—and he grinned in sheer relief

It sluiced the gummy dryness out of his mouth a lot better than a suck of tepid rubber-tasting water from a camelback. He'd done a fair impression of a SABA himself, just now, and it had worked. For now. He made himself file the whole thing on the *ongoing psychological damage* memory chip and move on with an effort of will.

Instead he looked around the inside of the aircraft.

Well, this beats the hell out of sitting buttcheek to buttcheek in webbing seats in a Herky Bird on a twelve-hour troop lift full of eau de piss and Red Bull, he thought. *Not to mention your conventional Misery Special in coach. I wonder if Adrian Brézé needs an ex-cop long-term? Could be worse jobs after this is all over . . .*

"Were people really shooting at us?" Leila said. "I wasn't sure."

"Uhhh . . ." *It's usually better to tell kids the truth.* "Yeah, but they weren't trying to hit you. Just the car. And maybe me and Cheba."

"Mom and Dad will both be angry at them," Leila said. "They were shooting *close* to us."

"And then they'll be *soooorrrrrreeeeee,*" Leon said.

With that both the children seemed to lose interest, looking around at their transportation instead. Apparently they were much less impressed than he was.

"Mom's plane is a lot bigger than this. It has a pool," Leila said, looking up from her tablet. "It's called *Le Misérable Excès.*"

"It's an Airbus 380," Leon said knowledgeably. "Really cool. We have our own bedrooms and there's this game room where the walls are screens and you can play interactive *Doom* and stuff. Hi, Peter! You look like you're feeling a lot better than you were before."

The slight sharp-featured blond man was a little older than Eric, but . . .

Looks younger, Eric thought. *No, not younger when you look in his eyes.*

He spent years on Rancho Sangre as Adrienne Brézé's bloodbank and fucktoy and tame researcher knowing that anything he found out would help them. *He's pulled his tours too, and he managed to turn it around on her, which was outstanding.*

Another advantage of this arrangement was that you didn't sit waiting for eight other aircraft to take off; they were climbing to thirty thousand feet within seconds.

Peter Boase grinned when Eric mentioned it.

"Do you think the Council of Shadows was in charge of setting up the deregulated civil aviation system?" he said, his voice still carrying a trace of the flat Upper Midwestern vowels; he was from Minnesota originally. "To make us all suffer?"

"Nah, just feels like it," Eric said.

The men laughed; Cheba looked at them blankly for a moment. Peter produced a paper sack from the refrigerator.

"Here's lunch. Take-out from La Casa Sena."

"They do take-out?" Eric asked, going over to the kitchenette and looking in the fridge. "Damn, real Mexican Coca-Cola with cane sugar, not that corn syrup crap the Iowans make us drink."

La Casa Sena was a place on Palace Avenue, just up from what had been the residence of the Spanish, Mexican and American governors, and was now a museum. The restaurant had been the fortified home place of a rich landowner once, back when the Apache raided all over New Mexico and far south of Sonora. It was a big two-story 18th-century adobe built around a courtyard, with a wine store and some fancy clothing shops as well as the eatery. He'd been there exactly twice; once when he was still trying to make it up with Julia, and once on police business, the investigation that had gotten his partner killed and himself disappeared into the world of the Council-Brotherhood war.

It wasn't the most expensive place in town by a long shot, but you could blow a couple of C-notes on dinner there and if you started hitting the wine list the sky was the limit. There was an old joke that Santa Fe was a city where ten thousand people could buy the state and fifty thousand couldn't afford lunch. Some people got nauseated after an adrenaline rush; Eric had always found it made him ravenous. At least he could do something besides stuff an MRE in his face this time.

Peter grinned: "Hey, it pays to have connections; there's takeout for *us*. Maybe we'll all die horribly, but we'll do it in style."

Eric nodded. "Beats maybe dying horribly while you're eating crap. Beats it all to hell."

"Right. And you wouldn't *believe* how nice it is to just say you need lab equipment and it appears. No meetings, no budget reports, no root-canal work, it's just *there*."

"What've you got?"

"Well, we've got a Bose-Einstein condensate particle . . . oh, you mean the *food*." Peter looked at a menu from the bag: "You want the grilled local organic chicken with basil pesto, *poblano rajas*, grilled onions, asadero cheese, heirloom tomatoes, and chipotle mayo on focaccia or the BBQ pork po'-boy, with jicama–cabbage slaw, rattlesnake bean–sweet corn salad, on a multigrain hoagie?"

Eric took the po'-boy and bit into it. Cheba took one, chewed thoughtfully, swallowed:

"This . . . *es como una buena torta de barbacoa*," she said, then went back to English: "Not bad . . . what did it cost?"

She'd been thinking of opening a shop to sell Mexican handicrafts when this was all over, assuming they survived, or possibly a restaurant. Adrian Brézé had agreed to get her a green card and start-up money as her price for helping with the raid on the great house at Rancho Sangre in California. Peter read it off; the young woman swallowed wrong and started to cough, so Eric pounded her helpfully on the back.

"Only problem with this trip is what's at the end," he said. "Going up against people with precognition and telepathy and all that good shit just makes me nervous."

It also makes me likely to die, but hey, goes with the territory, he thought to himself, keeping it silent because the others were more-or-less civilians.

Peter smiled. This time it wasn't just pleasant; there was something of a shark's grin in it as he tapped what looked like a tablet.

"We've been working on that prescience-blocking field."

"We?"

"Well, Dr. Duquesne and me. The Brotherhood moved us from the place in Sweden to their big base in Ecuador . . . they wanted us to camouflage it for them. Which we did. They've got lots of engineers and technicians, but not many real scientists for some reason. It's odd—if I had the Power, I would *so* have been using it experimentally."

"What's it like, the base?"

"It's in the crater of a semi-extinct volcano, burrowed into these amazing natural caves . . . there's even a monorail."

"Do they have their own nuclear reactor?" Eric said.

Peter frowned. "No, a geothermal unit . . . why?"

"I watched a *lot* of old movies on my phone while I was doing stakeouts. You would not believe how boring being a detective is. Anyway, what's that?"

"It's the *new* prescience-blocking generator. The first one, the one that Harvey, uh—"

"Stole."

"Stole. That was a test bed, jury-rigged. This is the production model for small-scale concealment. We put in a big one for the base; they had protective Wreakings, but they're much happier now."

He grimaced slightly. "Though I think some of them thought it was . . . cheating."

"What were they like?" Eric asked curiously. "I haven't seen any of their bigwigs, and the grunts were all in-and-out, real concentrated on business."

Peter frowned. "They seemed like people trying very hard to be good, but it doesn't come naturally to them."

Eric shrugged. "That's me, sometimes. Whatever works."

"And they were really concerned with being able to hide. I don't think things have been going well for them lately."

"Sort of a defensive crouch, yeah, I got that impression too. Not a good thing."

Cheba looked at the tablet. "It isn't one of those little computers?"

"We used the case from commercial tablets. It makes it inconspicuous."

"So, this is a machine that can do what the *brujos* do?"

There was a carnivorous eagerness to the question. Peter shook his head.

"I wish. No. No, that needs a lot of . . ."

He paused. "I can't explain without math."

"But hey, you'll give it a try, right?" Eric said patiently.

Peter flung up his hands: "The experiments I did at the Rancho . . . They need *modulation*, a control system as . . . as subtle as a human brain. One that worked *like* the human brain, or really like the Shadowspawn brain, on a quantum level. It's . . . it's like the difference between being able to play the violin and being able to make a loud noise."

"But," he went on, "we *can* make a really loud noise."

145

He tapped the screen. Leila and Leon were walking back from the cockpit as he did so; they stopped abruptly, their dark brows knotting.

"You're not there any more!" Leon said.

"I can see you, but you're *not there*!" Leila said. And added: "I don't like it!"

Peter stuck his hands protectively in front of the little machine as she pointed at it. "No! Don't hurt it!"

Cheba shook a warning finger. "You two be good! *¡Comportanse!*"

"C'mon, Leila, let's play some Angry Rodents," her brother said.

"This is going to be complicated," Eric said thoughtfully as the children put on their earbuds and VR glasses. "How many of those things do you have?"

"Fair number. At least one each, but don't lose them . . . or get them fried. We checked, and Wreakings *can* fry them, they just can't be very precise because the Power can't sense them. There are some attachments here; this is the underwater model, for example. Dive-rated. Rechargers, testing monitors . . . we've got some nice kit here. They have their limitations, but they sure do make it easier to *surprise* the other side, though."

"*Bueno*," Cheba said. She looked at the baggage rack, where her fashionista backpack with the built-in silvered machete rested. "There are some people, they *should* be surprised, you know?"

Dmitri's hands moved on the massive sniper rifle without requiring conscious direction; the three of them were lying in a little rocky declivity, with the barrel through the roots of a chamisos and Dale lying next to him with a little fiber-optic periscope peeping out to produce a picture on his tablet.

"Well, shit," he said. Then his head turned sharply after the departing plane. "*Shit*, did you catch that?"

Dmitri focused. "They're . . . *gone*. As if they stopped existing. As if they *never did* exist!"

Dale nodded slowly. "Yeah. Something really strange is going on here."

"*Beh pizday!* And we need to know what. Next time, no holding back."

He finished fitting the parts of the rifle into their foam-lined receptacles in the carrying case, snapped it closed and slung it over his back. Dale halted as they turned and started down towards the four-by-four.

"What?" Dmitri said.

"What just happened . . . the whole thing. Something Alpha Bitch said after I went for them at her brother's place. She said her kids were so pureblood that *they* might be screwing things up."

Dmitri snorted. "She is arrogant. They are too young, still latent."

Dale shook his head. "She said their future selves might be loading the dice *from a long time from now.*"

Dmitri stopped, winced, and shrugged. "That is a . . . disturbing thought. But what could we do about it?"

"Kill 'em?" Dale said. "Anyway, it's a thought."

They were all very silent as they drove away down the dirt track. Behind them a convoy pulled out of the gate of the National Guard base.

Dale Shadowblade nodded to the TSA agent at Albuquerque's airport.

"No, I've got no ID at all, and it wouldn't help you anyway. We psychopathic killers look like anyone else. Yeah, I've got a shitload of guns, knives and some China White in here, and a couple of grenades. I mean, I can't get addicted so there's no harm in the occasional line of blow, and I might need to kill someone, right? Yeah, it's more satisfying with your bare hands, but now and then you're in a hurry."

The agent blinked. "What was that, sir?" he said slowly.

"We're not the droids you're looking for," Kai said with a giggle.

"Have a pleasant flight, sir, ma'am."

"You do the scanner," Dale said to his lucy-cum-renfield.

It was easy enough to convince a mind it saw and heard what it *expected* to hear, but computers were simpler still.

"You need the practice anyway," he added.

They walked through the security line, and then through the scanners. The agent looking at the screen reared back and clapped her hands to her mouth in shock, then sat back again and burst into tears. Kai was grinning her usual nasty expression, and it got broader as they went into the concourse. She snapped her fingers with both hands, made a little prancing dance-step, giggled, and people began staring at their smartphones and tablets and shaking them or punching fingers at the screens and cursing.

Albuquerque Sunport was laid out in a T, the B gates to the right and the A to the left, with a big bronze statue at the junction. It showed an Indian—a shaman—with a feathered headdress, chasing an eagle in a flat-out run and looking like he was about to fall over.

"Looks like one of those Navajo pukes," Dale said. "One of the goodie-goodies who thinks they can keep you off with sand-paintings."

He grinned too, at the thought. *Maybe in the old days. Not anymore.* A lot of the medicine-men could manage a little Wreaking without really knowing what they were doing, but a modern Council adept was in a whole different league, like an assault rifle up against a spear.

It was fun to suddenly turn palpable in the *middle* of the sand-painting when you were nightwalking, and go on from there.

You know, it's really more fun when they believe in you beforehand but buy that Good triumphs over Evil shit. Then evil gets 'em and . . . yeah, that feels real good. Tastes good too.

"Looks like he's about to fall on his face. Or his ass, or both at the same time," Kai said, glancing at the statue.

Dale laughed. "That's appropriate. I'll handle this," he said.

Kai pouted. "Aw, I wanna—"

He clouted her alongside the head, making a hard smacking sound as the calloused palm struck, and she turned her eyes down. The action was a relief; airports had a bad aura, throttled rage and frustration. A man started to get up and come towards them, until Dale stared at him for a second; then he sat down again.

At the B10 gate counter Dale walked up to the agent at the computer.

"You got four last-minute cancellations in first class on the Alitalia flight to Paris with changeover in Atlanta," he said. "We're at the top of the standby list. In fact, we're the only people on it. Platinum premium boarding."

His eyes locked on hers, and he murmured, first in his own language and then in Mhabrogast. The agent's pupils expanded until the color was a thin blue rim around darkness . . .

"Why Alitalia?" Kai said, as they strolled down the Jetway.

They both had one small carry-on; he preferred to carry nothing but a few favorite weapons and some Wreaking paraphernalia wherever he went and just pick up anything he needed at the destination. Behind them there was a scrimmage around the counter, with the ticketing agent mumbling incoherently and would-be passengers waving their boarding passes . . . or trying, if they had them on their smartphones and tablets. Behind *that* there was another frenzy, as the Bank of America ATM began to spew cash out onto the floor.

"Better booze on the Euro airlines," Dale said. "And a better class of flight attendant. It's going to be a long boring trip and we'll need something to do. Flying . . . flying makes me *hungry*."

Kai giggled again. Then she almost ran into his back as he halted for a moment.

"What is it?" she said.

"Something else from bossbitch. She's got a job for me. And it looks like a lot of fun. A technical challenge."

CHAPTER TEN

Mitteleuropa

"Well, this is fucking nostalgic," Dale Shadowblade said.

The trail of smoke from the steam engine was a dun-colored plume in the distance, and the snow glittered in the moonlight.

"What?" Kai said.

"My granddad saw trains robbed sometimes," Dale said. "As a little kid. *His* granddad took him along the last couple of times as a treat just before the old bastard bit it."

"Oh." She searched her memory; he could feel her doing it like pages being flipped. "Like Butch and that Western shit?"

"Yeah, though Granddad said when they caught someone his graddad used to tie 'em to a tree and then cut open their bellies and pull out the guts a couple of yards, real careful not to kill 'em. So they could watch the coyotes having dinner."

Kai giggled. "Hey, that sounds like fun!"

"It does, doesn't it? I've never got around to it, always meant to, but he used to laugh himself sick when he told about the way they'd wiggle. Anyway, those trains would have looked like that one, all steam and smoke."

He took a deep breath; the smell of the countryside was different, wetter even with the cold, greener . . .

"Okay, you keep an eye on the body," he said, turning back to the Mercedes Sprinter van. "Bossbitch wants someone killed. Roll me in clover, said the pig."

There was still a slight smell of blood from the previous owners, but the back had comfortable foam padding. He lay down and crossed his arms on his chest. Kai closed the doors and squatted outside, smoking and cradling a little Austrian machine pistol.

Amss-aui-ock!

A twist of agony and ecstasy and a great snowy owl beat its wings, up and through the metal ceiling of the van. The night turned bright as he circled, full of rustlings and movement, the scurry of a field-mouse insanely distracting. He rose, banked, dove, then turned, exulting in the way his wingfeathers grasped the air like fingers in water. That left him flying at exactly the same speed as the train; there was a curve here that made it slow down a little. Another twist, and a chacma baboon fell to the top of the train.

Fingers and toes gripped, and the wind whipped at his grey-brown fur as the motion of the passenger-car jolted him. This was one of his favorite forms for climbing work; chacma baboons were nearly as agile as squirrels and with a hundred-pound weight and two-inch canines they were bad news in a fight too. There was more brain to them, too, which made things like maintaining purpose easier. A mutter of Mhabrogast . . .

Shit, he thought.

When you looked at it *this* way, the whole train lit up like a Christmas tree. With Wreakings, wards, and the personal patterns of adepts, like a chorus of flavors and smells, all of them bad to really bad. There was serious monster mojo here. He twisted again into his own base-form and began to pull not-see around himself. Tease out the threads . . . they were like a skein blurring the whole substance of the world around him . . .

The wind was cold on his naked skin. He shivered and sweated at the same time. Now for the most difficult part of all, one most Shadowspawn never tried. He checked his location again; not all that far from the bossbitch herself, her aura was unmistakable . . . and right, she'd be able to claim she wasn't thinking about anything but fucking her brains out and feeding while this went down.

And who's the smart one here? he thought sardonically. *Who's freezing his aetheric dick off, about to risk his life, and who's in a nice warm bed spanking the hell out of a really first-rate piece of ass?*

Feel the roof of the railway car. Feel the *quiver,* the way the matter existed not as a solid *thing,* but instead as a grainy foamy presence more like a note plucked on a guitar. Don't let the process become just instinct like walking through a wall, where it was easy to turn the bottom of your feet a bit more palpable as they came down. Control. Then sink into it, letting yourself match it—

—and fall through, a flash of darkness—

—and turn palpable again in a split second.

—and land in a crouch. He panted for a moment, the sound harsh in his ears. Dropping through a floor was insanely risky. If your timing was even a fraction off you ended up dropping right into the earth, or trying to go palpable again halfway through something. Both would kill you.

No sense in waiting. His don't-see-me was better than any Shadowspawn he'd ever met; that was why the Council had used him as an executioner, and that was how he'd met Adrienne. The downside was that you couldn't do much else but listen with the Power when you were hiding that hard, anything active showed right up and blew your cover.

On the other hand, hiding wasn't the only reason he'd been named Shadowblade.

Okay, there's Adrienne, making happy with lots of sound effects. Adrian, likewise, quieter, but a good time being had by all. And Arnaud on the other side . . . a trifecta of Brézés. I've never killed a Brézé before. It could get addictive.

His hand touched the door to the compartment. Not locked. Then there was a sudden unexpected wave of agony from within, as if someone had been dipped in liquid fire.

Dale Shadowblade grinned like a shark as he flicked the door aside and lunged.

There were screams coming through the thin wall of the compartment. Mixed with moans, and a smacking sound.

"Whose idea was it to put your *sister* next to us?" Ellen asked, jamming her thumbs into her ears and trying not to think of a series of memories that were unpleasant in a whole galaxy of ways, many less than straightforward.

Adrian grinned at her. "Any of my family who wish to do us harm, which is to say, any of them," he said. "Starting with her, and working on out to Great-uncle Arnaud, who I think did some of the scheduling for this trip."

Then he concentrated and began to mutter. Ellen felt a sensation like a fierce itch *inside* her skull. The sounds from next door dulled, until they were fainter than the droning whine of steel on steel from the wheels and the distant chuffing of the engine.

"You know," Ellen said, with a slow smile, "I was telling the truth about your hands and my bottom."

Hours later a scream of an entirely different nature woke her from a drowsing sleep, so loud she couldn't tell if it was psychic or physical or both. The muffling feel of the Wreakings clanging shut in her head was nearly as startling. She sat up in the comfortable but slightly narrow bunk. Across the compartment Adrian was crouched on his, alert and tensile as a great cat, the yellow flecks in his eyes glittering in the dim light.

"What was that?" Ellen said quietly.

"Death, I think," he said. "The Final Death. A nightwalker, a post-corporeal perhaps, in sudden agony and great fear. And close, close."

A fist thumped at the door. "Open!"

The rolling shutters were down over the lounge's windows, and the post-corporeals were there despite the fact that the sun was up outside and the train still in motion. They were also all within arm's length of the armored boxes held by their most trusted renfields, and they were snarling-angry.

"Arnaud Brézé was under my protection," Étienne-Maurice said. "It was made clear before we left Paris that all feuds were in abeyance until we arrived in Tbilisi, and we are not yet even in Istanbul!"

Ellen was uneasily conscious that they were snarling-angry at *her*, and at Adrian, as well as simply pissed off at having to be active in daytime away from their carefully arranged and usually underground home lairs. The renfields were coldly furious too; Arnaud's valet had been found dead face-down on the floor of the compartment too.

"Am I supposed to have killed my Great-uncle Arnaud?" Adrian said, reclining gracefully and lighting a thin brown cigarette. "And if I did . . . what objection would any of you have?"

He blew smoke towards the ceiling in that offensively arrogant way that only someone who'd spent a lot of time in France in the twentieth century could master.

Étienne-Maurice crossed his arms. "Because this train is under my protection," he said with deadly calm. "I would take any such action as . . . how shall I express it . . . a *personal affront*. Even a challenge."

He didn't have to add how many challenges he'd faced in over a century of existence, and how few of those challengers had survived.

"Then we should determine who *did* commit such a solecism, sire," Adrian said. "For it was not me."

One of the Tōkairin clan surged to his feet, hand going to the katana thrust through his sash. "You are a Brotherhood terrorist!"

"Well, yes," Adrian said with a slight smile. "But that is not relevant to the issue. *Your* motivation is obvious. Your cousin invaded my home territory and I—my wife, actually—killed her. Would anyone here have done differently?"

That brought unwilling nods. Ellen shivered a little inwardly, behind the shields that made it difficult to read her emotions. To Shadowspawn, that argument made perfect sense, which was an illustration of why hanging out with them was like swimming with sharks. The Brotherhood operatives who had a large share of that with blood made her nervous; these . . .

"Is this supposed to be a motivation for *me* to have killed *your* great-uncle?" the Tōkairin said.

Adrian shrugged expressively. "It is if you persist in trying to pin the blame on *me*. In any case, I have no motivation . . . well, I would have killed him if I had an opportunity in the normal course of events, he tried to kill me last year in Paris . . . but I have no motivation to do so *now* and *here*. Unlike my late great-uncle, I am not an impulsive or reckless man. I am attending the meeting in Tbilisi to make an argument; this would not have increased my credibility. And I fear my great-grandfather's anger . . . as who does not?"

There were nods, and a few smiles and laughs. Ellen became conscious of how sweat was trickling down her flanks as the ratcheting tension eased back a notch.

"*Ach*, so," the man in the SS uniform said. "But you might have had other motives . . . concealing a secret, perhaps?"

Adrienne spoke. "Arnaud was scarcely likely to confide in my brother. Insofar as he had a political position, he was aligned with *me*. Does anyone suggest that *I* killed him?"

"It is not impossible," von Trupp said thoughtfully.

"Well, any one of us *could* have killed him," she pointed out cheerfully, nibbling on a biscuit. "Is there anyone here who *doesn't* enjoy the process, other things being equal? Apart from you, Ellen."

Ellen shivered invisibly again. *Yeah, Adrian apart, who? And when he gets his blood up . . . How do you figure out a murder when everyone around cheerfully owns up to being a murderer?*

"Let us examine the . . . site," Adrian said.

No point in saying body *because there isn't one,* Ellen thought.

"Oh, I don't really think that's necessary—" Adrienne said.

The conversation became harder to follow after that, partly because some of it was telepathic, and more because the Shadowspawn started dropping into and out of languages she didn't speak. One of the many vile unfairnesses of their genetic heritage was that they could pick up languages with full fluency in a week or two simply by interacting with native speakers. The enlarged language centers of their brain, the part that handled telepathy, just *absorbed* it. Adrian spoke dozens. He claimed that he had the same faint accent in all of them . . .

When the dialogue started to include hissing snarls she slipped out unnoticed. Whenever she started getting too envious, she reflected that were advantages to *not* having the Power.

Nobody was guarding the compartment that had been Arnaud Brézé's.

"Why am I not surprised? These people . . . sorta-kinda people . . . couldn't organize an orgy in a whorehouse," she muttered. "Well, maybe that, but only because of natural talent in that direction, not organizational skills. If it weren't for their renfields they wouldn't have clean socks in the mornings and they'd always be running out of toilet paper and toothpaste."

It wasn't that Shadowspawn were stupid, though some were, about the same percentage as with normals. Adrian was brilliant . . .

And Adrienne is too, in that utterly skanky sneaky heh-heh-heh of evil laughter sort of way.

It was just that a lot of them *acted* stupid in this sort of situation. Stalking around each other with their fur bristling rather than getting on with things. Which was fortunate, in its way; if it hadn't been that way humans would all be in pens.

She slid in and closed the door behind her. The layout was identical to the compartment she and Adrian shared; a couch on either side that folded down into a bed, with an armoire-table between. Just as fancy, too, in a subtly different way. These wagon-lit cars were individual works of art, or at least craftsmanship of the highest order, put together like fine cabinetry.

All right, she told herself. *You've had years of doing Janette Bond stuff in Adrian's head and some real-world too, and you're good at seeing patterns anyway, you always were. What do you see here? Where are the details that don't fit? Pretend it's a painting and you're checking to see if it's a fake or not—you did that at the gallery in Santa Fe often enough. What doesn't fit? What's wrong?*

There was a sharp unpleasant scent in the air. Not blood; an aetheric body dissolved when it died, and evidently the valet had been killed in some non-leakish way. This would be the stomach contents, since the nightwalking body *did* oxidize food to create energy. Sure enough, there was a stained and damp patch on the sheets beneath the tumbled blanket. Ellen crossed to the window and flipped up the pull-down screen; the glass was sufficiently tinted to let a nightwalker enter the compartment, but most of them would hesitate anyway because you could *see* the sun outside, albeit a pale washed-out variety.

Black leafless trees were passing by, with glimpses of snowy fields and the occasional farmhouse beyond, like Bruegel's *The Return of the Hunters.* You forgot how *north* Northern Europe was until you were here in winter; because of the Gulf Stream it wasn't any colder than the mid-Atlantic states she'd grown up in, but it sure as hell was *darker* in this season.

The cause of death seemed obvious; a long double-edged silvered dagger was rammed through the bedding and into the mattress beneath.

And that's his monogram on the hilt. Someone killed him with his own knife.

She hesitated, then wrapped her hand in a corner of the sheet before she pulled at it—probably nobody was going to take fingerprints, but there was no point in taking chances. At least it was just silver, and not the alternative way of killing a nightwalking Shadowspawn, which was a knife with pre-activated glyphs commanding a Wreaking. Those were a lot more dangerous to the user. Especially a human, because if the nightwalker was strong enough and fast enough he could reverse it, which would be like the blade were running a couple of thousand volts right through *you*.

Then she frowned. There was more than one rent in the bedclothes. More than half a dozen, in fact, as if there had been multiple stabs. And why was the blade plunged deep into the mattress; until the nightwalker died or went impalpable the body would have kept it from going in that deep. And—

She ran a finger through a dry part of the sheet and rubbed thumb and forefingers together. There was some sort of dust or powder on the sheet, well away from what had been the edge, and it glittered. A quick glance aside showed a stack of envelopes, antique things with heavy cream-colored paper, but they'd do well enough. She took one, and used a sheet of the watermarked notepaper beside them to scrape as much of the powder as she could into the envelope and tucked the flap closed.

A first glance around showed only what a rather foppish, wealthy European born in the 1880s would have, with the unexpected addition of a modern Indian-made tablet. She tapped the screen, and found it had been playing Debussy through a set of wireless earphones as an accompaniment to a video file . . .

She shuddered and turned it off; on second thought she slipped it into her pocket, feeling as if her hands were dirty. There were the usual weapons, including an 1892 Lebel revolver with silver bullets in the chambers within reach of both the bed and the table, but no indication that any of them had been used. Something pricked at her attention. The pad of notepaper on the little table was *sewn* at the top, with a row of perforations below—just as usable as the adhesive type she was familiar with, but different, and it made it immediately obvious a sheet had been used. There was an elegant Montblanc fountain pen beside it, but no writing.

And exactly one sheet is missing from the top of the otherwise-virgin pad.

"Now, what are the reasons to kill someone? Kicks, with this crowd. Or fear. To stop someone from doing something . . . did Arnaud *know* something? Was he going to tell someone? It's right next to our compartment and one over from Adrienne's."

She picked up the pad and slipped that into her pocket as well. Another round of the compartment didn't show any sign of the missing sheet of paper, even when she went through the pockets of all the clothes outside the trunks. At last—reluctantly, and using the fountain pen—she began to lift the sheets. A corner of paper, yellowed from the equivalent of stomach acids—

"What are you doing here, *puta*?"

The words were in a woman's voice, flat neutral Californian-American, but accompanied by a short metallic *click*. Ellen's recent education filled in the rest, and she turned very slowly.

She recognized the figure in the doorway; Theresa Villegas, Adrienne's household manager. A renfield, but a very trusted one, from a family that had served the Brézés for nearly two centuries, since that branch arrived in California not long after the Gold Rush . . . Back on Rancho Sangre, the Brézé country seat on the central Californian coast not far from Paso Robles, there was an old story that a rattlesnake had bitten Theresa once.

The story said the *snake* had died.

"Looking around," Ellen said coolly, keeping her hands in view.

Theresa was a prim-looking middle-aged woman in a conservative business suit, with graying black hair and an olive complexion; in her hand was a small businesslike revolver, with the tips of the bullets shining a dull silver where the cylinder exposed them. The click had been her thumb pulling back the hammer of the simple single-action weapon. Ironically enough, Ellen was in more danger now than she would be with a Shadowspawn adept. The defenses Adrian had Wrought would keep the Power at bay long enough for her to run or get help.

None of it would help a damn with a nine-millimeter bullet traveling at over a thousand feet per second, and she couldn't Wreak to sabotage the weapon. The silver wouldn't do her any extra harm . . . but it wouldn't be any less effective than simple jacketed lead, either.

And Theresa had just exactly as much compunction about killing as Adrienne. Less, in fact, since Ellen was fairly certain Adrienne badly wanted to keep Ellen unwillingly alive for some time, possibly millennia. Whereas the renfield would be perfectly content to just kill her, for purely practical reasons and because she'd always disliked Ellen, who hadn't had what she considered the proper (abject) attitude for a lucy during her time at Rancho Sangre. Neither she nor Adrienne had read the Evil Overlord List, but the human was much more attuned to its pragmatic spirit.

"Returning to the scene of the crime, like a dog to its vomit?"

Said the bitch, Ellen thought but did not say. *Damn, I'm not nearly as scared as I used to be. Which is good . . . and a bit scary in itself . . . but just as grossed out.*

Instead she went on: "What exactly do you think Adrian will do if—"

"If I kill his lucy?" Theresa said.

"Wife," Ellen said with a friendly smile. "Kill his wife."

Theresa's finger tightened on the trigger, and for a moment Ellen thought she'd been overindulgent by giving herself the pleasure of puncturing Villegas' self-image; prodding the tiger, or in this case hyena, through the bars was only safe if there *were* good solid bars. Then it relaxed: the steel of self-interest proved strong enough for the flash of murderous hate. At some level someone like Theresa Villegas had to hate herself most of all, but human beings projected that outward more often than not.

"And of course what Adrienne would do to *you*," she finished cheerfully.

That didn't intimidate Theresa as much as she'd hoped. "Yes, she has plans for you." A gesture with the gun. "This would be a mercy, which is why I'm *not* going to shoot you . . . as long as you leave. Immediately."

Ellen turned her back on the renfield and continued to lift the sheet. There *was* a corner of paper there, and it *was* the same type as the notepad, as near as she could tell after the pseudo-body's pseudo-stomach acids had been at work on it for a few moments.

Why would a desperate post-corporeal eat a piece of paper? It would show up as soon as . . . oh. You'd have to root around. And post-corporeals start out as corporeals. The habits persist . . . look at this compartment, there's all the proof you need they really *really persist!*

"I will shoot you on the count of three . . . the *Doña* is usually rational given a little time to think . . . one . . . two . . ."

"All right, all right," Ellen said, straightening and tucking the pen away after wiping it on the blanket. "Have a *nice* day once she gets back."

She was still smiling when she closed the door of their compartment behind them. Then she sat and shuddered with her hands knotted together and pressed to her forehead.

I do not, not, not want to live this way! I'm spending most of my time around people who are like something out of a fucking horror movie! They all deserve to die! I hate these people! I hate the fact that I hate people and want to kill them!

A year ago she couldn't have imagined killing someone even in self-defense, much less enjoying the thought. She still had her pistol in her hand when the handle of the compartment door clicked. If it was the train staff, they simply wouldn't notice it—another thing she didn't like was *manipulating* people all the time, even if it was for their own good or just to stay out of their sight.

"It's me," Adrian said softly, probably sensing her emotions. "They have calmed down, for the present."

Ellen gave a shivering sigh of relief and gripped him fiercely as he came through.

"I adore you too, darling," he said, putting an arm around her. "But put the gun away first, *hein*?"

She took a deep breath and did. When she let them the reflexes she'd acquired about firearms operated automatically; and she hadn't actually *pointed* it at the back of his neck, anyway.

"What happened?" he asked.

"I'm . . . not sure," she said. "But here's what I found—"

When she finished they were on the sofa, her head against his shoulder. She could feel the puzzled frown in his voice.

"Theresa would not have threatened you unless she *truly* wanted you out of Arnaud's compartment." Then quietly: "And some day . . . we will have to have a little talk about that with her."

Ellen shivered slightly. Most of that sound in Adrian's voice was outrage that anyone should threaten her, which was heart-warming. A slice of it was sheer cold aristo arrogance, though. Even that was *slightly* heartwarming—his subconscious was indignant that a servant should threaten a Brézé, meaning her.

"I think . . . Arnaud was about to do something that Adrienne didn't want. Either she killed him or she had someone else do it."

"But what? Even by Shadowspawn standards, Arnaud was . . . whimsical. And as far as he had any politics at all, he backed Adrienne's faction."

"That's just it," Ellen said slowly. "Maybe he *learned* something."

"And then there is the means," Adrian said.

He took the envelope and rubbed a little of the powder between thumb and forefinger. Then he shook his hand, spitting a curse and rinsing it in the little compartment sink.

"This is powdered silver, prepared in a rather arcane and complex fashion. The Brotherhood use it sometimes, but it requires careful camouflage. If you can conceal it until a nightwalker shall we say slides into bed . . . the agony would be indescribable. Not fatal, but enough to thoroughly distract."

She brought out the tablet, notepad and pen. "Maybe if we held this paper up against the light, or scattered shavings . . ."

"Ah," Adrian said with satisfaction, laying them out. "I would not have seen this pattern."

He turned until they were facing each other and inclined his forehead against hers. "May I?"

She nodded, and made herself relax. Most importantly, she made her *mind* relax, concentrating on the warmth of his skin and the slight clean scent of his cologne and thinking of nothing in particular. A shiver went down her spine, and the whole sequence from the moment she opened Arnaud's compartment door flooded into the forefront of her consciousness. All at once, with everything she had thought/felt/seen/smelled/touched.

The memory ended, and his hand stroked her hair. "You were very brave," he said. "*And* very intelligent. That was dangerous, and you handled it perfectly. But now that you have, let me see if I can make a contribution."

He sat back, turned, and put his hands on either side of the notepad and closed his eyes. After a moment she could feel him humming; then he began to murmur—in Mhabrogast.

That always gave her a feeling like tinfoil between the teeth. It was illogical to think of an arbitrary collection of syllables as evil, but somehow you *did* feel that way when you heard it. Adrian had told her he had to ration his use of it because of the way it affected you if you thought in it for too long. He wasn't sure why; possibly it was the nature of the outlook the Power gave you, or possibly it was because the Brézé savants who'd reconstructed it in the Victorian period had colored their work with their own personalities.

After a moment he reached out, took the fountain pen and twisted it open with a single motion of his strong slender fingers. The ink in the reservoir dribbled down . . . and then began to sort itself, rolling in tiny beads across the surface of the paper without sinking in. When they did there were words on the surface, a single sentence written in an antique looping copperplate:

She knows, and she has—

Adrian sat back and sighed, rubbing at his temples. The last few letters in *another* trailed away, a scrawl that turned into a squiggle.

"A little more efficient than pencil shavings. Though probably a forensic laboratory could have done as much . . . possibly not, and in any event we do not *have* a laboratory."

"It's not exactly . . . straightforward."

"No, and that is *exactly* like Great-uncle Arnaud; even in his death he is exasperating!"

"What could it mean?" Ellen said.

"Obviously *she* refers to my sister. Though with Arnaud, one can . . . could . . . never be absolutely sure. But what is it that *she* knows? And what does she have? A plot, a plan, a weapon, a spy? It would be easy to go mad trying to figure *that* out."

They went through the files on the tablet; mostly those were Classical music, ebooks—few of them dating much past 1930—and amateur video, which she couldn't look at for long. Surprisingly enough Shadowspawn rarely abused children—humans didn't *taste* right before puberty—but Arnaud had pushed the envelope that way, to just barely adolescent victims. One section did have maps, including Adrienne's distribution plans for Trimback Two, the plague. It wasn't labeled, but she recognized it from things she'd overheard while she was Adrienne's prisoner.

"Arnaud wouldn't have crossed Adrienne for just anything, would he?" Ellen said.

Adrian shook his head. "Nobody not completely insane crosses her without good reason. Granted, though, if one *is* insane . . . I was being truthful in what I said to the others. He *was* always impulsive. And he became more so as time went on. His precognition was always very strong for one of so early a generation, but he relied on it rather than schooling or disciplining it, doing things simply because the idea welled up into his mind. Sometimes true prescience, sometimes simply whims. But whatever it was she knew, it was something we do *not* want her to know, and whatever she has, it will be regrettable."

"When could Adrienne have killed him?" Ellen said. "If we can pin it on her . . ."

"We cannot. Not directly. She brought in Monica and opened her mind to show that she was . . . ah . . . strenuously occupied at the time and completely preoccupied."

Ellen winced. "Poor Monica."

Adrian's mouth quirked. "She was actually quite proud."

"Like I said, poor Monica. So Adrienne didn't do it with her own hands . . . or mind. She had someone else do it."

"We may be jumping to conclusions ourselves," Adrian said thoughtfully. "But . . . yes, that *feels* correct. I cannot be more specific, not with an adept of her power muddying the waters."

"God, Shadowspawn playing cards with each other must be a joy," Ellen said.

"Chess is better. Though few have the patience for it."

"I thought predators were supposed to be patient?" Ellen said sardonically.

"More like spoiled housecats," Adrian replied dryly. His finger traced the paper. "I will show this to Great-grandfather. It would not be admissible evidence in a court, but the Council of Shadows does not . . ."

"Work that way, yeah. More like on moods, personal grudges, cabals, sheer desire to stick it to someone, that sort of thing."

"How well you know . . . them. It will be enough to divert suspicion from me, or at least muddy the waters. Still, I wonder *who* Adrienne brought in."

CHAPTER ELEVEN

Belgium

"We will be landing in Brussels shortly," the pilot said over the intercom. "Will everyone please take their seats and fasten their seat belts."

That was no surprise; the very slight falling-elevator feeling you got had started a few minutes before. Eric had talked with the pilot a little on the long flight; not much, and that was because the pilot himself didn't want to. If they hadn't both been graduates of the Suck, Eric suspected communications would've been strictly limited to "yes, sir" and "no, sir." The pilot knew there was something very odd indeed about Adrian Brézé and presumably about his friends, knew the pay was good, and had absolutely no desire to know any further details. His copilot was even more set on minding her own business.

"Please fasten your seat belts, and keep them fastened until the plane comes to a full and complete stop."

There wasn't much to be seen; they came down through layers of gray cloud that had a sort of psychic glumness to them, chilly and dull even when you only saw them through the porthole of an airplane window. It was the type of weather that made you want a cup of hot chocolate with some rum in it despite the fact that you were indoors and perfectly warm and comfortable. All you could see below the final level of cloud cover was a cluster of tall buildings to the south, and endless built-up area everywhere else.

They landed gently and taxied for a while; this aircraft was too small for the regular Jetways, but bigger than most of the other private aviation stuff it ended up among. A little electric cart pushed the gangway up, and the copilot opened the door to let in the wet chill and the rumbling whine of an airport.

"In a way this is even weirder," Peter said, extending the handle of his suitcase, while Leon and Leila solemnly donned their backpacks. "Weirder than the openly weird stuff."

"Weirder than what?" Eric said, shrugging into his coat and helping Cheba into hers. "My weird-o-meter started shooting blue sparks and making gurgling noises a while ago."

He also checked on his knives and coach gun, and discreetly made sure the others were doing the same with their weapons. In his experience a long spell in the air had a sort of stunning effect; the monotony, the noise and vibration, or whatever. He could feel something of the same effect now even though the business jet had been more comfortable than anything he'd flown in before. It took an effort of will to get up to speed again right away, and it was when you were logy that you most needed to be alert.

The copilot noticed the assorted instruments of destruction, and her high-cheeked Slavic face was absolutely impersonal as they walked past.

The time was only three in the afternoon in Brussels, but as they went down the ramp to the tarmac and trundled their luggage into the airport building the gray dankness was all-pervasive. It gave you a vague feeling that somehow it was bedtime already; even the twins were yawning, though they had slept most of the way across the Atlantic. The air outside was full of what might have been light rain or a heavy mist, and as they walked to the terminal, ridges of slush squelched beneath their shoes with a feeling that was halfway between a crunch and a splash. Getting miniature droplets of cold water flicked in your face at least had the advantage of being a little invigorating; Eric felt torpid and badly in need of some brisk exercise at the same time.

Peter seemed to be thinking hard as he hunted for phrases. "Before that—"

He visibly reconsidered using Adrienne's name in front of her children.

"—evil bitch came into my life . . . at Los Alamos . . . things were *real,* if you know what I mean. Well, someone who wasn't a scientist might have thought they were a bit strange, but they were what I was used to, going to work, hanging out with people I knew, and catching the odd movie . . . Then the evil witch carried me off to her lair at Rancho Sangre, and that was a complete nightmare."

Cheba nodded. "Worse because it was pretty, you know? Pretty town, pretty clean houses, pretty farms and the beautiful *Casa Grande*. And *her,* pretty like a snake."

The two former lucies shared a glance; Eric supposed that was something you had to go through to really understand, but he was perfectly contented to be on the outside looking in as far as *that* was concerned.

Helping Cheba get through withdrawal from the feeding addiction had been bad enough. It was worse than coming off heroin or meth cold turkey, though apparently while you were on it didn't do any particular harm. And the thought of detoxing alone, the way Peter had . . .

Peter made a gesture of agreement that turned into a wave at their surroundings.

"But Rancho Sangre was at least honestly beyond belief, like dropping into a movie. This . . . I've flown into Brussels before. Going to scientific conferences, mostly. Now I'm back here, in what should be a familiar place, but I'm not part of that old life anymore. It's as if I'm dragging a bubble of alien weirdness around with me, or I can see and everyone else around me is blind. And I can't go back, because I can't stop knowing what I know now about what's going on below the surface."

Eric chuckled. "Welcome to the club, *compadre*. When you're in the Suck you know it's a different world and that nobody can understand who isn't in there with you, but it's sort of obvious because everybody's wearing camouflage and carrying a gun and it separates you. This is more like being a cop, and especially a homicide detective—we used to say homicide roach, 'cause it gave you a roach's-eye-view of things. It's a different world in the middle of what everyone else thinks is the real world. It looks the same, but you know things other people don't, like adding a colored filter. Or taking one away."

Peter smiled a crooked smile. "Well, we're all in that situation now!"

"No," Cheba said vigorously, shaking her head until the black curls tossed. "For me, it is all strange. Everything is differently strange, the things you think are familiar are strange to me too. Some is just different; other things are twisted. It started when I left *Coetzala* for Mexico City. I don't understand how people live in a world of only buildings, like they don't eat beans and use the toilet . . . The twisted part . . . it's all different in sizes and sounds and colors. Nothing looks *real* to me, everything is like the pictures on a TV only it is my town that is like a little picture on TV in my head . . . and then I feel that it isn't real or this isn't real and I end up not knowing what real actually is. And *then* I met the *brujos!*"

She took a deep breath. "So I don't think about how strange things are too much, or it would make me crazy."

Looking around: "Why do we want to come to this place, Brussels, anyway? Big! Too big!"

The three adults and two children were a little lost in the sleek vastness of Brussel Nationaal/Bruxelles-National Airport once they made their way into the general concourse. Over twenty thousand people worked here full time, and hundreds of thousands passed through every day. Much of it, Eric reflected, might have been any major airport anywhere—shiny tile, shiny metal, shiny glass, overpriced goods and rows of metal and plastic seats carefully calculated not to be too comfortable, all amid a slight smell of burned kerosene.

All that was deeply reassuring. With Peter's little gadgets on their persons they wouldn't stand out to the eye of the Power, and there was plenty of crowd to lose themselves in. He let his detective sense fan out, that subliminal reading that flagged anyone who was looking for somebody in particular rather than just going with the flow. So far, nothing but his making a bunch of people who were obviously cops or security agents of some sort, like the creepy-looking plump little dude over there with the waxed mustache.

Of course there *was* one local feature you wouldn't see most places—

"And why is everything spelled out twice?" she asked. "One way that looks a little like Spanish, but isn't, and another way that looks a little like English, but isn't either."

Peter grinned; Cheba had spent a lot of time on their flight with a set of headphones and a textbook, doggedly polishing her spoken and written English. Both the men were hard workers, and they both found her a little intimidating that way.

"Because they speak two languages here, Dutch and French, and the Flemings speak Dutch and the Walloons speak French and they can never agree on anything. Starting with which language to disagree in, and mostly they never get past that part," he said.

"Sounds familiar," Eric said, thinking of New Mexico. "I haven't been to Brussels before when I transited through Europe."

"Isn't NATO HQ here?" Peter said.

"*Sí*, but it's administrative, not operational. We staged through Ramstein-Frankfurt. Doesn't matter much, when they let us off the transports it was usually only for an hour or so and we spent it lying down on the hangar floor with our packs for pillows or grabbing a smoke. You could be anywhere in the Suck Archipelago, except for the weather."

Peter said: "A lot of scientific stuff gets channeled through here too. So just about all *I've* seen of it is hotels and some excellent universities, which I admit beats an airport hangar. Even if the universities aren't as old as they look, despite the attitude Europeans put on. All that medieval and Renaissance stuff pretending to have been there for centuries."

"Hasn't that been here?" Cheba said curiously. "In Mexico City— that was the only big city I saw before this—there were ancient things from the time of the old *indios*, the pyramid, and old Spanish things, and buildings from the time of the Porfiriato, and the modern ones of glass, all mixed together and all looking as they are."

"This part of the world has been burned down or blown up or both so often that you can't tell what's original and what isn't. They try to make it look the same afterwards, but the same isn't the same, if you know what I mean. The first part of this airport was built by the Nazis during World War Two, for example. A lot of things around here were nothing but broken rock covered in the marks of tank-tracks at one time or another, mostly in 1945. Sometimes 1918 *and* 1945."

"They have really, *really* good chocolate here," Leon said, bringing the conversation back to practicalities.

His sister nodded vigorously. "I love the ones that are shaped like little seashells," she said with an air of heavy hinting.

Peter nodded solemn agreement. "Come to think of it, I remember those too, and they're completely authentic. C'mon, you guys, let's get some! There's bound be a shop selling them around here."

As the slight blond man led the two raven-haired children away, Cheba leaned closer to Eric.

She nodded. "Peter is like a brother," she said, which he found rather comforting. "Or the way they should be. Back in *mi tierra,* they were, well, focused on going to the city. And in the city, all the boys, they were *hijos de su tal por cual*. . . How do you say in English, ah! So short a word—assholes."

Then, seriously: "What do we do now?"

"I've got a list of inconspicuous hotels and we'll take a taxi," Eric said. "We'll start for Vienna in the morning as soon as we organize the transportation; I don't want to spend more time on the road at night than we have to. We should get there before these Council asswipes get their act together, they can't decide whether to have breakfast without fighting about it for a day or two. Easier to hide in a car than it is in a plane."

"Why are we taking the twins towards their parents at all?" she said quietly. "Isn't that where the fighting will be? The danger, at least, no? Why would Adrian want that?"

Eric had been looking at the children, smiling a little wistfully. They made them *feel* a little wistful—he'd always wanted some of his own, and being an uncle had confirmed the feeling, and he'd never see thirty again so the clock was ticking if he didn't want to be trying to ride herd on teenagers in his sixties. Although . . .

"Maybe not. I talked this over with Adrian. He doesn't want to use the children as shields . . . But it's possible they could be safer near their mother, or their mother and him, than anywhere else in the world. That's where she'd have more control over the other Shadowspawn. It's not like they've got any real discipline, and a lot of them tend to act on impulse. If they're right under her eye, they'll be more cautious."

"They may not have this discipline, but they certainly fear her."

"Yeah, but believe me when you're trying to get people to do anything, at least to do it effectively, discipline is a lot better. People act crazy when they're afraid. Anyway, we tried hiding them somewhere far away from the action, and look how that worked! Whoever came after us probably got reamed out by Her Supreme Evilness, but that wouldn't have been much consolation to us if he'd won. Or to her for that matter, if he'd ended up killing the kids as well as us."

Cheba frowned. "That is all true. But I have grown to care for them, and I worry that they might come to harm."

"Me too." He hesitated. "Though . . . Something I've been thinking about . . . Have you noticed how *much* you like them and how quickly it happened?"

She blinked, then her eyes narrowed. *Living proof that lack of education has nothing to do with lack of smarts,* he thought.

"Why shouldn't I like them? I have always liked *los niños,* and they are good children. Even when I was their mother's prisoner they did not behave badly. No more badly than other children. Well, other rich people's children."

Eric nodded. "I like them too, but I remember something that Adrian said. That Shadowspawn often leave their children to be brought up by others."

"You mean like, what is that bird that puts its eggs in other birds' nests, the cuckoo?"

"Yeah, and it would make sense for Shadowspawn children to evolve, to develop, in ways that made them real likable to the human adults— cute, appealing."

"*All* children *are* like that! If they weren't we would not feed them and clean up their messes."

"Right, if they weren't we'd strangle them instead. But maybe Shadowspawn kids are more like kids than kids are. To push our buttons, you know?"

Cheba shook her head. "I like them anyway. Even if that is true, they are not *pretending* to be good children. They are doing it by *really* being that way."

Leon and Leila came back, holding up a box in triumph. "Here, you should have some too!" Leila said; Leon nodded emphatically while he chewed.

Thing is, Adrian also told me that the human foster parents . . . A lot of the time, they're the first ones kids kill when they hit puberty. Because that's when they stop being naturally inclined to get along with anybody.

He took one of the candies from the box the girl offered. The shell was a dark, slightly bitter chocolate, while the interior had a creamy filling of hazelnut praline.

"Thanks," he said; it really was good chocolate.

Damn, he thought. *And they really* are *cute kids.*

"And Adrian wants me in Vienna," he said to Cheba. "You too, and Peter."

"Why? Me to look after the children and guard them, and Peter because he understands these machines . . . You because you were a soldier, and he needs you to fight?"

"A little. But also because I was a detective, and he wants me to detect. Let's get going, it's a long drive."

"How far?" Cheba said.

Peter glanced at his tablet. "About eleven hundred kilometers, call it six hundred miles, about the same as the distance between Santa Fe and Dallas. One long day's drive. In Europe that's a long way, just like in America a hundred years is a long time."

"Call it twice that distance, the way we're going to be driving, but we can take it relays," Eric said. Peter groaned slightly, and Eric went on: "Consider it the scenic route, professor."

"Talk about bad luck!"

Peter stopped talking abruptly and looked up at Eric and Cheba. The three were grouped around the Citroën seven-seater car by the side of the road, peering under the raised hood. Leon and Leila were happily engaged in snowballing each other, but the same anxiety showed on the faces of all the adults.

"I thought your machine would hide us, Peter?" Cheba said.

They were all carrying one of the little pseudo-tablets that concealed the wearer from the Power and they'd gotten fairly paranoid about making sure they were working. Even the children were wearing them, and had stopped complaining about it.

Peter was wearing a black Astrakhan wool hat with ear flaps. He ran his fingers under it and rubbed at his forehead. His explanations tended to emphasize the limitations of the equipment.

"Sure, what we've got will *hide* us," he said. "But I didn't say it would *protect* us, did I? Because it won't. Protect the car? Even more not. It doesn't make us invisible, either. Not to ordinary regular eyes."

"Or it could just be common or garden-variety bad luck," Eric said, taking a closer look the engine. "Christ, the fuel injector on this thing is shot seven ways, we might as well have been running wet cement through it. So much for high-end rentals and the synthetic crap they use for gas here. Shit."

"Do you want to bet on it?" Peter said. "Bet on this being luck instead of, you know, *luck*?"

"Normally, I might."

Eric looked around. It was as cold as you would expect in the run-up to Christmas, and they were in a world of black and white and gray. The white snow lay knee-deep across the lumpy fields of the little valley they were in; he'd been avoiding the autobahn and sticking to rural back roads on general principles, and much good it had done them. The asphalt of the little two-lane was black, flanked by banks of off-white snow where the plow had gone through; the ranks of pine trees on the ridges that flanked them to either side looked black in the dim light. The sky overhead was the color of a wet manhole cover, and the air had the damp mealy smell that made you expect snow.

"But here in Hansel and Gretel land, maybe not," Eric said. "I keep expecting to see a gingerbread house and a little old lady with a taste for veal."

Cheba looked at him, frowning in puzzlement.

It must be a major pain in the ass, he thought. *Not just having to work in another language, but not knowing all the references everyone else learned*

*when they were kids. Like everyone else was speaking a different language,
and in code. I guess that accounts for a little of the way she snaps at times,
that and everything else she's gone through.*

"A children's story about wicked witches," Peter said, filling in for her.
"A story that comes from around here."

"Oh. I think I saw a movie about that. There were many guns and
Gretel wore black leather."

"That's not the original version," Peter said, wincing slightly.

"One thing that's for certain," Eric said. "I'd feel awfully damn suspicious about anyone who stopped and offered us help about now."

Cheba nodded. "Or of *la policia*. Or of anybody. If this is *los brujos*,
that would be the next thing they did."

"Right," Eric said. "I think I saw a church steeple from that hill
back about half a mile, though it's hard to tell around here with this
wet thick air. I'm surprised the *people* here don't have moss on their
north sides."

"A church means a village," Cheba said. "Do we have time to get
there before dark?"

"We'll still be closer when dark hits than we would if we stayed here.
If it isn't just normal bad luck somebody *wants* us to stay here, and doing
what an enemy wants you to do is usually a really lousy idea."

"And it is only a few hours until the sun goes down," Cheba said
grimly.

They all glanced at each other again; their enemies were so much
stronger at night.

One of the advantages of traveling on Adrian's nickel was that he
didn't have to give a damn about the luggage, though the wastefulness
of it did make him twinge a little. Cheba cast a wistful look at the flat
ostrich-hide case with gold clasps that contained a lot of expensive girl

stuff. He couldn't blame her; this was probably the first time she'd had a chance to accumulate any of her own.

"Just weapons, money, and our camouflage tablets," he said. "Incidentally, Peter, how long before we have to recharge 'em?"

"Oh, not for at least twenty-four hours. And even that ought to leave us a margin, I've got some spare battery packs ready charged. It just needs some trickle current, it's a very economical application."

"Right, let's get going. Walking on this road . . . not so advisable either but we don't have much choice."

He checked everyone's clothes with a flick of the eyes; fortunately everybody including the kids had winter boots on, and they all had good parka-and–hood-style coats they'd put on when they got out of the car. They trudged on heading southeast; to the right the land rose into forested heights that probably would've turned into mountains if the cloud hadn't swallowed them. After a quarter-mile a fold in the land showed the ruins of a castle on a hill to the south, probably built long ago to dominate this valley and the passageway through it down to the Danube. Half the tower and the snag of a curtain wall still stood, though the war that blackened and cracked the stones might have happened eighty years ago or eight hundred.

"Was that a castle I saw back there? Hope to hell Franken-N-furter doesn't show up," Peter muttered, and began humming the tune to "Let's Do the Time Warp" as he walked.

I was right, Eric thought. *This really is Red Riding Hood country. That might've been funny a while ago. Now remembering all those old stories feels . . . different. Too many of them take it for granted the monster has a long career of eating people before they get their comeuppance. When it's for real, how do you know that* you *aren't the one who got the oven treatment before Hansel and Gretel showed up?*

Just about then it started to snow, big soft flakes that stuck to the shoulders and hoods of their coats and then to their eyebrows as the wind shifted into their faces. It cut visibility to almost nothing, and little rivulets of icy meltwater trickled inside no matter how tight you pulled the lace at the neck. Peter just sighed and dug his hands deeper into his pockets, clearly used to this sort of thing from the grisly winters of his upper Midwestern home. Santa Fe could get cold too and had the odd blizzard, if not as often; it was a skiing resort area in the winter. Plus Eric had seen every possible variety of bad weather at one time or another on his travels for Uncle Sam.

Christ Jesus, but I seem to make a career out of piling up bad memories to choke on later. The only compensation is the new *bad experiences aren't such a shock when they come along.*

Cheba looked utterly disgusted as she trudged, but then she had grown up in a sugarcane sort of place, and her time in the United States had mostly been in coastal California. She didn't actually say anything; one of the things he liked about her was that she didn't bitch and moan about stuff that couldn't be helped.

"I'll never feel the same about the Brothers Grimm again," Peter said as the wet cold settled into their bones, echoing his first thought.

"Who?" Cheba said.

Peter explained, in a way that had the Mexican girl laughing. The twins joined in, giving bits from their favorite stories—though the way Shadowspawn told them to their kids often had a disturbingly different perspective. Eric would've felt mildly jealous if he hadn't been worried enough to keep his hand close to the hidden grip of his coach gun whether or not that made walking harder. Everybody quieted down after they been on the road an hour or so, but none of them were going to collapse just from a few miles. The fall made it like walking in the middle of a snow globe, visibility cut to ten or twenty yards at most and sometimes only arm's-length. There was no sound at all except the muted hoot of the wind and the hiss of the flakes; it was quite enough to hear people's breaths and the scuffing crunch of their feet. The real limiting factor was how fast the kids could move. They were a bit too big to be comfortably carried piggyback.

As if to echo his thought Cheba caught his eye and inclined her head towards the children, who were tramping along with their heads down now, game little troopers but obviously feeling the strain.

He shrugged a little and raised a hand in a gesture as if to say *I know, but what can we do, stop and wait for it to bury us?*

With the weather thickening and the sun heading towards an early grave he lost track of the vague estimate of distance he'd formed. It was a bit of a shock when the church suddenly showed, a steep-roofed white stucco rectangle with a tall square tower, the black top sloping in and then swelling out again into a bulb before finishing in a long thin spire. Snow hid it again, then revealed a vertical shadow, then turned to a permanent reality, Central European but with a faint trace of Byzantium or Russia somewhere way back in its ancestry.

Don't zone out, Eric, he thought, disgusted at himself.

Around it the lights of the town glowed, blurred through the snow. Eric breathed out a silent sigh of relief. There hadn't been any traffic until they were almost on top of the place, but a few cars passed them now and a tractor went by pulling a wagon loaded with something under a tarpaulin. The village was a cluster of homes and a few shops with a small river running through it under an arched stone bridge

If the Santa Fe River back home had ever had any water in it, it would've been about the same size, which meant that in most of America it would've been described as a medium-sized creek. They got nods and a few calls of "*Grüss Gott*," but less inquisitiveness than a similar party could've expected in most American towns this far into the boonies.

There was a big Christmas tree in the town square not far from the church, with the lights twinkling on it already fairly bright as the short afternoon faded. There were a few other decorations spotted around the village, including angels blowing trumpets and pictures of an ethereal-looking blond child handing out gifts. A big Nativity scene wasn't much different from the ones he grown up with except that a second glance showed that the lambs were real-life breathing *lambs*, just about to be taken off for the night by a teenage girl with yellow braids.

He supposed that the statue standing nearby was Santa Claus or St. Nick, from the great curly white beard, but otherwise it was dressed more like the pope and for some reason there was a kid in a black steeple hat, a red waistcoat, and a green leprechaun outfit standing next to him.

Peter pointed to a sign that hung creaking over the street, too thickly coated with snow to show anything except that there was heraldry and gilt beneath it. The building it marked was well-kept, but looked so old that it was leaning a little to one side. A bit closer and you could see the marks where the ancient black oak timbers had been squared with adze and broadax, and how the patches of white plaster between the beams weren't quite regular.

Even a Southwesterner like him could tell the difference between fake half timbering and the real thing this close. For that matter, there were enough really old buildings in Santa Fe to recognize the somehow organic, grown-in-place look that amateurs using hand tools in a strictly local style produced, even if the details of that style had nothing in common.

"*That's a Gasthaus,* which means tavern or small hotel," Peter said helpfully.

"Yeah, professor, I have been outside New Mexico once or twice,"

Eric replied, with a flash of irritation. "I finished high school too, when I wasn't pulling my sombrero down over my eyes and sleeping against the adobe wall with a fucking burro standing next to me chewing on a cactus."

"Sorry," Peter said, flushing even more than the cold could account for.

"Sorry back at you," Eric said after a moment. "Worried, tired, hungry. Feeling a bit off, like maybe I've got a cold coming."

Not to mention fighting off a feeling of oh shit here we go again *without any concrete reason behind it. I've always trusted those feelings, and now I've had experts tell me that they're the real thing.*

Aloud he went on: "You speak any German? We're a little off the beaten track for much tourist traffic. All I know is some cusswords, from some German snake-eater types I met once."

"Only a bit—one of my grandmothers was German and she tried to teach me some when I was a kid. Oh, and I know the physics terminology, enough to help a conversation about that. Probably not much use here. There's almost always somebody who can speak English in a German town, though, even a small one."

The cold damp air was wonderfully enlivened with baking smells, rich with vanilla and buttery-nutty and gingery scents. It was long past lunchtime, and they'd just finished a long cold hike. Despite his general misery, that made part of him perk up.

"Okay, we need to get the kids warmed up and fed, and see if we can organize some transportation. We may be stuck here tonight from the look of the weather."

He let himself shiver, no longer forcing the unpleasant feeling of being core chilled out of his mind by sheer willpower, surprised at how bad it was.

I may not be twenty-two anymore, but am I an old man already? Can a couple of eight-year-olds run me into the dirt?

The inn *was* blessedly warm and bright as they pushed through the door and stamped the snow off their shoes. The common room featured a lot of carved wood that reminded him of Swiss cuckoo clocks, a couple of murals of fairy tales with an unfortunate prevalence of wolves and white teeth, and pine logs crackling in a big fireplace with wrought-iron andirons and a tile surround. It was all presided over right now by a wrinkled crone in a shapeless black dress whose nose nearly met her chin. For a moment he remembered his joke about Hansel and Gretel, but her bright blue eyes looked at them with alert curiosity as she put down her knitting, and then widened in concern at the sight of the cold, snow-soggy children.

"*Ha woesch! Wo' her?*"

They looked at her blankly; she clucked her tongue and continued into a flow of German, with a broad mooing accent that even he could tell wasn't anything like the standard form of the language. It sounded rather like a compassionate and elderly Teutonic cow. Peter looked baffled, but Leon and Leila immediately started chattering back at her in German that was apparently fully fluent—and from the crone's delighted smile, the same dialect she used. After a moment Leila turned to him:

"We told her that our car broke down," she said.

"She says that we're lucky it wasn't any farther away from the village," her brother added. "This is a lonely place, she says, and that they get snowed in a lot."

"And she says that dinner will be ready soon if we want to eat—and there will be *Kniadel*," Leila added eagerly.

"You mean *Knödel?*" Peter asked.

"*Ja, Kniadel,*" the old woman said helpfully, and broke into a new set of moos, evidently asking things like *where is your car* and *what about luggage* and *do you know these kids are wet and freezing?*

A comedy of languages and dialects followed. Luckily some younger members of the family turned up who spoke reasonable English, albeit apparently somehow learned from Englishmen who spoke a thick and adenoidal version of their own, which was absolutely indescribable on a base of deeply rural Swabian. The grandchildren of the crone had a couple of children of their own around the twins' age and size who could lend them some dry clothing. A message went off to ask around for someone with a four-wheel-drive vehicle to go fetch the luggage from the stranded car. Apparently with the weather this bad, there was no hope of getting the car itself fixed until after Christmas.

In the course of all that the ancient, her rather more than middle-aged son, and *his* son and daughter-in-law, took their coats, set them down in front of the fire to warm up and dry out, brought coffee and cream and plates of crescent-shaped biscuit/cookie things dusted with sugar and full of hazelnuts. Then they waded through a dinner of roast ham hocks done with mustard, horseradish and pickled chilies and accompanied by red cabbage, onion cakes and potato dumplings—which was what *Kniadel* turned out to be. Or *Knödel,* according to Peter. A bunch of locals trickled to in to have the same, mostly families, and mostly people who obviously knew each other from childhood; he supposed they were giving the housewives a rest before the big family dinners around Christmas.

"I suppose they'll be stuffing their turkeys soon," Eric said, and took a mouthful of the ham. "Dang, I expected German food to be sort of soggy and bland but this is pretty good."

"It's usually a goose, not a turkey, from what grandma used to say, her mother came from somewhere east of Munich, but yeah," Peter said.

"German food is sort of heavy, but after walking a couple of miles in the snow you realize why it got that way."

It was just the sort of thing you wanted in this weather, although Eric found himself tapering off long before he expected, giving it up and pushing away his half-full plate of the main course while the twins were already working their way through some cake full of cinnamon and nuts.

"*Liabr da Maga verrenkt, als em Wirt ebbes gschenkt,*" someone said disapprovingly as they took the remains of his dinner away; evidently that was a breach of manners here.

"I like it, this food," Cheba said, polishing off hers with gusto. "I like this place, too. It's different, but it's more like a place where people live."

"There's even a ruined castle!" Peter chuckled.

"That too, there was an old ruined hacienda near where I was born, burned by the rebels in my great-grandfather's time."

Leon turned and relayed the remark about the castle to the old lady as she put a bowl of whipped cream down by the cake. Her benevolent-granny's smile ran away from her face, and she said something guttural. Which was admittedly hard not to do in German, but it sounded more so than usual.

"She says that was the castle of the accursed von Trupps. And it's under a curse, too!" Leila added with ghoulish enthusiasm. "And they were, like, tremendously wicked and stuff, *très mal.*"

"Like us Brézés," Leon said helpfully, and the sister went on:

"Especially the last von Trupp, the mad baron. They say his master, the Devil, came for him in the form of a French magician in a black robe and stabbed him in the heart with a silver knife before he carried off his soul to Hell!"

One of the younger generation of the family that ran the inn started at the name, and then rolled his eyes at the repetition of the story.

"*Schmarrn! Heidezapf!* Superstition!" he said, in his odd hybrid accent. "In the days of the last Freiherr von Trupp there was plenty of bloody wickedness in the whole sodding country without bringing curses or any nonsense like that into the matter. The only truth in that story is that it *was* the French prisoners in the work camp there who burned down the *Schloss*. And killed the baron. They had good reason to do it, God knows; we were lucky they didn't come after the village."

Which started a ding-dong argument, involving granny (who would have been younger than the twins at the time) shaking her knotted finger in her grandson's face, but didn't make the table service any less efficient. Even his headache couldn't keep Eric from smiling slightly: with some slight differences in looks—darker, and desiccated rail-thin as opposed to solid brick outhouse—she was his own great-grandmother to the life, from what he remembered as a small child. From his parents' stories, the old biddy had ruled the whole family with a rod of iron until the day she died.

The *Gasthaus* had some rooms available, up under the roof and reached by a narrow twisting wooden stair that creaked beneath their shoes. Eric booked two of them, one for Cheba and the kids and another for him and Peter. The family of the old lady who liked stories about curses were obviously puzzled by the domestic arrangements of the strange Americans, the more so when they paid in cash from a thick roll of hundred-euro bills despite impeccable ID. The kids might just possibly have been Peter and Cheba's from their looks, but the ages were wrong and then there were their odd linguistic accomplishments. And they would've heard Cheba and Eric swapping the occasional phrase in Spanish.

Fortunately they were too polite to pry. When they had the children settled, the adults had a brief conference.

"You don't look so good, Eric," Peter said.

Eric sighed and slumped back, rubbing his hands across his face. "Yeah, I'm not feeling so great either. Started getting a little off about the time the car gave up the ghost, but I couldn't say anything then. Just had to bull through, there was no point in bitching. It's getting worse, though."

It was true; the headache had come on worse, his joints were aching, he felt hot shivery at the same time and he was beginning to regret dinner though he'd been hungry and justifiably so. It felt like the flu, but not quite. Cheba leaned forward and put her hand on his forehead—with two beds and two chairs the room was fairly crowded and half the space above was cut off by the slope of the roof. The calloused palm felt cool against the skin of his face.

She asked a few sharp questions in Spanish about how he felt, then made a sort of spitting noise of exasperation.

"*Paludismo,*" she said. "There is no doubt—I've seen it often enough before."

"She means malaria," Eric said, grimacing.

"*What!*" Peter blurted.

"I've had it," Eric said. "Got careless about my preventive stuff while we were down south of Kabul where the national bird is the mosquito, the stuff they give you brings on these bitching headaches. Christ, though, I had it treated to a fare-thee-well and the doc said it wouldn't recur . . . I suppose exertion and cold could have brought it on . . ."

"More *bad luck,*" Peter said.

Cheba looked frightened for the first time. "This is very bad," she said. "Malaria can kill."

Peter nodded. "Yes. We have to get him to a hospital."

Both of them looked at the Minnesotan. After a moment he flushed a little. "Oh, yeah," he said. "That's what *they* want us to do."

Eric grunted; he didn't feel up to speaking much. With an effort, and pressing his hands to the sides of his head, he managed to say:

"Primaquine . . . I need primaquine and quinine. Better . . . try to get them without any records."

Peter looked unhappy. "This is Germany. You can't buy a sandwich without leaving a record in triplicate."

"They might know, know that I've got malaria, or it might be just some general curse. Christ, just what I need, something that screws up my head."

It was coming on strong now, and even more unpleasant than he remembered. They helped him over to the bed, got a basin in case dinner left, and then undressed him. It was all a blur shot through with pain, which the aspirin didn't help much at all. He could feel the sweat running down his face and flanks, and someone wiping his face with a cold cloth. One of the worst parts was knowing that he'd soon be dreaming, and how well-stocked his subconscious was with some truly vile shit.

Vaguely, voices: *I must stay here and look after him; you will be better with the children.*

"Where the hell am I?" Eric asked. Then after a moment: "Oh, yeah."

What it *looked* like was the living room of Adrian Brézé's house back near Santa Fe, the place where the were-eagle had attacked them. It felt absolutely realistic, down to the smell of piñon burning from the fireplace. The most dreamlike thing about it was that he felt completely healthy; that was an enormous relief and at the same time gave him a twinge at how bad it would feel when he went back. One of the many downsides of being really sick was that it seemed like it would last forever.

He turned, and Adrian and his wife Ellen were sitting together on the couch. She flashed him a sympathetic smile, and Adrian gave a brisk nod.

"You are in my Memory Palace," Adrian said courteously; that meant he was effectively in Adrian's head. "And that is only possible because of the base-link."

That had involved donating a syringe of his blood for Adrian to step out and drink in discreet privacy. Despite the clinical nature of the exchange, Eric still felt vaguely embarrassed by the memory. He overcame an obscure impulse to come to attention and say *Sir*, and sat down on one of the chairs facing them instead. Adrian selected one of the slim brown cigarettes from the case on the cast glass table and lit it.

"It is extraordinary how invisible you are," the adept went on. "When I seek you with the eye of the Power, there is absolutely nothing. I can communicate with you, but you might as well be in China for all I can tell of your physical location; even the direction is obscure. It is the same with the others, even the children, and usually their direction is as plain as a compass heading. Where are you in fact?"

He filled them in on everything that had happened. When he had finished, there was a pause before Ellen filled it with a succinct:

"Shit."

Adrian blew meditative smoke at the ceiling. "Precisely. This is quite bad. Worse than I had anticipated."

Eric suppressed an instinctive *ya think?* Instead he said: "Who's doing this?"

"Immediately, I would say the von Trupps. Perhaps some of the more crazed members; there are some quite old post-corporeals in that clan, some still haunting the old castle occasionally, though they retain enough reason to go far before they feed for the most part."

"Not the Tōkairin?" Ellen said.

"Possibly both; the Tōkairin might . . . will . . . be supplying infor-mation, and then a little telepathic hint from the active head of the von Trupp clan to their ruin-haunting ancestors would suffice . . ."

"Not Adrienne?"

"Not directly. It does not have the marks of any adept she uses, those who are her close allies. But . . . In a way, yes, she and those like her are indirectly responsible. Just as she was for Peter's anomalous readings at Los Alamos. It is the way she affects, that the Council affects, that the nature of the Power itself affects the world. That feeling you get from the ancient stories, from the Odyssey or from fairy tales as they were before the Victorians had their way with them? The quality of arbitrary menace, malignant fate . . . As their sway in it grows, and they use the Power with growing recklessness, so the world becomes more as they would have it. Chaotic, fluid, a place where chance rules, and in turn is ruled by will."

His yellow-flecked dark eyes turned from contemplating something impossible to see and focused on Eric again. "I am very much afraid that you've fallen into . . . How shall I put it . . . A pocket where these new rules, which are very old rules, apply. A hint of what the world might become, if our enemies triumph."

You know, this mystical crap doesn't get any more agreeable just because it's true, Eric thought; Peter had said something similar, though with a more techy slant. *Very much the other way around, in fact.*

"This is God damned informative," he said aloud. "But what the hell am I supposed to *do?*"

Adrian nodded, appreciating the point. "You must get out of the area as quickly as possible; you need to get back to where there are more people, because there the . . . how shall I put it . . . inertia of things pre-serves ordinary causality for the present."

"Is there anything you can do for backup?"

Adrian shook his head. "Not at this distance. All three of you have as many protective Wreakings implanted as can be done without limiting your individuality. Obviously, someone is trying to trap you in that area, just as obviously you must get out. Back to people, but in getting back you must not take the most obvious route."

A frown. "Quite possibly those who are after you care nothing for the welfare of the children, either, and are not much afraid of me or my sister."

"Well, that just proves that they're pretty fucking stupid, doesn't it?"

Most of the time Eric Salvador and Adrian Brézé didn't have much in common, except a high degree of mutual respect. Right now their common smile shared worlds. Ellen glanced between them and rolled her eyes slightly.

"And I'll look after the kids," Eric said.

He could tell the other man controlled an impulse to let his eyes slide aside:

"I owe you a debt for that, you and the others," he said. "There is not been enough time for . . . to use a horrible Californianism . . . bonding between the children and me. They actually care more for Ellen, because they have spent time with her while she was my sister's prisoner. But I can tell a good deal from their auras, it is possible that with the right upbringing they could come to be human beings, or at least moral beings, to the extent possible for we purebloods. And in the end, they *are* my children."

Then Adrian frowned, lifting his head tilted to one side as if catching a distant sound.

"I think you had best return quickly. Here . . . With your personality matrix a little apart from those damnable machines of Peter's . . . I can sense a probability nexus approaching you."

"I'm in pretty rocky shape back there, but there is where the there is," Eric said sourly.

He took a deep breath, or rather the immaterial form of him currently dwelling in Adrian Brézé's mind did.

"Let's go."

He could tell it was much later than sunset when he woke in his own body, or at least regained a little consciousness there. Maybe it was the icy draft that did it, or perhaps the voice yammering—screaming—at the back of his head. He forced gummy eyes open, suppressing an impulse to whimper at the inrush of sick physical misery and the contrast to recent memory of perfect health. The window was open, and a little reflected light trickled past the figure that crouched there.

He couldn't make it out between the fever and the darkness . . . Except for the yellow eyes.

Am I awake? he thought, unsure for an instant whether or not he was in the evil dreams of fever.

And a calling hummed through the air, a sultry seductive music, a crooning in his head. It reminded him of something—the feeling you got looking out of a helicopter hatch or the edge of a cliff, telling you to throw yourself off. The voice was distant, as if he had his thumbs in his ears or there was white noise closer. Cheba stood between the beds; then she took a step forward towards the window, then another small step, slow and infinitely reluctant. All he could see was her back; she was wearing a big T-shirt, one that reached nearly to her knees.

Both of them ignored him, the woman and the monster, as if they were moving through some ritual in a place and time endlessly distant. He fought not to let his breath rasp as he made an arm heavier than lead and weaker than a child's move towards the nightstand between the beds. His fingers were like stale sausages that belonged to somebody else, every motion needing deliberate thought and an effort of will that made him sweat as chills rippled through his body.

Cheba stopped, and her head tilted back.

—and the yellow eyes moved forward—

—and Cheba's hand whipped out from where she'd held the knife behind her back—

—and slashed like a glint of moonlight—

There was an appalling scream, a squalling cry of rage. A shriek from Cheba too, as something struck her and she spun aside in a tangle of limbs and a spray of blood. That put her out of the line between his bed and the window. Thick and clumsy and distant, he still made his finger tighten on the trigger.

Thump!

Recoil wrenched the coach gun out of his hand like a blow from a hammer. Silvered shot cracked into plaster and shattered glass, and he sank back shivering and retching. There was another squalling scream, trailing away into the distance. Voices, feet pounding, anxious faces. He let it all trail away.

"If you call the authorities it is the same as killing us," Eric managed to say the next morning. "And we have to get out of this place, now."

He was conscious, just, and coherent, just, though there was a temptation just to look at the snow falling outside the window. A local doctor, an elderly man with white side whiskers that at home Eric would've classified as a '60s hangover, had waded through the snow to deal with Cheba's injuries and had been persuaded to cough up some medication for Eric as well. That he had anything for malaria was a stroke of luck, for once good.

Cheba's injuries consisted of four parallel slashes across her shoulder and back, the unmistakable mark of a cat's paw . . . But it would have to be a very large cat indeed. That was the biggest thing they had going for them, and they needed everything they could get. These were the most fanatically law-abiding people he ever *met*, and he could see it set a twisting in their guts to even think about not following proper procedures. Peter was in a quiet state of despair; if they were sent to jail or even just detained they'd undoubtedly have their shielding devices taken away, and that would be the end. Cheba was defiant, and fiercely stoic about the pain of her wounds, but she was also completely out of her depth here.

And so am I, Eric thought. *My brain feels like it was stuffed with red-hot Brillo pads.*

Leon and Leila were huddled in one corner of the room; they could be remarkably inconspicuous when they wanted to be. Now they quietly crawled under the bed and came up beside Gerta, the old matriarch of the family. She gave them a fond but distracted look, and then frowned as they started whispering urgently in her ears. She started to shake her head, then looked at Cheba again where the doctor was bandaging and swabbing. Her faded blue eyes grew metallic.

Suddenly she surged upright like a whale broaching, crossed her arms and began to speak. Her son and grandson tried to brush her off, failed, and then looked astonished when the grandson's wife joined in on her side. The doctor stood up, clicked his bag closed and went to the door, saying something alliterative with a lot of *ich* and *nicht* while looking at the lintel before going through.

Peter leaned close and whispered in Eric's ear: "He said, *I know nothing and I saw nothing and I heard nothing.*"

The argument went on for a little longer, with the old lady throwing around words like *drucksmulle*—which evidently meant something fairly dismaying—until the older man threw up his hands.

"We will do it," he said in English. "It will be a disaster of course, but we will do it."

His son nodded, also looking glum . . . but both of them looked a bit relieved as well.

CHAPTER TWELVE

Vienna

"Vienna is one of my favorite cities," Étienne-Maurice Brézé said.

The Orient Express halted a little after sunset in the *West-bahnhoff*, in a squeal of steel and a deep *shush-shush* of water vapor. Ellen hated to think how much it had cost, cost other people, to let this steampunk dinosaur fantasy function in the contemporary station, or the rail network as a whole. Where were the water and coal coming from? Not to mention clearances and the effects of the smoke; it had probably left a trail of at least minor disaster across Europe, turning people's lives upside-down . . . not that that would matter to the people who'd done it.

Sorta people. And maybe it would *matter; they'd view the video of people scrambling desperately to cope and not knowing what's going on and laugh themselves silly. Yeah, you would like Vienna,* she thought. *It went into a deep depression in 1918 and didn't come out for generations. So it's still basically the city of the Habsburg emperors. You remember it from when you had a body, not just a quantum-field imitation put together by memory.*

There was a bit of a crowd, drawn by the exotic antique technology, exclaiming and pointing behind a ring of policemen. The disembarking Shadowspawn and their retainers generally ignored them, apart from a few lingering glances that were probably hunting reflex and the audience probably interpreted as hauteur. They vanished in a cloud of flunkies, heading for their limousines and dispersing to palaces and guest suites and in a few cases top-end hotels across the city.

Humans have problems adapting to the modern age, because we evolved for the Old Stone Age, Ellen thought. *Shadowspawn do too, maybe more so because they're more specialized. They evolved when humans were scarce—I think that's why they have that addictive quality. It kept the blood source around . . . and willing to give them other stuff they needed, too. But now they've recreated themselves and they're in a world with* billions *of humans instead of just a few scattered through a wilderness, humans who don't know about them and are lousy at dodging or fighting them. They're like leopards dumped into a sheep farm.*

"Pigs," Adrian murmured into her ear; they'd agreed he could read her thoughts when open conversation was unsafe. "Humans are more like pigs—and I mean that as a compliment; pigs are much smarter and more formidable and adaptable than sheep. The comparison would be leopards hunting wild boar in the Old Stone Age, and leopards dumped into a confinement facility in Iowa now."

Ellen winced, and came back to the present when Adrian's great-grandfather spoke again:

"Though I do not like *this part* of it," Étienne-Maurice went on, aristocratic nostrils flaring.

The Westbahnhoff's original Victorian layout had been forcibly rearranged by Soviet artillery in 1945, and rebuilt and re-rebuilt since, with only a few preserved segments. It looked very slightly run-down now—most of the Eurosphere didn't have that burnished look that it had had on her first teenage visit as a student—but it was still cheerful and bustling, bright and *large*.

Which was why the Emperor of Evil doesn't like it, of course.

She imagined giving him an elevated finger as he stalked away, cane and robe and all with Seraphine in his wake, wearing a tall hawk-faced Somali beauty this time. Better still a load of silvered buckshot, the shocked scream of pain and then . . . At that she stopped and shook her head. Fighting when she had to was one thing; entertaining murderous fantasies for the pleasure they gave was another, and she didn't want to go down that road.

"I will be seeing you over the next few nights," he said to Adrian. "It would be . . . unfortunate for your ambiguous standing with the Council . . . if you were to disappear in the interim."

"I will be present, sire. I expect my children to join me here, in any case."

"Or join their mother, your sister," Seraphine said with casual malice. "Until then, descendant." She looked around. "Come, let us leave this vulgar excrescence, Étienne."

The post-corporeals were mostly like that, conservatives in a way that made small-town Alabama look like Upper West Side. Which produced a disturbing thought; would she still love Adrian the same way when *he* didn't have a physical body any more? She'd gotten used to his shapeshifting into other people and things, which besides being useful lent itself to some really interesting perversions, and you really couldn't tell when he was nightwalking in his own form, but . . .

It's sort of an abstract question now, she thought. *And I'll probably be dead of old age before he transitions, he could make a hundred easy in his original bod, and that's okay because with a thirty-year start we'll look about the same age . . . except that his* body *might be killed tomorrow and then I'd be married to a post-corporeal. That's . . . disturbing. Well, I could get used to a strictly nighttime schedule, I guess. We mostly live that way anyway . . . no tanning time at the beach together, though.*

"Let us walk to the hotel," he said quietly, when they were alone except for the staff. "I am a little tired of the . . . company."

"I know what you mean!" she said fervently. Then, as she took his arm: "Adrian, what would you do if I was killed?"

"Mourn," he said. And flatly: "After I had avenged you."

"Okay, good with the mourning and vengeance, but I meant . . . with my persona, my soul, whatever. If you had the opportunity."

Shadowspawn could sort of snap you up, especially if you were baselinked; the essential *you* would run on their wetware, and it would go on after your physical body died if they wanted it to, like a post-corporeal but inside the Shadowspawn's mind, in whatever environment they imagined. That had kept her sane while she was a prisoner at Rancho Sangre, and they'd used it frequently since . . .

"I would carry you, of course," Adrian said.

"I'm . . . I'm not sure I'd want that," she said. "Going on without a body."

"I face that prospect myself," he said.

"Yeah, I was thinking of that. But you'd still be . . . *real*. In a sense. For me it wouldn't really . . . I mean, even if you still loved me, I'd be part of *you*, more like a memory that you could revise—might revise even without being aware you did it. I don't think I'd want to just . . . go on like that. I mean, yeah, we're the dyadic unit, and yeah, you're the top and I'm the bottom, but that would be pushing things too far in the loss-of-control thing. Don't. If I'm dying, let me go and move on."

His eyebrows went up, then down in a frown. "What brought this on?"

"What, thoughts of violent death being on my mind? Recent experience, much? But . . . I don't think I'd want to be a figment of your imagination."

He smiled ruefully. "I see your point, my darling."

It was rainy and cold outside, and they put up their umbrellas; the baggage was being whisked unseen to their destination, which was a relief. Locals were out in force; early sunsets and this sort of miserable weather were nothing much to them. The air had a peculiar scent of damp stone and brick and something indefinable that she associated with European cities underneath all their local peculiarities; for some reason even with identical weather New York or Chicago *smelled* different. Though come to think of it, Boston was a *little* similar.

"I've been spoiled by the Southwest," she said. "My hardy Polish-German-Pennsylvanian blood got thinned and I became addicted to blue skies."

"Oh, your blood has no problems at all, my darling!" he said, and they both chuckled.

The splendors of nineteenth-century Vienna soothed her eyes, only occasionally interrupted by some more recent construction; they walked over the tree-lined Europaplatz, passed what looked like a big glasshouse and was probably a subway station, and down the Marianhilferstrasse to the eastward; literally downhill, since it sloped towards the Danube. The pre-Christmas crowds were dense and lively; this was the best of downtown Vienna's shopping streets, less tourist-haunted than the ones in the First District and attracting more natives and younger people. There were a few big department stores, but most were hole-in-the-wall size, the sort of idiosyncratic place that had been hollowed out by big-box competition in most of her native land.

"My God, they've got Cop.Copine," she said, looking into one of the windows.

"Not limited to Paris any more," Adrian said. "That silvered leather coat is quite fetching; the detail work on the back, particularly."

"Nice, but it would make me look like the Attack of the Forty-Foot Lamé Woman," Ellen said. "I've actually got tits, unlike that mannequin or the anorexic stork-waifs on the walkways. But those black leather pants with the zippers up the sides . . . possible."

"You should have them," Adrian said with a grin. "Now that you are Ellen Brézé, Scourge of the Shadowspawn. Are they not what a female supercommando would wear?"

"In a graphic novel, one doing serious fanservice," she retorted. "Those are the sort of pants you put on so you can take them off again."

"Or someone else can."

"Yeah, or *want* to take them off you. Still . . . tempting . . . they look flexible enough to actually move in and they'd go with those boots I got . . ."

They dodged in, though she felt slightly scandalized with herself. There was a moment of confusion because the salespeople assumed she was Austrian herself, but their English was fine. One thing led to another, shorts led to pants led to blouses, and time passed . . .

"Still, otherwise I'd just be worrying back at the hotel," she said. "Catholic guilt hitting, I suppose."

"It is a good thing you are not a *Hindu* Catholic," he said.

"Why not?"

"Because then you could be guilty in front of *hundreds* of gods . . ."

"Okay, we've been touristing this shop and now I've got to try those pants."

They felt like suede gloves for the legs. The staff made admiring noises when she came out of the changing room, adding a little sashay to her walk—sincerely, probably, from the envious looks some of them were shooting Adrian—as she examined herself in the mirror. They were tight, but also not confining; you really could move quickly in them, though it would be a sin to expose this butter-soft kidskin to rough usage.

Or some of them are just envying me, she thought.

The staff were showing a tendency to flutter around Adrian too, where he leaned against a wall with his arms crossed, long black cashmere overcoat hanging from his shoulders to show the trim outline of his waist and black shirt just open enough to hint at the hard swell of his pectorals.

Not to mention the truly tight butt and the dangerous, smoldering yellow-flecked eyes with their hint of menace and the way that lock of hair falls over his forehead. It's amazing a man can look so pretty *and so . . . so . . . so at the same time. Look all you want, boys and girls, but he's mine.*

She thought she lost a little of the status bank they'd built up when they gave the address for delivery—the Sabatier tunic and vest were irresistible too, but she didn't want to wear them out the door. The Hotel Imperial was definitely high-end, but . . .

"You two are so . . . so *young* to be staying there," one of the salesgirls said. "I mean, that's where they put elderly oil sheiks and Chinese politicians and . . . and people like that. Though their torte is amazing."

"I am older than I look," Adrian assured her in Viennese German; Ellen could just catch the gist.

She grinned. He was: about a generation older than he looked, in fact. Not quite a Bella-and-you-know-who situation, but it was there.

Then he shifted into something else; still German, but with an affected braying accent and ending with *Gnädige Frau,* which even she knew was pretty obsolete. That seemed to be a real knee-slapper, and had one of the girls hooting:

"I didn't think *anyone* our age could speak Schönbrunner Deutsch so well anymore! Just like my great-grandfather! *Just* like!"

Outside Ellen added: "Whereas you aren't at all like *your* great-grandfather, except your accent a little, thank God."

"Thank Harvey," Adrian said, his smile turning sad.

"You had something to do with it too," she insisted.

They went on past a small church, with an odd-looking assortment of derelicts around its side-entrance.

"I wonder what's going on there?" she said.

Adrian frowned for a second. "Homeless shelter in the basement," he said. A grimace: "I wish I had not done that. It's like licking a sick rat."

She winced; there were drawbacks to telepathy-empathy. Then she pointed out an imposing Neo-Renaissance pile to their left where the street opened out, all tall arched windows flanking a tall green dome, a little spoiled since this side was probably a lot less impressive than the front.

"Sorry . . . now, this *I* can tell you about. It's the Kunsthistorische Museum/Art History museum. We learned about it, and I've met people who work there. They've got some really nice Classical stuff, there's this vase by the Brygos Painter, sixth-century red-figure kylix, it's the Ransom of Hector and you could look at it for *hours*, I only saw it once when it was on tour to the Met in '16, but . . ."

"Ah, I will drop in and take it, and we can have it shipped home; just

the thing for the table by the vestibule, perhaps we could put mints in
it—"

"*Adrian!*" she began, then saw his grin. "Oh, you, you—"

She made to kick him; he pounced and pinned her wrists behind her
back to immobilize her for a long breathless kiss.

"Thanks. I needed that," she said as they went on hand-in-hand.

They saw relics more recent—a flak tower from the 1940s, now hous-
ing an aquarium—and past an enormous 18th-century barracks built
when barracks could be a work of art, four stories of restrained Palladian
giganticism.

"Beats a prefab," she said. "Why do our equivalents all look ugly?"

Adrian was startled out of his brown study. "In an imperial capital
they could afford aesthetics," he said.

Ellen rolled her eyes a little. "Not going to get guilty about the oppressed Carpathian peasants who paid for it, are you? And you think *I*
am a Catholic Hindu!"

"I will have you know my conscience is a delicate work of art requiring frequent lubrication and careful watering, wench. Besides, when that
was put up the peasants of the Carpathians were still being oppressed by
the Ottomans and were paying for the Sublime Porte's harem, not the
Habsburgs' architectural fantasies."

"What do you think that Adrienne has in mind next?" she said
abruptly.

"She plays a waiting game," Adrian said. "Partly because things un-
fold as she wishes."

"Well, that's *our* take on it. I'll give you any odds it doesn't look as
reassuring to *her*."

"Reassuring, and probably true. And it is partly because of the children. If she had them . . . then she would act more decisively. I think our

raid on Rancho Sangre was not totally unanticipated or totally unwel-
come to her—she saw it as a distraction while Harvey went rogue. But
it returns to bite her . . ."

"On her skinny androgynous ass."

He chuckled. "I have been told that mine is, as well."

"Nope, manly-type narrow muscular butt. Good luck to Eric and
Peter and Cheba, then."

"Good luck indeed. I do not like acting so through others, but . . ."

"General now, sweetie. Not supercommando."

His mouth quirked. "I must keep a watching brief. The thought in-
spires me to poetry."

"It does?" she said, surprised, as they came onto the Ringstrasse with
its busy one-way traffic and two-way trams.

"Something that Eric told me."

"He knows poetry?"

"Of a sort," Adrian said.

"This I *have* to hear."

Her husband nodded, cleared his throat and declaimed:

> *"Oh, I could have been a general*
> *And sent men out to die;*
> *But the sort of things that generals do*
> *They make me want to cry;*
> *Oh, I could have been an officer*
> *But they found I was too smart;*
> *They stripped away my rank-tabs*
> *When they found I could walk and fart."*

Mitteleuropa

Eric didn't feel as bad as he had, but even bundled up leaving the *Gast-haus* and going outside again into cold and falling snow was the last thing he wanted to do. Fortunately, doing things he deeply did not want to do was one of his oldest habits. He'd only been awake for a couple of hours, but the craving for more sleep was already unendurable. Doggedly, he made himself walk to the car—some German 4 x 4—and let someone push him in, then fumbled at the seatbelt. The blast of hot air from the heater was almost as unpleasant as the cold had been, but then when you were in the state he was, everything made you feel bad. All you wanted to do was get into the least uncomfortable position in bed and sleep as long as possible.

The old lady's son drove the car southward; at first for an hour or so over a pretty good two-lane road, with glimpses of snow on fields to either side, and then down a bit of a slope, then turning off through a gate on to what was probably a dirt track, a foot or two down under the layers of snow and ice. He was conscious enough to note that the burly white-haired German handled the deep fresh snow skillfully, not creeping, not going too fast and accelerating gradually when he had to. After a while he started to talk, probably as much to avoid thinking about what was going on and how horribly he was violating the sacred rules as anything else.

"This is the family's old cottage, you understand," he said. "My mother's grandmother—"

Which meant it had happened a *long* time ago, possibly a very long time.

"—lived there, her husband was a woodsman for the Frieherr back before the Kaiser's war and was called up in 1914. He never came back, but somehow she got a little gold together during the war—English sovereigns if you believe my mother's tale of what her mother told her! Given to her by a secret agent she sheltered while he was ill! Well, after the war when the paper money became worthless and a little gold went a very long way she bought the *Gasthaus* . . ."

Eric tuned out the rest; probably it was picturesque as hell in terms of small-town family sagas, but he didn't have the free RAM to deal with it right now. He got a vague impression of a small wooden building, black in a clearing with smoke trickling up from a chimney to merge into the falling flakes. Fortunately it didn't appear to be made of gingerbread.

"*Grüss Gott*," the German called after them as Peter and Cheba helped him in. "*Und Behüte dich Gott.*"

Peter shut the door with his heel after he'd helped Eric in and eased him into a chair; fortunately someone had come out and got everything going before they arrived, and it wasn't too uncomfortable.

"That means *greet God* and then *may you have the help of God*," he said. "Personally, I'd like to put off meeting God just as long as I can."

"It's Eric who needs God's help right now," Cheba said. "And ours, first of all."

They got him into bed. When Eric woke again he was wet with sweat but clearheaded, feeling weak and washed out but hungry. He wasn't good to be winning any Ironman triathlons any time soon, but from the way he felt, things would get better from here on. They'd made his bed up in a single main room that evidently occupied most of the cottage, and there was a fire of pine logs burning in a fieldstone fireplace, drawing well but giving a spicy tang to the air that was like and unlike the piñon wood he'd grown up with. Under that was the slightly musty smell of a very old wooden house that was kept up but not lived in much recently, seeping out of the ancient timbers as they warmed.

The interior had much the same feeling, a few modern touches around the windows, but the rest mostly crude carving like being inside a cuckoo clock of the type he'd seen taking his nieces and nephews to the International Museum of Folk Art back in Santa Fe. Someone had done this with the simplest of tools, on long winter nights when he couldn't work at his usual job.

Leon and Leila were playing in front of the fire, with some wooden toys that looked just as old but were carved in an entirely different style from the rest of the house, a monkey and some type of antelope and a rhinoceros. For a moment his mind wandered off wondering how they'd ended up here, but the cooking smells distracted him.

The door opened for a second and Cheba kicked it closed behind her; she had an armful of split pinewood that she emptied into the bin beside the fireplace, still favoring the left arm and shoulder where they'd been claw-raked.

"So, you are here again," she said. "It is the afternoon of the day after the day we got here—it gets dark so quickly! Come, I will help you."

"To hell with that, you got hurt worse than I did," he grumbled. Then: "Okay, I won't yell at you for a helping arm."

One of the things that had been added to the cottage was a small but modern bathroom, and it was inexpressible relief to get clean and get dressed. That proved well within his capacities, as long as he took it slowly. Peter served dinner, which was thick German bread and butter, and a pot of a sort of casserole-like thing made with ham, potatoes, onions, canned cream of broccoli soup and cheese on top.

"Minnesota cuisine, the classic hotdish," he said. "Minnesota cuisine minus the lutefisk."

"What is this *lutefisk*?" Cheba asked.

"You don't want to know," Peter said. "Not before you eat. The people from the *Gasthaus* certainly left us a well-stocked kitchen, but I think they use this as a vacation cottage now; there's a dozen pairs of cross-country skis up in the attic, and they've got a winter icebox. It makes me feel nostalgic. The back is covered with metal gauze but open to the outside to let in the cold, there were a few of those left in my hometown when I was a kid."

"Don't get too nostalgic," Eric said dryly.

"Seriously, this whole area does remind me of home a bit. And there's some damned odd stuff up in the attic bedrooms; somebody carved *R. Hannay was here 1916* and *who is this mysterious bugger v. Einem?* on the rafters."

"Why's that odd?" Cheba said.

"Well, Hannay isn't a German name; it's Scottish, I think. And the language is English, in 1916. When England and Germany were at war—and back then virtually no one in a little place like this would have known English."

He shook his head. "One of life's mysteries and going to stay that way, I guess. Like some more immediate ones—why they didn't turn us over to the cops, for starters."

The twins had mopped their plates with slices of dark pumpernickel and started in on some strudel. Leon looked up:

"Oh, that's because we told Greta what was gonna happen to you if they didn't help. Greta is the cool old lady."

"Not *all* of what was gonna happen," Leila said, licking her fork. "We could tell she wouldn't want kids talking about *some* of things they were going to do to you before they killed you."

"Ah . . . Thanks," Eric said; he felt a shivering chill that had nothing to do with any lingering plasmodium in his bloodstream. *Because I don't want to hear about them either.*

"Sort of like that stuff *Maman* likes to do sometimes," Leila said. "We could sort of see it ahead if you didn't leave. That's been happening lately. Just sometimes, you know? Seeing what's going to happen." She shook her head. "No, really what *might* happen, like sometimes in a video game, if you do one thing you get another? It seems like it's easier right around this place."

"It would've been like *Maman* having fun, but more gross," Leon amplified. "And of course we didn't want that to happen to you guys," he finished with a beaming smile.

Definitely a chill in the air, Eric thought.

The kids had evidently been running around in the snow most of the day, and didn't object when they were brought to the sleeping bags upstairs. When the three adults were sitting with coffee, Peter spoke:

"I did some scouting around here," he said. At Eric's raised eyebrow he grinned and waggled a reproving finger: "Hey, I may not be a deadly jarhead detective but I have done things that didn't involve staring at books or computer screens. I run and ski cross-country, and I used to hunt deer with my dad when I was a teenager."

Eric shrugged. "My turn to say sorry. What did you find?"

"It's open pine forest mostly, a lot less undergrowth than I'm used to, and with clearings here and there. The thing is that we're not all that far from the Danube cross-country, and it looks like good country for it."

"Cross-country . . . Oh. You mean on skis? I think I could hack that with another night's sleep, but what about Cheba and the kids?"

"The children have done a little of this thing with skis," Cheba said. "I tried today with Peter showing me. I can do it if I must, and I must."

Eric thought. *And God, it's a relief to be able to do that coherently.*

"I wouldn't go for it if we didn't have your little gadgets, professor, but we do. They'll look for us on the roads first and they'll assume we could be hundreds of miles away by now. But we've stayed here as long as we can."

His mind balanced distances and alternatives. Then he nodded: "If we can get to the river, we should be able to pick up some other form of transport, car, whatever. What's the but, though? I can see there is one."

Peter looked down at his hands spread on the table. "There are a lot of old bunkers scattered through these woods. I spotted four or five and I'm not an expert on that type of thing."

Eric rubbed two fingers on his chin; they skritched on coarse black stubble, which made him remind himself to shave tomorrow morning. "This is Germany, home of the bunker."

Peter's expression was grim. "They're old, but they're not abandoned. Not completely. The doors and firing slits and ventilators have all been welded shut or plugged."

"*Thou, oh evil manifest and invasive, get thee gone,*" Cheba swore in her Nahuatl-flavored Spanish. "I know why. *She* talked to me sometimes of their habits and customs. That is for the *brujos* to hide from the sun. The ones who live beyond death and have no real bodies often make such hiding places all around the places they haunt. That way they can go far from their home, almost until dawn, and have a hole to jump in at the last minute."

Eric hissed through his teeth. It made an unpleasant degree of sense; the main weakness of Shadowspawn who'd shed their bodies, the post-corporeals, was that they needed to hide during the daytime. If there was a network of cubbyholes like that spread around the place . . . then the limit wouldn't have to include time to get back to home base.

"Can we make it to the Danube, or at least the inhabited area, in one day?" Eric asked. "So we're not out in the countryside at sundown, when the little doggies come out to play?"

Peter shrugged and raised his hands. "I could, easy; I could do it by . . . oh, noon. But you're sick, and you haven't done much of this lately; Cheba's hurt and she's never done it before *at all*; and the kids are, well, kids. It'll be close. I suppose it all depends on how fast they find our trail."

"Not long," Cheba said. "At night, they can run as wolves to catch our scent, fly as owls to see. They know we left the village, and they are hunters. The Power makes the forms they take, but the forms are real enough—real noses, real eyes."

Real teeth, real claws, Eric thought, and sighed.

"I don't like it," he said. "But I got this nasty feeling it's our best bet. *Mierda.*"

The sun was just over the horizon, making the clouds go pale in the east, and Eric felt both bloated and very slightly queasy from the enormous breakfast he'd crammed down—ham, scrambled eggs, French toast, pancakes, left-over pastries—and badly in need of another four hours' sleep. A session of malaria was no joke. Cheba looked logy too, either from the pain keeping her awake or from the painkillers making her drowsy now. The kids were excited and looking forward to the day, but also a little sleepy—that was probably their Shadowspawn genes. Apparently the natural pattern for purebloods was to stay up most of the night, wake up in the middle of the afternoon and come fully active at sunset, whether they were nightwalking or not. The only one who looked fully ready to go was Peter, and Eric could sense tightly controlled anxiety in the other man. He didn't blame him, either, with this party of infants and cripples at his ass and some pretty literal bogeymen hiding in the woods. It said something for him that he hadn't found any occasion to suggest *scouting ahead* or something of that nature.

"These boots fit pretty well," the Minnesotan said. "But they're not *our* boots, and they're old, obviously just left here when people moved up to better. I warmed them up and rubbed them with some wax and bent them as much as I could. If anyone's feet start to hurt tell me right away."

He'd checked everyone's socks before they put the boots on too, making sure they were snug and smooth with no wrinkles. Eric appreciated that; if you took care of your gear, your gear took care of you. If you didn't, it would always fail at the moment you needed it most, and one of the worst point failure sources were your feet. That had been true in both his jobs, and it was just as important here whether he was going to chase or be chased; plus Shadowspawn *luck* always hit your weakest point when it was operating against you. On Peter's advice they'd eaten everything they could stuff down, and they were all carrying some food as well as the other essentials, and thermoses of hot sweet chocolate with a shot of brandy in each except the one for the kids.

There's absolutely nothing on earth that burns fuel like cross-country skiing and cold weather, Peter had said, dead serious.

Eric believed him, though climbing mountains in body armor and pack probably came a very close second. Peter had worked hard on getting the old skis in order too, and as they filed out he checked everyone's bindings one last time before putting on his own.

Eric glanced up at the sky, then gave the surface a careful eyeball. It wasn't snowing *now* though from the mealy smell in the air it might, but there were something like two feet on the ground, drifted in places. Slightly damp snow, the best kind to make a snowman out of. It would be impossible to get through on foot—not without snowshoes or skis. Impossible for people, at least. They'd squared away the cottage and locked the doors and left a couple of hundred euros on the mantelpiece;

small enough thanks for kindness that had almost certainly saved their lives. Saved them from a very bad death. Saved the kids too; he was starting to think it was really worthwhile to take risks to keep them from being raised to be the sort of person their mother was. For their own sakes, as well as to keep from unleashing two more monsters on the world.

"Okay," he said, a verbal placeholder to get their attention. "Peter will be breaking trail. Then you, Cheba, then the kids, then me on the tail. Don't talk unless you have to. Don't waste any energy, 'cause we're going to need it all. As long as we can, we'll do forty minutes and then a ten-minute rest. Steady does it, we don't work up too much of a sweat. We may need to go real quick at the end. Leon, Leila, if you can, ah, *tell* that anyone's coming after us, sing out right away, okay?"

Because I'm sure as shit going to pay attention if I start feeling that prickling crawly feeling, too. Funny, it doesn't help all that much now that I know it's real, because now I'll have to start wondering whether I'm really feeling it or just getting nervous.

They nodded. Peter dug in his sticks and slid off across the clearing with an economical-looking motion, skis slightly angled out, pushing off the inside edges like a skater getting started. Cheba followed, imitating him as best she could and touching her left pole lightly; the gouges in that shoulder must still hurt like hell, and the scabs would break any time she had to do anything strenuous with it. The children came next, moving smoothly in a way that showed they had done this before but still having to take more strides; there was just no way around the fact that their legs were shorter. Maybe that made the fact that one of the adults was sick and the other was clawed up and had never been on skis before yesterday a little less crucial, since they couldn't have outpaced the children anyway. That was looking on the bright side. The darker side was that they might need all the speed they could get if push came to shove.

"And speaking of pushing, *compadre*," Eric muttered to himself. "*¡Vamanos!*"

Shove—slide, shove—slide, use the poles for balance and to keep the arms swinging. He'd done this before, there was a Nordic-style trail just above the ski basin that overhung Santa Fe and his ex-wife, Julia, had been an enthusiast; he'd gone along for her sake, and because it was a lot less monotonous than running on a treadmill at the gym. The problem was that he hadn't done any for six years, since she left to find herself, and he hadn't liked it enough to keep it up afterwards plus the negative associations. He was fit when he wasn't sick and physically capable, but this used a particular set of muscles and they were going to make him pay.

Breathe in, hold it for the slightest second as he moved, breathe out. The cold damp air felt lousy, and then very slightly better as his body warmed up. Into the shade of the trees, mostly pretty big pines seventy or eighty feet high, clear of branches to above head height. Farther up they were as much white as green, last night's fall clinging heavily to the boughs. Whenever the wind stirred them little torrents would fall down, landing with pattering thumps. There didn't seem to be many birds, or much of anything else though they passed deer tracks, and a fleeting red streak up a tree might have been a European squirrel. And once what he was pretty sure were the marks of a raccoon, which would've been startling if someone hadn't once told him they'd escaped from fur farms here long ago.

His muscles ached, and so did his joints and his neck and his head. Forty minutes, and he felt like it had been going on for hours.

"Halt," he said, not too loud as they came to a convenient fallen tree, just the right height to sit on.

Peter was breathing about as hard as he was; breaking trail for the others was distinctly more effort than following. Eric might have felt guilty about that, if it had made any sense. As it was he just *wasn't* in any shape to spell the better skier, and his more experienced senses were better employed at the rear, since he couldn't be in two places at once. If someone was chasing them, they'd probably come up from behind. Cheba was looking a little gray, but had enough energy to keep the kids from skylarking—he didn't expect her to complain until she fell over.

Going to be an interesting life with that one, he thought as he unscrewed the top of the thermos. Then as he took the first sip: *Whoa, when did we decide she was going to be my own personal triumph of hope over experience? And she'll certainly have something to say about that herself.*

And: *Adrian, I hope you're watching over us. Because we're going to need it.*

"*Da ima okus govna!*" Adrian muttered.

"I have enough Polish to translate *that*," Ellen said sympathetically.

"Croatian, actually, but it's closely related," Adrian said, spitting into the fluted marble of the sink.

He tossed the blood bag into the waste container; let the hotel staff think what they might. She could see how he fought not to gag at the taste, gray-faced amid the splendors of the bathroom that went with the Hotel Imperial's suite. The sharp coppery metallic scent certainly didn't smell very appetizing, but then warm blood didn't attract either . . . for her. He'd shared the subjective experience of fresh blood with her telepathically, and . . .

Wow. Just wow. Just as good as being bitten, in its way. And when you throw love into the bargain . . . better still, love and sex into the bargain . . .

"Here," she said, laying a hand on his shoulder. "Just a sip to clear your mouth."

He looked up at her sharply, and she shook her head. "No, it's not the addiction getting away from me. Just a *sip*, darling. I'm testing my blood regularly, don't worry. Condition fully controlled."

Having a monogamous relationship with her meant that Adrian had to use stored blood fairly often, particularly if he was Wreaking; there was a limit to how much she could donate. The way drinking the stuff made him miserable was a proof of love too, in its way. He kissed her palm, then took the hand and touched his lips to the inside of her wrist. That gave her a tingle, both because it was Adrian and then the sharp little sensation and—

"*Ah.*"

A wave of fire up her arm, cool and sultry-warm at the same time, and a tinge of blue around the edges of her sight. It was like the instant you tipped over into orgasm, but so *long* . . .

She made a whimpering sound as he lifted his lips from her skin, and they clung together for a while.

"God, that has got to be one of the *best* things in the world," she said.

"Yes," he said. A wink. "And the best cure for nausea . . ."

Ellen laughed. "Come on. You've got work to do."

When he lay down on the bed he crossed his arms on his shoulders and closed his eyes. The relaxation that followed was beyond sleep; more still than death, despite the slow, shallow once-every-thirty-seconds breaths.

"And I'll watch over you while you check on the kids and our friends," she murmured, stroking his forehead. "Always."

CHAPTER THIRTEEN

Mitteleuropa

"It's been dark a while now," Peter said.

"Yeah," Eric said, sternly suppressing an impulse to add: *No shit, Sherlock.*

The air had gotten a little warmer over the course of the day, which just made the dank cold more penetrating and the skiing harder, and now it was freezing again. They'd never seen the sun all day, just a brighter blur to the gray-white cloud southwards, and it had never gotten all that high either.

He looked over at the children; they were sitting on a low stone wall slumped against each other, with Cheba crouched in front of them coaxing them to take the last of the formerly hot and now luke-warm chocolate. Their skis stood against the wall beside the adults, and on the other side was open ground—pasture, he thought—and evenly spaced leafless trees that probably lined a road. Beyond was a knuckle of open ground cloaked in dwarf junipers, and a mile farther off, a broad brimming river. The lie of the land hid the actual bank, but he had a feeling that there was a town there, or at least a hamlet. He wanted to push them all on right away, but he made himself wait and even forced himself to stop looking at his phone for the time. Having the kids collapse into a groaning heap on the road wasn't going to do anyone any good.

"How are you feeling?" the Minnesotan said.

"Like crap," Eric said shortly; his energy level had hit the point where he had to mentally flog himself to keep moving some time ago. "And it won't do any good in the whole God damned world to think about it."

He'd keep going regardless of how he felt until he fell facedown and couldn't move, because right now the alternative was that they all died, badly enough that it would be a relief by the time it happened.

He probably wasn't important enough for the enemy to keep his personality around to torture for centuries, but that wasn't really a very big consolation. A lot depended on how long it took the opposition to stop looking at the road out of the little town, and how quickly they traced them to the cabin and picked up the trail from there to the woods. He pulled out his tablet and checked the map—as long as he didn't engage the cell phone function, there was little chance of anyone using it to track him, but it still made getting lost a lot harder. It was full dark now, without moon or stars, but fortunately there seemed to be a little reflected light on the underside of the clouds and the patches of snow on the ground helped.

"Okay, there is a town over there, Stepp-something-on-the-Danube. Let's get—"

A sound came, faint in the distance but unmistakable. A long drawn sobbing howl, a little like a coyote's but not much; cold and deep and infinitely malignant.

"Wolf," Peter said. "Not much like the ones I heard on Grand Isle, but definitely a wolf." A moment later: "Wolves, plural."

The grinding misery of recent fever and all-too-present exhaustion had muffled Eric's alertness. That, and the sweat that kept turning into cold beads under his clothing. Now some sort of bug seemed to be scuttling over his skin amid all that. He yanked out his coach gun.

"Go!" he barked. "Push it, and don't stop."

Peter swung across the waist-high stone wall. He and Cheba each took a child by the hand and started walking quickly across the field towards the road, despite sleepy mutters of protest. At least the kids were weren't afraid of the dark, and saw in it like cats. Eric looked westward, the opposite direction from the infinitely distant and absolutely theoretical Vienna. Where the protecting sun had vanished. The ground of the meadow was awkward beneath his boots as he followed the others, snow thin and patchy and wet enough to clump. They'd been right to abandon the skis, but if they had to run the kids would have to be carried, and even a short slender eight-year-old was no joke. He wished desperately that he could reach up and swing down night vision, except of course that if he needed it the things that were after them could screw it up with a thought.

It was like the inside of a closet. By the time the leafless beech trees along the road loomed up like shapes of darkness in darkness, Leon and Leila were leading the two adults. Eric tried to keep looking in every direction at once; there wasn't any sign of a car on the road.

There wouldn't be, he thought, fighting not to let the breath rasp in his throat.

They trudged, and trudged and the apprehension built, rather than relaxing until he could taste stomach acids at the back of his throat. Something flitted through the air above him, or he thought it did, and that was almost a relief. It was gone by the time he could pay attention to it, and his heart beat so hard he could've sworn he felt the ribs flexing to its hammer.

"Center of the road," he said. "Hell with traffic, fast as you can. I don't think this bunch are going to be as restrained as the ones we met back in New Mexico."

"Hungry," Leon said suddenly. "They're saying they're hungry."

"I wish *Maman* were here!" Leila said suddenly, then turned her head down and trudged again. "Or Papa."

"I wish they were both here," Leon said.

Vienna

Adrienne bared her teeth as she paced on the faded, priceless carpets; it was the instinctive gesture of a species that bit their prey, and paralyzed them by it too. Dmitri lolled in his chair, ostentatiously refusing to be intimidated.

The Palais was a property she'd bought through cut-outs when it came on the market in 2006 and the locally dominant Sorgách family owed the Brézés a favor; it was early 18th century but fully renovated down to the fortified sub-basement and escape tunnels and a small but well-equipped mortuary-style crematorium to deal with the empties. It was also conveniently located in the Josefstadt District of central Vienna, which put it outside the Ringstrasse but near the excellent hunting-grounds of the university and its tasty herds of students. The basic architecture was Baroque—Fischer von Erlach had been the architect, back around 1710—but this upper apartment had been redone in a more Classical style, pale plaster and Chinoiserie wallpaper and spindly graceful furniture with cream-silk upholstery.

Normally she quite liked it, but right now she had an impulse to throw a teapot through the Schönfeld painting of the 17th-century noblewoman stopping at an inn. And this was *not* the time of year she usually liked to visit Central Europe; it was around sundown, but you could barely tell.

I could have gone out nightwalking today at high noon and gotten nothing but a sunburn, she thought sourly; which was an exaggeration, but a pardonable one. *I* was *born in California, after all . . .*

"Dale is taking care of it," Dmitri said. "With the von Trupps, especially the older ones . . . well, my name *is* Russian. Yes, yes, that is obsolete thinking, merely human prejudice, but we are not speaking of Progressives here, Adrienne Juliyevna," he said.

"A point," she said grudgingly. "But only because it becomes increasingly annoying as my children approach the decisive point. It would be *intolerable* for them to reach Tbilisi! I will not be put in a position where I have to choose between alternatives of that sort!"

"Dale's more likely to keep them under control."

"More likely, not very likely. But the von Trupps do not love the Brézés. Particularly, as you say, the older generation . . . Great-grandfather spoiled a number of their schemes."

Dmitri shrugged and spread his hands in an expressive gesture that an American would have thought of as Jewish, but which was actually simply the body language common in the old Romanov lands. She took the meaning: *what can we do?*

"You were the one who suggested that it was your children's future luck thwarting us," he said. "Logically, it would be protecting them at the same time."

Adrienne snarled and hissed, but she was careful not to direct it at her associate-subordinate. That pointed it at Monica, as she came in with a tray of pastries and coffee.

"Eeek!"

She managed not to spill it, and put it down between the Shadowspawn before retreating behind Adrienne's chair. Adrienne stuck her fork moodily into the sachertorte.

"The more I consider it, the more I think involving the Trupps was a mistake," she said.

"Dale was much in favor. He thinks he can even keep your former lucies alive, as well as safeguarding the children. One of the lucies at least."

"He has been strange since he killed Arnaud. That was done efficiently . . . but . . . I do need to get the children back, and I would very much like to reacquire Peter, if only long enough for a thorough probing of his mind, but . . . you will excuse me."

He nodded and left. Monica breathed a sigh of relief. "Leon and Leila aren't *really* in danger, are they, *Doña?*" she asked anxiously.

"I hope not, but this tit-for-tat is getting out of control; I intended it to preoccupy Adrian and distract him, but it is rebounding on me and *his* little gambit is rebounding on *him* . . . he should not have sent his retainers on such an unorthodox path. That bunch of von Trupps still think of themselves as werewolves in the classic sense. Too many hours spent with the Brothers Grimm in their impressionable years."

Indecision wasn't something she was comfortable with. "I will have to intervene . . . but I cannot *locate* my children more than approximately . . ."

She snapped her fingers. "I have it! I will focus on the *von Trupps*. There is nothing shielding them, that rural bunch are quite sloppy about it, and they are the immediate problem; to watch them is to solve the problem, or at least if they do not sight the children there *is* no immediate problem. I can . . . supervise from a distance, bend the probabilities if I must, blackpath anything those wood-dogs do."

She checked her reserves; that musician yesterday had been the last full feeding, but the social whirl here in Vienna was strenuous. *Hmmmm. Not quite full-up . . .*

"When was the last time I fed on you? More than a nip to set the mood, I mean."

"A week ago, about a quarter-pint," Monica said. "I'm getting rather, umm, anxious for another, actually. I'm sure my red-cell count is fine."

Withdrawal from feeding addiction was like that from heroin, only rather worse. Adrienne preferred to keep her regular lucies just on the verge of real suffering from it, as a training aid. And the begging and pleading was so charming . . .

"Come here, then."

"Oh, goodie!" Monica said, with a slow smile.

"No games, I just need the blood for some Wreaking. Don't pout, either."

The lucy sat beside her on the couch, leaning backward across her lap and embracing her, nestling her face into the Shadowspawn's shoulder, bending her chin back to present the neck. Her aura trembled and her heart began to race, stimulating the predator's reflexes even though Adrienne wasn't particularly hungry right now—it was better to feed *before* you did any serious work if you didn't want to kill the victim that time, because Power-depletion meant you might lose control. Adrienne licked the taut skin—a pureblood's saliva was antiseptic and promoted clotting when exposed to air, and besides that it was fun. Then she clamped a hand to the base of the human's head and curled back her lips to present the micro-serrations in the inside of her incisors; fangs would have been totally impractical, of course.

"Bite me, *please*," Monica breathed, muffled and tense.

"You asked for it," she said, and struck.

Her growl mixed with the lucy's moan; the first mouthful was always incredibly sweet, like a wine-and-cocaine cocktail . . . in this case a nice fruity Beaujolais Nouveau. Her victim's mind opened like a flower at the rush of pleasure.

"No, no, take more," she murmured as Adrienne withdrew and pressed a finger to the small wound.

"Later. Have some sachertorte. I'm going to be hungry when I come around, and you are the ultimate comfort food."

Mitteleuropa

They had to get somewhere with lights and people. He *could* see a faint glow in that direction, northeastward, but that was because everything else was so damn dark. There was an odd flicker to it, too. After ten minutes the figures ahead of him slowed, so that he nearly ran into them with his head swiveling backward. His mind felt as if it were encased in a sheath of hard flexible glass at the bottom of the sea, and he knew that it was pressure on the Wreakings Adrian Brézé had implanted there; panic and despair beat at it, emotions not his own but ready to flood his mind like a tide race through a canyon to make him run and run like a witless beast until the teeth closed. His amulets were all warm against the skin under his clothes, just short of pain. The blackness buzzed and throbbed with malign intent, like a million hair-fine tentacles swarming and probing from all directions.

"Keep moving," he said.

"*Los niños* can't," Cheba said.

"Carry them," Eric said, and she and Peter each took one; he needed to stay free to fight as long as possible.

He hated to say it, and not just because of the way Cheba gasped when Leila was boosted up piggyback and the weight came on her injured shoulder. Fairly soon he'd have to spell her or she'd collapse, and the thought of going into action with a kid riding on his back was just what was needed to make this nightmare complete. They moved down the road at a slow jog. Over the crest, and now it was downhill, which helped a bit. The air was thick but not actually foggy, and the lights ahead were much brighter; he could make out streetlights and windows. Nothing very tall, it wasn't a city and there weren't any skyscrapers. The biggest structure was some sort of old-looking white stucco mansion on a hill, with modest-sized floodlights in the grounds, but the whole thing was definitely three steps up from the nowhereville they'd stayed the night before last. And there were still Christmas decorations up, and now he could hear noise like revelry at the end of an infinite tunnel—

—and big wings cut the air overhead. Just a rustle and a flash of pale feathers, but the children squealed in alarm. He pivoted, arm flung out and aiming entirely by instinct. The muzzle flash from the twin barrels blinded him for a second, and most of the silvered shot pattered into the boughs of the trees as the muzzle whipped upward. Twigs rained down, but a long white barn owl feather did too . . . until it vanished with a subliminal sparkle. There was a crashing and then a thump somewhere out there in the dark, accompanied by a feral squall of anger and fear. Eric thumbed open the coach gun as he jogged on, ignoring the ache in his abused wrist and grinning a little as he shook the spent cartridges out and replaced them with two more from his left pocket.

That had sounded awfully like what you'd get if someone turned from a bird into a human being in midair without really meaning to, and then fell thirty feet through a big beech tree until they hit the ground. The grin turned to a snarl as a wolf howled again, this time shockingly near; whoever it was, *whatever* it was, was thoroughly pissed off. And others answered it, a pack, not right on top of them but not all that far away either. He snapped the gun closed by jerking upward, the hard metallic click obscurely comforting.

"He's saying *I'm hurt, Mommy,* and *come and eat, come and eat, eat, eat,*" Leon said, his voice high and quavering.

Wait a minute, Eric thought. *The bastard is thinking like a wolf as much as a man right now. And wolves are pretty much a dog with attitude. Werewolves especially, I guess.*

Aloud he gasped out: "Faster. Just for a bit, as fast as you can. Then when I give the word, kids in the center and us facing out."

"It'll attack," Peter rasped.

"We want him to. Got . . . to finish this one . . . before the others get here. Before he gets ahead and blocks us. Making him do what we want, not what he would want to do if he was thinking about it."

Tactics, and his detective's feeling for the psychology of macho asshole perps. And if he was wrong and they failed, they'd be overrun and ripped to pieces. A lumbering dash, the fall of their feet and the sobbing of their breath loud in the night. The ants were crawling on his skin, all right, and it felt tight enough to split under their little sharp feet.

"*Now!*"

Dogs can't resist chasing something that runs, especially when they smell fear. Let the wolf rule the man. Let the man go apeshit because he can't stand to lose face or let the others laugh at him. C'mon, do the wrong thing, you son of a whore! Make that son of a bitch!

"Now, stop!"

He knew he stank of raw terror, and he suspected the others did too; having these things chase you through the night was an ultimate fear built right in, and something deep down knew those weren't just wolves. Perhaps this was the irrational source of the fear and hate wolves had always aroused, the way the ancient masters had used their forms to hunt men.

The children went down and huddled on the ground, clutching each other. The three adults made a protective triangle; there was a *shing* as Cheba's machete came out. He couldn't see six feet, but he could hear paws rutching on the wet pavement with its patches of snow. Then he could see, see the glowing yellow eyes above the snarling muzzle; the nightwalker had been careless to leave them like that. He fired just as the eyes lifted in the killing leap, then clubbed blindly with the silvered steel barrels, flailing into the strobing afterimages that the twin streaks of fire drew across his vision. Metal cracked against bone, thudded into something like hard upholstery.

Weight slammed into him and he went over on his back, tensing his muscles as he fell so it wouldn't knock the wind out of him. A hundred and eighty pounds of wolf tried to anyway. He got his hands up just in time, the fingers locking in fur over muscle that felt like living metal. Slaver sprayed to his face, and the harsh animal musk and stink filled his nose, and the blank yellow eyes were like windows into a world of fire. There was a flash of fangs amid a sound like baseball bats being slammed together or God's own castanets as the great jaws snapped close enough that the hot wind of it fanned his chin. Blunt-clawed paws scrabbled at him, and he could feel his grip slipping.

There was a whirring sound and a *chunk*, and suddenly the salt of blood filled his eyes and nose and mouth, blinding and choking. Cheba was shrieking as she drew back for another roundhouse swing, but he could feel the weight of the wolf on him lurch as someone kicked it between the haunches, very hard. It was distracted—only for a second— but he used that to jam his right forearm up under its chin, locking the arm so that its lunge just pushed his shoulder back into the ground. The other hand stripped his knife out from the sheath under the tail of his parka, and he reared up to drive it home. There was a familiar soft, heavy resistance as it sank, and he ripped upward with the silver-threaded blade up and across in a convulsive heave to open the body cavity and cut the arteries.

Something flashed within his head, a silent scream of astonishment and mortal terror like some soundless blast of mental lightning.

And then there was . . . nothing. Sparkling in the night for the briefest instant, more sensed than seen, and then even the wetness of blood on his face and hands was gone. Even the scent of it, vanishing like a dream when you woke.

"I couldn't shoot, I couldn't shoot, it was too close," Peter was saying.

"Fuck that, let's *go*," Eric rasped, halfway between reason and a snarl. "Kicking it in the balls was a real good idea. The rest of them are coming, and even odds ain't my choice here. Three on one just barely worked with Rin Tin von Hitler there."

More howls broke out, as if to punctuate his words; the children's bodies were tense and shaking a little as he helped pull them up. They all moved out at the fastest walk the little ones could manage, trying to control their breathing. Leon was hiccuping, and his sister had stifled a whimper before it quite began. Eric stuffed the coach gun inside his coat, and Cheba tried twice to wipe her machete before it sank in that the blade was as clean as it had been the last time she oiled and sharpened it. Her first try at sheathing the tool/weapon nearly took off an ear.

"Careful with that, *querida*," he said, and guided it home.

"They're coming," Leila said. "They're changing, and they're coming. They're *angry* now. Not just hungry."

"And they've got the whole damn night," Peter said.

Cheba grinned in the darkness, a flash of white teeth. "Not so much, it is nearly midnight."

"How time flies when you're fighting for your life," Peter said.

Okay, Eric thought. *They can't identify us with the Power. All they've got is their senses. Animal senses. Got to break trail somehow. Think, you dumb bastard! Right, let's get into town and cover our smell with lots of other people and gasoline and stuff.*

It wasn't a very big town, though bigger than he'd first thought, denser and thicker built than an American settlement covering the same area, all low-rise except for church steeples but packed together. There were a lot of decorations up, but they didn't seem particularly Christmasy, except the ones which *were* Christmas ornaments. There were a lot of evergreen wreaths, and as they approached the outskirts and moved over to the side of the road to give way to traffic, fireworks started bursting overhead. More and more of them as they walked into town, everyone and his dog out in the yard setting off rockets, plus some bigger official-looking ones from farther in. Enough bottles of champagne were being cracked to make him a little nervous about the fireworks even now. Some of the sky-rockets plunged into the clouds above and were just flashes of diffused light, though others burst in multicolored splendor lower down. There were Catherine wheels and Roman candles as well in the town square and in the park around the big building on the hill. The noise seemed slightly muffled for the first instant, then burst through into his perceptions as if they were pricking a bubble of silence that had encased him.

A lot was going on. For some reason a laughing, cheering and rather beer-full crowd were pouring molten lead from a little teacup-sized holder into a big pot of water. In other places, doughnuts were being passed around and steaming drinks ladled out, and an enthusiastic band was playing "The Blue Danube" and people were waltzing.

His mind raced as he actually *recognized* someone.

"Hans! Hans Schenk!" he called, half shouting.

The German commando—ex-commando, now—looked around in surprise. He was a decade older than that night on the slopes of the Hindu Kush, and wearing some vaguely nautical-looking uniform, with a walrus mustache and much less hair on top of his head under the peaked cap. There was a lot more of him, too, but he still looked as strong as an ox, with thick wrists and shoulders to match the modest beer gut. He also had a semi-paralytic drunk's arm looped over his shoulders, and some probable subordinates in sailor suits were trying to round up a few others and get them moving. The drunks were of both sexes and mostly middle-aged, and all looking as if they'd be very, very sorry tomorrow.

"Eric!" the other man blurted after an instant of blank surprise, and then dawning comprehension. "Eric Salvador! What the devil are you doing here? I thought you were a policeman, in that town of yours with the mountains and the opera!"

He spoke excellent English, accented but with the flatter, harder vowels of a North German rather than the ripe Schwarzenegger style of the locals.

"Hans, I don't have time to explain and you wouldn't believe me if I did. I'm here with these folks, and we need to get out of sight and out of town right now, it's a matter of life and death, and I swear we're not in trouble with your authorities. Can you help me?"

The forty-something German froze for another instant or two, his eyes flicking to Cheba and Peter and then the children. "Life or death? Well, we've seen that before, you and I, no? Follow me."

Two of the semi–sailor types picked up Leon and Leila, and the whole nautical-looking party plus several drunks pushed through the crowd. Despite the small absolute size of the place, they were managing to make enough noise to blend with the fireworks and the music into an overwhelming blur. That would probably mean they were hidden from sight and scent as well. It didn't take long to get down to the docks, where something like an enormous, elongated white rectangular barge with a sharp prow was tied up; it had glassed-in observation areas and lots of windows as well. All in all, it looked like a medium-sized hotel reincarnated as a boat, which was probably exactly what it was.

"Behold the Erzherzogin Cecilie," Hans said. "Management had a flash of inspiration and thought a Christmas and New Year's tour would be just the thing. Bloody fools, and bloody dangerous, and it's three-quarters empty because most of the people who could afford a ticket realize that."

He took a closer look at the five of them as they went up the gang-plank, then swore in German. "You weren't joking, were you?"

"Not even a bit," Eric said.

"Please tell me that you have documents," Hans said. "Even these days, that makes things a lot easier here."

"Valid passports, Hans." Eric started to go on, then felt himself doing a slow buckle at the knees. "Got to get out of here," he mumbled. "Got to *go*."

"Let's get you to bed," the German said, guiding them to a couch.

"God in Heaven knows we've got plenty of empty staterooms. Though I hope you don't mind heading for Vienna, because that's where we are going."

Eric Salvador didn't precisely lose consciousness, but he did lose most interest in his surroundings. Far and faint and muffled, the wolves howled. He supposed that sometimes the luck had to be crazy good, as well as crazy bad.

Vienna

Adrian Brézé blinked awake.

"Extraordinary," he said softly, his face turning northwestward. "They were not there to the eyes of the Power. To be unable to detect my own children, the strongest blood linkage of all . . ."

"Where are they?" Ellen asked, snuggling into his shoulder.

"On the Danube, and heading this way, assuming they are on the boat, and that it is safe. They will be here soon. Before the ceremony for Arnaud."

"That's wonderful!" she said.

"Yes," he said. Then, slowly: "But that was . . . perhaps too easy. As if I were pushing with the wind at my back. I had to be careful not to make myself too obvious . . . though that section of the von Trupps are not exactly highly skilled. Still, their instincts are keen enough."

"Luck? You were *luckier* than you expected?"

"Exactly."

CHAPTER FOURTEEN

Vienna

"Here they come!" Ellen said.

It was a cold sunset hour, with the streetlamps blurred streaks through what couldn't quite make up its mind to be fog, a light drizzle of very cold rain, or sleet. She was a little surprised at how eager she was. Leon and Leila were cute kids, but she was even more eager to see Peter—who'd become a close friend during their common captivity on Ranch Sangre—and Cheba, though the younger girl was sort of prickly and difficult sometimes. And she was glad to see Eric's battered and slightly sinister face too. Adrian was wonderful, but you needed people besides your sweetie. People you didn't despise and hate and fear, that is.

"They were virtually here, and still I could not sense them. Then *ping*

237

and they were there again," Adrian said, still a little bemused by it; it must be like someone being able to switch his vision on and off.

Peter's little technological marvels were all switched off, of course, since it would never do to have the Council's Shadowspawn confronted with an open and blatant contradiction between what they could see and what they could sense. They would find out eventually, but the trick had to be protected as long as possible.

"The wonders of modern technology," Ellen said, holding his arm as they stood just outside the doorway of the hotel, occasional cold drops flicking into their faces under the awning. "Shadowspawn tend to get kind of dependent on their special abilities. I'm all for cutting them off and giving them a bit of a glimpse about how us peasants live. Nothing personal, darling."

He smiled a little wryly: "Objectively speaking, I approve and agree entirely. My *emotions* feel as if the ground has vanished from beneath my feet, or as if I'd gone blind."

Ellen laughed. She was feeling a little bubbly anyway, now that the children and their friends had arrived safely—though there was a certain irony in using the word *safe* in this context. The limousine they'd dispatched for the trio of adults and the two children pulled up in front of the Hotel Imperial, which was a 19th-century neo-Italian Renaissance pile on the Ringstrasse, originally the Prince of Württemberg's Viennese pied-à-terre, topped with a stone balustrade and allegorical animal figures from the prince's heraldic arms. Two doormen in top hats and pearl-gray suits dashed forward to hold umbrellas.

Ellen hugged Peter and Eric; she gave Cheba a handshake. Contrary to seriously time-lagged but still widely believed folklore, Mexicans were actually a little more reticent about that sort of contact outside a very close circle than Anglo-Americans, who'd gone from hugging nobody to hugging everybody over the past century. Adrian gave both the men a firm handshake, actually bowed over Cheba's hand and kissed it—he had the sort of looks and air that could carry that off—and stooped to exchange the oddly formal-looking French kiss on both cheeks with his children.

"My friends, I am in your debt," he said; she noticed again that his diction had gotten a little more formal even in English since they arrived in Europe and started hanging out with the older Brézés.

The men nodded; Cheba gave a feral grin. "You *are* in my debt now, *jefe*," she said. "And I like it much better that way."

"How are you?" Ellen said to the children, who'd always seemed to like her . . . hopefully not in a culinary sense.

Though she wasn't entirely sure how much they'd known of what happened on their mother's estate. She knew that they knew that Shadowspawn drank human blood, at least; evidently it was usual to start them on small sips a few years before puberty, which was when the Power really kicked in along with the surge of hormones—she supposed that had evolved to keep children from being too uncontrollable. Adrienne had called it the *latent period*, and she'd heard Adrian use the same term.

They yawned and beamed at her at the same time. "We had all sorts of adventures, and then a fun ride on the boat," Leon said. "Were you there, Papa? I thought you were."

"I was watching," Adrian confirmed. "And helping as I could."

The three who'd shepherded the children shared a glance, and small nods. Those turned to looks of alarm when Leila added:

"*Maman* was there too, I think."

"Sometimes I could hear pieces of ice hitting the hull outside my room on the boat! It was all pretty cool, like that story we read, *The Sea*

Wolf. Things could get really dull at *Maman's* place, and this trip was a lot more fun."

Peter made a choking sound; Eric snorted but very softly. Cheba gave them both a symbolic whap on the back of the head, wincing a little when she moved her left hand.

"And Hans told us all sorts of funny stories about the things he did when he was a soldier and knew Eric," Leila said in turn, giggling as they came into the lobby. "Hans is cool, *vraiment.* This looks like a nice place."

The Hotel Imperial had been a hotel since the Princes of Württemberg decided they needed the money more than the building about a hundred and fifty years ago, through a number of extremely discriminating restorations. One of the things that hadn't changed was the swarm of uniformed flunkies that ushered them in; they and their predecessors had greeted everyone from Greta Garbo through Adolph Hitler to Simon Wiesenthal, and it was still used for the stodgier sort of visiting panjandrum.

Ellen mentioned the Hitler connection, and Peter laughed as they were swept into the splendors of oxblood marble and porphyry columns beneath the blazing chandeliers and up the sweeping staircases beneath huge portraits of bemedalled and mustachioed grandees from 19th-century Mitteleuropa and their long-gowned diamond-decked consorts.

"I looked it up. Before the First World War old Adolf . . . well, actually young Adolf . . . did odd jobs here, carrying out garbage and stuff when he couldn't make enough selling postcards to pay for a doss-house. He didn't come back until he'd done the rape-Austria thing."

Adrian laughed aloud himself at the anecdote, with a sardonic note to it. Ellen did too, but felt a small twinge that took her a moment to identify. It wasn't that Adrian didn't genuinely loathe tyrants of the

Hitler-Stalin-Pol Pot type, it was that some part of it was . . . Well, one big reason von Stauffenberg and the other Junkers had finally decided they had to kill the man they called "the Bohemian corporal" was pure *de haut en bas* contempt for prole effrontery. Her husband wasn't consciously any sort of a snob, and he'd spent most of his life *risking* his life in rebellion against his inheritance, but somewhere deep in there a hundred generations of aristo arrogance lingered. You didn't have to be a Shadowspawn to assume you were a different, and superior, order of being.

You can take the boy out of the Château, she thought. *But you can't altogether take the Château out of the boy. On the other hand, it is so worth it.*

Of course, the aristo thing had its upside. He hadn't had to use the Power to get them the Maria Therese Suite, with its four adjoining bedrooms and sweeping view of the Ringstrasse and the Opera House. All it had taken besides money was his personal presence. That utter and sublime conviction that everyone was eager to get him exactly what he wanted, and of course that he deserved it. Throw in a charming smile, and it almost always worked.

Ellen hid a slight smile of her own at Cheba's reaction to the Rococo splendors of the rooms, though she kept it well hidden. The Mexican girl had excellent natural taste; she'd seen that during her convalescence after the Rancho Sangre op, not least in the sort of thing she'd hypothetically chosen for the folk art import store she dreamed of opening someday. And this Belle Époque display of lux—complete with gold tassel embellishments on the swags of the looped curtains, eighteen-foot ceilings with gilt plaster work and a view of the Opera House from a great corner window—was an excellent example of its type.

You'd have to be an old-fashioned pickle-up-the-ass modernist prig to disapprove of it on principle. Still, it was obviously love at first sight for Cheba. People who grew up practicing austere simplicity simply because they couldn't afford anything else rarely embraced it as an aesthetic principle.

Adrian had also arranged a complete new set of baggage and its contents to replace the ones lost in Germany, which had probably been torn to pieces by the teeth of a pack of very annoyed von Trupps, not to mention copiously peed on. Cheba was pleased, though a little disconcerted by the fact that the butler service the hotel laid on had already put everything in place in the cupboards and drawers. Ellen helped settle in the children, a process itself helped by the discovery of the complimentary imperial torte waiting for them.

Can't blame them for that, she thought, *nibbling a bit of it herself. By God, the Viennese may have all their glories behind them and be living off memories, but one thing they can still do world-class is chocolate, dark and not too sweet.*

A single gesture from Adrian had made sure everyone understood that for all his Wreakings they couldn't talk frankly here. Eric and Cheba had made slightly stilted but perfectly genuine expressions of thanks for the *laying on of hands* that accelerated their recoveries. The new set of dressings Hans had put on Cheba's claw-wounds had been spotted with new blood when she took them off.

Cheba even took a moment to thank Ellen, since she knew where the blood had come from to juice Adrian up before they arrived. Ellen still had a bit of that mellow, drifting sense of utter peace you got after the ecstasy of a feeding, the way it made absolutely anything feel so good and everyone seem lovable. Cheba would know a little of what that was like, but she couldn't know how much more intense the high you got from the bite was when it was of your own will and with love, without that nasty undertone of fear, guilt, self-loathing and dread afterwards.

Ellen felt more than a little sorry for her.

"Your man, he is a good *jefe*," Cheba said seriously in a quiet aside as they walked towards the elevator.

Even if he is a blood-sucking brujo, went unspoken. She continued aloud, in the same undertone:

"And you, you also do not forget those who help you."

All in all it made dinner rather fraught, though Ellen found she had an excellent appetite.

After all, she thought as they were bowed to their table, *in a way I'm eating for two. And Eric and Cheba are making up for lost time—the Power can force their bodies to heal faster, but cell division has to have something to work with. Peter's the only one who might be worrying his stomach closed. And the kids just shovel it down, unless it's pretty loathsome; though their table manners are absolutely superb for their age.*

Which was fortunate; the maître d'hôtel had looked a little dubious at seating children that young. This place was on the high end of stuffy-formal.

Interesting how Cheba absorbed that sort of formal thing like a sponge, since she started out basically as a peasant with lizards in the thatch. She's actually a bit better at it than me, by now, and I was the first in my family ever to go to university. Look at the elegant way she handled her napkin there, or the little serious frown over the wine list.

The hotel restaurant was about the degree of high-end stodgy-conservative you'd expect, but nonetheless impressive; red and gold, snowy linen, glittering silver and crystal and an atmosphere of subdued old-money sybaritism designed to make you feel like a pre-1914 grand duke. Ellen worked her way through briny grilled octopus with wasabi and ginger-orange sauce that put her in mind of a makeout session with some sort of sea nymph, a small bowl of richly sweet lobster bisque with a bite of Armagnac and a tiny little floating lobster pancake, and finished by splitting the double entrecôte of dry aged Austrian beef with peppercorn sauce, sauce ravigote, and onion potatoes with Adrian. It was tender, but not so tender that it didn't have an interesting texture, and it tasted like the earthy Platonic essence of grilled steer, one that had lived on a low-stress regimen at a bovine spa in the Alps with plenty of organic grass and gentle aerobic exercise and moo-yodeling classes. She'd never heard of the Austrian red wine that went with it, but the grapes had died happily too and Adrian gave it a glance of surprised respect.

"My goodness," she said, patting her lips with the napkin and hiding a small belch. "There was more aged Austrian beef in that than there was in the last Conan movie. Wonderful for the red cell count."

Her eyes met Adrian's, and even with the tension there was an exchange of flirtatious subtext that stopped just short of him doing that Shadowspawn snap-of-the-teeth thing, a gesture expressing a combination of predatory sexual interest with a rather different type of appetite. That wouldn't have been tactful with Peter and Cheba at the table; Adrienne used it too, and when *she* clicked her ivories at you it was usually a prelude to a starring role in some spectacular and quite involuntary piece of sadomasochistic kink. Which had been bad enough for Ellen, and worse for them.

In a way it was a pity they had to be so discreet, because it was a good idea for the kids to be exposed to a more positive role model for . . .

Well, predator-prey relationship relationships, I suppose you'd call it. They're purebloods and they'll have the, um, needs, she thought, around a mouthful of iced *Milchrahmstrudel. It's not as if they're going to have all that much difficulty finding human-type people who* want *what they have to offer. I hope they get something as good as Adrian and I have, but just learning to avoid that whole vicious lethal exploitation thing would be a nice passable good-enough. And of course if Adrian and I have kids too . . . deal with that when we come to it.*

"Do you two think you could stand a Ferris wheel ride without losing that dinner?" Adrian said to his son and daughter.

"Oh yes, Papa," Leila said, her brother nodding agreement as he chewed.

"Should we be—" Cheba began, then stopped before she could say:—*wasting our time that way.*

Ellen was morally certain that someone had nudged the other woman under the table, though she wasn't certain who.

Peter, Eric or Adrian? she thought. *Hmm, Peter or Eric, I think. Probably Peter. He's got a sort of brotherly vibe going there. Wonder if Eric has figured out that he has the serious-type hots for her yet? And under that tough marine/cop/divorced thing, I think he's a lot more sentimental than she is.*

"Yes, that sounds like a good idea," Cheba said, her voice neutral.

She really isn't a very good liar, Ellen thought. *Not bad, but not very* good *either. Too ferociously straightforward.*

The concierge was a little surprised that they intended to walk to the Wiener Prater; like most Europeans he assumed that Americans didn't have functional feet. He did supply umbrellas, which were useful, a list of the attractions of the park which were still open this time of year, and some completely unnecessary directions.

"If we are to stop Harvey, we must get this matter of my uncle's killing out of the way," Adrian said abruptly. "And I received a message, a telepathic message, suggesting a meeting to discuss just that. No names, but it is supposedly one of Adrienne's principal supporters who wishes to turn on her."

I notice he didn't say murder, Ellen thought mordantly. *Where there is no law, there is no murder—just killing. And among Shadowspawn . . .*

The crowds out enjoying the splendors of the Ringstrasse were considerably thinned by the light drizzle. The cast-iron streetlights made a watery glimmer as they reflected on wet stone, like an Impressionist cityscape done by someone with undiagnosed myopia. The children ran on a little ahead, doing an occasional two-footed jump into a puddle. Ellen, Adrian and Eric Salvador all did occasional expert checks for tails and other forms of surveillance; Peter and Cheba were a little more obvious about it.

My name is Ellen . . . Ellen Bond . . . I mean, Brézé, she thought, conscious of the comforting outline of her derringer and the weight of the knife under her coat.

And it's even more comforting that Adrian's here.

He walked easily, not quickly but with a springy grace, his hands in the pockets of his dark coat and a hat—hats were fashionable once more—slightly tilted over his brow.

"Why do you trust whoever sent you this message?" Eric said bluntly.

"I don't, of course," Adrian said. "But there are ways of . . . authenticating . . . telepathic messages. We do not use them very often, because it requires some lowering of barriers, of defenses, on the side of the one wishing to show truth."

A mirthless grin: "Of course, one of the ways around that is simply to change your mind after you sent the message. But I can say with some confidence that the sender meant what they said at the time they said it."

Eric's snarl had the same savagery: "Hey, just to make our heads hurt a little more, couldn't one of you guys get another one to put the mojo on him so he believed something during a conversation and switch it back afterwards?"

Adrian nodded crisply. "Yes, that actually can be done. It almost never is, because it requires letting down *all* your defenses and allowing another to control your mind. The only person I would allow to do that would be Ellen, and she does not have the capacity. And I am unusually non-paranoid, for a Shadowspawn purebred."

Peter snorted, and spoke without turning his head. "Not long on trust, you guys, are you? And I thought John le Carre novels were bad!"

Adrian gave him a small sly smile. "Well, le Carre was—"

Peter pummeled his own temples. "God, how I always hated all-explanatory, non-falsifiable conspiracy theories! And now I'm living in one! You have *no* idea how offensive this is to a scientist."

Ellen held up a hand. "No, *don't* tell me le Carre was one of you, lover. Even if he was."

"No, my darling, I shall cruelly torture you by leaving you in suspense. And here we are."

The Prater had been an amusement park for more than a quarter of a millennium, or rather longer than the United States had existed; large chunks of it were still open even in the depths of winter. It was the sort of place that only really closed down for the apocalypse or a Russian invasion, and which featured a main avenue much like the Ringstrasse except that it was straighter. Ellen felt a slight pang as they walked through the cheerful crowds, many of them youngsters even at this hour, but many also good solid burghers just enjoying themselves among the restaurants and food stalls, the mimes and jugglers and haunted houses.

She would have loved it herself as a kid, but her family had never even made it to Orlando; some of the rides looked truly spectacular, the two-hundred-foot-high Ferris wheel in particular. It was well over a century old, too, though the gondolas were a fortunately much younger product of an early 21st-century restoration.

"Thank you," Adrian said at the Ferris wheel's ticket booth.

This time it wasn't all old-world charm, or even the thousand euros. She could see something flicker in the attendant's eyes as he changed his mind about telling them the ride was just now closing down. There were fifteen gondolas on the great wheel; they saw Peter and Cheba and the children into one. The great machine clanked and rumbled as it advanced to the next position.

Eric took a step back into the shadow. He had a gift for being inconspicuous, possibly just his training as a detective, or possibly his trace of the Power magnifying it. Two sets of footsteps approached. For a moment Ellen didn't recognize the dark hook-nosed man in the lead—his hair was cropped close now, and he wore a casual-elegant dark suit with a camel's hair overcoat draped across his shoulders cloak-fashion. He took a last puff of the cigarette he held between thumb and forefinger and flicked it away. His lucy/renfield, Kai, walked behind, silent and blank faced in her blue skirt-suit, one hand casually inside her open purse. Adrian nodded and extended a hand.

It wasn't invitation to shake; they touched fingers in a gesture Ellen had seen among Shadowspawn before. Without looking back at her Adrian said:

"It is him, and in the flesh."

It was easy enough for Shadowspawn to imitate each other in aetheric form, as long as they had some DNA for a template. A nightwalker who was really expert at imitating auras could fool even another adept unless there was direct contact; that was one point of the gesture. Dale Shadowblade flicked his eyes to her and Eric, then inclined his head and motioned to the gondola. They all climbed in and the machinery swept them up, up and up until even through the wet winter's night the Prater and the greater Vienna beyond were a sweep of multicolored beauty.

Faintly, she could hear the delighted laughter of the children from above. It seemed—and did—to come from another dimension, one where normal things existed and monsters did not stalk the waking world.

"I will speak to you through her," Kai said, and in French.

No, not Kai, Ellen thought.

The voice was hers, and even the slightly slurred nasal urban working-class East Coast American accent, but the whole tone and cadence were different. It was hard to tell in the darkness, but she thought the girl's pupils had expanded until they swallowed the iris and left only pools of black. Beside her she could feel Eric tense very slightly, like a hunting dog pointing. Adrian shrugged, indifferent to eccentricity and used to it.

"What do you have to say?"

"That Adrienne did indeed commission me to kill your Great-uncle Arnaud, for a beginning."

Adrian shrugged again. "I had assumed that. You will of course be unwilling to state that before the others."

Kai chuckled, and Ellen shivered a little at the grating sound. *I've hated Kai ever since I met the vicious little bitch,* she thought.

Among other things she'd acted as a Judas goat luring victims for her master and participated in the kills.

But right now, I can actually feel a little pity for her.

"Unwilling to die? Most certainly!" Dale said. "At least the Final Death. But possibly the body's death, if I can get out from under *her.*"

"Then what use are you to me? You confirm something I already know, and give me no proof to use."

"It is simple; demand that she produce me to prove my innocence. Furthermore, you may now swear—and demonstrate—that Dale Shadowblade agreed that Adrienne ordered him to kill her great-uncle, while he was under his brother's protection on the train. That ought to be reasonably safe for you, if done in public and with care."

The assassin lit another cigarette and looked out over Vienna. There was an interval of silence that felt like a steel string bending.

"Why?" Adrian said softly. "Any of us would have killed Arnaud, under the right circumstances. But why would she compel another to do so, and at such a crucial time?"

"He was the weak link. He was her original conduit to her great-grandfather, some time ago. It was a long considered plan, you understand. But he was developing . . . very strong reservations about her plans."

"What sort of reservations? About Trimback Two?"

Dale shrugged. It was oddly disconcerting to have the body language in a conversation coming from one person, while the actual voice came from another. It produced an odd mental stutter, and made it that much harder to analyze the meaning of either. Doubtless that was part of the purpose of a tactic weird even by Shadowspawn standards.

"Not so much that as the little subplot you discovered considering the Brotherhood rogue and his bomb. Indeed, his last words to me were about that. He did not save his life, but it did make me think. Adrienne is very clever, but perhaps not as clever as she thinks, and she has a tendency to think of others as mere chess pieces for her cunning hand to move. Using this Harvey as a chess piece takes arrogance to the borders of folly, given his record—Shadowspawn who underestimated him before tended to die as did Tōkairin Michiko and her grandfather. And using her great-grandfather so, that lies beyond those boundaries into outright madness."

"Ah," Adrian said. "That has puzzled me. How does she plan to remove herself and her principal supporters from Tbilisi at the crucial moment without alerting the Council?"

"She does not. Somehow, she plans to preserve herself—and her favored ones—*through* the explosion. Too clever by half, eh? And it makes everyone in her party far too dependent on her for survival at the crucial moment. I do not find "trust me" a very convincing argument. Perhaps her definition of *rival* extends further than she says."

Adrian spread his hands palm down, a gesture that said: *you have a point.*

"And you wish from me? Protection, perhaps?"

Dale Shadowblade laughed, a dry chuckle; horribly, Kai echoed it in a shrill giggle with exactly the same rhythm, like the very same sound moved up several octaves.

"The only protection for me is for Adrienne to die the Final Death, and to stay very much out of your way, my . . . friend. With the plague unleashed, you will have enough to occupy you for a good long time, I think. I wish to avoid the Final Death as long as I may."

The wheel turned as they talked, which Ellen hoped wasn't too symbolic, or too much of an omen, and came to a stop at the entrance. Dale and Kai stepped out and walked away without another word, past the knot of park officials standing and arguing with each other, waving pieces of paper and tablets.

"I'm sorry if there's a problem, *meine Damen und Herren*," Adrian said smoothly, in faultless Viennese German. "I am truly sorry if we have violated any park regulations, but my children would have been so disappointed to miss this historic ride. We've come all the way from California, and our time is so limited. We have nothing like this at home, after all!"

"Oh, you *are* a smoothie!" Ellen murmured as they walked past, putting her arm through his. "You didn't even have to spread any more cash around. Unless you were just telling them we aren't the droids they are looking for?"

"No, no Wreaking. And while you can bribe some Austrians, it would be very risky to try it on a petty scale, openly and in a mixed group. Too much *ordnungsliebe*, even this far south and east."

He turned his head to Eric; unless someone was using a directional microphone on them they had plenty of privacy. And, of course, Adrian could fry any such electronics. The crowd had thinned out, even before they left the Prater itself.

"What did you make of that conversation we had?"

Eric's scarred and battered features knotted in a scowl. "My initial expert response? Fucked if I know. For starters, I don't know French. This Apache guy does?"

"Shadowspawn are very old-fashioned—it is the formal language of diplomacy and high politics among us. Partly because so many of the post-corporeals are old enough that they grew up thinking that way, and partly because of the role the Brézés played in the original discoveries. And languages are easy for us. A week or two to acquire full native fluency, and the process doesn't require much conscious effort. You can force it down to an hour or two with a Wreaking."

Eric made brushing gesture. "Okay, so maybe it was better that I was focusing on his body language—and hers. Christ, that's creepy, that ventriloquist dummy thing they were doing. Now, granted, I only met this guy once and he was naked and trying to kill me, but he didn't give me the same . . . vibe then. If this was the first time I'd seen the guy I'd say he was a badass, right, but a lot less rough-hewn about it than my first impression back in Santa Fe if you know what I mean."

"You know, that's true," Ellen said thoughtfully. "And I did meet him a couple of times when I was Adrienne's lucy. I mean, this time he hardly gave me any of that *I want to rape you and torture you and kill you and drink the last gulp of your blood as you die* that I got before. He barely bothered to hide it then. Adrienne thought it was funny to dangle me in front of him like a steak in front of a mean dog."

"He would know that it would anger me, not amuse me," Adrian observed.

"Yeah. And it that could be because he was concentrating on business this time. The dynamic with Kai seems sort of different too; there was always a lot of terror there, but it was a . . . comfortable terror, if you know what I mean. Something's happened to Dale."

Adrian made a thoughtful sound. "His shields were like diamond plating on steel. His aura revealed absolutely nothing; but then, that is his reputation. He made his name as an assassin of other Shadowspawn, and would have to be exceptionally good at concealment of all types."

"I'm going to circulate a bit among the other humans attending," Eric said. "Something doesn't *smell* right here."

CHAPTER FIFTEEN

Vienna

"**W**hy do Shadowspawn have funerals?" Eric asked Adrian Brézé, just after sunset a day later. "I mean, for starters there's no body, not with the old ones like him."

He was more or less getting used to the nocturnal sleep cycle; it seemed to be easier for him than it was for Peter or Cheba. Of course, according to the Albermann test he had more of the *H. nocturnis* genes than the average, though not all that much more. That might account for it.

He preferred to think of it as just being adaptable.

"After the first death, the death of the body, it's quite common to have a party," Adrian said seriously. "Often both the killer and the victim will attend."

"You're kidding, right?"

Ellen shook her head sadly.

"*Mierda*," he said. "And anyway, there isn't much question about the afterlife, either. I mean, they *get* one, but then it ends."

Cheba smiled an unpleasant smile. "Maybe. Maybe not. Maybe there is a hell for them, after this spirit form is killed."

"I certainly hope so," Peter said. "And I'm speaking as a guy who decided there was no Santa Claus when he was four years old."

The limousine wasn't particularly large by American standards, but it was still having problems negotiating the narrow streets. They were a bit winding, too, and fewer of the buildings were what he'd come to consider Viennese-looking, which was to say fewer of them were symmetrical and stuccoed with a lot of flamboyant ornament. A few had half timbering like that little village where they had been snowed in; more were brick or stone in irregular masses, here an overhang, there a pointed arch. Then Ellen saw him frowning a little out of the window.

"This is the old part of town," she said. "Old by local standards, that is. Richard the Lion-Heart was held prisoner not far from here."

"Yes," Adrian said grimly. "And it has been a . . . meeting place of sorts . . . For a long time too. Not quite that long, but for many generations."

The car stopped, let them out, and drove away. A flicker of curiosity passed through Eric's mind; what had the driver thought of it all? He looked around the . . . he supposed you'd have to call it a church. It certainly had the same form as a church, Austrian Baroque Catholic variety, and a lingering smell of incense. He was willing to bet that it *had* been one a long time ago. It was full of formally dressed Shadowspawn in suits or robes for various weird costumes, something like a couple of hundred of the most powerful adepts on earth.

Nearly all of them would be delighted to kill him in some hideous fashion, but at least he wasn't running away from them through the snow with wolf-form fangs inches from his ass and a civilian, a girl and two kids to look after and him sick into the bargain. It was a lot easier to view the enemy objectively now that he wasn't on his own; not that Peter and Cheba and even Leon and Leila hadn't done their part. You didn't feel nearly as much like a rabbit at a coyote party when there was a friendly adept around.

So seeing Adrian Brézé again had been pure deep relief. Eric was reasonably satisfied with the way he had coped on his own; after all, he was still alive and so were those he was supposed to be looking out for. It had still been far too damned close for comfort. And he and Cheba were feeling fine physically now, thanks to that same friendly adept.

"And funerals in church?" he went on.

He remembered Rancho Sangre, the Brézé estate in California. That had a church, or what had once been a church . . . And lavishly built in the same neo-Spanish fashion as the rest of the place, what he privately thought of as the Zorro Revival style. It hadn't been used as a church for a very long time, if ever. The sign outside said it was a community the-ater. From his brief spell undercover masquerading as a renfield button-man for an allied family of Shadowspawn . . . well, they certainly put on performances there. Not exactly Shakespeare in the park, though.

The Council weren't actually Satanists anymore. On the other hand, they hadn't forgotten their roots either. They kept a lot of the ambience and trappings.

"This is a church," Adrian said. "But not to the Christian God, that's merely camouflage."

Ellen nodded, her face stark behind the net veil attached to a little round black hat. "It's only a century or so since they started surviving death," she said. "Before that, they were just people—bad, murderous people with psychic powers."

"And take a gander at some of the details," Peter said grimly; he'd been looking closely. "This . . . this so-called church . . . Maybe it was a church once . . . isn't what it looks like at first glance."

At first glance it looked like a typically gaudy example of Counter–Reformation Baroque, Austrian-style. The exterior had a turreted dome flanked by two towers, all white and yellow stone; that looked positively restrained when you walked into the interior, a blaze of gilt stucco, porphyry columns, colored marbles in every shade from cream to Imperial purple, and contorted murals done in the style of El Greco, only plump and pink to match the carved plaster.

Then you saw what the murals and statuary actually portrayed. Eric felt an impulse to clap his hands over the children's eyes, followed by one to squeeze his own shut.

I've seen a real lot of really bad shit, he thought. *Even more as a cop than I did in the Suck. That . . . that's just plain . . . nasty.*

Beside him Cheba gave a sharp intake of breath—he suspected the sight was even worse for her, given her time at Rancho Sangre. Even though she probably wasn't all that religious, the blasphemy would hit the small-town Mexican girl a lot harder, though the obscenity and cruelty were bad enough.

Ushers in formal pearl-gray suits with black carnations in their buttonholes showed them to their seats; thankfully Adrian had a block to himself, so his retainers didn't have to rub elbows with those of the other Brézé lines. From the glances he was getting out of the corners of their eyes, the feeling was entirely mutual. He leaned forward to whisper in Adrian's ear, but the other man forestalled him:

"No, we won't have to stay for long. It is necessary that we put in an appearance. Take the opportunity to familiarize yourself with the players."

He did, including Dale Shadowblade, who was sitting on the other side of the aisle not far from Adrienne's party. He kept his face impassive, but he could feel an involuntary bristling at the sight of that slab-sided, high-cheeked, hook-nosed countenance.

So is he going to deliver, or was that all some sort of elaborate set up?

The memory of that face snarling at him, the outstretched clawed hand, an impalpable blow like a ripsaw of pure malevolence made tangible . . .

And I blasted some silver shot into him, or at least sort of into him because he was only sorta-kinda of there. And he's an Apache pretty much, not one of these old-school stiff upper lip Euro types. Odd that he's not paying me more attention.

Étienne-Maurice Brézé took the lectern, dressed in a black silk robe picked out in crimson embroidery at the cuffs and hems and neck. A roll of organ music sounded through the big church, a sprightly mocking tune before he began:

"My brother Arnaud Brézé was one of us," the master of the Council said. "A vampire, a werewolf, a malignant sorcerer, cruel and murderous . . . and stylish. His body of the flesh perished many years ago, and he became entirely a creature of darkness, among the first generation to survive the body's loss since the first Empire of Shadow ten thousand years ago and more. Now his aetheric form has perished as well. Just as one might expect, his death came at the most inconvenient possible moment and has cost and will cost us all a great deal of trouble. Would he have wished it any other way?"

Laughter ran through the church, the merriment of devils, and Eric shivered slightly. The thing that had once been almost a man went on:

"Let me begin my tribute to my kinsman with an anecdote. When my brother and I were torturing our father to death—ah, the lost merry times of youth—"

Eric tuned out the speech and studied the faces instead, as closely as he could without being utterly obvious. Adrienne Brézé had a pleasant social smile on her face, but he could see her eyes flicker once or twice towards Dale Shadowblade as if puzzled. Slightly puzzled, more than a little angry.

He jolted back to awareness as the cool irony in Étienne-Maurice's voice change to something much flatter and more matter of fact. The tiny hairs under his collar bristled a little.

"—But this leaves the matter of killing a Brézé while under my protection. This constitutes *disrespect*, and I am . . . annoyed."

Those blank yellow eyes him came to rest on Adrian. There was a small quiet rustle as many more joined them. Eric made himself aware of the location of all his weapons, sat very still, and for the first time in several decades actually prayed. It was easier, somehow, in this obscenely desecrated place.

Adrian came easily to his feet, the fingers of both hands resting lightly on the back of the pew in front of him. He inclined his head slightly, then spoke:

"The matter is simple: Adrienne Brézé ordered her follower Dale Shadowblade, well known to you as a killer of our kind, to kill Arnaud. This I heard from his own lips yesterday. I will now drop my shields long enough for you to know that I speak the truth."

The plan had been for him to do that in a flash and then get them back up again before anyone could do anything seriously manky. Adrian looked intense for a moment, staggered, then swore in some language Eric didn't recognize and put his hand to his head. Ellen put her hand on his arm, then turned and nodded slightly to the others with a small tight smile.

Stage one, Eric thought. *And—*

Dale Shadowblade leapt to his feet. "It's true!" he shouted. "And she plans to kill you all!"

The not-really-a-church erupted in a chorus of screams and shouts and howls; some of them were quite literal howls or shrieks as the night-walkers and post-corporeals reflexively changed as they scented danger and animal instinct overrode muffled intelligence. Hands—and in several cases, claws—reached for the Council's assassin. He seized Kai, pitched her slight form at the nearest assailant and bolted out the door.

"Seize him! *Alive!*" Étienne-Maurice shouted.

Shadowspawn might not know much about discipline or organization, but they got fear and domination down like a treat. Even so, Adrian was in the first wave after the fleeing man. Something huge and furry raised a paw to smash Kai down, some sort of weird cat striped and spotted at the same time and the size of a horse, but Ellen stepped forward and swept her behind herself to tumble into the pew, then skipped backward brandishing her curved silvered knife to discourage any random violence. Cheba and Peter had their weapons drawn as well, and the Mexican girl shoved the children down as they tried to stand on the seat and crane their necks to see the action.

"What the fuck was *that* son of a whore!" Eric blurted.

"Liger," Peter said, holding his coach gun in both hands. "Lion-tiger hybrid, biggest cats in the world, they grow over a thousand pounds—"

"Later!"

That was a God damned rhetorical question, professor!

Eric had been told what his part was, and he'd studied the ground, both maps and Google Earth. Running out into a night full of man-eating monsters with their blood up was still one of the harder things he'd ever done, but he did it. And the renfields could kill you just as dead, which meant he had to keep an eye out for the human servants as well. It was deep dark once he was past the lights of the "church," and the streets were narrow and twisty. It was a good thing that he had a lot of experience in making the map in his head correspond to the real terrain.

"This way!" he heard Adrian's voice call the Wild Hunt that had boiled out of the building with fangs bared and fur bristling.

And he could *feel* the same thing, like a compass pointing in his head combined with a snarling eagerness for blood. Some part of him— one that wasn't counting turns and jogging carefully down slippery cobblestones—was uneasily conscious that this must be the way the wolf pack had felt as they chased him and the others through the snowy woods. The bestial snarling reinforced the impression, except that this time he was running *with* the pack, more or less, even if for purposes of misdirection.

It was a profoundly disquieting sensation, and he felt sorry for any bystander who got in the way. Or even for anyone who observed it, not least because no one would ever believe them and they would probably go nuts thinking about it. Somewhere a faint hint of zither music from some busker died with a scream and a crash of splintering wood.

A manhole cover clanged down. *Cutting it close,* he thought. Something flashed down out of the night, a huge shaggy-crested white-breasted eagle of a type he'd never seen before. There was a glimmer as it dove through the iron disk, turning impalpable for a critical fraction of a second. That was apparently a bravura display of night-walker skill; the Shadowspawn in bird form would have to turn palpable again *really quickly* to avoid a fatal plunge into the solid fabric of the earth beneath the tunnel's floor. Transitioning back to human form, or some favorite four-footed attack machine, in the fractional second before their momentum carried them across the height of the tunnel.

Whoever it was carried the trick off, but it didn't seem to help much. There was a shot from below, a racking animal screech and then two more discharges echoing away underfoot. Then dead silence. He drew his own coach gun, levered up the manhole cover with his left hand and dropped through. It wasn't much of a drop, particularly since he wasn't overburdened with gear, and he landed with flexed knees in something wet and truly unpleasant. There was a low reddish glow from caged utility lights at inconveniently long intervals, brighter pools fading into shadow. The stench was stunning, but there was enough adrenaline in his system that it didn't bother him.

He trotted forward. The sewer was an arched tunnel, with smaller openings feeding into it on either side, each contributing its loathsome flow. Suddenly Adrian was trotting up beside him, and farther back a yammering broke out—human shouts and whoops horribly mixed with wolf-howl, tiger-snarl and a grunting boom he'd heard only once before, on a training exercise in northern Australia.

"Saltie," he said.

"*Crocodylus porosus,*" Adrian said, with specificity worthy of Peter Boase.

Not very long ago according to an Aussie he'd met in a bar in Darwin, a saltwater crocodile weighing about two tons had bitten an eighteen-foot section of teak decking from the side of a yacht in the Coral Sea. It was just the sort of thing you wanted to meet in the sewer.

"This is going to take careful timing," Adrian said.

"Doesn't it always?" Eric replied.

They weren't exactly friends, and he didn't know if they ever would be. Technically speaking they weren't even of the same species, or subspecies, and he strongly suspected that he'd find some parts of Adrian's life rather squicky. At that moment, though they were operating on exactly the same wavelength.

The sewer was sort of a flattened egg shape with the point upwards; Adrian broke left and he went right, both of them splashing through the shallower portion. Eric bared his teeth. *His* part in this would actually be more difficult than fighting. A glimpse of movement ahead, and he pushed forward at a run, waving Adrian back with his left hand. Through a dark patch, and then into another pool of dingy red light. Another flicker of movement, and this time it was a man in soiled evening dress, standing with his right foot advanced and his left arm tucked into the small of his back. The right was lowering the pistol into a formal range-style aim, and behind the muzzle broad brown face split into an exceedingly nasty smile.

It would be just like the son of several bitches to aim for his face. Best to shoot soon, before curse-wreaking bollixed even the Stone Age excuse for a weapon.

The coach gun bucked in his hand and pellets whipped the foul water to froth and scored runnels in the mold on brick and concrete. A flash and a flat elastic *bang*, and something overwhelming punched him in the gut. He made a strangled sound somewhere between pain and *ooof!*

"He is mine!" Adrian Brézé shouted, his voice high and harsh.

A great black wolf with yellow eyes rose from the boiling ruck of men and monsters. It blurred, and became the semblance of a man. Étienne-

Maurice stood naked, only the eyes the same, flinging out both arms with the hands backward.

"Hunt!" he shouted at his great-grandson.

The living Brézé went forward, around a gradual curve. He aimed and shot with the same fluid sureness. A degree of silence fell, breaking into another predator babble as he returned dragging the body by one ankle, much of its weight supported in the filthy flow down the center of the sewer. His great-grandfather stepped forward and touched the still warm flesh.

"It would've been far more elegant, not to mention more entertaining, to take him alive," he said dryly. "As I ordered, and so that information not be lost."

"I'm sorry not to fulfill your order, sire," Adrian said politely. "But I was concerned that he might flee in nightwalking form if I hesitated even an instant."

"Ah, yes," the Lord of the Council said. "That odd hesitation to lose the body of flesh, as if the garment mattered."

He straightened and spoke to carry: "I sense from the dying mind the chaos of death. The aetheric form born of this body is no more; there has been a Final Death."

Adrian moved aside, and flicked a kick at the nose of a leopard that was sniffing at Eric Salvador's form. He went to one knee and pulled the man's arm over his shoulder, bracing himself to help lift the solid muscular weight.

"Armor stopped it," the New Mexican wheezed. "Hurts like fuck, though."

As he spoke the horde of Shadowspawn in their varied forms parted for the great thirty-foot, four-ton bulk of the saltwater crocodile to flow endlessly forward, half submerged. There was a surge that sent the dark water curling up the sides of the sewer, and the cavern jaws closed on the body. A flick of the great sculling tail sent droplets spattering and the reptile vanished into the darkness with its prey.

"Just keep walking, Monica," Adrienne said.

She did, struggling to control her breathing. For one moment and one long cold considering look like a strip of ice laid on the inside of her breastbone she'd thought that the *Doña* was going to leave her there in the ongoing riot. Most of the crowd in the church . . . sort of a church, and her mind stuttered as it refused to process images . . . had bolted out after the fleeing Dale Shadowblade. Many of the rest were either cringing back against the walls, walking out *through* the walls, or arguing with each other. A few had collapsed to the ground and were hugging themselves and shivering; those would be the lucies and pets.

I know how they feel, Monica thought.

She felt another rush of liquid-loose-in-the-lower-belly fear too as Adrienne halted near her brother's pew. The folk there tensed, and their hands went to weapons—all except the children, whose faces blossomed with smiles.

"'Allo, *Maman*," Leila said, waving. "Have you come to take us back? 'Allo, Monica! Tell Josh and Sophia 'allo from us!"

"We have been having a lot of fun, but we miss you," Leon added. "And the dog. Papa is busy a lot of the time."

"Not yet, my darling little weasels," she said. "I've just come to pick up something for a friend."

Her hand darted out in a blur of speed, latched onto Kai's collar and wrenched her out from where she cowered on the floor between pews, casting the slight form into the aisle in front of them with a casual and astonishing display of strength. She dodged Ellen's knife with almost contemptuous ease.

The young woman landed with a thump and then an *ooof!* of expelled breath. Peter made an abortive lunge, but Cheba pulled him back. She had a little gun in her hand, the silvered barrels glinting between her fingers.

"No!" she said sharply. "Guard *los niños!*"

"Excellent tactics, my little chocolate drop of delight," Adrienne chuckled. "I'll be seeing much more of you later, and you too, my svelte blond boy toy."

She blew Cheba a mocking air kiss, twiddled her fingers at Peter, then turned and kicked Kai with vicious precision just as she started to get up. Monica winced a little in sympathy; she knew *exactly* how that felt, especially when it took you by surprise rather than as part of a scenario.

And this was far too chaotic for play. Even with most of the crowd gone, the church still resounded with snarls, howls and shrieks of pain interspersed with babbling and pleading. Some of the Shadowspawn were fighting, or just attacking in reflex, with instant hungry malice; Monica averted her eyes from some of the things going on in the pews and on the floor. That could've been *her*. They walked quickly, Adrienne leading and pushing Kai ahead of her in an agonizing arm lock.

A few cold-eyed renfields looked at her, then flicked their eyes aside. They'd be the ones in charge of guarding their masters' possessions. One yellow-eyed nightwalker with a black silk top hat gave a snarling hiss and reached for Monica. Adrienne pivoted on one heel and thrust out her free fist, the little finger extended. She spat something in Mhabrogast and dark light seemed to explode behind Monica's eyes. When it cleared the elegant Edwardian clothes lay vacant across the marble and polished wood, and a rat scuttled for the walls.

Adrienne snickered and gestured, and the rat gave a despairing squeal as its fur caught on fire. Flame and the hard stench of burning hair all vanished as it plunged into the stone of the wall, leaving a blackened spot on the plaster.

"Don't run, Monica. It's undignified, and also it is so *stimulating*. Later, and not in public."

She forced herself not to dash; Adrienne was already bright-eyed in a way that told how true her words were, and the last thing she wanted to do was start a stampede in her direction. Then they were outside in the chill damp. A car pulled up, but not the one they had arrived in. It was a Mercedes S600 limousine, looming in the narrow street like a sleek black yacht. The driver popped out and held the rear-opening door open; he was dressed in something halfway between a chauffeur's outfit and a ninja costume, smiling very slightly beneath the mirrorshade glasses that she knew were also night goggles. It was David Cheung, one of Adrienne's renfields Monica liked even less than she did most of them, but an inexpressible relief now. So was the light machine pistol in his right hand, and the way he scanned the ground behind them.

Monica abandoned her brisk stride and dove, tumbling into the back compartment in a headfirst plunge that might have hurt if the interior hadn't been so luxuriously padded, panting in sheer relief. Adrienne threw Kai in and swung in after, seating herself with her usual slinking grace. She kicked off one shoe and pressed the foot between Monica's shoulder blades, pushing her into the thousand-knot Turfan carpet that covered the limousine's floor as the door swung shut with an almost inaudible but very solid chunking sound.

"Just relax down there for now, *chérie*," she said. "I need the room up here to deal with our guest, and it will be a little while before your talents are called for."

Kai scrambled away and crouched against the opposite door, her eyes huge and her hand fumbling with the lock despite the obvious futility of it. The limousine didn't have anything as plebeian as seats; the rear was a U-shaped set of couches upholstered in buttery off-white kidskin, like the fantail of a yacht, with a scattering of throw-pillows.

"Dale won't let you kill me," she said, her voice a thin reedy whisper.

"You flatter yourself, little snack," Adrienne said.

Monica couldn't see her Shadowspawn from where she lay on the floor, but she knew that steel and velvet tone of voice. It made her shiver, and her skin roughen all over, but that was familiar and welcome in its way.

"But in any case, we need to have a little talk before we consider such ultimate pleasures as your death. Why, we've hardly gotten to know each other at all! First, let's disorganize your mind a bit. It makes dealing with those tiresome Wreakings easier. Hmmm . . . pain, I think. Lots and lots of pain."

To the air: "And yes, David, you can watch over the monitor. Am I not the very model of a sensitive and caring employer? But I will be very annoyed if there are any traffic accidents; remember to multitask. I really do wish to be in Istanbul shortly."

Then she sprang. There was a tumbling thrash of limbs, human cursing and the shrill *nocturnis* snarl, and then a despairing wail. When the motion ceased, Adrienne had the girl in a feeding lock, one leg behind the small of her back, the other hooked across her knees and both wrists in her left hand. Her right clamped the victim's jaw and bent it back until the neck was a tight arch.

Monica smiled, relaxing and sighing, propping up her head on one elbow. They were out of danger, and . . .

Ooooh, but that looks sexy, she thought, touching her tongue to her upper lip. *Really, really hot.*

And it made her remember that first terrifying time when she hadn't known what was going on. She still had bad dreams about it, but most of the time it was as if it had happened to somebody else, that lost house-wife from Simi Valley whose car had broken down south of San Luis Obispo. That was before she'd realized what a turn-on fear could be, of course. Her own, that is.

I was so inexperienced and naive then, of course. I still usually don't like watching this side of things when it's not me on the receiving end, but I'm going to make an exception for you, Kai.

It was what human beings like them were for, after all, as mice were for cats. And she had never liked Kai, who had always put on airs be-cause she had a small dose of the Power. And Dale Shadowblade was frankly terrifying, but not in a *good* way like the *Doña*, and Kai had been his assistant as well as victim. Generally speaking she didn't find other people's fear all that stimulating, but the girl was making a lot of fuss about nothing anyway. Probably.

And it feels really sexy too, being held like that, after the first couple of times. Come on, you little bitch, you're no blood virgin, and it's better than you deserve.

Adrienne chuckled again and whispered in Kai's ear, "Did Dale ever tell you that if you're habituated to a single Shadowspawn's feeding for a long time and then get bitten by another the pain is *almost* as intense as the pleasure for a while? This is *really* going to hurt and then you'll beg for more."

"Please, please!"

"Is that please *yes*, please *no*, or both . . . ? Name of a dog, but I am vile! Also more of a Californian than I thought—making out in the back seat of the car . . . Now scream for me, you little minx."

The tip of her tongue traced the taut skin, and then her head moved with the swift predatory grace of the feeding bite like the final pounce of a cat on a mouse it'd been toying with. Monica winced and stuck her thumbs in her ears at the earsplitting shriek of raw agony; it had to be even louder for the Shadowspawn, and they had such sensitive ears, but Adrienne was smiling as a trickle of blood dripped past her working lips. She really appreciated a good heartfelt scream.

Kai's body arched in a galvanic spasm, then slumped. Released, her hands went trembling to the Shadowspawn's shoulders.

"Hurts . . . don't stop . . . *hurts* . . ."

After a while Adrienne lifted her mouth, panting a little, with a thread string of blood dangling from one corner until she licked it up.

"Tasty! Now open your mind," she crooned.

She licked the neck clean—something in the saliva made a feeding bite clot with unnatural speed and guarded against infection—and shifted until she was facing her victim, forehead to forehead. There was a sharp vinegary scent of sweat and fluids as Kai sobbed and clenched arms and legs around Adrienne.

"That's right, spread wide inside . . . oh, this is a well-traveled path . . . tsk, Dale, that's a clumsy set of Wreakings, undo *here* . . . give in, give in, right to the core, that's right . . . What's that? You actually said *I wouldn't touch her twat with a Taser?* So naughty, isn't it, Monica? Mmmm . . . now, let's run through what Dale's done since that little job on the train . . ."

Having your memories riffled like that set up an intolerable inward itching; it also gave you this *suffused* feeling of being filled beyond your capacity like tissues just before they tore. Plus it was really humiliating . . . which could be a lot of fun in an odd fashion once you were used to it and put your mind to cultivating the right attitude.

Like an inner equivalent of the crawling and foot-licking, and that's re-

ally satisfying, she thought. *Kai probably* is *well experienced that way, though this is all rather* abrupt.

"Your brother did *what* to you when you were twelve?" Adrienne laughed. "Oh, my, that's entertaining—but do let us concentrate on business, don't just free-associate . . ."

After a few moments of silence: "Dale must have *learned* something from Great-uncle Arnaud when he killed him; he definitely seems to have changed his behavior after that. A pity he didn't tell you what it was that he learned, precisely. Perhaps he soul-captured Arnaud for a really prolonged, enjoyable interrogation internally? Dangerous . . . but Dale always was excessively non-risk-averse. *Vraiment,* it is a puzzle . . ."

Kai flopped backward when the Shadowspawn broke the link, mouth working and tears leaking down her cheeks as she covered her face with her hands. Adrienne rubbed her hands and looked around:

"Now, we do have a Taser here somewhere, do we not? Let us literalize the metaphor! And when we reach the manor we're stopping at, you can show David some appropriate gratitude, Kai. He is growing quite excited, and it would be cruel to deny him. Travel can be a broadening experience, don't you agree?"

CHAPTER SIXTEEN

Turkey

Harvey Ledbetter grunted and stretched as the engine noise stopped
and they stepped down into the open stained-concrete expanse of
the warehouse.

"The problem here is that we can hide the . . . package . . . from the
Power but it's going to be a bit harder to hide it from the fuckin' Turkish
police. Who have prob'ly been put on the QT by the Council's puppets.
And we don't want to put ourselves in the hospital with Wreakin' too
much to throw them off."

He didn't mention the other possibility; either collapsing with a burst
brain vessel, or going unpleasantly mad and having to be killed by your
friends.

"Adrian got the Brotherhood to drop some hints too," Farmer said. "He told us that before we went after you. No details, of course."

A sly grin. "After all, there was a remote possibility you might turn us."

"Not hard to slip information in as from the CIA or some other nefarious source," Anjali said judiciously. "Terrorists with nuclear weapons make people nervous, oh yes indeed."

They walked through the dimness to the front of the building and its magnificent view of a blank brick wall across the street. Bursa was one of the biggest cities in western Turkey. Mt. Uludağ towered over it to the south, and the hills around were forested; that and the parks and gardens around the mosques and palaces had given it the nickname of Green Bursa in the old days. The old days hadn't included a huge clutch of automobile and textile factories, or the run-down industrial district where they'd parked the bomb.

The corner office had dirty windows. It was also cold and smelled seedy, of ancient tobacco and machine oil and tired electronics and far-from-fresh socks.

For some reason this sort of neighborhood seemed a bit more depressing than the equivalents he'd grown up around, and God knew Texas had *depressing* in plenty. Even in the Hill Country of his birth where at least the background looked fairly good. Though that had been all right here, too, from what they'd seen coming in. The snow lay thick on the higher pines, and there were ski resorts where Europeans and the newly prosperous Turkish glitterati cavorted. Down here it was mostly just chilly rather than freezing.

They grew olive trees around the town, which meant you never got *really* cold weather. Not by Jack Farmer's standards, at least; Harvey and

Anjali disagreed. Even the discomfort had a certain instant-nostalgic charm now, though. When you didn't expect to live much longer . . .

Well, hell, most of the things I like doing can't be done when you're old, *and, Harvey, you are old for this job. And you never really were afraid of being dead, right? Afraid of dying, but that's only logical, as the Science Officer said.*

Harvey seated himself in the absent manager's swivel chair and put his feet up. "Okay, let's get logical here. We want to be hard to check up on. What's the easiest sort of marine traffic to check?"

Anjali and Farmer looked at each other. "Anything where there are computerized records," Farmer said.

"Which means all commercial cargo shipping through regular channels," Anjali said; computers were easy enough to fix with the Power, but there were so many of them and it left traces. "I am presuming you went overland for that reason?"

Harvey nodded. "Yeah. Shipping's a bottleneck. You two got it off that container ship in Europoort-Scheldt easy enough, because nobody with the Power was looking. But there are ways around that. What we need is a purchase, not a charter, and under the table," he said. "Something just big enough; the god damned thing—"

He avoided saying *nuke* or *bomb* most of the time, just basic field-craft.

Not being evasive or euphemistic, no sirree, not us.

"—only weighs a couple of tons, anyway. We want it shipped on something you'd look at and not think *cargo*. Something just big enough to have a hold that'll conceal it. "

The two agents looked at each other again. "You mean one of those tourist sail-cruising things, what're they called..." Farmer hesitated.

"Gulets," Anjali said.

"Yup." Harvey nodded. "They were mixed cargo boats before they took to ferrying two-ton, two-tone Teutons around to soak up raki and court skin cancer. Now, good old straightforward stealin's out. Nobody may notice a truck going missing if you're careful, but a ship, even a little one, that's a hog of a whole different bristle. We need to show a little more finesse this time."

"We are experts at finesse," Anjali said.

"As long as it involves kicking guys in the crotch," Farmer added. Then: "No! I was kidding!"

"Jack would put on weight if you did that," Harvey said. "And he'd get too meek and mild to be useful. Okay, you pick a gulet up in Bodrum and meet me in Istanbul."

"Why there?" Jack said. "It's out-of-the-way, and it'll take time."

"That's where they make 'em. Not as many ripples."

They both nodded; an adept sniffing along their trails would be more likely to spot a disruption if the thing they affected was unique rather than one among many.

"Both of us?" Anjali said. "You can manage the . . . package . . . alone from here?"

Harvey chuckled. "Darlin', I've been fifty-nine for a couple of years now and I ain't dead. Remember, no Wreaking unless you really have to. I'll see y'all in the city the city."

That was a joke of sorts; Istanbul was a Turkish corruption of *is tin polin*, which was what medieval Greek-speakers had called Constantinople. *The* city. Anjali got it and actually smiled slightly; Farmer just scowled and grunted, which was not much of a change. Harvey went on:

"There's what, fifteen million people thereabouts? Good place to hide."

"Where?" Anjali said. "It is, as you said, a somewhat large city."

"Karaköy, the docks."

"Address?" Farmer said.

"You don't need to know. Dock that sucker, and I'll be there. You won't be able to miss me; I'll be the man with the twenty-five kilotons. Then we load up and sail for Batumi. From there . . . almost home."

"Istanbul is an interesting city," Adrian said, looking out at the darkening streetscape. "It gives one perspective, the layers of history and the sense of time."

"Yeah, interesting when it doesn't have a nuke somewhere in it," Ellen said; they were fairly sure of that, at least. "That makes it . . . sort of more interesting than it should be. As in, it might turn into an overdone layer cake any second."

They were speaking English, which was a bit of a relief, though her French had improved vastly over the last year—which had been, subjectively, five or six. Even though she could switch to thinking in it with a mental effort, shifting back to her native language brought a subtle feeling of relief, like a pressure you didn't notice until it was gone.

She picked up one of the deep-fried *paçanga böreği* pastries from the plate between them and nibbled on it. The dough was flaky and dotted with sesame, the filling air-cured beef seasoned with cumin, fenugreek, garlic, and accompanied by hot paprika, carmelized onions and bell peppers. It had an almost carnal richness, and the proprietor of the little hole-in-the-wall restaurant with battered plastic furniture had beamed with pride as he set it and the bottles of Efes Pilsen beer down before them, roaring with laughter as Adrian said something in incomprehensible glottal Turkish.

The other customers were mostly local workingmen, and after some frankly curious stares were mostly noisily occupied with their own affairs, including loud games of cards and puffing away to add to the fug of tobacco smoke. The Karaköy District had once been the foreign quarter, Galata, on the north shore of the Golden Horn. It was overwhelmingly Turkish and Kurdish now and had been for generations, but from here you could see the outline of the Christea Turris, the ancient Genoese-built tower that dominated the skyline, like part of a castle in a storybook.

The area had some tourist traffic, but it was mostly workshops and business offices and shops that sold electronic parts, plumbing supplies and just about everything else. The red-light district was around here too, mostly staffed with Slavic types these days with additions from the more recent influx of Syrian refugees.

Ellen suspected that if she weren't sporting a wedding ring, what locals would consider respectable garb, and an obvious husband who they'd all assume from his looks and even more from his speech and cigarette was Turkish . . . then the atmosphere would be a lot less relaxing. For starters, there was only one other woman present, and she was thirty years older and worked here. Night was falling, along with the cold rain outside, and there was a steady grind and hum of traffic and clank and rattle from the fast trams on the Galata Bridge just to the west.

"The you-know-what adds a certain spice, eh?" Adrian said, probably leaving out the word *bomb* because nearly everyone in the world knew *that* much English. "If anything, that makes the city *more* fascinating. The glitter of transience . . ."

"You are insane," she replied. "Or male, which is much the same thing." She hauled her mind back to business. "Would Anjali Guha and Jack Farmer turn on you? They fought with you to get your children back. And we don't *know* that they have. They've just . . . disappeared."

Adrian lit another of his slim brown cigarettes, looking out. "They fought with me against Adrienne; their commitment to the struggle against the Council is absolute. With Harvey . . . It would depend on what he told them." He sighed. "You must understand . . . it is so easy for you humans to be good."

Ellen blinked, surprised. "It *is?*"

"Comparatively speaking. Guha and Farmer are like many in the Brotherhood . . . they have enough of the Shadowspawn genes to Wreak on a limited level, but not enough to feed, or nightwalk, or survive the body's death. But that means they still have many of the . . . the drives and motivations of Shadowspawn. Mingled with human, fighting it, sometimes twisting together to create things worse than either."

Ellen nodded, grimacing a little. From what she'd heard, that was what was likely to make the more unpleasant types of serial killers. The Stalins and Hitlers and Pol Pots, too. Monsters driven by appetites they could neither suppress nor really satisfy and usually didn't even understand themselves.

"My kind don't work well in hierarchical organizations, save at the top," Adrian said.

"So the Council is a complete feuding, squabbling chaotic mess that only accomplishes things because it has magical powers, and the Brotherhood is the same story only with slightly less chaos and less magic. Yeah, I know it's not really *magic* magic."

"Exactly. Have you noticed how many mad dictators prefer to work through the night and sleep late each day? And some good men such as Churchill, who had the same pattern and always went his own way and relied on intuition . . . Such cooperation as Shadowspawn show is largely the product of the human part of their heritage. Guha and Farmer . . . have made a *conscious decision* to be on the side they are. If Harvey can somehow convince them that his plan will *work* they might well turn again. If they believe that will advance the ends for which they fight, you see? But I had nobody else to send."

"And they and Harvey fought together, didn't they?"

"That too. We are capable of some bonds."

She turned and touched the backs of her fingers to his cheek for an instant. "Yeah, *you* are. The Brotherhood isn't giving you much support."

"The Brotherhood, what is left of it after generations of defeat, is busy preparing for Trimback Two. Thanks to you, they have the pattern for the vaccine. If they can preempt Adrienne with it . . . her plan can be turned on her . . . the whole nature of things revealed in the process. The inner circle of the Brotherhood are understandably . . . focused."

"Don't they *care* about a *nuclear bomb?*"

"Not as much as you would think," Adrian said grimly. "They are . . . they think of it as being commanders and generals in a long war against great evil."

Ellen remembered the Hôtel de Brézé, and the way the post-corporeals made their un-lives an endless psychopathic revenge against the living without even realizing their own motivations. Or for that matter, the way Shadowspawn like Adrienne reduced themselves to cartoons, willing stereotypes of wickedness.

"Well, yeah," she agreed . . . more or less. "I'll go with the *against great evil* part, yupper, no dispute."

"And commanders, they would say, must be prepared to make great sacrifices."

"The problem there is I come from a long line of people, like for example Polish peasants and Pennsylvania coal miners, who ended up on the receiving end of *necessary sacrifices.* Other people decided it was necessary, and we got sacrificed. Making a sacrifice is really pretty easy, when you're the one holding the knife."

"They think in terms of campaigns. Good men . . . or at least men on the side of good . . . burned Dresden to the ground and annihilated Nagasaki. Even if Adrienne somehow uses the bomb to destroy her Shadowspawn enemies, that makes so many the less of the powerful Council adepts—and makes it more likely that Brotherhood can turn the Trimback Two option on her. The lives of *billions* are at stake. And you have met my great-grandfather, and Adrienne. What do you think the world would be like when they are as they wish, demon-gods openly worshipped and feared?"

"Euuww. Complete and total euuuwness," she said . . . lightly, but with an underlying creeping feeling she knew he could sense.

"What is one small city to that?"

"That's . . . cold."

He smiled crookedly. "*I* am trying to prevent it. I have persuaded them to help. Though I have my doubts whether that was the right thing to do; and they doubt even more."

She clutched his hand fiercely. "You have doubts? Welcome to the club, you *are* human."

"Remember what I just said? Many of the uppermost in the Brotherhood *can* feed, do feed. Mostly on cold donated blood, which believe me is unspeakably unpleasant, and they *can* nightwalk. They are . . . lucky, and cunning and strong, and tend to survive where others die. Inevitable in a group where death is more common than life. And the life the survivors have is hard and dangerous and full of constant fear."

Ellen suddenly looked at him. "Adrian," she said. "If . . . let's say all this turns out well . . . wouldn't Shadowspawn tend to rise to the top, anyway? People with a lot of the genes, at least? I mean, we can't undo the knowledge that the capacities exist."

Adrian laughed. "What do you think has been happening through-

out history, my darling? Why *did* the heritage persist, given all the dis-
advantages it also carries? A tenth of Asia is descended from Genghis
Khan, the geneticists have found. The great sin of the Council . . . of the
Brézés . . . was to separate out the bloodlines. Let them be mingled."

"Eh?" he went on, and kissed her fingertips.

His phone played a snatch of Debussy. He brought it to his ear, listened, and his face became a motionless mask of cast iron.

"They have found it," he said. A crooked smile. "You will not stay
behind, *hein?*"

"What, and wait for the fireball to come find *me?* If it happens, I
want it to be quick, and with you."

"And with you," he said, dropping a note on the table.

"That too."

"My, but I spend a lot of my time in disused warehouses," Ellen said,
controlling her breathing.

That really did help . . . though just ignoring the fear as much as you
could was even better, treating it as something that happened outside
you and not worth much attention. A big part of learning to handle things
like this was realizing that fear just wasn't as important as you'd thought
before you experienced a lot of it. Though she suspected doing that was
something she'd have to pay for in the long run.

"Inside your head and in reality too," she went on lightly.

"An old warehouse or disused factory is the ideal if you need abun-
dant space that is inconspicuous," Adrian replied. "This group would
attract attention in a hotel."

"Unless you stuck a camera crew in a corner and pretended that this
band of hardcases was making Bond film twenty-nine."

The dozen Brotherhood operatives sitting and talking quietly or working on their kit were a mixed lot. There were eight men and four women: Europeans, Turks, two who looked as if they came from below the Sahara—the one with the ritual scars in particular—an a couple of East Asians and uncharacterizables. Half of them were smoking, too. If you had the Power, you could do that without worrying about the consequences. Getting cancer was a matter of bad *luck* . . .

They all wore clothes that were dark, rugged and practical without shouting *deadly supercommando secret society SWAT squad;* besides that, to anyone who saw them the only thing they all shared was ages ranging from early twenties to early middle age.

No, not quite the only thing.

They shared a hard-faced toughness, more a mental than a physical quality, though they had the tensile readiness that showed they were at home with violence too. They had a weird collection of weapons, tailored for the sort of thing they usually did. Nothing automatic, nothing complex except for one futuristic-looking and very massive sniper rifle; the firearms were simple cut-down break-open shotguns with twin barrels or those even more cut down coach gun things or revolvers, along with plenty of blades of various types and a couple of crossbows and martial-arts-style thingies. The silver plating on the blades and silver-jacketed ammunition wouldn't be necessary for Harvey Ledbetter, or Farmer and Anjali if they'd gone over to their old boss, but they'd work just as well as naked steel and lead, and it was what they were used to.

She checked her own gear; revolver and a couple of knives, and there was a Kevlar lining to her bush jacket, light silver mesh here and there, and various harmless looking objects that were actually amulets with embedded Wreakings. She wouldn't need the silver, none of the people they were going after could nightwalk, but the amulets might well come in useful. All three of them could Wreak on a level that made them nightmares to a human normal like her.

Couple of tabs of valium would be welcome too, but we'll have a stiff brandy and a quiet cuddle afterwards instead, and Adrian can have a sip of blood, which is really *soothing . . . for both of us. Christ, Harvey, why did you have to do this? I like* you *and you saved my life. Also you're too smart and tough for comfort if you're not on my side.*

Then she went over the plans again; the target was yet another old building, one dating from the 1930s and an early example of Bauhaus Industrial with a flat roof.

"Ah, it looks as if things are about to move," Adrian said with satisfaction.

Two newcomers walked in, and they *were* past middle age, though slim and vibrantly fit. One was a man who had the tell-tale yellow flecks in dark eyes that often showed up with a heavy dose of Shadowspawn blood; very much like Adrian's, in fact. The woman's eyes were pale blue and her white hair cut to a cap of curls, but she gave off the same subliminal crackling sensation Ellen had come to associate with adepts. The genes for appearance weren't very closely linked to the ones that controlled the Power.

"We've located the device . . . or at least, we've located the place Harvey Ledbetter has been using and we cannot locate the device with the Power," she said, in a crisp British accent with an overtone of something else. "Which is itself a valuable clue."

Nobody's using their *names,* Ellen noticed; though the team had introduced themselves. *Paranoid, what?*

"Is there going to be interference from the Council?" one of the grunts said.

Adrian cleared his throat. "Probably not, this time," he said. "That is the most I can say. The factions there are like a knot of adders."

"What a surprise," someone muttered.

The looks Adrian got were almost as sidelong as they'd been at the Hôtel de Brézé or the church in Vienna. Her husband had always been an independent operator . . . or loose cannon . . . even by the standards of the Brotherhood's decentralized operations. Plus he had close family links with the enemy's upper echelons. And she suspected there was an element of sheer envy at his command of the Power.

"Ledbetter is an outlaw," the Brotherhood woman went on.

Brotherhood woman, Ellen thought mordantly. *They haven't bothered to make their terminology more inclusive, have they? Why am I not surprised? It's a different world in here. And once you're inside, nothing outside seems really real.*

The adept went on: "If Guha and Farmer are with him, they are too. Lethal sanction regardless of collateral damage is authorized. Don't hesitate; it doesn't take long to throw a switch."

Even his hard-bitten crew winced a little at that; she did herself. One little switch, or with this crowd just a flash of thought, and you became an ionized gas. She *hoped* Harvey wouldn't do that with so many civilians around . . . but then, she hadn't expected him to go rogue like this in the first place. Even Adrian hadn't, and he'd grown up around the Texan. It might be some subtle mental influence from Adrienne or one of her minions; yet another hellish thing about the Shadowspawn world was that you could never quite tell for certain whether *anyone's* mind was entirely their own. Mental compulsion could be extremely subtle, extraordinarily so, a matter of imperceptible nudges at the probabilities of individual decisions.

"What's our insertion?" another asked.

"Vertical."

"Helicopter?" the man said dubiously. "Noisy . . . and very complex."

Complex meant vulnerable.

"No, we've arranged something rather less noticeable," the man with the yellow-flecked eyes said. "Bless the tourist trade."

Adrienne frowned at Dale Shadowblade. "Why are you speaking French so often?" she said.

"Practice." He shrugged, keeping his face to where the sun had set before he arrived.

Adrienne returned the gesture at the man's back. Her ally had always been taciturn; playing up to the Apache Devil stereotype, perhaps.

"Do you want your toy back?" she said, nodded to where Kai huddled in a corner, hugging herself.

"I suppose so," he said. A smile: "You seem to have been educating her."

"There are times when roadside diners are just what suits the mood," she said with another shrug.

Kai scuttled over behind him with a lunge . . . but did not, Adrienne noted, touch.

"Thank you," Adrienne said absently as Monica handed everyone coffee and retired to the corner—she hated being around other Shadowspawn.

As well she might, Adrienne thought. *She has the most* appetizing *mind, like the aroma of fresh blueberry muffins.*

"It went well at the warehouse?" she said, sipping the coffee. "I was glad to have you ask for a written précis of the plan."

Which you usually don't, she added: Dale was a loner and arrogant even by the standards of her species. *But worth the trouble to cultivate. Arnaud . . . Arnaud could have been a problem. And when a person causes you problems, remember: no person, no problem.*

Dale shrugged again. "There is no point in taking chances. I do not think this Brotherhood rogue will notice that his plan worked . . . that is, he will think it was all by his own efforts that the local gendarmerie believed his tale of terrorists and smugglers."

"It ought to be entertaining to watch," Adrienne said. "Monica, the pastries."

"The consequences of Vienna have not been too . . . unfortunate?" Dale said.

"No, Great-grandfather was seriously annoyed with me, but I managed to convince him that you had exceeded your instructions, and I was suitably chastened by your Final Death; excellent bit of camouflage there, by the way. It is not easy to deceive a Brézé adept. Adrian is up, though there is suspicion because he apparently killed you before you could be questioned; I am down, but not irredeemably so, and court favor with the Council will shortly no longer matter much. If at all. How do you find post-corporeal existence?"

A shrug. "Much better than nonexistence," he said, and left.

Adrienne laughed. The hotel had an excellent view. The city glittered before her, the long curves of the Bosporus bridges bright to her night-adapted eyes. She grinned happily and nibbled a baklava as another set of lights began to drift across the sky, an airship running with its engines off.

There were few things so entertaining as watching an enemy make a mistake. And if you had subtly guided the enemy into that mistake . . . why, that was the honey glaze on the flaky pastry crust. Though . . .

"That was odd," she said.

"*Doña?*"

"Kai didn't make him angry."

"That you hurt her?" she asked, surprised.

"No, that I *touched* her; he would have been able to smell her blood in me, and me on her. We generally hate people touching our things unless we're very close, and I took some of his Wreakings out of her mind, which he would also be able to sense—now he'll have to spend hours looking for booby-traps. He should have thanked me for getting her out of the church, but done so resentfully. And snarled at *her*, that's why she was so charmingly torn between relief and fear when I turned her back over to him."

"That's not very logical, he *left* her there."

"Don't be dense, Monica, you're not stupid. What has logic to do with it? I am speaking of emotional patterns and you've been around Shadowspawn long enough to know what we're like."

"Well, you *are* all very territorial. About your lucies, particularly."

"Exactly. Instead he was indifferent, though to be sure he's a very self-controlled man. Hmmm. It should have needled him worse than if I'd killed her. Not that it's important, but still . . . Not that she's much of a prize. A little of the Power, yes, but not a really interesting personality. Much easier to corrupt than you, for example."

Stung, Monica protested: "I am *extremely* corrupt! Why, then-me would have absolutely hated now-me, if I could have seen me back then . . . you know what I mean?"

"Translated from Buffy-speak, yes."

"So I'm just . . . corrupt in a *nice* way."

"Fairly corrupt, not extremely, and I've been working on it for a decade. Evil I can do myself; perverting innocence is much more fun."

Monica beamed. "I feel really guilty about it sometimes. I know you like that."

"Very much. It tastes like paprika," she said, and propped her feet up a little higher. "Fetch me . . . no, popcorn! There's going to be a bit of a show."

"Ummm . . . I don't think we have any popcorn here."

"Oh, *merde*. Well, some brandy, then."

CHAPTER SEVENTEEN

Istanbul

The Zeppelin Company had long ago diversified into everything up to and including kitchenware, but since the turn of the century it had also taken to making airships again, mostly for the tourist trade. Ellen had even seen one during a holiday in San Francisco, taking a stately tour up the Napa Valley. They were midgets compared to the giants that had once bombed London and circumnavigated the globe right after World War One, but still nearly three hundred feet long; there were pivoting engines in pods, and the controls were all digital and fly-by-wire. Ellen knew that in fact it was gossamer-fragile and light, but instinct said it was a massive hulk hovering impossibly overhead.

It loomed like some great prehistoric night-creature over the roof, not like an aircraft at all. The buzzing throb of the engines died down to a low growl just sufficient to hold it in place, and a rope-ladder dropped from the gondola along with a grapnel cable. Someone tied that off. Adrian went up first and Ellen right behind him, glad that she'd always been athletic—she was a runner and tennis-player of considerable merit, and she'd learned more recondite skills since. Adrian moved like a leopard in the night, nearly running upward, and paused to give her a hand through the hatchway.

The seats had been removed inside the gondola, except for the pilot's; it was surprisingly small, after the huge bulk of the lifting body, no bigger inside than a minor commuter jet. Fourteen people crowded it, and she put an arm around the solid slimness of Adrian's waist as they both gripped handholds on the walls. It was always a bit of a shock when something reminded her that he was actually below average height. The air had an electric crackle, and that distinct fruity scent of Break Free gun oil, and very faint powder residues that apparently never entirely came out of clothing.

It's my imagination that I can smell the blood. I'm glad the Brotherhood approves of showers and soap and deodorant, she thought. *They can be sort of self-punishing at times.*

The cable slipped free. There was a curious rising-elevator sensation, and a rumble and splash as water ballast cut loose. The pilot chuckled.

"Never thought I'd get a chance to actually *do* this," he said.

In a thick Australian accent, what she thought of as a *roip* way of talking; he was a man in his thirties with a thick shock of yellow hair beneath the headset.

"Always thought the higher-ups were bonkers for putting me through fuckin' Hindenburg school, and here I am floating over to a bunch of clowns with fuckin' shooters and whizz bangs."

Adrian leaned forward. "Can you do a silent approach?"

"Come upwind and drift down?" A shrug. "I can try it. Tricky, though. All things considered I'd rather be back in Borroloola snogging the salties."

The big aircraft spiraled upward, and lines crawled over the screen's GPS unit. That looked patched in and clamped in an improvised mount; someone had liberated a military-grade model for this.

"Here we go," the pilot said, and cut the engines.

Silence fell, broken only by the whine and click of small electronic components. Lights and streets and buildings drifted by beneath, shockingly close; the hills north of the Golden Horn were coming up, and they were scarcely higher than the modest height of the tallest towers.

I wonder how they're handling the police and air traffic control, Ellen thought, the words drifting through the tension in her mind. *I wonder how many laws we're breaking?*

The thought was remote. That whole world, laws, regulations, the mechanisms of civil society, seemed so distant now. And more than remote—she was thoroughly enclosed now in the cystlike prison of the Council-Brotherhood War—but the real world seemed so unreal once you knew how the world really worked. A false front, a reassuring story told to children, a Potemkin village, a world pulled over the world's eyes. It was a profoundly unsettling thought, when you let yourself dwell on it, so most of the time she didn't.

Of course, so is the fact that you're floating in a balloon towards people who want to shoot you, she thought. Then: *Wait a minute . . .*

"This thing won't *burn*, will it?" she asked.

The pilot grinned without turning around, though there was little he could do while the zeppelin was free-floating at the same speed as the air that bore it up, with nothing for the control services to bite on. She could see his reflection in the glass of the gondola's windows ahead of him, ghostly and pale.

"No, don't worry about us doing a Hindenberg. It's helium in there"—he jerked a thumb upward—"not flammable. Skin's not doped with rocket fuel, either."

She blinked. "Rocket fuel?"

"Just a bit of an exaggeration. It was iron oxide and aluminum and cellulose acetate on the outside of the old Zeps, though. Burns a treat. This lady's all composites and synthetics, strong and fireproof. Mind you, it's all too thin to stop a bullet. Like riding in an empty beer can that way."

Adrian chuckled at that, as did most of the group. One—the tall thin black woman with the Yoruba teardrop scars below her eyes—glanced at Ellen and shrugged as if to say *what can you do?*

The pilot glanced at the screen, where high definition pictures flowed from the radar-laser scanners. A spot steadied on the roof of the building that was their target. "Coming up. I'll have to restart the engines to hold us over the roof, there's a bit of a breeze."

Adrian shook his head, an abstracted look in his yellow-flecked eyes. "No. I will go down on a line and secure it. You can winch the craft in after the assault group rappels down. Is everyone clear on that? Objections?"

Everyone looked at him then; even Ellen, though she knew he wasn't as reckless as he sounded sometimes. Because . . .

"You'd have to be dead lucky," the pilot said. Then: "Oh. You *are* dead lucky, right, sport?"

Adrian nodded. "Perhaps lucky enough. Then again, perhaps not, *hein?*"

That brought a chuckle; this time the scarred woman, whose name had been something like Abayomi, joined in. Ellen gave his arm a single brief squeeze as he knelt by the door and opened it, reaching around and down for the wire cable with its lock-loop on one end, casual about the hundreds of feet of open space below him. The light of the city poured in, but the breeze surprised by being gentle, if cold.

Because we're floating with the air, she realized. *At the same speed as the wind so we don't feel it.*

Below, a dark street crawled by, with pools of light where the streetlamps cast puddles that glittered where the beams struck standing water and damp pavement. The rain was still falling, turning the glitter of windows and cars beyond watery and shifting. With the hatch open she could hear the murmur and rumble of traffic, and the shushing white-noise sound of the rain itself on miles of rooftops and pavements and the tin-roof drumbeat on the zeppelin itself.

Adrian looked at her and nodded once as he snapped a hook to link the line to his body.

"Give me the word," he said crisply.

"Right," the pilot said tightly, his eyes moving between the GPS screen and the inward-slanting window ahead of his position. "Coming up . . . we're going to cross right over it."

"Just about . . . *now!*"

Adrian leapt into the darkness, trusting in qualities of mind and muscle and bone to stop at just the right moment where the moving line draped over the roof. Ellen's heart seemed to lurch in her chest, even before the weight coming on the line made the vast gossamer fabric of the airship bob and dip. Then there was a solid *yank*, a groan of protesting trusses, and the football-field bulk of the zeppelin swiveled in the air as the line turned its nose into the wind.

"We're solid," the pilot barked, and reached up for the emergency gas valve, yanking on it to balance the weight that would be leaving the airship. "As long as the bloody thing doesn't tear loose. Go, go, *go*!"

The Brotherhood troopers swung out; each hooked on, locked an arm and a leg around the cable that swooped out in a long curve into the night and slid away. Ellen had never actually done a rappel like this in reality, though some of the rock climbing had come close. In the dreamspace of Adrian's mind, yes, often, and in conditions far worse . . . and it would work just like real training, if she didn't think about it and paralyze herself.

Hubbie's waiting for me, she thought, and let her body act as it *thought* it had done a hundred times before.

A jerk as her weight came on one elbow, the hand on that arm locked under the other armpit, her ankles crossed on the cable below with the soles of her boots clamped on it to slow the descent and keep the cable from burning through the leather jacket. There was gear specifically for this, but they didn't have it and you didn't need it for a short drop . . . if you were strong and willing to take risks.

Rushing night, a flash of exhilaration, then dark shapes looming. She released about six feet up, landed and rolled on the asphalt surface of the rooftop, grunting slightly as she slammed into a ventilation duct. Luckily that was the corner—it hurt, but it didn't boom much. The black shape of the dirigible above them bobbed upwards, hauling the cable more nearly straight. There was a hiss of released gas, but the pilot didn't bring the airship down too far. They'd need to get back on board. She rolled back to her feet, felt an inner tickle that was Adrian checking on her—he'd installed a Wreaking to let her know when he did that, and another that could shut him out if she chose. Right now she hadn't the *slightest* desire to do that.

Someone pointed to the camera pickup over the central island that held the stairwell; the building was about three stories high, too little for an elevator.

Adrian made a gesture with thumb and forefinger, as if shooting it out: *I've taken care of it.*

The black woman knelt by the door. It had an access keypad and a biometric scanner, quite state-of-the-art, but Ellen had noticed that Istanbul had a full share of the mod-cons, which had rather surprised her. Turkey was apparently quite a modern country, at least this part of it. The Brotherhood operative reached out one slim-fingered hand and closed her eyes. There was a *click* and the door opened slightly as the deadbolts withdrew. Adrian paused, frowning.

There . . . are . . . human . . . traces . . . below . . . carefully . . . shielded, he *thought* at them all, the word/symbols freighted with meaning beyond their content—a cold wariness, alert and hard and quite merciless. **But . . . no . . . trace . . . of . . . Ledbetter . . . Guha . . . or . . . Farmer. They . . . have . . . been . . . here . . . but . . . I . . . cannot . . . be . . . certain . . . if . . . they . . . are . . . now.**

Everyone looked slightly surprised, as far as she could tell in the dark among a group so stone-faced. Of course, Adrian's sensitivity was far greater.

You . . . said . . . Ledbetter's . . . shielding . . . was . . . very . . . good, someone pointed out.

Ellen unconsciously rubbed at her forehead. She didn't like telepathy, even the somewhat distanced relay version Adrian could provide despite her lack of the genes that would let her do it herself. She liked the real thing even less—she'd experienced that in his mind, while he was soul-carrying her. It was too much like talking to someone by whispering in each other's ears during an embrace, naked. Nice with Adrian some-times. With people in general, no. Especially Shadowspawn people, who tended to get so obviously *hungry* around her.

Most of the time Adrian . . . well, his motto was *if you have a message, text it*. Adrienne felt the same way, oddly enough. Telepathy had low bandwidth, especially at a distance. But there were occasions when it was useful.

The building was three stories, but it had only one logical place to put something the size of the bomb. That was in the loading dock on the ground floor. One of the Brotherhood operatives secured the rooftop door with a wedge jammed in next to the hinge, and they went down the stairs in a very quiet rush; someone was always looking up the stair-well and someone down, and the second-story door was dealt with equally quietly.

I don't think I'll ever really love the Brotherhood, Ellen thought. *But I do respect them.*

"*Halt!*" someone shouted as they came out into the echoing spaces of the ground floor.

There was nothing but darkness, shadows and concrete pillars. She dove for cover behind one of them, ignoring the pain of landing elbows down on a hard surface. It took a moment before Ellen realized that she was hearing through her base-link with Adrian as well as through her ears. Their connection grew stronger under stress, and what she was get-ting now included his knowledge of Turkish.

"Halt or we will open fire! This is the gendarmerie and you will re-ceive no further warning!"

Oh, shit, she had time to think, before the roaring, stuttering, strob-ing flicker of an automatic weapon cast its jerky shadows. The deadly keening ping of ricochets sounded, all the more nerve-racking because the danger was so random. Seconds later there was a single, louder, bang and an inhuman shriek of agony. A round had misfired or ruptured and a chain of explosions had shattered the weapon and probably most of the man wielding it.

That was why Shadowspawn didn't use automatics when they fought each other, and the Brotherhood didn't carry them either. One of the adepts with her had lashed out with a preset Wreaking on reflex.

Grenades flew. More of the automatic weapons opened up, in panic: the police ambush hadn't been set with attack from above in mind. Generally terrorists didn't drop out of the sky on Zeppelins. . . .

A megaphone began to bellow something from outside. It cut off in a feedback squeal and then the big soft *whump* of gasoline going off in a rare fuel-air explosion. Ruddy light shone through a window, and screams sounded from the street. The volume of fire grew.

"No! Don't kill them!" Adrian shouted.

Her heart lurched as he stood erect and spread his arms wide; the lisping whine of Mhabrogast as he shouted made her want to clap her hands over her ears—even though she had a revolver in the right.

Lines of tracer swung towards him . . . and then stopped. The world *twisted* and men leapt to their feet. They were dressed in black helmets and body armor, their faces anonymous under their night vision masks. They all tore off their goggles and threw them away, as if they'd stopped working—or were showing them something different, different and intolerable.

One kept tearing at his face as if something was clinging there; only the leather gloves he wore prevented him from ripping it away. Another simply stood rocking back and forth, tears flowing from his eyes. Two more just ran, their screams echoing over the slap of their boot soles on the concrete.

"Secure them!" Adrian snapped. "They must have been decoyed here somehow. They're bystanders, not players!"

He moved forward, shouted another phrase in the *lingua demonica*, his voice utterly different—deep and harsh, but somehow also like the chittering of a rat the size of a wolf. Another police commando erupted out of a utility room, tearing off his earphones and batting at smoking spots on his uniform; the smell of scorching polyester was added to the medley of stinks. Behind him communications equipment shorted out in a spectacular barrage of yellow and red sparks and a crackle of burning plastic.

The Brotherhood commandos sprinted forward. They seemed to know exactly where the Turkish police were hiding, those who weren't stumbling blind or rolling on the floor as they fought with private de-mons. Mostly they just touched them, and the Turks lost interest or slumped unconscious. The less Power-endowed used hypodermics.

There was a bustle of action. "Clear!" one of the operatives said at last. "They're barricading the street outside, though. And the airship will have to leave. No amount of Wreaking can hide something that size for long."

Adrian nodded. "The bomb?"

"There's been no one here but the gendarmes for hours at least."

Adrian was snarling—literally—when she came up to his side, hol-stering her pistol, and then gasping with relief when he needed not hold the Wreakings in operation any longer. The snarl wasn't simply anger; she could feel the frustration and self-reproach. And even in the darkness he looked a little pale. Wreaking on that scale without time for prepara-tion would be draining even for an adept of Adrian's capacities. They needed a little privacy. Even when it didn't involve sex, she felt feeding was far too intimate to let anyone else watch if it could be helped.

"Remember what you said about Harvey," she said.

Some of the tension went out of him. There was even the faintest trace of amusement in his voice when he spoke:

"It is much easier to appreciate his dashing redneck savoir-faire when you're not on the receiving end."

"Sir," one of the Brotherhood operatives said. "This was under the windscreen wiper of one of the trucks. Old model, but a substantial semi-tractor. I get an impression that it came from the east—there's a residue that smells like that curse the Council put on the area."

The note read, *Sorry I couldn't show you and Ellen around Istanbul, but I've got Georgia on my mind.*

"Let me see this truck," Adrian said.

While he examined it, Ellen kept her back to him and her eyes busy. Despite the temptation; his face might have been a disreputable angel's when he concentrated that way, but it wouldn't do him any good to have her mooning over him and it *might* to have her watching his back. There was a long silence, broken only by the muffled sobbing of one of the Turkish SWAT team.

"They are expecting backup soon," one of the operatives said, after a few words with the crying policeman. "Even if you got their communications before they called an alarm."

Adrian sighed again. "And it would tickle Harvey's fancy no end to have us waste more time and more of the Power. This is the vehicle, there is no doubt about that."

One of the others placed her palms against it, and concentrated. "I feel absolutely nothing, she said dubiously. "No linkages, no trace of flexion in the world-lines beyond what you'd expect for one anonymous vehicle. It is . . . Just *there*."

Ellen couldn't resist the snicker that she mostly smothered. "Now you know what it's like being a normal," she said.

"That is the effect of the new . . . Technique," Adrian said; even here among Brotherhood loyalists he didn't say *machine*. "Even now that it has been removed. That portion of its existence has been, mmmm, *cut out* of its history as far as the Power is concerned."

He turned. "Deal with the gendarmes; get them out, implant short-term amnesia, and plant some suggestion of psychotropic gasses. After the Bangkok Strike, that will be credible enough. We should torch this truck, otherwise someone from the Council might notice. We cannot have them getting a hint of the Boase Effect."

One of the team nodded. "Sir, we have to evacuate as soon as we've done that. There are far too many of the enemy around, and they have the Turkish government under close control."

He nodded. "I and my companions will carry on the search. Back to the roof, the lot of you." Only Ellen heard him add: "For whatever good it will do."

"What about us?" she said, as the Brotherhood operatives withdrew; one of them was limping and swearing, though that was the limit of their injuries.

"Eric and the others are down by the docks. That was an excellent thought of his. Come, we can do some work along the way."

He walked over to the wounded Turks. One . . .

Ellen swallowed and let her eyes slide out of focus. "Is he dead?"

"Not quite, but beyond hope." Adrian went down on a knee and touched the man's forehead; the body went limp. "Help me with this one."

Fortunately the ambush team had all had the usual first-aid supplies with them. They did what they could and then Adrian levered the semi-conscious man upright. Ellen took an arm over her shoulder, her nostrils wrinkling with the smells of blood, scorched flesh and gear, and body wastes. They walked the man out. The street outside was the tail-end of chaos as policemen chivvied the last of the local civilians away; a medium-sized truck with official markings was still burning despite fire-extinguishers. An ambulance pulled away as she watched, and machine-pistols turned towards them.

Adrian pulled out ID from a pocket, held it up and snapped orders in Turkish. Ellen was close enough to see the look of relief on the nearest faces; paramedics ran forward with a gurney, and a squad rushed past the two Americans.

"What did you tell them? And how did you explain *me?*" she asked, as they walked past briskly; a police noncom went ahead of them, waving others aside.

He continued ahead as the pair turned left, down towards the Golden Horn to the south.

Adrian shrugged. "I told them I was a *Milli İstihbarat Teşkilatı* officer."

"What's *that?*"

"The Turkish equivalent of the CIA and the FBI, combined. It's a useful cover." He smiled bleakly. "Harvey taught me that one. It's appropriate, no? Let's see if the others have managed to blunder as badly as we and the Brotherhood."

Peter Boase held up the tablet, the screen glowing with high definition pictures of Harvey Ledbetter and his two presumed accomplices.

"*Have you seen these people?*" he asked, one of the half-dozen phrases of Turkish they had learned. Then: "*I don't speak Turkish. Yes or no, please?*"

Eric didn't speak Turkish either; he was good with languages, but no

Shadowspawn to pick them up in a few days. He did, however, have a knack for telling whether people were lying or not. He was also usefully intimidating, scowling with his hands in the pockets of his overcoat, the scabs and bruises on his face adding a little gravitas. All that helped, but trying to do detective work in a place where you didn't speak the language and didn't even have some interpreter sweating by your side was still a nightmare.

"No," the Turk growled, and started to push past Peter into what might be the entrance of a rooming house, or some really cheap apartments. "I have not seen them."

"Yes, you did, my friend," Eric said. "Didn't your mama ever tell you that lying was a sin?"

As he spoke he put his left arm on the door frame, barring the local's way. With the same motion he brought his right hand up and fanned out a crisp spray of bills with a gesture like a stage magician's.

He hadn't done that before because money was like a gun. Which meant it wasn't a magic wand that always made people do what you wanted. In this case, if you offered the money before you knew whether the person actually had the information needed, you muddied the waters beyond repair. If nothing was what they had, chances were they would make a determined effort to sell you disguised nothing.

The man had been sporting a scowl to match the New Mexican's; that faded as he looked down at the bills. He didn't smile—the sensible man wouldn't, when a foreigner waved that sort of cash under his face. Danger and gold went together a lot more certainly than love and marriage ever had, and this looked to be the sort of neighborhood where people were acutely aware of the fact.

He did look as if he were thinking things over, though, unconsciously chewing for a second on his substantial mustache. Then he gave a jerk of his head, motioning them through into the foyer. That was a fairly fancy name for a dark dingy little expanse with a staircase leading upward, and a slight whiff of either human or cat urine under a reek of cheap disinfectant. It made a good place to do business, though. Under all the differences of detail—the building was basically stone, and might be a thousand years old—it made him sort of nostalgic for some of the things he'd done as a homicide roach. Even little Santa Fe had plenty of places like this, and Albuquerque still more.

"Bingo," he said softly, as the man took the tablet.

The Turk grunted, and surprised him by expertly manipulating the touchscreen to enlarge the faces. Then he surprised Eric again by speaking in comprehensible if thickly accented English, the type that got meaning across without necessarily being able to master the tense structure:

"Yes, I see him, and him, and her, the dark woman. She is wearing scarf on head and long coat, but she look from like a hawk and everyone else dog, bad woman I think. Think she have gun. Man with yellow hair too; bad man, cruel man. Old man meet them on dock, truck with—"

The man's English failed him, but not his command of information technology. The fingers of his right hand danced on the screen; Peter sighed, and Eric swore fluently in Ladino Spanish. Even more surprisingly, the Turk chuckled appreciatively at one of the riper phrases. The screen he showed was of a big flatbed with an integral crane . . . Perfectly suited for lifting a heavy load, and with modern controls one operator could use it; there were video pickups on the business end.

"Old man hires six to make fast on gulet," he said. Then with a slight frown: "He speaks very good Turkish. Not like Turk, but good for foreigner."

"A gulet is a type of local sailing craft," Peter said. "It would have a diesel, too. Small enough for three people to operate, if they knew what they were doing and didn't mind taking risks."

"Joy to the fucking world," Eric snarled sotto voce. Then, to the other man:

"When?"

The Turk plucked the money out of his hand, then rubbed his thumb over his fingers in a meaningful gesture. Eric produced more, but before the man could reach for it he leaned close and whispered with their noses almost touching:

"When?"

He wasn't trying to scare the guy; from his own instant appraisal he judged that that would take a lot more than getting in his face. He did want to make sure that he wasn't dismissed as some foreign pansy who could be dicked around with impunity.

"Just now," the man said with a smile, and added street directions.

Eric tossed the money over his shoulder as they turned and dashed out of the building. It was a petty gesture, but satisfying. One glance at the man had told him that he wouldn't grovel for the money meta-phorically, but at least he'd have to do it *literally*.

Adrian stopped. Eric was standing and glaring out to sea as if he was looking through the sights of a missile launcher across the crowded docks of Karaköy.

Peter slumped expressionless against a bollard, staring at a gulet al-ready small in the distance towards the east, its hull and masts white against the blue of the Asian shore. Adrian stood and panted with his hands on his hips, long practice forcing him to take slow deep breaths and keep his shoulders back to let his lungs expand. Ellen was not far behind, carefully guarding his path; the Brotherhood operatives were gone, having been lent grudgingly for a single operation. The quayside was crowded with a simulacrum of maritime life, little in the way of freight or fish, but plenty of big ferries and some cruise ships as well as pleasure craft of all shapes and sizes.

Adrian turned to a young dockworker who was coiling rope.

"So, brother," he said in perfect idiomatic Turkish. "Did a gulet just cast off from here?"

"Yes, the *Çahanoğlu*, Bodrum built, mostly teak, thirty meters. Strange though, no real crew, just three foreigners and a container in the hold that they hired some men to help stow. That is a waste. This is the prime cruising season down along the coast, and that is too much ship for two men and a woman."

He shrugged, evidently not overly disturbed at the perils of some foreigners, or their obvious lack of good sense. "If I were still living in Hamburg, I would want to go for a cruise this time of year as well. Winter there is not as cold as Erzurum, but you can go for months without seeing the sun. No wonder Germans are all mad."

"That is very helpful, brother." Adrian shook hands with him, and slipped across a discreet wad of bills as he did. "Now, if you could help me find a gulet of my own . . . No, no crew is necessary . . . Also, no formalities, I am in a hurry . . . May God witness what I say, that would be a help to me, and I would be thankful. Grateful, to anyone who helped me."

"By God, it is good to find a man who knows what he wants without filling in forms," the local said, covertly glancing down to see the denominations in his palm and trying to hide his surprise. "My father's brother's paternal cousin—"

Turkish used separate, specific words for kin terms like that, much more precise than English.

"—has a good one. But it has just been refitted for the season. . . . A substantial deposit will be necessary with no, ummm, *formalities*, you understand."

Which meant no papers, permits or licenses.

"And something will be necessary for the officials, to explain the need for haste and help them be reasonable."

The Turk shrugged one shoulder and made an expressive gesture with thumb and fingers, the *for bribes* as plain as speech and much more discreet. Adrian nodded. He might not be able to bribe the local bureaucrats himself without a time-consuming dance or using the Power; he didn't know which ones were susceptible, and like any transaction corruption required some degree of trust.

"Your uncle would not lose if he chartered it to me," he said.

Which, as they both knew, meant *sold under the table*. Nobody in their right mind was going to assume they'd get their valuable property back under the circumstances. Adrian reminded himself not to try and bury the problem under money. Too much would excite suspicion. Just enough to be very tempting . . . The men would assume something illegal was going on, which would explain the cash and the haste.

He mentioned a figure with a percentage bonus for haste. The man nodded, turned and walked quickly away with a pleased and eager step. Adrian began to laugh, staring out to where the waters of the Golden Horn reflected the lights of towers and bridges. The cold brackish water had the stale harbor smell, unattractive in itself but hinting at voyages and adventures. A probe with the Power revealed absolutely nothing, which was significant in itself.

I must be very careful here, Adrian thought. *I will do nothing but waste energy if I seek the impact of the bomb itself on the world lines, even my own. Perhaps if I focus entirely on certain other things—*

"What exactly is so funny?" Eric growled, unconsciously rubbing a belly still bruised by the shot in the sewers of Vienna.

Adrian slapped him on the shoulder. "That all my life, or at least all my life since he took me from my parents, Harvey has been advising that it is a very good idea to be careful about deciding what you want before you set out to get it."

"*¿Qué?*" Eric said in frustration.

"One of the things I wanted to do after I married Ellen was take her on a sea voyage. We have no time for a real honeymoon, you understand. It was more the nature of convalescence combined with the commando school. Come, we need a gulet of our own for this pleasure cruise in the footsteps of Jason seeking the plutonium fleece."

"I'd prefer a missile boat with some heat seekers and a couple of autocannon," the New Mexican said flatly.

Adrian shook his head regretfully. "Not with my sister in the mix. An aircraft would be extremely unwise, even more so." A full-throated laugh. "It is ironic. She actually loves modern technology, and I am glad to use it. But together . . . contending together . . . We dare not rely upon it."

"Except for Harvey and his fucking bomb, and that thing shielding it."

Adrian sobered and nodded. "Yes. Except for that."

"And I just accomplished *zip*," Eric snarled; Adrian could feel the self-reproach radiating off him.

"On the contrary. We now know for sure that Guha and Farmer are helping him. Bad news, but good intelligence."

CHAPTER EIGHTEEN

The Black Sea

Ellen was a little nervous about the gulet, and the more so as preparations for departure went on through the night until the very slightest paling appeared in the east and the city lights lost some of their harsh brilliance.

"They're asleep," she said, climbing back up the steep staircase to the chilly darkness of the deck, somehow emphasized rather than relieved by the lights of the city. "At last, at long last. Over-excited. It happens at their age."

Adrian nodded, abstracted. "And their blood doesn't help. This is the middle of the day, for them."

"Afternoon nap, then. Is the ship okay?"

"Our *Tulip* is a sweet little thing and should serve us well. We're about ready to cast off."

She wasn't nervous of the ship itself. It was a pretty enough craft, essentially a biggish schooner with two masts, a sharp bow, a cruiser stern and a low deckhouse that was the only break in its long smooth lines. She was no expert on boats, but the slim sleek shape of the *Lale*—the word meant "tulip"—appealed to her aesthetic sense in a way that made her confident Adrian was right about her being a *sweet little thing*.

In her experience objects that looked perfectly suited to their purpose usually were, and she could tell how something *looked* at a glance. It was one of those cases where aesthetics were extremely practical.

What bothered her was that Adrian was the only one aboard who really knew what he was doing. Sometimes his omnicompetence was irritating, sometimes reassuring, and sometimes both at once; and sometimes it was a bit disturbing because it reminded her of how much older he was than he looked, since not even his abilities would have enabled him to learn all that by his mid-twenties. This time it was a little of all of those. It was reassuring that he was an expert sailor, but the only thing she'd ever done in boats was ride in them, and she had about as much seamanship as she did skill at polo. The others . . .

"Eric?" Adrian said, when the owner's scratch crew had finished carrying bundles and boxes below and departed pocketing sums big enough to be satisfying but just short of being large enough to excite suspicion. "Do you have any experience with oceangoing vessels?"

"I'm from New Mexico. Lots of beach, no ocean."

"You were a marine. . . ."

The dark stocky man shrugged. "Mostly I was a marine in fucking Afghanistan. I used to see kids in the villages make little boats out of wood chips and straw and float 'em down the irrigation canals sometimes, and that's my nautical experience. But hey, I've got the training, so you ram this sucker on a beach and I can land and set up a perimeter. If I had a squad to do it with. Getting us there is the squids' business."

He and Adrian shared a smile, leaving Ellen baffled.

"The engine?" asked Adrian.

The ex-policeman gave a slight quick nod. "Now you're talking, diesel engines I can handle. Trucks, generators, armored vehicles, and my dad ran a garage and I helped him all through high school. This one can't be all that different from what I've worked on."

"I hereby appoint you chief engineer. Go take a look."

"Aye-aye, Captain," the man said, snapping off a salute and disappearing below.

"Peter?"

The scientist had been looking around in admiration, tracing the rigging with his eyes. "I've sailed a small boat on the lakes when I was a kid," he said. "Emphasis *kid*, emphasis *small* boat. As in, one hand on the tiller and one hand on the rope. I can safely say that I understand the hydrodynamics of tacking. Also, I've read all the Patrick O'Brian books and I can talk about Napoleonic-era British frigates by the hour."

"Better than nothing, and we won't be using the sails unless we must. A rig like this can be handled from the decks in any case, and it's all high-geared winches. Familiarize yourself with it, as far as you can."

Peter's eyes traced what was to her a cat's cradle of complexity soaring up to the masts. "Looks pretty simple," he agreed. "No flying sails, nothing fancy."

Eric stuck his head out of a hatchway. "Full tanks, and she's ready to go. Danish-made marine diesel, it's old but it looks like it's been well kept up. I'll be hopping like an eight-armed monkey if it needs anything but the on-off switch, but I'm pretty sure I can keep it going. It's got a pretty good outfit of spares and tools, as far as I can see."

"Good. I could sense that the owner believed the description he gave, but he might have been mistaken."

"Right, you can detect lies but not dumb ignorance?"

"There is a dark cloud to all silver linings."

Cheba came on deck and crossed her arms. Adrian looked at her and visibly decided not to ask about her maritime experience. She nodded and spoke.

"This boat—"

"Ship," Adrian said.

"—this *boat* has plenty to keep us going for weeks. I think it was meant for a dozen people. Rich people. There is enough space for that many in the cabins. I will start breakfast in a few hours. Huevos rancheros. Also I will make coffee, lots of it. These *moros* know about coffee, at least."

"I suppose I could do an inventory of the paintings in the staterooms," Ellen said mock-helpfully.

"If it comes to a fight, Peter and Cheba and Eric will be absolutely essential. You three get some sleep if you can, we will be standing watch and watch. From the description the ship has more hull speed than Harvey's; it was worth a few hours till dawn to avoid trouble with the harbor police."

They nodded—they had been up much longer—and disappeared.

Adrian put an arm around her waist. "I will show you the bridge."

That was in the glassed-in front part of the deckhouse just forward of the rear mast. The interior was polished russet wood, and the wheel might have come from a galleon on the Spanish Main; there was a semi-circle of built-in couch at the rear done in colorful cushions and Turkish kilims. Besides the scents of wax and cloth, there was a faint undertaste of cinnamon and musky incense. After all the Barbary Corsair Oriental decor the touchscreen controls flanking the wheel were a little incongruous.

Adrian brought them up and ran her through the menus. "In theory we could run the engine room from here," he said. "But the electronic controls were all added on later and I do not fully trust them. When these fail, it's always at the worst possible time. We will need Eric. But most of the routine tasks are not very complex. Here, take the wheel."

She did, with him standing behind her and resting his own hands lightly on the wheel as well. She was half expecting it when his teeth lunged for her throat, and she stifled the scream as the overwhelming strength of his body pinned her against the wood—

"Okay," she murmured some time later. "Okay, that's it . . . no—"

His mouth clamped on her neck and fire ran out to the tips of her toes. So tempting . . .

"Adrian! *Earwax!*"

A heart-stopping moment, and he released her. "Sorry," he murmured. "I thought . . ."

"I was. Honey, it's the hint of danger that gives it that edge, but that *was* the edge. It's a good thing everyone else was asleep. Sort of fun forcing myself not to yell, too."

"And fortunate that there were so many rugs and cushions here," he said, helping her untangle the clothing, particularly the parts that had been used as impromptu restraints.

"Yupper. I *like* the odd bruise, but in moderation."

They had just time to shower and change before everyone was stirring. The engine was a quiet rumble beneath their feet as the *Tulip*'s sharp prow turned down the Golden Horn, Adrian threading them expertly between everything from cockle-shell pleasure boats to giant bulk carriers. All the adults crowded into the wheelhouse once they were out of the harbor proper, holding their plates and eating while Adrian explained the controls.

Cheba raised an ironic eyebrow at her before soberly concentrating on the lesson, being uncomfortably acute as usual. Adrian was an excellent teacher, and he was right; she *could* read the ship's passage through the water through her palms on the spokes of the wheel. They could also see the children running up and down the deck, with shouts of *"avast!"* and *"belay!"* and waving of imaginary cutlasses.

My God, is Leon really trying to walk like Johnny Depp? she thought, feeling a spark of brightness.

The morning was clear and chilly, whipping escaped strands of her platinum hair around her face when she leaned it out one of the windows and bringing a flush to her cheeks. The water of the Bosporus was a dark purple blue streaked with white foam. There was a long, slow corkscrew motion to it, and sunlit bursts of spray came flying down the deck each time the bows broke free. The *Rumeli* lighthouse loomed over to the west, an octagonal white spike on the edge of Europe catching the sun rising out of Asia. Then the coastline fell away to east and west as the Black Sea opened up before them. Besides cooking the promised breakfast, Cheba also proved to be the best at holding a heading.

"Keep the bow so," Adrian said, his finger tapping the little icon of the ship that moved along a line on the navigation screen. "The radar alarm is set, and for the present Harvey cannot deviate much from the shortest course to the coast of Georgia; if he did, we would get ahead of him. Peter, Eric, you spell her. I want you all to get the feel of it."

He yawned and stretched like a drowsing leopard. "Let us sleep for four hours, no more. If there is danger it will come in the night. My sister will take a hand in this pursuit."

Ellen hadn't been conscious of how tired she was until she stumbled and almost fell on the steep companionway down to the row of cabins. Now . . .

"You know, I really wish it was just the two of us," she said as she collapsed backward onto the bed.

She was barely conscious of her husband undressing her and drawing up the covers; it was a very comfortable bed, and the linen sheets smelled of lavender.

"Then we would be even more tired," he whispered in her ear. "But I know what you mean. Sleep now, my darling. Sleep, and dream well."

"Adrian's after us," Harvey said, squinting into the rippling brightness of the noon-lit sea.

They'd moved bedding into the wheelhouse of their gulet; that made it easier to trade off, and anyone in the Brotherhood was used to sleeping in the daytime. It was safer then. Running a ship the size of the *Çobanoğlu*, plus keeping the vital but jury-rigged shielding device going around the bomb, was brutal for only three people. Guha gave a protesting mutter as he spoke, started to put a pillow over her head, and turned one bloodshot eye on him from a nest of blankets and quilts.

Harvey grinned to himself; that was safe enough since he was at the wheel and facing away from them. They'd bought what amounted to an oceangoing sailing yacht, with luxury accommodations for three or four couples and more Spartan ones for as many crew and attendants. And here they were, rigged out like a perpetual sleep-over combined with a labor camp. At least there were showers and a kitchen within reach, and enough storage space for baggage that they could simply throw dirty laundry overboard in a weighted bag. Though when it came to it, he was the only one who could really use the kitchen. Jack Farmer was barely up to grilling hamburgers into tough gray discs, and Anjali Guha could turn any ingredient known to the human race into a glutinous mass.

Well, I didn't choose them for their culinary skills, he thought. *'Sides which, I* am *here and I always did like eating my own cooking.*

"You're not probing, are you?" Farmer asked in alarm.

"Nope, just passive, but I recognize his mind. We spent a long time together, and we're base-linked. I can tell when he's scanning for me. Plus of course I taught him, back in the when. There were them as reckoned nobody that pureblood could be turned to the positive side of the Force, and I did see the force of the argument, so I built in some failsafes back when he was just knee-high to a ravening beast. Hopefully he ain't noticed that he has a real problem with penetrating any disguise Wreakings I do. Case of age and treachery beating genes and strength. Of course if he has noticed, we're just back to hiding like hell which we do anyway."

Anjali and Jack exchanged glances. They'd worked together a long time too, and like anyone else in the Brotherhood they'd heard a great deal of gossip about the team of Ledbetter and Brézé. It was lurid and long, and most of it was even true, including the fact that they had managed to kill no less than three of the high Council adepts, not to mention a large quarter of their followers and retainers and relations. More, they'd worked with Adrian personally in California last year and seen what he could do. During that final battle against his sister's renfields he'd used his mind like a mass of flying razors, like some Lord of Shadow out of the ancient myths ripping men's lives free of their bodies with a single snarling thought.

Anjali spoke: "You seem very calm about that."

Harvey nodded. It was a perfectly reasonable question, a professional inquiry and not panic.

"Well, if it was just us, we'd be doing some stretching exercises. So it was nice and comfortable when we bent over to kiss our collective ass good-bye. Adrian is one of the two strongest adepts living, and he's a smart little bastard besides. The upside is that his sister is doing the best she can to stop him, and she's the other of the two strongest living adepts."

Another glance between the two younger operatives. "Are you sure that it is you who are manipulating her, rather than she who is manipulating you?" Anjali said.

"Sure? Oh, *hell* no!" Harvey said, laughing at the thought. "I mean, just think about that for a moment. If I was sure it was me on top, it'd be dead certain she was the one calling the shots. That's a question that can only be answered in retrospect, possibly from the afterlife, which would be difficult because there isn't one. The big advantage I have is that I'm *not* sure who's diddling who. If it were Adrian I wouldn't even have that, I wouldn't even try to string *him* along this way."

Jack rubbed the soft blond bristles on his chin. "She's smart too," he pointed out.

"Yeah, just as smart, but she was raised on the other side. With the usual disadvantages."

They nodded. That meant solipsistic narcissism, and the bone-deep arrogance of those who thought of themselves as physical, living gods. If it weren't for that personality pattern, the Empire of Shadow would've returned full-fledged long ago, given the power imbalance. Harvey wasn't quite sure how much of it was genetic, and how much of it was due to the Council's origin as an alliance of black magicians.

He'd come more and more to the environmental side of the Force as time went on. The example of Adrian strongly suggested genetics were not destiny.

But Satanists almost had to think that way, whether there was an actual Satan to model themselves on or not. There wasn't, but humans were a very plastic species and could shape themselves into a pretty fair approximation of demons, with sustained effort. Naturally enough, their children tended to catch the contagion by osmosis. Shadowspawn more or less had to be like cats, but they didn't have to be nasty ones.

"That doesn't mean we can't be overconfident too," Anjali said. "On the other hand, we must not paralyze ourselves."

Jack snorted. "On the one hand, on the other hand, on the one hand, on the other hand, and so it goes round and round until we disappear up our own assholes with a wet plop."

"Keepin' in mind that the question can be sort of academic. Worst case, we *are* being her instruments for wiping out a lot of the Council. That wouldn't be so bad."

"It *wouldn't?*" Anjali said, in what was almost a squeak.

"Fellas, that would mean we get to *wipe out a lot of the Council.*"

"For her purposes," Jack said.

"For her purely *selfish purposes.* We're thinking in terms of winning the war first and foremost, and she's not. Concentrate on that *wipe out a lot of the Council* bit. There just ain't no downside to that; Adrienne may be smarter than her great-granddaddy, but if she takes over with our nuke she'll have a lot fewer adapts working for her than he does. Plus, it just sort of sets a good precedent."

Farmer smiled, a remarkably evil expression. "So we're in a *heads I win, tails I win really big* situation here, with some *and bitch, you did it to yourself* thrown in?"

Anjali frowned thoughtfully, and then smiled herself; her smile was much more restrained, but held an equal degree of sly wickedness. For a moment they all shared the pure pleasure of doing unto someone else they truly hated.

Think of it as a bonding experience, Harvey thought.

"Dude, that is diabolical," Farmer said. "I think we made the right decision."

"I do try," Harvey said. "And the Brotherhood knows about her plague, and she don't know that we know, so that's taken care of 'cause we have the vaccine stockpiled. Whereas if the dinosaurs on the Council were to do their EMP thing, we would just be purely so screwed. It's a case where *very evil, very powerful and very stupid* actually is more dangerous than *very evil, very powerful and very smart.*"

"Can you tell specifically what Adrian is trying to do?" Anjali said, bringing the conversation back to tactics.

"His Wreakings do tend to have that certain tangy barbecue flavor," Harvey said. "Right now I'd say he's just trying to find us and our little bundle of joy. If he starts trying to cast bane, I'll know it's him. Problem is, in that event we're really going to need that help from the would-be bitch goddess of the universe."

"Let's hope he doesn't find us, then," Farmer said.

"Well, about that . . . So long as he knows where we're headed he really don't have to know exactly where we are for a while."

"But? Oh wise one, enlighten us," Anjali said sarcastically.

"Sailin' straight into Batumi ain't our only option. This gulet is a mite more flexible than your average container freighter. Those giant floatin' shoeboxes need a lot more infrastructure."

CHAPTER NINETEEN

The Black Sea

Adrian stood on the prow of the *Tulip*. It was rising and falling with a long, very shallow sweep; the wind was out of the north, and the gulet motored along at a conservative nine knots, foam breaking from the prow in a broad V. The wind was cold on his naked form, and the stars that shone so many and bright above were somehow even colder. The burble of the diesel was oddly reduced by the intense silence of the night, the distances drinking it down; they were well off the usual shipping lanes, and there were not even the lights of an aircraft to disturb a scene that might have seen *Argo* making home from Colchis. Moonlight glittered on the waves, making a sky-road that seemed to dare the ship to take the upward path to worlds beyond the world.

"I don't like this idea," Ellen said. "I particularly don't like us splitting up. What is this movie, *Teens Die Because They Shower And Fornicate In Scary Old House/Cabin in the Woods, Part XVII?* Is this the seagoing version where we split up and dive into the water instead of doing it in the basement with candles and monsters?"

Eric and Peter were jarred into laughter; Cheba looked at them with a mixture of incomprehension and disgust.

"Only Adrian is diving into the water," she said. "And what is this about a movie? And we have plenty of monsters."

Adrian shrugged, as Eric leaned close and whispered into Cheba's ear.

"I don't like it either," Adrian said to Ellen. Then he smiled slightly. "In a sense, we're not—I am still in the stateroom."

She prodded him with a finger. "Don't you try to soothe me, buster," she said. "*That's* you, and I don't want to be married to a comatose body."

He was nightwalking, of course, but with his aetheric body this palpable the finger felt just as it would to his physical one.

"We need the data. Harvey is concealing himself far too well, Peter's device is working very well indeed . . . and I think some other force is seeking to thwart me as well."

"*Her.*"

"Probably. But I cannot be sure."

She sighed and stepped back. He stroked a strand of bright hair from her forehead.

Peter had an aluminum case in his hands, attached to an improvised harness of webbing. "This is ready to go," he said, as Ellen took it from his hands. "It's fully waterproof to two hundred feet and it's powered for twelve hours."

Adrian looked up at the sky. "Just put her nose into the wind if the weather turns dirty; and that can happen very quickly this time of year. There's that sea-anchor ready if necessary."

The slight blond man nodded. "We're taking turns monitoring the weather channels."

Adrian kissed his wife lightly on the lips, smiled at them all, turned, and ran out the bowsprit. A leap, the whisper of Mhabrogast through his mind, and he *twisted* . . .

And a dolphin clove the water. Down into the mild warmth . . . up again, soaring, his eyes flexing automatically to see through air as well as water, down again, threading air and water like a needle, a delirium of fluid speed, the water tasting of fuel (foul) and not-quite-salty enough and fish (*fish! fish!*). Vision was sharp, but hearing was the *world*. He hung in infinite space, and around him was a galaxy of sound-stars, the dull red booming of ship's motors, the creaking hiss of the wooden sailing ship, the distant rumble of waves on shores, the creaking whistling surging tide of *life* down to the voices of far-distant swimmers and the song of a distant pod of his own kind.

Sound not through ears, but heard with his whole body as its instrument. Sound like the touch of feather-light fingers on every object, even the surface of the abyssal depth below.

"Adrian!"

He heard that too. Ellen's voice was a thing of richness, a sculptured solidity of rolling form, a tower of location that was precisely *there*. There was no gap between the sound of a thing and the thing itself; they were *one*, as scent was to a wolf. He soared out of the water again in a twisting leap that was a dance of love and longing.

"Here, Adrian!"

He remembered being a man; that was easier in this form than in many, simply because there was so much more brain to work with. The problem was that he didn't remember it in the same *way*, while the Shadowspawn consciousness curled at the base of the brainstem struggled to assert itself. After a moment it did, and he rose out of the water, dancing on his tail with more than half the sleek torpedo-shaped body in the air, rolling an eye at her and grinning. She leant down on the ladder that had been thrust over the side, and extended the harness.

He hated the thought of it interfering with the flow of the water over his skin, but it was necessary. She slipped it over his head and cinched it around his trunk behind the forefins with a single movement, and he nuzzled at her. She had no scent—disconcerting to his memories, for most forms had better noses than men or even Shadowspawn—but the very sound of her heart outlined her form. He felt an overwhelming impulse to passionately bite the saucy flauntingness of her beautiful dorsal fin, which caused a momentary mental stutter, starting with the fact that he still knew at some level that she didn't have one. The dolphin part of his consciousness then decided it didn't care . . .

A hand smoothed his head; he whistled and dove.

Ellen stared out over the ocean and took another bite of the burrito without bothering to taste it. She supposed it was a burrito; there were various things including meat inside something like either a tortilla or a pita. She needed fuel if she was going to worry effectively.

"Thanks, Cheba," she said. "I should take a turn at that. So should Peter—he's not busy with the engines."

"I cook better than you do," Cheba pointed out, and handed her a cup of strong coffee to go with it. "None of the men can cook, except the *jefe*, and he does not have time even when he is not turning into something strange or fighting or doing the things he does."

"Peter can cook."

"He can cook things I do not like, they're all . . . what's the word, food with no real taste, too smooth . . ."

"Bland."

"*Sí*, bland. I need to have something to do, anyway."

Ellen's mouth turned up wryly. She hadn't had time to get *really* worried yet; Adrian had only been gone for an hour or so . . .

"But I don't like the look of that at *all*," she said suddenly.

A fin had just broken the surface for an instant, creamy off-white in the moonlight, with a little curl of foam to either side. Then it turned and bored towards the *Tulip*, the fin vanishing and nothing but a huge pale streak showing through the water, fading as it went deeper. She went to the rail and looked over. Then the whole ship lurched and shook, as if it had brushed over a rock . . . though she knew that there was nothing below but very deep water and the seabed. She dropped the half-eaten wrap and the coffee cup overboard with a yell as she pitched forward and the rail struck her across the waist and she started to topple. Cheba grabbed her by the back of her jacket's belt and heaved backward, enough for her to stagger back to equilibrium.

"Thanks!" she said fervently. "Whatever that is I *sure* don't want to go swimming with it!"

Eric came boiling out of the hatchway. "What the hell was that?"

"I don't know," she said.

Peter came out of the deckhouse as she pointed to the other side of the vessel; the little ship had an effective autopilot. The fin showed again, and he leveled his binoculars.

"That is a big shark," Cheba said. "A very big shark. There are sharks like that off Veracruz—one of my mother's cousins saw them there and there was a picture in the newspaper of one that ate some *touristas*."

"Uh, guys, are those things supposed to live around here?" Ellen asked.

"Fuck if I know," Eric said. "That's a big-ass shark, right? As in *Jaws*?"

"It's a Great White," Peter said. He let the binoculars hang on their strap, and his fingers danced across his tablet doing some impromptu research. "Ah . . . no, they don't have them in the Black Sea. Not more than a few miles away from the Bosporus, at least."

They all looked at each other. The children came out, sleepy in their pajamas, and the three adults made simultaneous preventative grabs as they headed for the rail.

"Hello, *Maman*!" Leon called, and he and his sister waved.

"*Mierda*," Eric said.

"That's Mom," Leila said cheerfully. Her small, still slightly chubby face went abstracted for a moment. "She's feeling . . . well, she's a fish, she's really funny when she's a fish. It's *Maman*, but not, you know? She said you have to be always careful with her when she's a big fish."

"Big fish just bite without thinking about it," Leon amplified, reciting his safety lesson. Then he snapped his teeth together: "Chomp! Chomp!"

Peter began whistling a tune; after a moment Ellen recognized it as "Farewell, Ye Ladies of Spain."

"Stop that!" she said.

"Okay," he said equably and shifted to the theme from *Jaws*.

"Dammit, I know I started it, Peter, but my husband is in the water with that thing!"

"Except for this boat, *we're* in the water with it," he said soberly.

Eric smiled, or at least showed his teeth. "Or vice versa," he said, and disappeared as the fin circled, easily keeping pace with the ship.

The half burrito lay heavily on Ellen's stomach. A few minutes later

Eric emerged again, taking something wrapped in a length of plastic out of a sack of the same improvised-looking devices.

"Cousin of mine used to go midnight fishing for rainbow trout this way in Lake Bonito, over by Alamogordo," he said. "That is one honking big fish, but the principle's the same. I made up these on general principles 'cause we were on the water."

He did something to the package, a jerking motion, shouted: "*¡Oye, tu! ¡Puta! ¿Qué es tu pinche problema?*" and threw it with a hard snapping motion that showed he'd played baseball once.

"Uh, Eric—" Peter began, as Cheba stifled a startled giggle. "Maybe that's not—"

The fin darted away abruptly; then there was a muffled booming and the dark water behind the *Tulip* abruptly rose in a shattered bulge of white a dozen feet across. A huge pale shape tossed ahead of it, writhing.

The children winced and Leila put her hands to her head. "Ooooh, that *hurt*," she said. "That really hurt, *vraiment*."

"*Maman* is mad now," Leon said. "Really, really . . ."

A grating sound came up the hatch from the engine room. Eric's grin—shark-like itself—turned to alarm, and he dashed for the hatchway, swinging below. The three adults peered through the moonlit night, and something heaved below the water astern. Not a shark this time . . . but it was an even paler dead-white.

"Oh, that's not right," Peter said. "That's just not *right*."

"What is it?" Ellen asked; he had his binoculars to his eyes again.

They were a type with wide lenses, designed to trap the maximum amount of light, and as he put it *unbuggerable*, since there were no electronics.

"That's a sperm whale," he said. "*Physeter macrocephalus*."

"You mean—"

"Moby Dick-style whale. The giant-squid-eater. An *albino* Physeter macrocephalus. Melville got the idea from the one that sank the whaler *Essex* in 1822 by ramming it with its head, that's the way the bulls fight each other. That one was supposed to be eighty feet long and would have weighed about seventy tons, which is a bit less than half what this ship displaces—"

"Jesus, will you stop lecturing!" Ellen shouted, as a tall spout of water and air plumed into the air at a forty-five-degree angle from the huge pale bulk.

Immense flukes lifted and struck, and the sea fountained away from them. The noise of the diesels turned to a tooth-grating howl for an instant and then died away into grinding and clashing sounds, then silence. Eric reappeared.

"Cylinder blew. Freak accident," he said bitterly, wiping at a grease-mark on his cheek. "What the—"

The stern of the ship heaved upward. Cheba grabbed a child, and Ellen did too. All of them were thrown to the deck with bruising force; Leila squealed, then called:

"Wooooopsie!" in a voice filled with innocent glee.

The *Tulip* heaved again as the great bulk rose close enough to the bow to throw a chaos of white water along its flanks and over the rail.

"Don't worry, she won't do anything that would hurt the children," Ellen gasped as cold foam drenched her.

If she's thinking straight. If not, she may be very sorry *when she shifts back to human . . . humanoid . . . form after she's smashed the boat and swallowed us all whole.*

From what Adrian had told her and what she'd experienced while he was soul-carrying her, a nightwalker wasn't just wearing an animal suit. The Power manufactured an aetheric body based on a DNA sample, from blood or a bite of flesh or any body fluid that had cells in it; adepts called it *taking on the beast*. You got the animal's senses and strengths, but you also got a lot of its basic nature, and you had to think with its nervous system. The adept's personality and memories remained, but they had to work through what the form provided and maintaining a sapient's purposes could be hard in some of them.

That's why she switched to the whale. Sharks have tiny little brains. They swim, and they eat, they make little sharks, as Peter would remind me. Cetaceans have big brains, they think better, especially the types with teeth. She probably memorized a note to herself: if anything strange happens and your tiny shark brain feels things are getting away from you, turn into a whale.

"Can you get the engine running again?" Ellen asked.

"Yeah," Eric said. "I'll take about an hour, with someone to give me a hand."

"Look on the bright side," Peter said. "That thing could smash the boat, but she doesn't want to. And she'll have to go away before dawn, or at least turn into something that breathes water and go deep. Whales don't have hands."

The white whale had dived; everything was silent for a minute, and Eric turned to go below again and begin his repairs. Then *Tulip* lurched again, more softly this time. The stern dipped and stayed down, as if a heavy weight had been attached to the keel at the rear.

"What the hell . . . Much as I hate to say it, maybe you should get another of those little explosive fishing devices," Peter said.

"I've got plenty of them—" Eric began.

Something came over the side of the ship, rearing into the air like a giant questing snake. Ellen froze for a moment before she realized what she was seeing. It was a tentacle, three times the length of her body and thicker than her ankle. She stared at it wide-eyed and open mouthed until it fell like a living rope. Then she screamed, as it fell across her leg and the barbed hooks that lined it bit. The suckers gripped with agonizing force, and the living cable began to pull her towards the rail.

She tried to draw her revolver, but her eyes were streaming with the pain and the salt water that had surged across her face moments before, and she knew she was just as likely to shoot her own foot. Something flashed through that haze; it was Cheba and her silvered machete, hacking at the tentacle and screaming:

"*¡Muérete, tú! ¡Pinche cabrona! ¡Muérete!*"

That wasn't just the needs of the moment. Cheba didn't remember her time at Rancho Sangre very fondly. Something went *click* behind Ellen's eyes; she had a weird sensation of feeling pain *twice*, in her leg and in her outstretched tentacle, of feeling her rage doubled and going *both* *ways* . . .

My tentacle? Do I have tentacles? Lots of them, and I'm seeing the ship from below, and the water's too warm and the light hurts and . . . Oh, God, I so did not want ever to be touched by her again! And this is one of the reasons, the way it fucked with my head!

Cheba and Peter were hauling her back as the tentacle let go and whipped away. Eric took one look at her leg and started bandaging with skilled speed.

"Don't knock me out!" she said, though the hypodermic he pulled out of the medical kit looked very tempting. "I am not going to be unconscious with *that* around!"

"It won't, just takes the sting out at this dosage," he said, a little indistinctly.

That was because he was pressing the bandage down with one hand and pulling the cap off the hypo with his teeth. He spat it to one side and administered the painkiller with brutal dispatch, simply jabbing the needle into the thigh of her injured leg through the pants. It was rough, but at this point she scarcely noticed the sting. She *did* notice the wave of relief; the pain didn't go away, but it became a lot less important. With both hands free Eric finished dressing the wound quickly.

"Not as bad as I thought—" he began, then snatched up his coach gun and shot again, deafeningly right over her head.

She looked up and felt her mouth drop open. A mass of tentacles gripped the rail and slid forward like writhing black pythons to seize anchor-points, securing themselves with the adhesive suckers and the barbs and hooks that lined them. Something huge was pulling itself over and onto the deck, something like Cthulhu on steroids. Its glaring eyes were the size of bowling-balls a foot across, pupils like S-slits of blackness. The curved beak like a giant parrot's gnashed in the midst of the whirling chaos, and the central mass was bigger than a bear, with weight enough to make the drifting *Tulip* heel and loose things slide and bump as they tumbled across the deck. Cheba was shrieking Spanish maledictions again and hacking as the tentacles came probing, and Peter was struggling with a shotgun and shouting as well. It took an instant before she realized he'd been shouting something in Latin:

"*Mesonychoteuthis hamiltoni, Mesonychoteuthis hamiltoni!* Colossal squid! Fifty feet long, weighs tons, *fights* sperm whales! Damn! Darn! *Shit!*"

Both barrels of the shotgun blasted silver buck towards the monster. Ellen realized the anesthetic was affecting her when she heard herself ask:

"You're a physicist, Peter . . . why do you know the Linnaean names of giant squid?"

"It's a hobby, it's a hobby, *die, you bitch, die!*"

That was directed at Adrienne-the-monster-squid, not her: he fired again. There was another soundless blast of noise inside her head, and the tentacles abruptly withdrew like a video being played backwards. The colossal squid—something deep in her mind noticed how appropriate the name was—slid away, and the ship rocked upright again. A sudden silence fell, and they could hear the waves lapping against the hull beneath the brilliant stars.

"Wow!" Leon said softly; the children were clinging to each other near the door to the deckhouse. "*Maman* is *really* angry with you, Ellen! Not just playing!"

"I should get the engine going again—" Eric began.

Then the *Tulip* lurched once more. It felt different, more of a monstrous *tugging*. Noises came through the hull, as much felt through her body as heard, sharp metallic rending and crackling sounds and then something like a big taut wire breaking. Then a tentacle broke the surface again; it was hard to see by moonlight, but it seemed to be brandishing something. It flexed like a whip, and the object turned through the air and thudded into the forward mast with a heavy metallic clatter and fell to the deck. It was round and disk-like, a couple of feet across, lobed . . .

"Son of a *bitch*!" Eric shouted, then a long sentence in Spanish, then: "She twisted the fucking propeller off the shaft! So much for *no hands*, professor."

"The *whale* didn't have hands," Peter pointed out reasonably. "The squid has *tentacles*."

Silence fell again. "Guess she found a way to attack the ship that didn't endanger the kids," Ellen said thoughtfully. "Ah . . . Peter . . . Adrian went over how to raise the sails, didn't he?"

"Yeah," Peter said. "But I suspect we're going to have a sea anchor hanging off our keel."

"Not if I have anything to do with it," Eric said.

He lofted another of the improvised grenades over the side. This time the explosion took a little longer, went off deeper and hit the underside of the *Tulip* like a huge padded hand whacking it on the belly.

"Not going to let her get at the rudder," he said. "That would be . . . bad."

"I hope Adrian gets back soon," Ellen added, then: "I think I could use a nap. Someone give me a hand? And *not*"—she specified with slightly drugged precision—"a tentacle. Definitely no suckers. Suckers *suck*."

"I think he's not in the area anymore," Harvey Ledbetter said, taking a deep breath. "I'm not sure, *can't* be sure if he's using one of those new personal shields. I wasn't getting any direct sensing, just . . . a feeling we were being looked over by the Power. Now we're not. Took off in a hurry, which is a comfort."

"*Something* destroyed our electronics," Anjali said.

That wasn't as serious as it might be; not getting lost was a very minor Wreaking, requiring merely sensitivity to the earth's magnetic field.

"And wrecked the fucking engine," Jack Farmer said.

"Those were probably him. Nice deft subtle touch, no more damage than essential."

"Which leaves the question of why he didn't screw with the shield device. Even if he can't locate it precisely, he knows it's here. Fry the electronics and it's all over."

Harvey leaned on the wheel of the ship, looking out over the bow and the white curve of the sail, brilliant in the moonlight. He laughed heartily, breathing in the clear cold sea air; they'd opened a window, because the deckhouse got a little fusty with the three of them living in it.

"We got a fail-safe there," he said. "Which is that Adrian, thanks to my careful upbringing, is sort of a soft-hearted and humanitarian little bastard, a real nice guy. Which incidentally proves it's possible for a Shadowspawn to be that way, which some disputed. I was right and they were wrong and I get to sing the *'I was right'* song."

Farmer looked at him, baffled. "Yeah, that's why he's trying to *stop* you . . . us . . . from getting the bomb to Tbilisi. Which *incidentally* proves having mostly human genes doesn't necessarily make *you* a nice guy. So if he blew the shield mechanism . . ."

"Every adept in the Council would see that fireball rushing out of the future," Harvey went on. "And then . . ."

"They would go as the saying is, *ripshit*," Anjali said thoughtfully. "Every screw and bolt in this ship would break. The wood would rot and splinter. Our eyeballs would boil and our hair catch on fire while we suffered strokes, heart-attacks and scrofula. And . . . and they would turn on Adrienne, to begin with."

She looked at him narrow-eyed; Harvey could feel her questioning, besides seeing the reflection of her face in the glass of the cockpit. As he'd said, it was impossible even in theory to be sure whether he was his own agent or hers right now. Nobody in the Brotherhood could ever be fully confident of their comrades, and the consequences of betrayal were one reason Brotherhood agents tended to have relatively short lives and long, tortured deaths.

"You're right," he said. "And then guess what?"

"Well, they'd know about the shield—the first real advantage we've ever had. And then Trimback One," Farmer said, and began to laugh as well. "Trimback One would be back on the table."

"Good and proper," Harvey agreed. "Which would mean *hundreds* of nukes getting tossed around. Upper-level air-bursts for the EMP effect, granted, but still massive casualties, and then everything would just purely go to shit. Oh, a hell of a lot more than one groundburst in Tbilisi. Plus the Brotherhood can *beat* Trimback Two, maybe even win the war for good, but not with Trimback One."

The two younger agents began to snicker themselves. "So he can't destroy the shield," Farmer said. "He can't even sink the ship."

Anjali clapped her hands together. "He must *capture* the bomb and keep the shield going until he dismantles it! Whereas if we set the bloody thing *off* the Council lords will have only seconds of warning, if that!"

"Like Sauron and the One Ring at the Crack of Doom," Harvey said with immense satisfaction.

Farmer scowled. "Why didn't you explain this in more detail?" he asked.

"Keeping y'all on your toes," Harvey said blandly. "Worked, didn't it? He can't sink us, but turning this thing into a drifting hulk would work."

"It works both ways," Anjali said. "Adrienne is limited in how she can attack *him* if he has her children along . . . and he probably does."

"Probably, and on a boat not much different from this, I'd guess," Harvey said. "If Adrian's nightwalking in a marine form, pro'bly a dolphin or an orca, that limits his range. He'd come right after us after that little hoedown in Istanbul . . . or at least I would have, in his position, and I trained him."

He released the spokes long enough to rub his hands for an instant. "We got Mutual Assured Destruction, folks! And if we don't lose, we win."

Harvey turned utterly serious. "Now we've got to plan how to hold him up once we get ashore. Hold him *just* long enough."

Anjali and Farmer looked at each other. "You don't want us to go to Tbilisi with you?" Farmer said carefully.

"You particularly want to come?" Harvey asked. "'Cause when I set the timer . . . if I get a chance to do it that way . . ."

Chances of getting out alive will range from slim to absolutely none, went unspoken.

"We are willing to take the risk if it is crucial to the mission," Anjali said flatly, if not enthusiastically; Farmer grunted and nodded.

Harvey shook his head. "I can't fight my way into Tbilisi. With every adept in the *world* there? I wish! And I can sneak as well alone . . . maybe better. What I need you to do is hold up pursuit as long as you can, pick up some local assets and use a few tricks I can give you. Which considering you're going up against Adrian . . . and maybe the Brotherhood . . . is plenty risky, believe me."

Also unspoken was that Adrian and the Brotherhood would kill them cleanly if it came to that, or in Adrian's case even let them surrender. Both were extremely unlikely in the convocation of demons gathering in Tbilisi.

"We should be ashore in a spot I know around about noon, with some services laid on. No nightwalkers to worry about, at least."

"Small mercies," Farmer said, and they all laughed again.

The dolphin came barreling out of the depths, its body flexing in an up-and-down rippling motion, aiming at the location of the periodic explosions. The colossal squid skulking at a safe distance barely had time to register the motion before the beak hit like a fifteen-hundred-pound battering ram moving at over twenty miles an hour, all concentrated behind a hard punching surface a couple of inches square. The whole gelatinous mass of the monster's form flexed and rippled in shock as the force propagated through it.

Adrian heard himself grunt—at least, that was how his *Tursiops truncates* body and brain interpreted the shower of bubbles and pulsed sounds it emitted at the stunning impact. He twisted away by reflex through the forest of tentacles as the squid thrashed helplessly and drifted downward. A swift gliding curve like a fighter jet brought him in for another attack run.

The squid *sparkled* and reformed. Without silver it was very difficult to do lasting damage to an aetheric body, if the guiding intelligence preserved enough presence of mind to go impalpable and switch back again despite the shock and pain of a wound; that reset the form to default in a fraction of a second. Then its tentacles darted out for him, malign intelligence sparkling in its giant eyes, ready to rip and rend with arms intended to do battle with eighty-ton sperm whales ten thousand feet beneath the surface.

Tearing a body in half often *did* kill, persuading the hindbrain it was dead before the intelligence could recover.

Amss-uui-ok!

The tentacles closed on the sperm whale where the dolphin had been, but the black giant threw itself forward, its scores of tons carrying the squid effortlessly along, its thick skin and protective blubber shrugging off the terrible barbed grip. A third of the whale's eighty-foot length was jaw, lined on the lower side with massive teeth. They began to close—

—and the great white shark flashed by, twisting to take a huge bite as it did, its rows of bone saw ripping out a semicircular chunk—

—and the orca flexed to pursue—

—and the other orca maneuvered, and Adrienne's sardonic:

And . . . this . . . is . . . ridiculous . . . we've . . . done . . . it . . . before . . . and . . . it . . . just . . . wastes . . . the . . . night! i . . . am . . . taking . . . my . . . bat . . . and . . . ball . . . and . . . going . . . home!

He responded with a wordless snarl of rage after the echolocation of the disappearing black-and-white shape, and fainter came: **nyah . . . nyah . . . can't . . . catch . . . me!**

The urge to pursue was overwhelming, but he fought it down; it *was* getting towards dawn and their speed and strength *were* too closely matched. He suppressed the impulse to cast a malediction after her as well. A battle of Wreakings would drain them even more, and already the blood-hunger was gnawing at him.

This is a distraction. Time to go home.

Home was where Ellen was. He turned and surfaced briefly, disappointed but not surprised to see that the *Tulip* was under sail—the high chance that the engine would be destroyed was why he'd picked a vessel with sail backup, after all. Then he drove towards it with powerful strokes of his flukes, leapt . . .

. . . and transformed.

A naked man went to one knee on the deck, looking down a grand total of six shotgun barrels full of silver shot; he could feel the cold menace in the cartridges, enough to wound even his aetheric form to the very edge of probable recovery, particularly as depleted as he was. Adrian grinned wearily.

"Commendable vigilance, my friends."

It would be simplicity itself for Adrienne to take his form, and only a little harder to mimic his mannerisms.

"Griffyndor," he said.

Their faces relaxed as the prearranged password activated the confirmation Wreakings in their minds. "Ellen?" he said sharply, noticing that she was gone.

"Hurt but not too bad," Eric said crisply. "I patched her up and gave her a shot of joyjuice."

"Good. I must—"

He staggered a little as he came to his feet. Peter started towards him with a look of concern on his face, then stopped when Adrian held up a hand.

"No!" Then more gently: "Not now. Don't come closer until I have . . . refreshed. I've been using the Power rather extravagantly."

Eric followed him below to his stateroom; the ex-policeman didn't completely relax until he saw the eyes of Adrian's blood-body open and heard his sigh. From his aura he still found the sight of two apparently identical bodies merging mind-boggling and unpleasant in equal measure, but he nodded and holstered his coach gun.

"Yeah, it's absolutely you," he said.

"You weren't sure?" Adrian said, sitting up; he was dressed except for his boots.

Ellen rested beside him, her eyelids opening slightly; he could feel how deep her sleep was, urged by the narcotic, but that was wearing off.

"There's *sure* and then there's *absolutely completely sure*. How'd the mission go, boss?"

"I slowed Harvey down, and I have a better idea of where he's headed than he thinks—he is not the only one who took precautions against something like this long ago."

Eric nodded. "Yeah, that extra bit never hurts. Cheba's cooking up something . . . don't know what to call it, clock-wise, but it'll be ready in about an hour."

"That will do nicely. We can plan then. And now, if you will excuse me for a little . . ."

He felt better, although the wounds to the aetheric body usually transferred to the physical one as stigmata for a little while; that meant the equivalent of bruises and scuffs. And he was ravenous, of course.

Ellen was resting, and in any case in no fit state to accommodate him; he reached into the cooler and took out the plastic pint container of blood. Warming it made it slightly less nauseating . . . at the cost of increasing the subsequent headache.

"Best to rip the bandage off quickly," he muttered to himself and drank it down, trying to avoid holding it in his mouth.

He'd heard Englishmen describe pouring beer down their throats without touching the sides, and did his best to do that literally. He didn't succeed, and spent a long moment in silent misery, fighting the impulse to retch—if he vomited, he'd have to do this *again*. And he tried not to breathe through his nose, either. The closest he'd ever been able to come to describing the scent of old dead blood was dog vomit on a hot day, combined with stale diapers and sulfuric acid. The taste was similar, with an overtone of rotten bananas.

He supposed his remote ancestors had evolved the aversion because the Power was so sensitively dependent on complex amino-acids and whole-chain proteins in the blood; the Shadowspawn system didn't so much digest it as incorporate it directly. Refrigeration and the preservatives and anti-clotting agents in blood-bank supplies actually kept it quite usable, but they didn't trip the receptors for *fresh blood*. Nor did it have the intoxicating tang that strong emotion gave blood, the subtleties that made a fine Bordeaux like Concord grape juice by comparison.

If it wasn't vile, it would be as boring as baby formula, he thought. *Still, I'm not drinking it for pleasure. Consider it a penance, Adrian. Stop hesitating and get it over with.*

There was a reason adepts who didn't take blood by force didn't Wreak more than they absolutely must, either, and why those in the Brotherhood had such a powerful taboo against drinking living blood at all. A drug that actually made you as powerful as it made you *feel* was addictive on a whole series of levels. This stuff wasn't going to tempt anyone to vice.

When it had settled he swallowed a second pint. That was as much as he could possibly hold down, and enough for what he needed to do, though no more than that. A stiff shot of brandy helped too, though it was a sin to use *L'Essence de Courvoisier* as mouthwash. The hints of plum and apricot did sooth his abused mouth, not to mention the alcohol. He took a second, sipping at a more civilized pace, and sat down beside Ellen; she was under a coverlet, and he ran his hand through the air over her injured ankle.

Yes, painful but not too serious, he thought.

Normally he would have let it heal conventionally, with perhaps a little Wreaking to ensure that there was no scarring or internal adhesions. Now . . .

He finished the brandy, set the glass down on the sideboard, twitched up the blanket and gently laid his hands on the bandage. She stirred in protest.

"No, lover, you've just worked hard," she said.

He smiled at her sleepy face and tousled hair. "And we may both have hard work ahead tomorrow. We can't have you limping or leaving a blood trail when you need to be Ellen the Scourge of the Shadowspawn."

He took a deep breath and calmed his mind. Healing required a process that basically convinced your own body that it had suffered the injury itself, then duplicating the process of Power-assisted cell division.

This was going to hurt.

*   *   *

"Will . . . will it hurt?" the woman said, and Monica pulled a chair up and sat across from her and her husband.

The guest stateroom was compact but comfortable . . . though the porthole was far too small for anyone to squeeze through and the door could be securely locked from the outside. Adrienne Brézé hadn't done anything as pedestrian as hire a local craft for her impromptu sea voyage. Months ago she'd had her yacht—the *Morey*—sail from San Diego through the Panama Canal, across the Atlantic and wait for her in Istanbul on the off chance that she would need it; of course, her hunches were of a different order from those of ordinary mortals. It was a modified Grand Banks schooner originally built to order in Oregon, three hundred tons and two tall masts, with ample room to pick up a couple of lucy candidates and all the special features she desired.

Hunting and killing is all very well, but one-night stands tire after a while, she'd said. *You want something more emotionally complex. And I don't want to leave a trail of floating empties across the Black Sea. That would be . . . uncouth.*

"Ummm . . ." Monica said, wondering how to put things tactfully.

You poor dears. It'll take a while to adjust.

"Well, not the feeding so much," she went on, trying to be reassuring without an offensive chipperness. "At first there's only a little sting and you feel . . . detached, accepting . . . And later, after a couple of times, it gets really, ummm, *nice*. A major rush, better than anything including . . . well, better than anything. You start craving it quite a lot after a couple of days without."

Worse than cigarettes or even heroin, in fact, but there was no need to go into that just now. The couple sitting on the guest room bunk were quite young . . . though no younger than Monica had been when her car broke down passing through Rancho Sangre that evening so long ago.

They'd gone into the wrong . . . or right . . . café in Istanbul on their honeymoon and caught Adrienne Brézé's eye as she prepared to depart, and ended out stumbling after her in a daze of Wreakings. It was touching to see how the young man kept his arm protectively around her shoulders, despite his own terror.

Right café, Monica told herself firmly. *Pretty soon, being a lucy is going to be the luckiest thing in the world. It's all for the best in the long run. I'm sure we'll be good friends eventually . . . it will be nice to have some company again, people who understand.*

"Th . . . that doesn't sound so bad," Jessica said hopefully.

Monica sighed and went on gently: "But other parts of it are probably going to hurt a bit, yes. And be . . . stressful. You should just keep thinking *I can do this* all the way through and it won't go too badly, though. It takes a while to get used to."

Jessica Bertsch whimpered slightly and gripped her husband Todd's hand; *his* eyes flicked to her and then to Dave Cheung leaning in the doorway with a Glock in his hand. They were both extremely frightened, of course; your first glimpse of a nightwalker transforming evoked primal terrors. A hundred and fifty thousand years as the prey species of *Homo nocturnis* ensured that the genes remembered, besides the way it knocked the world out from beneath your feet.

Then there was the kidnapping, the armed guards and the prospective violation.

"The *Doña* is going to be, ummm, very hungry when she wakes up. She's doing a lot with the Power tonight, you don't need to know the details yet, but it makes a Shadowspawn ravenous. Our blood is the fuel for the Power. Though they eat normal food as well, of course."

"She turned into . . . a tiger," Todd said; his voice held the peculiar tone of someone who had no doubt that they'd seen something but still didn't really believe it. "A tiger. And she walked through the wall. And her body was still there."

"They can do that, yes. It's called the aetheric body, and when they come out it's called nightwalking. And . . . umm, they can read your mind, too, so . . . no fibbing! It has to be a completely honest relationship. And they can do a lot of other things. Right now, though, you need to focus on getting through your first feeding."

"And you . . ." he said.

"Oh, yes, I've been a lucy for ten years now. So you see, it isn't that bad. What I'd advise is that you, Jessica, be right next to her when she comes back from nightwalking and re-enters her body. She'll just go for your throat then, and after she's drunk a pint or two of your blood you'll be . . . sort of glassy and spaced-out for a while. That will be the drug in the bite getting a hold on you."

Todd Bertsch was a graceful-looking man, with wavy dark-red hair and freckles and a body that looked like a gymnast's, shown to advantage in the briefs that were all either of them wore. He also looked mutinous. Monica smiled at him and spoke reassuringly.

"No, really, Todd, I understand your concern and it's very sweet, but that's safest for her. Then Jessica will be quiet while the *Doña*, ummm, well, she's going to be feeling playful by then. Excited. When the *Doña* has been at you for a while and fed again on you she'll be more relaxed and less . . . well, a bit less dangerous for Jessica when it comes to playing. So you'll be protecting her this way, really."

That would appeal to his feelings, and had the advantage of being true. Monica patted the sobbing woman on the shoulder.

"It's all right to cry and be scared, honey. I was too and I cried *all the time* at first. But this whole thing is natural. Just remember you're serving this *need*. It can be quite satisfying if you think of it that way, feeling your blood draining into the hunger. It's what we humans are for, like flowers for hummingbirds. It can be beautiful as well as terrible. The *Doña* is really the nicest Shadowspawn there is, too."

"There's more of them?" Todd said.

"Oh, *thousands*. All over the place, little bunches everywhere. They run the world, pretty much. I mean, who could stop them from doing anything they want? They just don't let people know, though I understand that's going to change soon."

She looked at her phone; it wasn't long before dawn. "Come on, let's get things ready."

Dave Cheung motioned with the gun. Todd glared at him, but they both rose and walked down the corridor, through the sitting room and into the stateroom of the *Morey*. Which was named after the giant eel, a voracious ambush predator.

It was part of the stern of the ship and ran its full width, darkly lit by light reflected off the surface of the water and coming through the outward-slanting windows that made a semicircle at the rear. The panels and floor were African rosewood, and there was an oval king-sized bed and a few other items of understated furniture and some Tabriz carpets. Adrienne looked almost childlike as she lay with the cream silk coverlet drawn up under her chin and her arms crossed on her shoulders.

Jessica checked at the sight of the delicately carved ebony X-shaped frame with the restraints and the clamps bolted to one wall, and the various toys. Her eyes seemed focused on the whip, then took in some of the other things.

"Shhh, shhh, it's all right," Monica said. "That's for play, later; I mean, *I* spend a fair bit of time tied up like that and it's really quite stimulating when you're used to it, and it makes your blood sort of . . .

tasty. Todd, get her to lie down here on the bed, that's right. Then you sit here, in this chair next to the bed."

He jerked as the renfield gunman secured him to the chair with a padded restraint built into the arm.

"There, you sit beside her, Todd," Monica said. "This is just so you don't get in the way when the *Doña* goes for her. Things could get . . . out of hand if you did that, it's a natural impulse, but . . . I mean, really bad. Never, never try to interrupt a feeding, it, um, sets them off. You can fight and resist afterwards, she quite likes that sort of game."

Jessica's brown eyes were wide, and her dark skin had roughed as if with a chill, though the chamber was at a perfect mild seventy degrees, with a subtle scent of flowers. Dave gave her a wink as he left, and Monica scowled at him.

It's their first time, she thought, annoyed. *Don't spoil things, Dave. It should be dark and awful and terrible, but . . . pure and wonderful too. Really, sometimes I think you have no class at all.*

Of course, he wasn't really a lucy, though the *Doña* fed on him now and then; basically he was a renfield, a helper-worker. Monica looked at the time again, moving towards the door, and wondering if she should have warned the Bertsches about the *special thing* Adrienne could do to you with her mind. Technically it involved stimulating certain centers in the brain with jolts of the Power, though it certainly didn't *feel* like it happened in the head. They'd certainly be experiencing that in the next couple of hours, but . . .

No, it'll be such a nice surprise and help them come to terms with things. It feels so much better than you'd expect from hearing someone talk about it. Though it does sort of change your self-image.

Not long to dawn . . . could Adrienne have been delayed, so that she'd have to spend the day in deep water?

No. She's here, she's close.

There was an unmistakable flavor when nightwalkers approached, if they weren't hiding and you'd experienced it before. A chill, a feeling of being *lost* somehow, even in the most familiar place, as if the world had changed around you to another place with completely different rules. The couple looked about wildly; they didn't know what it meant. Adrienne Brézé entered her lair through the wall, flowing, twenty-two feet of reticulated python marked in blue and green and black. Jessica gave a series of hiccupping moans and shook in terror too paralytic for anything louder as the head reared over the foot of the bed and then slid under the sheet, winding itself around her body coil upon coil. Monica shivered herself and licked her lips; she knew exactly how that coiling embrace felt, so cool and resilient and irresistibly strong.

The snake sparkled and disappeared as Adrienne returned to her own flesh-body. Jessica tried to scramble up as the yellow-flecked dark eyes opened and turned to look at her with a smile, but Adrienne pounced in a blur of speed, arms and legs trapping her and mouth lunging for the neck with the lips rolled all the way back from the teeth. Monica slipped the door closed as the victim screamed once, high and desperate, and her husband shouted in helpless anguish.

The door was nearly soundproof, but Dave was looking at a screen set in the desk of the sitting room outside. Monica marched over and tapped three times on the screen, locking it out of internal surveillance mode. The sensors were keyed to her fingerprints, of course.

"Hey, what do you think you're doing?" he protested.

"Whatever I please, because she *listens to me*, Dave."

The man snarled at her; she wasn't impressed, having been snarled at by people who did it much better.

"Where do you get off being so high and mighty?" he said. "She—"

"*She's* a Shadowspawn adept, *I'm* a favorite lucy . . . and you are just a *creep*, Dave. You are a . . . a *toad*. Show a little respect for people's feelings!"

He met her eyes for a second, then glanced aside. She went on briskly:

"Go and tell the captain she's back. He knows what to do then. And tell the cooks . . ."

She thought. "A late lunch for two here. And something for the Bertsches in their cabin, something rich and special with plenty of liquids. They're going to be shaky and they'll need to talk things over and have some privacy."

He nodded and stalked out. Monica nodded to herself as she sat and brought the screen live, setting it to turn on the camera and record, and began to compose her daily message to Sophia and Josh, composing her face into a smile.

Somebody had to keep up standards around here.

"We had a wonderful time in Istanbul. I'm sending a file of pictures and *yes*, there will be *presents*. I saw Leon and Leila with their dad in Vienna and they say *hi!*—"

CHAPTER TWENTY

The Caucasus

"There it is," Ellen said grimly, as the Tulip came to a stop half a mile offshore.

The wreck of the gulet they'd been chasing lay on the low muddy shore, both masts broken off and lying forward in a tangle of rigging and sails. A huge ragged hole in the shoreward side gaped empty; past this spot the coast rose to low jagged cliffs. The wind was off the land, cool and smelling of green and damp earth. Up above the waterline was a section of planking and beams, its edges matching the hole in the ship's flank.

They were well north of Batumi, the main port of Georgia; somewhere close to one side or the other of the border with the secessionist Republic of Abkhazia, an irritated triangular piece of land thrust like a sore thumb into the westernmost Caucasus Mountains. She'd vaguely recalled reading headlines about troubles here all her life. If she recalled correctly, they'd started *before* she was born, back when the old Soviet Union broke up.

A quick tap on the tablet had produced more articles about multi-sided conflicts than she'd wanted to see or had time to read, including the usual massacres, double-dealings, reciprocal ethnic cleansings and convoluted feuds involving Circassians, Abkhazians, Dagestanies, Chechens, Georgians, Armenians, Russians, Turks, and a clutch of other ethno-linguistic groups mostly about the size of a moderate high school district. All with histories of mutual hatred stretching back to mythical times, and all wrapped in absolutely contradictory narratives, with each minute groupescule insisting with fanatical intensity that their version was the capital-T Truth. Most of the differences between them looked invisible or deeply trivial to an outsider, though you'd be well-advised not to say so.

Stalin had come from near here, and apparently the only time the locals weren't bashing and knifing each other was when they all cringed together under the knout of some mad-dog tyrant and his secret police.

"That was clever," Adrian said grudgingly, looking at the wreck of the ship. "But then, Harvey always was. There are no cargo facilities here. That puzzled me for a while, I thought this location might be *dyezinfor-matsiya*."

"Subtle guy, Harvey," Eric said.

"Blasting a hole in the side of the ship to get something out is sub-tle?" Peter asked.

"Yeah, it's subtle *thinking*," Eric said admiringly. "Outside the box, and how! Don't confuse that with subtle *execution*. I'd like the guy, if I weren't on the other side. Sorta."

Adrian nodded: "If you just beach your ship and hack a great hole in the side, then it all becomes much simpler. Use the segment of hull as a ramp, then a skid as you drag it up with a truck . . ."

It was an hour after sunrise, and the weather was about like Pensacola at this time of year—humid and mild, above-freezing chilly at night, in the fifties right now and not likely to go much higher, windbreaker weather. The low coast was intensely green; as they got closer she could see dense pine forest, the mouth of a small river and what looked like a run-down orchard of some sort of fruit tree, small with round-trimmed tops. The undergrowth was waist-high at least, and a few of the trees were dead. There was open ground beyond, glimpsed through the vegetation, and then—

She gripped a stay and shaded her eyes with her right hand against the morning sun. Very far away to the north and northeast were the blue-and-white line of a range of snowcapped mountains, the peaks seeming to float in the sky; they reminded her of the Colorado Rockies, and must be immense to be visible at this distance. The sight was quite lovely, the white of the snow very faintly tinged with pink deepening to red as she watched.

It was all very pretty, and empty, and unutterably discouraging, a feeling like being very tired and having a lump in your stomach at the same time. She'd been hoping that they could catch Harvey at sea; the ocean was very big, but didn't have many hiding places on the surface. That shore, that *land*, looked very big and very easy to hide in, and they were running out of time.

An image haunted her, of a human shadow cast forever on a concrete wall by the burst of nuclear fire that had vaporized its maker. When she'd seen it in a collection of photographs she'd been mainly interested in the aesthetics, the stark black-and-white formal composition. Now . . .

"The Caucasus," Adrian said. A wry twist of the lips: "And the ancient homeland of my species, or close enough."

"Where next?" Eric said.

"That is also clever. Harvey had a truck waiting here, but we do not because we were following him and didn't know exactly where he would land. We can track it to the nearest road, and presumably they will be heading for Tbilisi . . . but walking after them is not really practical."

"You can't hex out the direction?"

Adrian nodded at Peter. "You did your work well. No, the bomb is a hole in the world. More than that; it is an *invisible* hole in the world. As is anyone standing within a few feet of it, particularly if they are touching the casing."

Peter shrugged, smiled and blushed. "Hey, once I sussed out the principle, the applications sort of leapt out. Professor Duquesne did as much of the work as I did, or more."

"So we need to get ashore, organize transport, and try and catch them before they get to the city," Eric said.

He was apparently doggedly indifferent to discouragement. So was Cheba, who appeared on deck with the last load of the carefully selected gear and baggage she'd packed.

Okay, they can do it, I can do it. Never say die, until you die.

"Good man," Adrian said softly, then nodded. "Let us be about it. I am focusing on Harvey himself as much as I can, but I am getting only a vague southeastward heading even when he is away from the device . . . he shields very well. Or he would have died long ago, fighting powerful adepts. Fortunately we know roughly where he is going."

"Yeah, I want to get off the beach as fast as we can," Eric said. "Let's not be more obvious than we have to be, we're sort of exposed. What about this ship? Want me to open the scuttling cocks?"

Ellen winced. The *Tulip* was a handsome enough product of human hands and minds that casually destroying it offended something deep in her; also there was an irrational reluctance to casually dispose of something that had served them well, even if it was only an inanimate tool. Also—

"Not much point," she said. "The masts would be above water even if we did, and the other ship, Harvey's, is right there and the only way we could get rid of it would be to burn it, which would be *very* conspicuous. And think of the time. I suppose eventually the police or whatever will figure something out, but by then it won't matter one way or another. This is all going to be resolved in the next couple of days."

So if there's a world left by then, we'll worry about it then.

"Yeah, not worth the trouble," Eric conceded. "And you're right, I don't want to attract attention. The locals might get antsy at a bunch of mysterious armed Americans—"

Cheba gave a small snort, but continued stacking the gear.

"Hey, you wanted that green card bad, *chica*, so get used to it— Americans wandering around. Better to avoid them if we can. This isn't *Expendables Twelve*."

"And the people we rented the *Tulip* from can get it back if we just leave it here," Peter said. "The ownership documents are still there in the cabin."

Cheba grinned without looking up from her work. "Yes. Of *course* the officials and police here will send a boat worth lots and lots of money back to some foreigners . . . how do these what, Georgians, feel about Turks, *jefe*?"

"They hate them," Adrian said succinctly. "Not as much as Armenians do, that would be impossible, but fairly emphatically."

"Yes, back to some foreigners they hate if they find it with nobody on board, with no permission, and they would *never* just throw the papers into the water. Those people we got it from knew they would never see it again, that is why the *jefe* paid so much."

Peter winced. "You're such a cynic, Cheba."

"What is this place you lived in once where people act like that? I would like to live there too, except that there is no such place," she replied.

Eric chuckled. "Translated: what planet do you come from, professor, and how many moons does it have? So, boss, we bug out right now?"

Adrian nodded as he stood with his hands in the pockets of his light waxed-cotton jacket, staring at something none of the rest of them could see. His children crouched at his feet, watching him with their heads cocked on their sides and identical frowns on their faces. *They* looked as if they were trying to follow something interesting but more complex than they could really grasp.

The *Tulip*'s equipment included a big yellow plastic cylinder that held an inflatable boat, and the rest of them unlashed it and pushed it over the side, anchoring it with a line secured to a ringbolt. Lettering on its side specified the contents.

"Woof," Ellen said, dusting her hands. "That's heavy!"

"Needs to be," Eric said. "I recognize the type, it's pretty much a CRRC. You want to do the honors?"

He handed her a line hooked to a little lever arrangement on the casing. She gave it a firm yank, and the ends blew off the tube and a seam along the top cracked open, all with hissing *brack* sounds, like an aerosol can in a fire. The boat within unfolded like a flower in stop-motion photographs, and in a few seconds it was a black rectangle about twelve feet long by six wide, bluntly pointed at one end. Peter went down the rope ladder and balanced expertly.

Eric looked slightly surprised, but handed down the outboard motor with the shrouded propeller as the other man reached up.

"Whitewater rafting," Peter said by way of explanation, as he secured it to a plate at the stern. "The SEALs use these things; you ever try out for that?"

"*Mierda*! Do I *look* completely loco? You have to love to suffer and have a suicide complex to even apply for the teams." A snort. "Actually I did apply, but I met my own personal IED before I could try for the qualifying course."

Cheba and Ellen looked at each other and shrugged; the Mexican girl tapped a finger on her temple and wiggled the others. They formed a chain and handed the gear down into the boat; it didn't take long, since they were carrying only essentials, mostly in knapsacks. Hopefully they could pass for backpacking tourists.

"Okay, ladies . . . hey, boss!" Eric called. "Ready to go?"

Adrian shook his head, a little as if he were emerging from deep water. "Very tangled . . ." he sighed. "There are too many powerful adepts gathering, too many already near. They . . . step on each other's Sight, confuse the inner eye."

He handed down the children, and Eric started the motor as he slipped easily into the boat. The engine burbled, and water foamed up behind the stern; spray came over the bows, cold in Ellen's face. She put a hand on the cooler full of bagged blood that was her special responsibility; in its way it was as much ammunition as the half-moon clips of silver bullets in her pockets.

It's odd, she thought. *This is dangerous and uncomfortable, but there's something comfortable about it . . . well, Adrian's here, but . . . you know, I'm with all my best friends. Well, not exactly all my friends, there's Giselle back in Santa Fe, but we're all close somehow. It's . . . not comfortable, it's comforting.*

Peter killed the throttle some distance from the land; the boat slid onto the shore with a *shrrrussh* sound as the fabric rasped over the gravel of the beach. Ellen braced herself against the forward surge. Eric hopped out and grabbed one of the loops at the bow, bracing himself against the greasy sideways motion of the flat bottom on the muddy gravel. Everyone else followed, and the adults all grabbed on and pulled the craft forward beyond the wet dirt. Then the backpacks and duffels were handed out and distributed. Eric and Adrian bent to examine the drag marks near Harvey's beached ship.

"Yeah, you were right, they had some sort of rig with a winch," Eric said. "See, that's a spade jack's mark where they planted it to brace the vehicle. Looks like they used a chain saw to crack the structural members from the inside, cut through on the top and most of the way on the bottom, then put a loop of the cable around one of the strakes and pulled. Then they switched the cable to drag the load out of the hold onto the section of hull, refastened it to that timber there and dragged the whole thing up like a sled, then switched the cable onto the container again and pulled it up onto the bed of the truck up a standard double ramp. Looks like a two-axle job to me, military from the treads, but not ours. Big but not huge, six-tonner maybe."

"Agreed," Adrian said. "They probably . . . yes, several local helpers. They would be hired, no knowledge of what the cargo is."

He knelt by the track and extended a hand, closing his eyes and touching the ground lightly.

"You are right . . . I can See the truck before they loaded it . . . a GAZ model. Old, battered, the engine is knocking."

"Yeah, not much doubt about that around here."

"And a local . . . his interior dialogue is in Georgian . . . nervous, afraid . . . he sees Harvey laughing . . . then the shield generator comes too close."

"We can follow the tracks with the Eyeball Mark One," Eric said. "That'll get us to a road, at least."

They trudged on up towards a narrow, overgrown lane with puddles standing in the ruts of the truck that had born the bomb. Leila took her hand and swung it as they walked. That led through the orchard, which turned out to be an orange grove, which from the look of it hadn't been tended or harvested in a while, and the ground was dotted with the rotted remains of fruit, filling the air with an over-sweet scent. The field beyond was equally scruffy, though comely enough in a disheveled way, looking like neglected pasture; it was bordered and dotted with trees, and her art-student eyes identified oak, ash and hornbeam. There were a lot of birds, including a flock of a big finch with spectacular rose-red plumage and a group of pheasants that burst out of some bushes as they passed, skimming off across the landscape in a thrumming clatter of wings.

The overgrown lane from the water fed into a slightly less overgrown dirt road bordered by big plane trees. Adrian took a stance and murmured, the whining, grating syllables of Mhabrogast.

"There will be cars down this road, the first in about twenty minutes," he said. "Even on local roads we could be in Tbilisi in a few hours. If we are not on the right side of the border, that could make for complications."

"Can we get them to stop? They might not want to pick up so many hitchhikers," Peter asked, then held up a hand. "Okay, okay, don't laugh at me!"

None of the others did, though there was amusement in Eric's voice as he said: "One way or another we will, professor."

"Wait," Adrian said. "There is something else . . . a Wreaking, it's familiar but I can't quite place . . ."

"*Cover! Cover!*" Eric shouted.

Ellen promptly dove for the ditch at the edge of the road, ignoring the mud and water, landing with an *ooof!* mainly because Leila came down on top of her. She got her revolver out and the girl arranged beside her first, not least because while the twins were on the whole well-mannered children they had an instinctive tendency to snap when startled or frightened. Then she saw what Eric had seen—or what he had heard before they were visible. Two armored vehicles were coming out of the tree line to the northeast, crackling through saplings and brushes, the heavy wheels humming as the diesel engines burbled. They were low-slung boxy shapes with wedge fronts and eight big wheels, the weapons in the skeletal remote-operated turrets probing as the operators within turned their joysticks and watched the screens.

"Fuck! BTR-90s!" Eric said, some piece of military acronym-ese she didn't recognize.

They were all armed, but they were armed with things like coach guns and revolvers full of silvered shot, or knives and Cheba's machete; weapons designed to fight nightwalker adepts. Against soldiers with modern weapons, they didn't seem like much.

Plus I don't think any of us want to hurt ordinary human type people. Not that there's much choice now.

"*Jefe*, over to you," Eric called. Then: "Shit!" as something went by overhead and a crackle of explosions came from *behind* their position. "Grenade launcher and heavy machine gun on each of those APCs. *Do* something!"

Adrian came up to one knee, began a pass with his hands . . . then stopped and toppled forward, clutching at his head. Something like a flush of liquid nitrogen seemed to run through Ellen's chest and belly as she saw the contorted agony on his face, and the twin trickles of blood from his nostrils.

She crawled along the ditch, hauling the cooler of blood. The grenade launcher chattered again, a series of dull *thumpthumpthump* sounds, and the next line of explosions was much closer. Something slashed through the leafless branches of the tree above her, showering her with bits of twig.

"Adrian! What's going on?" she asked sharply.

He looked up; his eyes were bloodshot too, and he grated around a hissing snarl: "Old Wreakings . . . childhood . . . like hooks in my head . . . *damn* Harvey! I will not let them harm you and the children, I *will* not—"

Then he screamed; it was an instant before she realized it was in Mhabrogast. He slumped backward as the last syllable sounded, his body arching and then going limp. Eric cast a glance over his shoulder: *we're all going to die now* was plain in the frustrated anger of his expression.

This was obviously no time for shyness, or bottled blood. She tore open the neck of her jacket with her left hand and put her right hand behind Adrian's head. He was making small whimpering sounds and his eyes had rolled up until only the pink-tinged whites were visible, and his hands twitched in a random way that made her heart clench. She took a deep breath and brought his mouth up to touch the skin at the base of her neck.

For a moment she thought he was too far gone even for that. Then his arms closed around her with bruising force and she felt the sting of the bite, sharper than usual with the desperate need.

"Ah. *Ah.*"

She closed her eyes and shuddered; not even fear of death could make the sensation any less overwhelming. After a time she couldn't have judged he gently laid her down and stood, his face a mask of blood—hers and his own, running from nose and eyes and dripping off his chin beneath the red grin of his mouth, the coppery smell of it rank. Her whole body felt warm and almost liquid, but she craned her neck to follow him as he walked forward.

The turrets turned towards him. His hands came up to either side, fingers crooked and then moving in patterns that hurt the eye to watch while he shrieked falsetto abominations in the language of demons, the war-magic of a Lord of Shadow. She felt a sharp pain, as if something had reached into her head, clenched and tugged towards the place behind her eyes; beneath that was pride, and also an impulse to pound her head on something hard until she didn't have to listen any more. At times like this you realized that the Power was simply *wrong*, chaos and Old Night let loose on earth.

One of the low-slung vehicles slewed sharply and then halted; there was a muffled *bang* from its engine compartment, followed by black smoke and low red flames. The turret on its top pivoted and fired six times into its companion, shredding all the wheels on one side, then blew up with a rending *crang*. Pieces flew, some of them trailing smoke. Soldiers poured out of the machines. Some of them fled wailing, stumbling, falling and rising to run again or just crawl with foam dribbling from their lips. The rest began firing . . . at each other. Bullets sparked off the armor of the war-machines in little pale flecks of light, and then the survivors threw aside their assault rifles and fell on each other with knives and teeth, bestial howls and cackling laughter. After a moment nothing moved but the wisps of smoke drifting on the breeze and carrying the acrid stink of scorched metal and heavy oil.

The first Empire of Shadow had lasted for a hundred thousand years of cannibalistic sadism. You could see why.

Then another man crawled out of a hatch, hobbled and lurched over to the other machine—one of his feet wasn't working—and crawled inside the rear hatch. He screamed with pain as he reappeared hauling a slight limp figure, but he dragged it twenty yards before he collapsed.

"Wait," Eric said as Adrian began to walk forward towards them. "*Jefe*, those things are burning, they're stuffed with explosives and fuel, they're going to *blow*."

Ellen flogged herself into motion, ran up beside Adrian and held up a bag of the blood. He took it, ripped off the top with his teeth and poured it down his throat, then spat redly.

"Safe enough for a minute," he rasped.

They all followed, into the stink of burning and the raw smell of death, blood and urine, feces and ripped meat. It was Jack Farmer and Anjali Guha, both wearing some sort of camouflage-patterned uniform. The American's right foot was canted at an angle inside its boot, and tears ran down through the grimy sweat on his pug face as he cradled his unconscious companion's head and shoulders.

"She's dying," he said dully as Adrian and the others came up. "She's bleeding inside."

"Twenty men just died because of you," Adrian said, his voice unhuman. "A million more may die tomorrow."

Farmer didn't answer. Adrian didn't speak either; instead he knelt and touched the sleeping woman. After a moment she jerked slightly and her breathing slowed from a rapid shallow panting to something deeper and slower. Adrian's face ran with sweat, diluting the trails of thickening blood.

"Heart," he said hoarsely, and clutched at his own chest. "There—"

Farmer looked up. Adrian shook his head and spoke: "She'll live now; I did just enough. Open your mind, I need the details."

There was a moment of silent communion; Farmer ground his teeth and grunted hoarsely, as if he'd been punched in the gut.

Adrian nodded before he went on: "And don't either of you ever cross my path again," he said, in a low rasping growl she couldn't even *imagine* disobeying.

"We won't," Farmer said, and turned his face away.

"Boss, we've got to *move*," Eric said.

Adrian nodded, wiping at his face with one sleeve, and his expression human once more, as if great dark wings had faced away from about him.

"I need some water. And . . . yes, there will be a van in a few minutes."

CHAPTER TWENTY-ONE

Tbilisi

I am getting sick of hotels, Ellen thought, glancing out the window as they all sat down around the suite's table.

Tbilisi was a city of moderate size, about a million and a half people, on the same order as Philadelphia if you subtracted the suburbs. Over millennia it had grown along the steep banks of the winding Kura River, which had been navigable all the way to the Caspian until the Soviet engineers and dam-builders got to work on it. There were hills to the north and lower, more distant ones to the south, and the area along the river was mostly trees and walkways, with a jumble of older buildings and narrow streets around it, lined with pleasant older buildings including some very odd-looking churches with octagonal towers in their middles.

Even good hotels.

They were staying at what had been the Hotel Majestic just before the First World War; it had been refurbished (including filling in bullet-holes) in the early years of the century and was now the Tbilisi Marriott. The exterior was a very nice provincial Beau Arts, pale stone cladding and engaged pillars with arched windows; the interior was slightly bland upper-level business traveler international standard.

The main merit was that it was right downtown on Rustaveli Avenue. Under other circumstances, she'd have enjoyed staying there, taking walking tours of the city with Adrian and visiting vineyards and historic buildings and enjoying the way Georgians burst spontaneously into choral song in places like elevators, rather like inhabiting an operetta. As it was—

I like to travel, but not to conventions for monsters. Not in the wake of a nuclear weapon. Not to conventions for monsters and in the wake of a nuclear weapon. I want a holiday. And it's comforting to have Peter and Cheba and Eric along, but I'd like to have it with just me and my sweetie sometimes. Though we seem to have acquired some kids, of course. Okay, back to business.

"Farmer thought the yield would be about twenty-five kilotons," Adrian said.

The table between the five adults was scattered with their tablets and tourist maps of Tbilisi and the surrounding area. There was also the remains of a Georgian dinner, sent in from a local eatery: round *khachapuri* cheese-stuffed breads something like a yeasty pizza, spinach with walnut and pomegranate-juice sauce, spiced *kupati* sausages made of pork, garlic, cilantro and *more* pomegranate and touches of cinnamon and cloves, and other dishes as well—the local cuisine favored lots of small *plats* and had never met a pomegranate it didn't like. They'd split a bottle of local red wine, which had been excellent in a hearty sort of way, and were now gnawing on elongated things made of thickened grape juice and nuts and looking at the map with frustration.

The children had taken theirs off to their bedroom to watch the third *Ender* movie. It was all eerily calm, considering the business and the risk that they might all get vaporized in the next day or two. Though she supposed that getting excited wouldn't help.

Adrian prodded at the map with a finger. "Harvey carefully gave Farmer and Guha no idea of precisely where he planned to put it, but it must be reasonably close. Within miles, not tens of miles."

"Does it have to be close?" Cheba said. "It is a *nuclear bomb*!"

"Okay, thing is, nukes aren't magic," Eric said, hunched over the map, tracing distances with a piece of string and a pencil.

"Which is a change from dealing with Shadowspawn," Peter said. Then he raised a hand to Adrian: "Yes, I know the Power isn't magic. But it *feels* like magic. You *talk* to water in a special language and it flows uphill."

"Walks like a duck, quacks like a duck, who gives a fuck if it's not a duck?" Eric agreed. "Back to nukes. I did a course on the effects of nukes when I made sergeant, it's sort of academic now but you still do it, Cold War hangover I guess. They're real powerful explosives and the radiation's bad news, but guys have survived within less than two miles of a *fusion* bomb's ground zero just by sitting in a slit trench. And that's a multi-megatonner we're talking about, one of those big mothers they made in the 50s. Forty times the size of the plutonium job we're facing, or more."

Peter nodded. "Eric's right."

Cheba looked a little dubious; Ellen *felt* that way, she'd always thought of nuclear weapons as a one-per-city apocalypse, but between them the two men didn't make mistakes about that sort of thing. Peter went on:

"I'm not an expert, but I studied the effects a bit at Los Alamos—you really can't avoid it there unless you do that deliberately, like Victorians hoping sex would go away if they didn't talk about it. Earth or stone stops the immediate pulse of radiation pretty quickly. Then there's the blast, overpressure and shock waves and the flash heat. The flash heat can vaporize you close up or give you bad burns quite a ways away, but any solid barrier will give you a high degree of protection."

"You don't want to be underneath the fallout plume either," Eric pointed out. "That's a longer-term problem, though. Short form, you're close, you're toast. It'll kill you with the blast wave, or get you with the radiation, or fry you to a fajita, or pulverize you with high-velocity bits of everything, or you get caught in a firestorm when the buildings go up. But even a little farther away, and some pretty basic protection can get you through, though it's a good idea to keep up-wind and run fast."

"Harvey will take no chances. This is his one opportunity," Adrian said.

Eric nodded: "So if you want to be sure . . . with a twenty-five-k bomb, put it no more than a mile away, and even then not with any terrain features in between."

"Shadowspawn are more vulnerable to the radiation, aren't they?" Ellen said. "I've heard you say that."

Adrian tapped his fingers together, leaning back in the chair. "Yes. Especially the aetheric body, nightwalking or post-corporeal. About . . . roughly, about as vulnerable as unshielded electronics are to EMP. That is not the mechanism, you understand, but the effect, in range and so forth, is about the same."

Peter nodded. "I think the *actual* mechanism that randomizes things is—"

He started to lapse into mathematics, then stopped as everyone groaned. Adrian smiled slightly as he went on:

"It tracks very closely. The Council did some experiments . . . using Shadowspawn under sentence of death . . . in the 1950s, around the Soviet nuclear tests. It was simpler to hide in the middle of a continent, and the Soviet government made secrecy easy, with the Council in control."

"I'll bet," Peter said. "The Soviets used to set off nuclear tests upwind of cities like Semipalatinsk to see what fallout did to civilians, and that was without evil sorcerers sticking the Power in. So the effect on aetheric bodies is *like* EMP?"

"Closely similar."

"Ah," Eric and Peter said together. "After you, professor," Eric went on.

"Okay, that limits it too," Peter said. "EMP is short-range when the explosion is low-altitude."

He went into details that flowed over Ellen's head; Adrian apparently had the same problem:

"Just the results, Peter."

"Ah . . . three miles maximum. Less if there's a building in the way. Really, the EMP for a ground burst is about the same radius as the blast effects."

"That simplifies matters a little," Adrian said. "And Shadowspawn who are corporeal are only slightly more vulnerable to radiation than normal humans, but they could not escape in aetheric form if they feared a nuclear weapon had gone off nearby. So it will be close, to kill the corporeals with blast and heat and the post-corporeals with the gamma radiation. Not more than half a mile from the Rustaveli Theatre, I would say."

"And we know the target is this Rustaveli place?" Eric said, tapping a pencil on the little *cultural landmark* symbol.

"Rustaveli National Theater, yes. That is the only location where all the adepts will ever be in one place. You understand, Shadowspawn do not *like* being concentrated so, it makes our prescience much less effective. Think of it as being in a dark room with plugs in your ears, a lot of background noise and a large group of your worst enemies. They will keep it to a minimum. There need be little debate; the *fix is in.*"

"So a mile around *here*," Eric said, tapping the spot on Rustaveli Avenue . . . which was right in Tbilisi's historic downtown. "Above ground location . . . top floor, if possible. But the thing weighs what, a hair under two tons? Bulky, hard to handle on your own."

"If that bomb goes off there, a hundred thousand humans will die, minimum," Adrian said grimly.

"Yeah, it's bad," Eric said. "The way the hills surround that area, that'll focus it. Whooosh!"

He made a welling-up gesture. Ellen winced. She didn't like the clinical way he was talking about it . . . but it wasn't that he didn't care. It was a technical area he knew something about, the way she did the evolution of perspective, and that was how he discussed it.

"I thought you said there were simple ways to protect yourself?" she said.

He shrugged his thick shoulders. "Simple if you know 'em and you've got the stuff you need and you've got warning. If you don't, you die. Or if you're just too damned close. That's right in a city center. Lots of people just too damned close."

"And we've got too many places to look," Peter said, peering at the map and then dancing his fingers across his tablet. "I mean, jeez, look at the number of buildings!"

Adrian shook his head. "If the bomb were not shielded . . . but then, it wouldn't be here."

He frowned. "Let us first eliminate the obviously unlikely ones. Then . . . I think you should search, and I will try a search for the right *people*. Harvey is very skilled, but lacks the raw power to compel large numbers to forget. He cannot take the bomb with him when he deals with them, and must be outside its influence. He can hide himself, but not the ripple effects of his interactions. Someone may notice something."

"Yeah, there are a couple of angles. Like, construction companies— did anyone rent a crane last day or two? Pain in the ass investigating without knowing the local language, but I can try."

"Me?" Cheba said.

"I need you to guard the children," Adrian said.

She nodded grimly and made no foolish objections; that would be dangerous enough, and she had nothing to prove—not when she'd attacked a giant squid with a machete not forty-eight hours before.

When the others dispersed to get some rest, Ellen looked a question at him.

"No," he said, shaking his head. "I do not think it would *work*, taking them with us as shields. Too much is at stake, and my sister . . . she loves them in her fashion, but she is ultimately a solipsist."

"Yes, and—"

She stood very still for a long moment. Adrian waited, his eyes locked on her.

"We're starting at the wrong end. Look, Adrienne is planning on being *there*, at the meeting, right?"

"Yes, she must."

"And she's going to blow it up while everyone's doing the UN From Hell bit . . . she must know when Harvey's going to blow it up, that is."

"Yes."

"Look, lover, we've got to find out *how she plans to survive that.* If we find out that, we'll find out where the bomb is, or get a lever on it. We can work *back* from that."

He seized her, and the kiss left her breathless. "And that will be for you and me."

"That was a stroke of genius you had," Adrian said, looking around the interior of the Rustaveli Theatre.

A few Shadowspawn lounged there already, and a slightly larger number of renfields seeing to the arrangements. Ellen winced as they walked past the manager, who was middle-aged and portly and probably normally a dignified-looking man. He was looking down at the body of one of the theater attendants, with tears trickling down his cheeks.

A renfield cuffed at him and snarled in Russian; probably *get rid of that and be quick about it*, because after a moment he bent clumsily, grasped the dead woman's wrists and began to drag her out.

"I really do not like saving this bunch from getting fried," she said. "If only they didn't have a city as a human shield."

As a theater, it all looked quite nice, in an old-fashioned way; about eight hundred seats, with three levels of boxes extending around to the horseshoe-shaped section at the rear, and a broad stage. On that workers and technicians were erecting . . .

Yup, that's an altar, she thought queasily. *Carved altar. And they're putting down a waterproof surface around it. And those scared, cute-looking people at the back in the handcuffs are going to have a starring role in the production, so they're making them watch, and the carvings show what's going to happen to them . . . though I doubt they really believe that, because some of the things are impossible without the Power and nightwalking.*

"I know what you mean, but needs must," Adrian said.

He walked over to one of the renfields. "The seating arrangements," he snapped.

The man looked like he wanted to object; he glanced into Adrian's face and tapped his tablet instead. A printer nearby spat out hard copy, and Adrian took it without thanks.

He's usually unfailingly polite to waiters and ticket agents and bellhops, Ellen thought. *But here, I can see why he's a bit . . . abrupt . . . this time.*

"This is the Brézé area; this is the speaker's podium below the altar," he said. After a long moment:

"I can think of only one way for her and her supporters to leave the theater fast enough to catch the others by surprise."

"How?" she asked, baffled; that had been puzzling her.

He looked down. She did too . . . and then remembered Adrienne walking out of walls in Rancho Sangre to take her by surprise.

The bitch loved it when I screamed in shock. I got so I twitched every time I saw something moving out of the corner of my eye.

"But isn't that dangerous?" she said.

"Hideously," Adrian said. "One mistake and you suffer the Final Death."

Then, a deep breath. "Come, we do not have much time."

Night was falling. Tbilisi wasn't *very* cold, but it smelled like it might snow, mealy and damp and densely overcast. Eric looked up at the building.

"That would be perfect," he said.

It was new; still under construction, in fact. In the States it would be a middling office building, but it was larger than average here. This was mostly a low-built town, even more so than say Albuquerque.

"And the contractor couldn't figure how his computer lost the file," Peter went on. "That was a good idea."

He looked up at the building again. "We've got to decide quickly. And I don't want to go up against someone who can Wreak without an adept."

"Not to mention the way Adrian always talks about him. That is one serious badass and I want the odds in our favor," Eric agreed. *Thank God Peter isn't trying to be Action Man.* "Time to get backup."

He took out his phone. Under his stoic exterior he could feel the sweat trickling down his flanks. Unless he missed his guess, up there was a nuke with a man sitting by the controls ready to hit the switch.

He tapped the number. Then again, then again . . .

"Shit! Boss isn't answering! I'm getting full bars here, too!"

"Back to the theater," Peter said. "He may be somewhere reception is bad."

They turned and trotted, pushing through the crowds on the sidewalk and ignoring the throaty Georgian imprecations in their wake. It was only a third of a mile, anyway. They were running against the clock and they'd better win, or they'd be trying to outrun a fireball, and failing.

"What do you want?" the manager said, in heavily accented English.

He was slumped behind his desk in the cheerful, cluttered office whose walls were posters where they weren't bookshelves. There was a stale smell in the air, as if he hadn't bathed in days, or as if he was exuding a heavy musky scent of despair.

Adrian replied in gargling Georgian. He didn't just speak it; his body language adapted, gestures growing wider, hands moving more fluently. Ellen could see whatever he was saying break through the apathetic misery of the man's demeanor, until he virtually flung himself at a file and brought out a roll of old blueprints. He and Adrian spoke quickly and traced their fingers over sections of it, then the man took a pen and sketched rapidly. Adrian nodded, and spoke again.

The man walked quickly out the door without looking back. Adrian snarled a laugh.

"Occasionally virtue is its own reward. I could not have gotten cooperation like that by compulsion—not without time, and Wreaking."

"What did you tell him at the end there?" Ellen asked.

"That he should leave, get his family, and head south as fast as he could. And I laid a minor Wreaking on him, to fool a casual probe with the Power."

She looked down at the plan. "That's not marked as a passage," she said.

"It isn't; nor will there be any records or municipal permits—though with money, you could do that anyway here. But that man . . . his name is Botso . . . says that there *was* construction here last year. Very mysterious, with government agents telling him to ignore it. This is a very old city; there are many unrecorded catacombs. He has marked where he thinks the entrance is. Come, quickly."

Her breath caught; they were heading to confront Adrienne in whatever lair she had prepared. *I thought I killed her last time. Maybe I can* actually *do it this time. Hooray, as long as I survive it. Vengeance is sweet but I'm not suicidal about it.*

Down, down. One spot where Adrian's arm stopped her before she could turn a corner.

"What?" she said softly.

"Tōkairin retainers. Where they are keeping Michiko's body . . . perhaps to make a point during the deliberations."

She winced. She didn't in the least regret shooting Tōkairin Michiko, who had been a murderous sociopath with the powers of a junior-grade goddess and who'd been trying to kill Adrian at the time, not to mention Eric Salvador. Still, the thought of passing by the physical shell, gradually decaying in its deep coma was . . .

Creepy. But I am the Connoisseur of Creep by now, and that's relatively minor.

Down, until the lighting looked as if it should have *Installed During the Reign of the Red Czar* written on it, and the masonry might have come from long-vanished incarnations of this city—the Tbilisi of the Ottomans, or the Safavid Shahs, or Queen Tamar the Great. Until they were in a corridor of old rock and crumbling mortar, with a single bulb hanging from a wire. She looked around: nothing but dimness, dampness, and a smell of old wet stone running into a dead end. He looked around.

"Solid rock for many yards in all directions except above us," he said. "Guard me."

She gulped slightly and drew her revolver, trying to be conscious of the long corridor and the ceiling at the same time. Training and Wreakings made it harder to come upon her invisible and impalpable . . . but not absolutely impossible. Ellen controlled her breathing and pushed fear away, not denying it but denying it the attention that turned into a feedback cycle. Instead she opened her senses and simply waited.

A click. "*Got* it," Adrian breathed. "Oh, that was clever, of her. And dangerous, to us."

Ellen looked down; a square trap-door showed in the corridor's floor. "Booby-traps?" she said.

"Of course." A grin. "But I *am* one of the two most powerful adepts . . . slightly more powerful than the other, and there are times when brute strength is useful."

He levered the trapdoor up and dropped through, the glow of his pen-light showing through. "About six feet down. Come."

She sat on the edge, felt his hand on her shoes, then slid through. He didn't precisely catch her; it was more a matter of a guiding hand, and enough experience to land without a dangerous shock. They were in a small square room, rather like a largish walk-in closet. This looked more recent, with the marks of power-drills on the walls, and a low tunnel led off. Adrian headed into it and she followed, stooping, the skin between her shoulder blades itching. As they went she tried to imagine how this related to the structure above.

"We must be about below . . ."

"The main theater," Adrian said, and stopped.

Ahead of them was a blank oval steel door. Adrian leaned palms and forehead against it. "Oh, clever again," he said. "This can only be opened from the inside, once it is closed. The locking mechanism is much too massive to move with the Power. And it is silver-plated on the inside, and to either side. I must . . . I must try to go around."

They looked at each other, appalled. Nightwalking thorough solid rock for any distance was utterly disorienting. Not quite suicide, but close enough. She opened her mouth to start an argument she knew she would lose—lose, and be left with the body while God knew what happened to the real Adrian. Then a familiar sensation came over her, a coldness, and a little implanted *ting-ting-ting* feeling at the back of her brain.

"Nightwalker!" Adrian hissed, his hand going to his knife.

There was a *chunk* from behind the door, and it swung slowly open. Dale Shadowblade stood there, in nondescript dark clothing . . . and then he smiled, and changed. So swiftly and skillfully that the clothing didn't fall away during the transition, though it was baggier on the slim dark man.

"Why are you taking on the seeming of the man you killed?" Adrian asked.

His great-grandfather's brother smiled. "Have you not guessed yet, my old?" he said in impeccable, old-fashioned aristocrat's French. "Name of a black dog, I should have thought it obvious by now. Yet even your sister, far more suspicious, did not guess."

"Arnaud!" Adrian said.

"Indeed, Arnaud," the man . . . or what had once been a man . . . laughed. "Now post-corporeal once more. I killed your sister's Apache . . . Apache in both senses of the word . . . not he, me."

"The powdered silver . . ."

"Self-administered, so that when we grappled he was paralyzed by the sudden pain."

"And it *is* possible—"

"To reinhabit a body vacated by the death of the aetheric form? Yes. Not even a prolonged process, though far from easy. I became interested because possession was one of the few myths that did not seem to have its roots in us. Most said that it arose because we could take the seeming of our victims when we nightwalked, but I suspected otherwise. That savage of your sister's gave me the empty body to use. Observe . . ."

The two Shadowspawn locked eyes; as she watched, expression drained from both of them, and Arnaud's eyes became blank glowing yellow. Communication flowed between them, sensed but as impalpable as if it was water that moved through sand.

Adrian stirred and shook his head. "My God, it is true," he said. "We all underestimated you, it seems."

"Yes. And now I shall flit away, a mosquito too elusive to skin as a wolf or shoot from an elephant's back like tiger. Adieu, *mon cher*, and I very much hope we never meet again."

He sauntered away down the path they had followed; Ellen tracked him with her pistol, and he looked over his shoulder for a moment to blow a kiss from his fingertips as he vanished into the darkness.

Adrian shook his head. "He showed me what he had done. Impossible to lie at that level . . . no time!"

They stepped through into what might have been a dungeon once, or a section of long-disused sewer or storm-drain dug in the palmy days before the Revolution.

"Her coffin is within," he said.

"A coffin? She's in a *coffin*?" Ellen said. "Adrienne wouldn't be caught *dead* in a coffin. Well, you know what I mean," she added defensively, as he snorted.

The chamber was long and round, cut from the living rock; water glistened here and there as their flashlights moved across a surface that still bore the scars of the drills. Nobody had ever smoothed them, but a mesh of new-gleaming wire covered the whole interior except for the roof.

"See," he said, directing the little light upward. "They entered in the body, and left as nightwalkers, closing the door behind them. Arnaud . . . Dale Shadowblade, they thought . . . locked it behind them. Then the only way to enter would be through the solid roof."

"Wouldn't they be afraid of being buried alive? The bomb . . ."

"This is solid rock and deep. And they could always dig themselves out from the outside afterwards—one can be in two places at once. My sister likes bombs; let us proceed."

More than a dozen of the elongated boxes stood on frame bases. They didn't look all that much like coffins; more like featureless footlockers of the appropriate size. One in the center stood on a higher frame than the others, with the Brézé arms in a golden plaque attached to the upper surface.

"Vanity," Adrian said. "At a guess, this is an abandoned effort at an extension to the sewer system. Easy enough to expunge it from the re- cords . . . and arrange accidents for all who knew of it. But the time, the patience for such a plan . . ."

"Maybe she did something like this anywhere there *might* be a full Council meeting," Ellen said.

"My sister likes bombs. Let us oblige her."

They removed their backpacks. Eric and Adrian had made them up; simple blocks of semtex plastic explosive, with mechanical timers. They placed one on each of the . . .

Coffins. It's traditional, so let's call them coffins.

Then Adrian stood by his sister's, and laid one hand on the back of Ellen's neck. "Time to bargain," he said. "And from a position of strength, for once. Let her be obliged to drop into a bomb-ambush of her own."

The world seemed to blur. For a moment she could see another place—the theater above, with the last screams of the sacrifices just dy- ing away, and the intoxicating—

It's intoxicating? Oh, damn, I hate it when I get confused like this!

—scent of the blood filling the air, along with the vinagery smell of Shadowspawn excitement and the aggression crowding bred.

sister . . . i . . . have . . . your . . . body.

Anger/fury/barely restrained amok rage. Then a weird amusement, and: **bargain?**

quickly!

A sense of internal movement, of personalities emerging from layer upon layer of defenses. An intimacy of perfect hatred from Adrian and a bone-deep reluctance to engage on this level, layers of complex emotion from Adrienne that made Ellen queasy even at this remove, flashes of memory about Adrian that made her squirm with an effort to unknow.

The knowledge that falsehood had become impossible for an instant.

here . . . it . . . is . . . location . . . under . . . your . . . mentor's . . . control . . . can't . . . stop . . . now. beyond . . . my . . . power . . . my seeing . . . five . . . years . . . ago . . . date . . . time . . . place . . . you . . . have . . . twenty . . . minutes . . .

so . . . do . . . you . . . now . . .

The powerful, malevolent consciousness turned to Ellen for an instant:

and . . . you . . . will . . . die . . . soon . . . i have . . . seen . . .

The link broke. Adrian's breath was ragged and his face sheened with sweat; for a moment his throat worked as if he were about to vomit, then he controlled it. They ran from one coffin to the next, setting the timers and hitting the buttons. Then they dashed out the door and Adrian paused only long enough to kick it closed behind them—as much to augment the force of the blast when-if as to fulfill the letter of that literally unspoken agreement. Pounding back up the corridor, and he stopped and linked hands. Her foot hit the stirrup running, and she soared upward and landed . . .

. . . just in time to see the flash of the katana, but far too late to do anything. Anything but feel the huge impact as it flashed down between neck and shoulder, and the coldness, and the beginning of darkness. A scream felt through the mind, of rage and grief beyond all bearing, and a huge *grabbing* sensation on the inside of her head.

No, Adrian. Let me go. Let me die.

"Mother of *God*," Eric blurted, when he saw the limp figure over Adrian's shoulder. "What the fuck—"

"No time, you were right, *follow me.*"

They dashed through the street and into the building. Eric flung himself at the door in a running leap, feet first. The hoarding over the opening came free in a screech of nails, and he fell down with bruising force. He ignored the impact that wooshed the air out of his lungs, the pain of sharp things gouging through his clothes, have to *move move move.* Adrian leapt over him, and Peter caromed into him just as he started up again. They went down in a cursing tangle, saw Adrian lay his burden down and dash up the stairs heedless. They followed, without time for thought.

Story after story, push the legs like pistons, suck breath, ignore the body's protest. The top, nothing but scaffolding and boards around the edges, an empty echoing concrete space lost in shadow and darkness save for one portable light. Harvey looked up from the long container and held up his hand, his craggy face underlit into an iron idol of regret and unmoveable determination.

Deadman switch! Eric knew in a moment of despair, and thought he could see the thumb begin to relax.

"*Mogh-urdak-tzee, tzee!*" Adrian screamed, his hand shooting out in a claw, a bottomless rage in his voice.

"Ufff!"

Eric grunted as if punched in the stomach. Behind him Peter tripped on the last tread of the stairwell and fell full-length. He *knew* that it was *impossible* to move, that the world was frozen in one eternal moment in time. His thought returned to bite itself on the tail, over and over, then broke free as breath returned to him.

And Harvey froze, his thumb holding the contact closed. The edge of the Wreaking had paralyzed Eric Salvador; defenses or no, he didn't like to imagine what it must be to have it thrown like a lance of burning ice directly into his brain.

Adrian walked over and took the mechanism from the older man's hand, examined it, made a motion over it and set it down.

"I am sorry," he said, his voice a rasp but with a gentleness in it. "I did not want it to come to this. I owe you very much, my brother, I owe you my soul. But you are too dangerous . . . and Ellen was killed."

"Sorry 'bout that too," Harvey said. "Real sorry. Never wanted—"

Blood burst from his lips and eyes. He went rigid for a single instant, then fell, limp and dead.

"Jesus," Eric whispered, clutching at his own chest, feeling the distant echo of a force that tore the veins loose and flooded his chest. "*Jesus.*"

Peter came up beside him, wheezing. "We've—"

"*Name of a dog, what is that?*" Adrian cried, throwing up a hand as if to shield himself from something in the sky.

An instant later the cloudy night outside became white light, frosted like the inside of a bulb, but bright, harsh, flat. Adrian dropped to his knees and clapped his hands to his head. Eric waited to die . . .

Wait a minute, if the bomb had gone off I'd have been dead before I knew it. It's only fifteen feet away, for fuck's sake. My brain wouldn't have had time even to register the light.

"We lost?" Peter said.

The light faded, changed color, slowly died like the world's biggest parachute flare. Shadow returned, darker than ever. His head snapped to the gaps in the hoardings, and behind them was no light at all, none of the diffuse glow that a city always showed. Adrian laughed, soft and bitter.

"No. We won. We saved this city. We even saved the corporeals at the theater, though I wish we had not. Somehow *she* concealed another weapon."

"That's a high-level airburst, it must have blanketed most of Georgia and chunks of Armenia and Azerbaijan," Peter said, going to the edge and peering out through a crack in the plywood. "Yup, city's blacked out. High enough it wouldn't do much damage otherwise, though. Maybe a statistical uptick in the cancer rate."

"Your sister had a backup plan," Eric said.

"Yes," Adrian said. "I should have expected it. An intermediate range missile, a confederate of hers in control of some Russian commander; she would not chance a ground burst that might strike too hard, but a high-level one, yes. Probably part of Trimback One, ready to go, and somehow she got another shield. It makes no difference. No, it is *better* than merely stopping the bomb. I felt my great-grandfather die, and Seraphine, and many another, and the souls they had imprisoned. Now the real war begins, and we have the advantage. Harvey would have been happy to see this."

"Wait a minute," Eric said, his mind slipping a little from the diamond point of concentration. "You said Ellen died? Then who was that you were—"

"Come," Adrian said, an infinite weariness in his voice. "We must get to Cheba and the children. The city will be in chaos, and soon Adrienne will strike what she thinks is the killing blow on the world."

CHAPTER TWENTY-TWO

Brotherhood safe house, Kars, Turkey

"I don't want to live without a body!" Ellen said.

Or thought she said; the words came out as a very faint croak, and she wanted to scream with the sheer pain they caused. For a while she was mostly conscious of pain, an infinite number of different kinds. After a while the general weakness and the feeling she was made out of hollow straws and the ache in her head and the savage sore throat gave way to panic at the way her sight was blurred. The sword had hit her in the *neck*, razor-sharp and driven by skilled, hate-filled strength. Her throat must have been cut almost to the spine, maybe *through* it, instant massive exsanguination and death within a second. How could it have damaged her *eyes* and left her alive?

"You have a body, my darling," Adrian's voice said. "Just . . . not the same one. But a body of flesh and bone."

Wait a minute, that must be true. If I was in Adrian's memory palace, I'd feel fine. Perfect. I feel like absolute verge-of-death crap. And . . . disconnected? As if I were wearing something too tight?

Infinitely gentle hands eased a tube into her mouth. "Here, take some water. Sleep."

When she woke again her first thought was: *Oh, shit.*

Cheba was sitting beside her bed, watching a *telenovela* on her tablet. When she saw wakefulness, she turned and called: "*Jefe!*"

Adrian came in, smiling at her with a constraint in it. She could see better this time, though her eyes felt grainy and dry.

"Oh, Adrian," she said. "Did you do what I think you did?"

The voice came out; it was a hoarse rasping whisper, as if her vocal cords had been idle for months . . . which they had, she suspected. She couldn't move; an attempt to raise her hand merely made her fingers flutter for a little. But she was conscious of her body in a way she never had been before, as if she could feel the cells dividing and dividing again; as if she was riding in a car, and the car was her, and the stalled engine was just beginning to turn over again. The room around her was plain institutional beige, but it *glowed* with potentiality. She could feel, feel . . . *everything*.

"This is weird," she whispered. "I'm weaker than a kitten, but I feel . . . I feel as if I could squeeze the world like *putty*."

Adrian sat beside the bed and raised her head again. This time there was lukewarm chicken soup in the feeder he put between her lips; she tried to suck (and why did she move her tongue so carefully around her incisors?), and some of it dribbled down the side of her mouth. The rest went into her throat, and it tasted inexpressibly good. She could feel it all the way down, as if it were warming up her very being.

"Let . . . me see," she said, the rasp a little less painful.

"Very well," he said, not trying to argue.

He reached to the bedside table and held up the mirror for her to see. The face looked . . .

Like a concentration camp survivor, she thought. *No, like someone on life support since I . . . killed her. Well, victor and the spoils. God, this is . . . Do I want this? But consider the alternative . . .*

And underneath the damage of months in coma, it was a perfectly good face. Not the mostly North European one she'd been born with; smaller-boned, high cheeks and tilted eyes, small delicate nose and lips, raven hair cropped close in a hospital cut and skin the color of ivory just touched with amber.

And eyes black-dark, with tiny yellow flecks swimming in them.

"It's a good thing I'm so feeble. I can't freak out, I'm too tired. Later."

Adrian laid her head back down and took her hand between his; strength seemed to pour from it.

"We won," he said, leaning close so that she could meet his eyes. "You did. We saved Tbilisi; a million and a half men and women and children live because of you. You *deserve* this new chance."

Standing behind him, Cheba said dubiously:

"Is it really her, *jefe*?"

"Yes. Her persona, her memories and all they made of her. The body . . . carries it. I didn't know if it would work, there was not *time* to do anything but . . . hurl her, throw her essence, hoping that Arnaud had remembered rightly. But it worked."

"Well, there's a massive oversimplification," Ellen croaked, and closed her eyes, trying to feel around the interior of herself.

It was a jumble. She could remember everything up until the sword hit, even her last thoughts. But she felt not merely ill, but *odd*. As if she were seeing the sensation of touch, or as if sensations she had no names for were crowding in, demanding attention, or as if she had grown two new arms and ears on her feet. When she opened those slanted, gold-flecked eyes again she motioned towards the door with a glance. The Mexican girl smiled at her, nodded, and slipped out. She closed the door behind her gently.

But it isn't just that I want some privacy with my husband, Cheba, though I do. I could smell *you. Smell your blood.*

And Cheba smelled so *good*.